W9-CNI-454

Mirror, Mirror

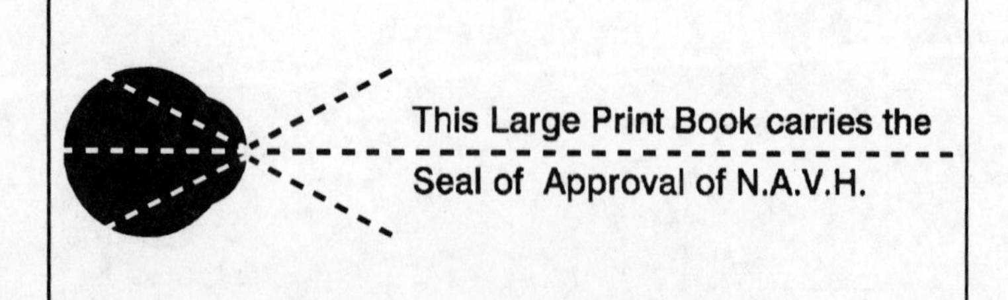
This Large Print Book carries the
Seal of Approval of N.A.V.H.

Mirror, Mirror

J. D. Robb
Mary Blayney
Elaine Fox
Mary Kay McComas
R. C. Ryan

THORNDIKE PRESS
A part of Gale, Cengage Learning

GALE
CENGAGE Learning®

Detroit • New York • San Francisco • New Haven, Conn • Waterville, Maine • London

Copyright © 2013 by Penguin Group (USA).
"Taken in Death" by J. D. Robb copyright © 2013 by Nora Roberts.
"If Wishes Were Horses" copyright © 2013 by Mary Blayney.
"Beauty, Sleeping" copyright © 2013 by Elaine Fox.
"The Christmas Comet" copyright © 2013 by Mary Kay McComas.
"Stroke of Midnight" by R. C. Ryan copyright © 2013 by Ruth Ryan Langan.
Thorndike Press, a part of Gale, Cengage Learning.

ALL RIGHTS RESERVED
This is a work of fiction. Names, characters, places, and incidents either are the product of the author's imagination or are used fictitiously, and any resemblance to actual persons, living or dead, business establishments, events, or locales is entirely coincidental.
The publisher does not have any control over and does not assume any responsibility for author or third-party websites or their content.
Thorndike Press® Large Print Core.
The text of this Large Print edition is unabridged.
Other aspects of the book may vary from the original edition.
Set in 16 pt. Plantin.

LIBRARY OF CONGRESS CATALOGING-IN-PUBLICATION DATA

Robb, J. D., 1950-
Mirror, Mirror / By J.D. Robb, Mary Blayney, Elaine Fox, Mary Kay McComas, R.C. Ryan. — Large Print edition.
pages cm. — (Thorndike Press Large Print Core)
ISBN 978-1-4104-6266-4 (hardcover) — ISBN 1-4104-6266-8 (hardcover) 1. Large type books. I. Blayney, Mary. II. Fox, Elaine. III. McComas, Mary Kay. IV. Ryan, R. C., 1937- V. Title.
PS3568.O243M57 2013
813'.54—dc23 2013029749

Published in 2013 by arrangement with The Berkley Publishing Group, a member of Penguin Group (USA) LLC, a Penguin Random House Company

Printed in the United States of America
1 2 3 4 5 6 7 17 16 15 14 13

CONTENTS

Taken in Death

J. D. Robb

In memory of Tom Langan,
a one-in-a-million hero

When a child fell into her power, she killed it, cooked and ate it, and that was a feast day with her.

THE BROTHERS GRIMM

Good and evil we know in the field of this world grow up together almost inseparably.

JOHN MILTON

Prologue

The evil witch killed Darcia. Henry knew it because he'd seen Darcia on the floor, and all the blood. He'd wanted to shout and cry and run. He'd wanted to fight, a brave warrior, a knight in battle, like the hero in his favorite stories. But he couldn't. Everything felt funny and sleepy and wrong. He knew he was under a spell. The evil witch's magic spell.

And when he looked at Gala, his twin sister, her eyes were like the blue glass in the vase with white flowers on the table.

The evil witch had cast a spell on them so they were like the zombies in his vid game, so he and Gala just shuffled along and the words he wanted to say came out like low, creepy moans.

The spell made his head feel thick and too big. And under the spell he was really scared.

She made them wait, the evil witch, while

she packed stuff in their special going-on-a-trip bags. Waiting, he thought the spell started to lift. Though his head still felt big and thick, he remembered the secret in his pocket.

The witch took them out of the house, and told them to get in the back of the car, to lie down, to sleep.

He wanted to run away, to grab Gala's hand and run, but the spell made him get in the car. They lay down together, Henry and Gala, and shivering, held each other close.

Maybe the witch would take them to a dungeon or a tower and lock them up. But he didn't sleep because he had the secret, and something he could do. If he could just say the words.

When the witch said, "We're going to have such fun! We're going to live in a special place made of sugar plums and chocolate icing," he didn't believe her.

He saw a tear slide down Gala's cheek, and he tried to comfort her inside their minds.

I'll protect you, Gala. I won't let anything bad happen to you.

We'll protect each other, her mind said to his.

He wanted to cry, too, but he had to be

brave. He had to take care of his sister, and find the way home again.

Because evil witches lied. Even when they looked like Mommy.

CHAPTER ONE

In her long leather coat, her choppy brown hair wind-blown, Lieutenant Eve Dallas stood in the sprawling living space of a three-story town house on the upper-crust of the East Side. The dead woman wore blood-soaked pajamas covered with dancing puppy dogs. She lay on her back, one arm flung overhead. The blood trail and spatter told the tale, clearly.

But for now Dallas gave the uniform standing by the go-ahead.

"The nine-one-one caller states she's a friend of the victim. She identifies same as Darcia Jordan. The wit — Elena Cortez — and the vic are nannies. The vic's employers —"

"If she's a nanny, where are the kids? Is this her residence or place of employment?"

"Ah, both, sir. She works for Ross and Tosha MacDermit, who own the place. We did a search through, didn't find any kids.

No sign of struggle or disturbance anywhere but here. But there is indication some clothes and toys were packed up, taken out. Two kids, one male, one female. Twins, age seven."

"Peabody." Dallas turned to her partner. "Get their names, descriptions, photos out now. Get the Amber Alert out, now."

"Lieutenant, the parents are, according to the wit, on vacation. We haven't been able to contact them, so it's possible the kids are with them. It didn't seem like —"

"I don't care what it seems like or doesn't to you, Officer. The nanny's dead and the kids are unaccounted for."

"But protocol —" The cold fire on her face had him dropping that ball.

"They've got a security cam on the door. I want the disc. Keep the witness close. I'll speak to her shortly." Turning her back, Eve stepped to the body. Opening her field kit, she verified identification first.

"Victim is identified as Jordan, Darcia, age twenty-nine. Single, no offspring. Employed by Ross and Tosha MacDermit, as Parental Assistant. Is that the new term for nanny? The victim has multiple stab wounds. Throat, right shoulder, chest. Defensive wounds on the palm of the right hand, on the right forearm."

Frowning, she eased the neck of the ruined pajama top down slightly. "Hell. There's a small pentagram carved just above her heart. Shallow cuts, but a clear pattern. Possible ritual slaying."

She used her gauge to determine time of death. "TOD, straight-up midnight."

"Alert's out."

Eve nodded at Peabody. "Take a look."

Bending down, Peabody studied the occult symbol. "Crap. You think ritual?"

"I think the killer took the time to cut this into the vic."

Peabody, her square face full of worry, glanced toward the stairs. "I'm going to do another search. Kids hide."

"Go ahead. Closets, cabinets, under beds." And remembering another young survivor, added, "Bathtubs, showers." Standing again, she scanned the area.

"A lot of valuables, electronics, easily portable. Check for jewelry, cash," she called out to Peabody, then took the disc the uniform brought her.

She popped it into the living area's wall screen. "Run disc," she ordered, "begin twenty-three thirty. Scanning speed."

All quiet, she thought, studying the camera view of the entrance, the sidewalk and street beyond. Just an ordinary fall evening heading to the end of 2060 in an upper-class East Side neighborhood.

At time stamp twenty-three fifty-four, she saw the late-model, black, four-door sedan slide to the curb.

"Freeze image, enhance. Run that plate," she snapped to the uniform. "Continue, standard speed."

She watched the woman — tall, curvy, blonde, late thirties, long black coat, high boots — get out of the car, cross the sidewalk to the entrance door.

She flicked a glance up, toward the camera, smiled — slyly. And rang the bell.

"Lieutenant —"

Eve held up a finger to silence the uniform, watched the woman speak. A lip reader might get the words, even though the woman turned her face. Then she smiled again, stepped forward out of range.

"Scanning speed."

In her mind, Eve saw what happened inside, away from the camera. A strike out with the knife, catching the throat. A step or stumble back, a hand thrown up. Another strike with the knife, cutting the hand, the arm, the shoulder, driving the victim back. Two hacks into the chest, and the coup de grace, the second, killing slice of the throat.

And using the tip of the knife, after death,

to mark the dead.

She slowed the run again when the woman — red coat now, a large travel tote over each arm — led two absurdly pretty redheaded kids with glazed eyes out of the house.

They went without protest, swaying toward each other like miniature drunks, and climbed in the backseat. After stowing the totes in the trunk, the woman slid behind the wheel.

Eve clearly saw the woman throw back her head and laugh before she pulled away.

"Vehicle data, Officer."

"Yes, sir, that's the thing. The car is registered to Ross and Tosha MacDermit. And that woman, sir? That's Tosha MacDermit." She held out his PPC, showing Eve the woman's photo and ID data.

"I recognized her from when we accessed the data to try to contact. That's the vic's employer, Lieutenant. That's the mother."

"Why didn't she let herself in? Why kill the nanny instead of telling her to get out? Does the wit know where she and the husband are?"

"Not exactly. A second honeymoon deal. An island, maybe South Seas. She wasn't sure. She was pretty hysterical."

Employers, Eve thought, and brought up the data on her own PPC, began to scan.

The wife was employed by the UN as an interpreter, held dual citizenship, and that would require some untangling of red tape. Husband, a self-employed artist.

"Start a canvass, Officer. Knock on doors. Find out where the MacDermits are supposed to be, when they left, when they're due back. Find out if anyone saw her come home last night. If they keep their car on the street or in a garage. Get some answers."

"No sign of the kids," Peabody said as she started downstairs. "No sign of burglary — a lot of visible valuables up there. I found this." She held up a long black coat. "In the master closet. It looks like bloodstains. Smells like blood."

"It would. The killer wore it while stabbing the nanny. Left that behind, traded coats. Bag and tag. The security disc shows the mother arriving about six minutes before TOD, ringing the bell."

Peabody, bending over to pull an evidence bag from her kit, jerked back up. "The mother, but —"

Eve gestured to the screen, backtracked, zoomed in on Tosha MacDermit's face.

"That's the mother. And here . . ." Zipping forward, she ran the section showing her leading the two children out.

"Why kill the nanny?" Peabody wondered.

"An affair with the husband?"

"An always popular theme." Thumbs tucked in her belt loops, Eve took another hard scan of the room, the blood patterns, the body. "She may have done him, too, elsewhere. Kill the cheaters, take the kids, and leave. But she doesn't take any valuables?"

"Done with them," Peabody suggested, "done with the cheaters? She could hit, or have already hit their financials. At least it's really unlikely the kids are in any danger. She's their mother."

"Look at them." Eve zoomed in again on each pretty face. "That's not just getting-woken-up-in-the-middle-of-the-night groggy. Look at the pupils, at the way they walk."

"Drugged?"

"They had to walk out the front door, which means walking right by the nanny's dead and bloody body. I'd think that might cause a little bit of upset. Instead, they look . . . slack, empty."

"Maybe she gave them something so they wouldn't get upset, give her any trouble — maybe not even really understand the body and blood."

"Maybe. She's an interpreter for the UN. We need to start pushing there. He's a freelance artist."

"Sculptor primarily, if the third-floor studio's any indication. A good one, too. Fairy-tale stuff with an edge."

"We need to find out where they went, where they are, and if the husband's still alive. Let's take the wit outside. Grab the disc, log and seal."

She stepped outside into the stiff breeze that tugged at her coat. It skimmed back through her hair and chilled her hands. She never remembered gloves until it was too late.

Bystanders gathered just outside the sidewalk barricades. She scanned them with eyes the color of good Irish whiskey, and cop flat. And spotted the witness in the back of a black-and-white.

"If she's hysterical," she told her partner, "you take the lead."

But Elena Cortez's hysteria had shifted to watery shock and grief. She stepped out of the car, wringing a damp cloth hankie in her hands.

"I'm Lieutenant Dallas, Ms. Cortez, and this is Detective Peabody. Tell us what happened."

"I don't know. I don't know. I came with the children —"

"The children."

"Sasha and Mica. I'm their nanny. They're friends with Henry and Gala, and Darcia . . . Darcia and I . . . we're friends." She sucked her breath in three times as she pressed the hankie to her mouth. "Good friends."

Fat tears spilled out, down her thin face. "We walk them to school together, and I waited on the corner, down there" — she pointed south — "but she didn't come. And it was cold, so I took the children to school, and I came back to see what happened. She didn't answer when I texted her, so I came to see. Maybe she's sick, I thought, or one of the children. She wouldn't forget. We walk them every day to school, and the MacDermits are away."

"Where away?"

"I — Somewhere warm and important and romantic. They come back tomorrow. They have their tenth anniversary. It's a special trip."

"Okay, what happened when you came back here, to see?"

"She didn't answer. I worried a little. I don't know why I did it."

"Did what?"

"I tried the door. I don't know why, it's always locked, but it was . . . impulse? I don't know, but it wasn't locked. I just pushed it open, and I called out. I stepped in, just a little. I saw blood, then I saw Darcia. I saw her on the floor, with the blood."

She pressed both hands to her face. "I should have gone in, looked for the children, but I shut the door, very fast, and I called nine-one-one. I started to run first, but I called nine-one-one, and they said to stay. So I stayed."

"You did exactly right," Peabody told her gently, as the tears fell faster, faster.

"The children? Did he hurt the children?"

"The children aren't hurt, as far as we know. Elena," Peabody continued, "do you know anyone who'd want to hurt Darcia?"

"No. No. No one."

"How did she get along with her employers?" Eve asked.

"They're family. She's been with them since the twins were babies."

"Did she have . . . a special relationship with Mr. MacDermit?"

The insinuation went over Elena's head as she smiled a little. "She loved him. He's such a nice man. A big kid, she said sometimes. When I bring the children over, he always makes us laugh. He's a very important artist, but he's very nice. And a very good father. Not all men are such good fathers."

Eve had reason to know the truth of that.

"And his relationship with his wife?" Eve asked.

"Oh, they . . ." She stopped, eyes widening.

A cab pulled up, and its rear doors flew open.

"They're home! Oh God, they're home."

So they were, Eve thought. She stepped forward to intercept them — the big, broad-shouldered man with a mane of wild red hair and fierce green eyes, and the tall curvy blonde.

"What's going on?" The blonde tried to push by Eve toward the house. "What's happening? Where are my babies?"

"That's exactly what I want to ask you."

CHAPTER TWO

As his gaze tracked — police vehicles, barricades, then fixed on Eve's face — Ross MacDermit wrapped a beefy arm around his wife's shoulders. "They're in school, Tosh — relax. What's going on?" he demanded of Eve. "Did something happen to Darcia? Our nanny?"

"Again, your wife has that answer."

"I don't know what you're talking about. What's happening here? Where's Darcia? Ross, contact the school, make sure Henry and Gala are okay."

"I'm talking about you coming home a few minutes before midnight last night, Ms. MacDermit. And when Darcia Jordan let you in, you stabbed her to death."

The woman's ice-queen pale face went sickly gray. "What? What? Darcia —"

Once again, Eve blocked the woman's push toward the house. "Then you drugged your children and brought them out to your car, put them inside, and took them to another location. Where are the children?"

"Our children?" Her eyes, wild with fear, wheeled toward the house. "Henry. Gala. Somebody took our babies?"

This time it took Eve and Peabody to hold her back, and several uniforms to restrain Ross.

"Your home security clearly shows you arriving at eleven fifty-four last night, six minutes before Darcia Jordan's death."

At Eve's words, Tosha let out a wailing sob. "No."

"And the vehicle you drove is registered to you. It clearly shows you departing, at twelve twenty-three, with the children."

"That's impossible." Ross bellowed it as he fought to jerk free of the uniforms restraining him. "We were in New Zealand, for God's sake. What's the time difference? God!" He squeezed his eyes shut. "Seventeen hours ahead, seventeen ahead," he murmured, the words shivering out like a prayer. "At midnight in New York we were in New Zealand having drinks by the pool with a couple we met at the resort. Dom and Madeline Porter, from Oxford, England. I have their contact information. I have the contact information for the resort. The cocktail waitress can confirm, the towel boy can confirm. We were in New Zealand. We were halfway around the damn world."

"We'll check on that, and we'll have your security disc analyzed. Until that time . . ."

Eve trailed off as Tosha had gone very still, and the tears glazing her eyes seemed to freeze. "Ross." She groped out for his hand. "Maj."

"No. No, it can't be. It's all just some horrible mistake."

"Who is Maj?" Eve demanded.

"My sister." Tosha shuddered when she said it. "My twin."

Because she wanted them both contained, and wanted to move quickly, Eve took them through the small gate, across their own rear courtyard, and in through the kitchen.

"Check the alibi," she told Peabody.

"I think, damn math, I think it's maybe the middle of the night there. Or tomorrow. Either way, I'll wake somebody up, get it started."

The MacDermits huddled together, hands locked, in a sunny nook where Eve imagined the family typically had breakfast.

She slid in across from them.

"There's no data on a sibling, Ms. MacDermit, much less a twin on your official information."

on both children, and another on Maj. We have the vehicle she was driving, and every cop in the city will be looking for it. We'll arrange the wire so that if she tries to contact either of you, we'll know. But the more I know about the person who took your kids, the more ammunition I have to find her. What happened to her?"

"She was committed to the Borj Institute for the Criminally Insane in Stockholm," Tosha told Eve. "I testified against her, and I told what happened to the police, to the psychiatrists, to everyone."

"What did happen?"

"She came to kill me. To end me once and for all. Papa had punished her that day because she took my new doll to the garden and burned it. She marked it with my name, and burned it, and he took her new doll away, and she was confined to her room. She couldn't go outside to play or talk to friends. For a week, he said. She was so angry, and she came to kill me."

Tosha pressed her lips into a thin, trembling line. Her eyes, an arctic blue, pleaded into Eve's. "I . . . saw inside her mind, and I knew. I ran outside and I hid, and I made my mind still. But hers wasn't still. She couldn't find me, and instead she went to Papa's room, and while he slept, she stabbed

"No, there wouldn't be. I . . . You can contact Wanda Sykes. She was my legal representative when I came here, here to New York. And, and Markus Norby. He's police in Sweden. Paul Stouffer, who was with Child Protective Services there. And, ah, Dr. Otto Ryden, he was the psychologist assigned."

"Assigned to what?"

"The case. I was legally permitted to omit Maj from my data, to legally change my maiden name — Borgstrom — after . . . after Maj killed our father. She killed Papa like she killed Darcia. She tried to kill me. We were twelve. I haven't seen or spoken to Maj in over twenty years."

"You're identical twins."

"Nearly. She has a birthmark. Here." Tosha touched her fingers between her left breast and shoulder. It trembled there. "It looks like a pentagram. A sign of witchcraft. I know how that sounds," she went on when Eve said nothing. "I can only tell you she's evil. She has a darkness in her, more than a sickness. They said she was sick, but . . ."

She lowered her hand, once again gripped her husband's like a lifeline. "I think she hated me even when we were in the womb, for being part of her, for preventing her from being the only. The One, she would say. There can only be one. Now she has my children. You have to find our children."

"We already have the alert out. Where do you keep your car, your four-door black sedan?"

"In a private garage on Fifty-seventh," Ross told her. "What difference does it make? What difference? We have to find Henry and Gala."

"We're looking. The alerts are out, and we're already looking. Everything you tell me, everything we learn, is going to help. You say you haven't seen or spoken to your sister in more than twenty years, yet she arrived here, in your vehicle."

"I can only tell you she's very smart and full of hate. Still, we shared a bond, as twins can. We would know what the other was thinking or feeling. She would hurt me whenever she could, so I learned to *know* when she meant to, and hide from her. And to keep my mind very, very still so she couldn't find me. She'll hurt our babies. She'll hurt what's mine. Please."

Tosha reached across the table to grab Eve's hands. "Please, find her before she hurts them. They're only seven years old."

"We're going to set up a tap. She may contact you, may demand a ransom."

"It's not money she wants. She wants to

bring me pain."

"If she hurts Henry and Gala, I'll kill her."

Tosha turned her face into her husband's shoulder at his fierce and quiet words. "I never thought she'd find me, us. I should never have left the children. I should never have left them."

Peabody came back in, gave Eve a nod to indicate the alibi checked. "Is it all right if I make coffee?"

She spoke directly to Ross, got a momentary blank stare. "Yeah, sure. Ah."

"I'll take care of it."

"One minute," Eve said, and rose to have a quick word with Peabody.

"You said she killed your father," Eve began when she sat again. "Where's your mother?"

"She died giving birth to us. It was a very difficult birthing, complications, unexpected complications. Maj blamed me. If we had been one instead of two, our mother would have lived, she would say to me. I cam second, and so I killed our mother. I shoul never have been born."

"What happened to Maj after your father death?"

"What does it matter?" Ross explode "Sitting here isn't finding Henry and Gal

"Right now, there's a full, global alert

him with the knife from the kitchen. She stabbed his heart, and she cut his throat. She stabbed, and stabbed, and she made a mark on him, like her birthmark."

"She carved a pentagram on him?"

"Yes. And she . . ." A sob broke through though Tosha muffled it with her hand.

"What?"

"She . . . drank. His blood. She licked and lapped at it. Oh God. God, Ross. I can still see it. I saw it in my head, and I see it now."

"Tosh. Tosha. It's over." He took both her hands, pressed his lips against them. "It's done. I'm right here."

How many times, Eve wondered, had Roarke said those same words to her when she woke from nightmares?

They were never really over.

"What happened then?" Eve asked.

"I ran to the neighbor's house so they could help, but it was too late. They called the police, and the man, the neighbor, he went to our house. He found her on the bed with Papa, with the knife. He said she was laughing.

"They took her away, and I never went home again. I only saw her again when I testified. She said to me one day she would come for me and take all I loved. Now she has. They're only children, and so innocent.

She'll hate them for that, for their innocence."

"We're going to do everything we can to get them back safe. You said Stockholm. When did you come to New York?"

"When I was eighteen. I lived in the countryside, with a family in Sweden. They were good to me. But I wanted to be away, far away. There had been nightmares until I was almost sixteen. She'd come into my sleep. I can't explain."

"You don't have to." Eve knew exactly.

"Dr. Ryden helped me. He helped me learn to keep her away, and to keep my own mind from reaching into hers. But when I was old enough, I wanted to be away. I came to New York to live, to study, to work."

"Are you a sensitive, Tosha?"

"No, no, it's not the same. Only with her. And now, not even that. I don't feel her, I don't see her. If I did, I would have known she was close, that she wanted the children."

"You came home a day early?"

"Yes, we wanted to come home, to surprise Darcia . . . Darcia." She pressed her hand to her mouth. "Darcia and the children. We have gifts for them. Oh God, she killed Darcia. She was my true sister. My little sister, and Maj killed her."

Peabody set a cup in front of Tosha. "I

made some herbal tea. You should drink it. Your kids' faces are on every screen in the country now. Your sister's, too."

"I have another question," Eve began. "Do Henry and Gala know about Maj?"

"No." Rocking, Ross pressed Tosha's hand to his lips again, as much for comfort as to offer it.

"I didn't want them to know, or to be afraid, or to understand, so young, that there's real evil in the world. She's from another life," Tosha added, then stopped, went white again. "We're the same. We look the same. They'll think she's me, their mother. Oh God, they won't understand."

"She's got no reason to hurt them. Listen, *listen,*" Eve stressed as Tosha began to weep. "If she'd wanted to hurt them, to kill them, she would've done it here, right here in your home, where you'd come back and find them. She took them for a reason. She packed clothes and toys for them. Why would she do that if she only meant to kill them?"

Though her breath stayed rapid and ragged, Tosha nodded. "She . . . wants them because they're mine — and hers — we share blood, we share faces, bodies. We're almost the same. She wants them." She turned to her husband, held on, held close.

"She wants them, Ross. She won't hurt them as long as she wants them."

Only, Eve thought, until she gets tired of them. Or until they fulfilled her purpose for them. But she let the terrified parents hold on to that slim thread of hope.

It didn't look like a dungeon, or a tower. It looked like a bedroom — the two beds, the two dressers, the toys on the shelves. There was a bathroom, not like the one at home. It had only a toilet and a sink. And no door to close for privacy.

The rooms had no windows, and the only door was locked.

On a big red table sat a blue and white tea set with bowls of little cupcakes, and gumdrops and frosted cookies.

His stomach hurt, and his head.

"Mine, too," Gala whispered. "And I'm so thirsty."

They'd told each other not to eat or drink, but they were only seven.

"We'll have just a little bit," Henry decided.

But they were so hungry, and the pot held cherry fizzies instead of tea. So they gobbled up the treats.

"Is it a game?" Gala wondered. "Papa likes games."

"I don't think it's a game. Darcia . . ."

"Maybe it was pretend." Gala's eyes filled. "Mommy loves us. She loves Darcia. Mommy wouldn't hurt us or Darcia."

"It's not Mommy." Henry's handsome little face screwed into fierce lines. "She's an evil witch who cast a spell so she looks like Mommy, but she's not."

"Are you sure?"

"She said she'd hurt us if we didn't drink that stuff. When she stopped the car and told us to drink that stuff, she said she'd hurt you if I didn't drink, and hurt me if you didn't. Mommy wouldn't do that."

"No, Mommy wouldn't."

"It made us go to sleep, like a spell, so we woke up in here."

"I don't want to be here. I want Mommy. I want Papa."

"They'll find us." He took a deep breath. "They'll send a good witch to fight the bad witch, and to get us out, to take us home."

"How will the good witch find us here?"

"I don't know, but she will." *I can't say it out loud,* he said into his sister's mind.

The magic talk was a secret, even from their parents.

You can't say it either, or she might hear.

I won't.

I took the Jamboree to bed with me.

You're not supposed to!

I know, but I did. It's in my secret pocket, the one Darcia made for my pajamas. I'm going to send messages to the good witch to help her find us. We can't let the bad witch know, or she'll take it away.

But we don't know where we are.

She'll know! He heard the door creak. *Don't tell her!*

Maj opened the door, smiled broadly. "It's quiet in here. Just what are you two talking about?"

Gala curled her fingers into Henry's, and promised not to tell. "We want to go home now," she said to the witch who looked like Mommy.

"You are home. This is your home now. And look at this! You ate and ate and ate. Cookies and candies and cake. You'll get fat, fat as little pigs. Fat enough to eat." She laughed, and Gala no longer thought she looked like her mother.

"Fat enough to eat," Maj said again. "Yum. Yum. Yum."

CHAPTER THREE

With Peabody, Eve stepped back into the living area. The business of murder played out around them with the MacDermits safely tucked away in the kitchen with two uniforms. The morgue team had already taken the body, and the sweepers swarmed through the rest of the area.

"Get everything there is to get on Maj Borgstrom," Eve ordered. "Everything. Add in EDD if you need assistance there." She pulled out her own 'link as she spoke. "And arrange for the MacDermits to move into a safe house."

"On that."

Thinking fast, Eve contacted Dr. Charlotte Mira, the NYPSD's top profiler and psychologist. "I need Mira," she snapped to the dragon who guarded Mira's gates. "Don't fuck with me."

Mira's admin's face bunched up like a fist. "Lieutenant Dallas —"

"I don't care if she's headshrinking God, do it now."

If the clenched jaw was an indicator, Eve would have hell to pay later, but the 'link screen shifted to waiting blue. Seconds later Mira's calmer face came on.

"Eve?"

"Maj Borgstrom. She was committed to the Borj Institute for the Criminally Insane in Stockholm as a minor, about twenty-five years ago. Murdered her father. She's just killed her twin sister's nanny here in New York, and abducted the sister's twin kids — boy and girl, age seven. I need whatever you can find out from her doctors. Anything, everything. And I need it now."

"How long has she had the children?"

"Since just after midnight."

"Let me see what I can do."

"Fast," Eve added, then clicked off. She contacted the other ace up her sleeve — a man who had connections and sway everywhere she could think of in the known universe.

For the second time she drew an admin, but this one smiled at her. "Lieutenant, how can I help you?"

"I need to talk to him, right away."

Caro's smile faded, but she nodded briskly. "One moment."

It took hardly more before Roarke came on. She saw mild annoyance on his truly stupendous face, just a hint of it in those intense blue eyes.

"Sorry," she said immediately. "It's urgent. Who do you know in Stockholm? The heavier the weight, the better."

"Would the Prime Minister be weighty enough?"

"Sounds like it. Here's the deal." She ran it through for him quickly, hitting the high points, knowing her husband could and would connect the dots.

"I'll make some calls."

"Appreciate it."

"That's smart," Peabody commented. "Pulling in the big guns, medically and politically."

"We use what weapons we've got."

"I've got the safe house set up," Peabody continued. "The Belmont. It's close to Central. I didn't know who you wanted assigned. But with a kidnapping, the feds —"

"They'll be notified." She had another weapon there, in the form of her commander. Once again she pulled out her 'link and contacted one of her detectives.

"Jenkinson. I need you and Reineke on protection detail." She briefed him as succinctly as she had Roarke, gave him the location and the destination. “Bring in EDD to set up the tap, and move it.”

As she ended transmission, she turned back to Peabody. “Check in with the uniforms. See if we’re having any luck with the canvass.” And once again, she used the ’link, went through an admin, and quickly to Commander Whitney.

“Sir —”

“I’ve seen the alert, have the bare bones.”

Saved time, she thought. “I’m having the parents moved to the Belmont with Jenkinson and Reineke on first shift. I’m going to order a tap on their electronics, considering the possibility of contact or ransom demand, though I believe both are low. BOLOs have been issued for the suspect and the vehicle she was driving — which belonged to the parents, the MacDermits, and was kept in a private garage. I’ve asked Dr. Mira to contact the suspect’s medicals in Sweden, and I enlisted the aid of a civilian consultant. Roarke knows the Prime Minister over there, and may help cut through some of the international red tape to information.”

“I’ll arrange for the tap,” he told her. “I expect to be contacted by the feds at any moment.”

“Yes, sir. I fully intended to contact the FBI. However, as the suspect may have entered the country illegally, or, in fact, may be wanted in Sweden, I considered this may be an international incident, with international repercussions. With that consideration I'm unsure whether to have a conversation with the FBI or the HSO or Global."

Whitney's broad, dark face remained impassive, but she saw the acknowledgment in his eyes. "That is a consideration. The politics are complicated at this point. It may be best for me to contact the HSO, let the federal agencies hash out their food chain. I will, at this point, request Agent Teasdale out of HSO assist, if such assistance is warranted."

"Thank you, sir. I have the name of a police contact involved in the investigation, in Sweden, of the suspect's father's murder. A CPS contact, and a shrink as well."

"Give me what you have, and we'll deal with the international red tape."

"Thank you, sir." She listed the names. "I'll continue the investigation as primary until further orders."

She caught Peabody's smirk as she pocketed her 'link. "What?"

"You're riding the smart bus today. Angling for Teasdale on the federal side because we've worked with her before. We know she's solid, doesn't hot dog."

"And isn't an asshole," Eve finished. "Right now, it's still all NYPSD."

"Nothing on the canvass yet," Peabody reported.

"Nothing more to do here now, and no time to waste. We'll go check out the garage, see how she got in."

"Those kids have to be scared," Peabody began as they walked out to Eve's vehicle. "I know you said ransom's unlikely, but what else does she want them for? Because you're right. If she wanted to kill them or mess them up, she'd have done it in the house, left them like the nanny for her sister to find."

"Then the torture's over. Dead's dead, and ends it. Not knowing's worse than knowing. But that doesn't mean she won't hurt them."

"Kill them, dispose of the bodies."

Eve shook her head as she drove. "I don't know, but I can't see why she'd have packed stuff for them if she wanted to end them right away. How did she find the sister? How long has she known where Tosha lives, about the kids? When did she get out of the institution and how? Once we get those answers we might have a better idea what she's planning."

She pulled up at the garage, a three-level

building. Two for vehicles, from the looks of it, she thought, and top-level apartments, maybe offices.

"You've got the name Tosha gave us for the owner?"

"Bing Francis."

"Contact him." Eve studied the setup. Upscale security cams, swipe bar, scanner.

She held her badge to the scanner, watched the red beam play over it.

Dallas, Lieutenant Eve. Identification verified. Please place warrant for entry on scanner.

"I don't have one. This is a police investigation. I need to know how an individual posing as Tosha MacDermit, registered owner of the 2059 Class-A Orbit Sedan, New York license number Tango, Echo, Victor, zero, six, one, gained entry to these premises and accessed said vehicle."

I am unable to process this information.

"I bet. Listen —"

Even as she geared up for a pissing match with the computer, Peabody signaled. "The owner's coming down. He lives upstairs."

"Good enough. Disappointing," she admitted, sneering at the scanner. "But good enough."

He came around the corner of the building, a big man, heavy in the belly and with a wide, Irish face, keen hazel eyes.

"Bing Francis," he said. "You just caught me. I was about to head out. What can I do you for?"

"I need access to the garage."

"Well now, I sure want to cooperate with the police." Still smiling broadly, he spread his big hands. "But I gotta ask why."

"You haven't had the screen on this morning, Mr. Francis?"

"Can't say I have. Had my music going. Why?"

Eve drew out Tosha's ID photo. "You know this woman?"

"Sure I do. Ms. MacDermit. Come on now." He added a quick laugh. "She can't be in trouble."

"She's in serious trouble, and the person causing it got into this garage last night and took her car."

"Now, that can't be. Ms. MacDermit took the car her own self."

"How do you know that?"

"Well, she forgot her swipe, and couldn't remember her code. Just flustered, she was. So she asked me to let her in. People forget sometimes, it's not a crime."

"No, it's not. But it wasn't Ms. MacDermit."

"I was looking right at her." He tapped

under his eyes with split index and middle fingers. "Close as I am to you."

"Did you ask her for ID?"

"I *know* her." Irritation pinked up in his face. "She and Mr. MacDermit have kept their car here for more than five years now."

"Did she ever forget her swipe and code before?"

"No, but —"

"It wasn't Ms. MacDermit. It looked like her, but Ms. MacDermit was in New Zealand. That's verified. And the person you let in killed Darcia Jordan and abducted Henry and Gala MacDermit."

"What are you talking about?" The pink faded to dead white. "Darcia? She's dead? Somebody took those kids? I'm telling you it was Ms. . . . Oh sweet Jesus, sweet Jesus, was it a clone — that Icove thing? I saw the vid, and . . . you're that cop! You're those cops. The Icove cops."

"We're New York City cops," Eve corrected. "And no, she isn't a clone. She's Tosha MacDermit's twin sister, and she's dangerous. What time did she take the car?"

"God almighty. I didn't know she had a sister, much less a twin. If I had, I . . . I don't know. This is awful. Those are the damnedest cutest kids. And polite, too. And Darcia . . ."

"I know it's a shock, Mr. Francis, but we need to know what time the woman posing as Tosha MacDermit got the car."

"I guess, yeah, yeah, it was just before seven last night. And now that I know, I see she was off." Francis pulled a bandanna out of his back pocket, swiped it over his face. "Didn't sound like Ms. MacDermit so much."

"What do you mean?"

"The accent. The real one hardly has one, you don't much notice. But the one yesterday, it was a little heavier. And she laughed different." He rubbed his face again. "I gave her the start code for the car. She said how she just couldn't remember a thing — long day at work. I didn't think twice about it. If I had . . ."

"It's not your fault," Peabody told him. "You thought you were helping a client."

"Hand to God, I did, but those kids . . . Anything happens to them, I don't know how I'll live with it."

"I'd still like access."

With a nod at Eve, he used his own master swipe, coded in. "Anything I can do. Anything. She didn't get the boosters out of the trunk."

"The boosters?" Eve asked as the big door slowly grumbled open.

"Kid seats," Peabody told her. "They're young enough to need them."

"I figured maybe her and the mister were headed out for the night. Their slot's right over . . . The car. She brought it back."

"I can see that." Eve moved into the garage, and to the black sedan tidily parked between two others. "Do you have a log-in?"

"Absolutely. Just give me a minute."

He hustled over to a wall comp.

"Didn't bother to lock it," Eve observed as she opened the driver's door. "Get the code, Peabody, let's open the trunk."

She'd have sweepers process the car, but she wanted to take a first pass.

"She brought it back at twelve forty-six this morning," Bing announced, and shut his eyes as Peabody started to open the trunk. "Please, God, don't let those babies be in there."

"Booster seats — one pink, one blue. Maintenance kit, spare, first-aid kit." Peabody scanned the inside with a wand, then stepped back. "No sign of blood."

"She put them in the backseat." Picturing it, Eve moved to search through the back. "She either doesn't think she'll need the car or didn't have a secure place to keep it out of sight. But she's got them somewhere reasonably close, somewhere she can drive to, secure the kids, and drive back in under a half hour. That's good to know. Got a mini-disc here, sticking out of the backseat."

She drew it out carefully, frowned at it. "What the hell kind of disc is this? It's got a monkey on it. A monkey in a bathing suit."

"For a kid's toy. Like a kid's PPC, sort of. Plays games, does some limited communication, like an old-style walkie-talkie sort of. Also limited Internet access, depending on parental guidelines." Peabody shrugged. "Lots of kids have them. He probably lost the disc back there when he was playing with it."

"The car's so clean you could eat off the floor." Eve shook her head. "And it was stuck in the seat with just the edge sticking out. I think the kid planted it. How do we play this thing?"

"We'd need the toy — another of the same kind. I think there are a lot of them on the market."

"A Jamboree!" Francis shouted it, and this time his face flushed red with excitement. "I've seen Henry with that a dozen times the last couple months. He got it for his birthday. It's a Jamboree. My grandson has one. I got one upstairs. We play spy with them. I've got one."

"If you'd go get —"

But he was already running.

"Some luck." Peabody studied the disc. "If the boy really did plant it there, if he's got the toy with him, it could be a break."

"And she either doesn't know what it is, or doesn't know he has it. Get another team of sweepers on the garage and the vehicle, and let's get a copy of the security feed from Francis. She didn't take them far. She must have a place, a place she can keep two kids under wraps. Close by so she could case the house, get a sense of their routine maybe. That means she's got money enough to buy or rent. Where'd she get it?"

She stopped when Francis, breath heaving, ran back. Panting, he pushed a colorful little PPC into Eve's hand.

"You should sit down, Mr. Francis." Peabody steered him back so he could at least lean against the trunk of a bright red Urban Mini. "Catch your breath."

Eve fiddled with the toy a moment, searching for controls, power, then slid the disc in.

Giggling burst out, followed by singing — young voices, a boy and a girl. Eve felt her bubble of hope pop. It looked like Peabody had been right.

Then an adult voice cut through, laughing as well.

"Bedtime, you goofies! Henry, time to put that away."

"That's Darcia," Francis murmured.

There was some negotiating, some protests, some begging for a story.

"You already had your story tonight. A new story begins tomorrow! Let's go brush our teeth."

There was a click, a beat of silence, then another click.

"I wish I had a story now." The boy's voice, Eve thought, in a whisper. "Darcia said I could dream one, so I will. Mommy and Daddy will be home soon. I'm going to dream a pirate story. Good night, everybody."

Click. Pause. Click.

This time the boy's voice came on, a bare whisper, slurry, groggy — and music played over it.

"I'm Henry. The evil witch has me and Gala. She killed Darcia. Tell Daddy to come get us. I don't feel good. We had to drink it. It says second. Tell the good witch to come and bring Daddy. Please. We're scared. Tell —"

And silence.

"There's not much room on those little

discs," Peabody said quietly. "He probably ran out of space."

"Smart kid. Smart little kid." Eve glanced over, saw Francis still leaning against the trunk. He'd covered his face with his hands as he wept.

Eve jerked her head so Peabody would deal with him, and stepped out of the garage to play the recording again.

"Smart kid," she repeated. "You stay smart. We're going to find you."

Chapter Four

Eve handed Peabody the Jamboree Francis had lent them as she got into the car. "Limited range, right?"

"Yeah. I think probably a couple of blocks, maybe three or four tops."

"Hmm." Eve used the in-dash 'link to contact Feeney — her former partner, her trainer, and current captain of the Electronic Detectives Division.

He said, "Yo," as his weathered, hang-dog face came on screen.

"What do you know about a toy — what is it — jumbalaya?"

"Jamboree," Peabody corrected.

"Yeah, that."

"Nice little unit, some good features on it. Couple of the grandkids have them. I told them I could make them up something, but they had to have the store-bought."

"I bet you could," she murmured. "Can you boost the range on one of them?"

"Don't see why not, if I had one to take apart and fool with. What's this about? Is this about those kids who got taken?"

"Yeah. The boy's got his toy with him, and he left us a message disc in the car the kidnapper used to transport them. I need you on this, and I'm going to set up a command post at the crime scene. I think the kids are being held in the general area. Central's too far to make this idea workable."

"Give me the address," he told her. "I'll clear the time, bring a couple of the boys along."

"Appreciate it." She relayed the location, clicked off. "Peabody, pull in Baxter and Trueheart, and have them bring down what we need to set up at the crime scene."

"I bet if the boy got one of these for a gift, the girl's got one. Twins," Peabody pointed out. "It's more fun to play if somebody's got a second unit."

"We'll look for it."

"Maybe there's a way to find his frequency. We could try to contact Henry, use that to triangulate location."

"And if we do that when his crazy aunt's around, she hears it, takes the toy — maybe hurts the boy. He needs to try to contact us, and we need to be ready when he does."

She pulled up at the house, in front of the sweepers' van, and drew her signaling 'link out of her pocket. She scanned the text from Roarke as she got out of the car. "Good. It's good. We've got some juice in Sweden, and Roarke's got some data on the suspect. When Mira comes through, we'll have a clearer picture."

"Baxter and Trueheart will put things together and head in. It's weird working out of the crime scene."

"We make do." She walked in, skirted around the sweepers at work. "Go ahead and check the girl kid's room for the toy."

Eve did a quick walk-through of the first floor and determined that the living area, despite the blood spatter and pool, provided the best space for the work.

Still, she stepped off into the kitchen to read the data Roarke had accumulated.

"Found it!" Peabody walked in, waving the second Jamboree. "The kids' rooms are pretty tidy."

"Good. Feeney will have two to play with. Maj Borgstrom, incarcerated in institution for violent tendencies/criminal acts. She was treated by Dr. Dolph Edquist, deceased, and subsequently by Filip Edquist — looks like the first shrink's son. He's dead, too.

Open case they're calling a bungled burglary."

"Well, the evil witch couldn't have had anything to do with the second Edquist's death if she was locked up."

"She wasn't. Two years ago she was, by the second Edquist, deemed ready and rehabilitated enough for a transfer to a halfway house. She had to wear a bracelet. Eighteen months ago, a week before Edquist was killed, she walked out of the new facility, leaving her bracelet behind in her room."

"Well, shit."

"Two days before his death, the recently divorced Edquist made a cash withdrawal in the amount of whatever three hundred and fifty grand in U.S. dollars is in Swedish money, and had arranged for a private shuttle to transport him and a companion to Argentina. False identification and documents listing Edquist as Artur Gruber were found on the premises. But none of the cash. Also missing were an estimated eighty-five thousand in jewelry and other easily portable valuables."

"And another scoop of shit. She vamped the doctor."

"That's one way to put it." Eve leaned back against the kitchen island. "It reads he fell for her, helped get her into a less-secure facility, and planned to run away with her to South America. So she killed him, took the money, and whatever false ID he'd had made for her, and at some point made her way here."

"Why did she wait so long to take the kids?"

"She had to find her sister. Maybe she started the hunt while she was vamping the idiot doctor. She has to find them, scope things out, get a place she can keep them."

"How was he killed?"

"Stabbed. Like her father — and like the father, like the nanny, she carved her little witch symbol on his chest. The cops over there haven't been able to trace her. Edquist's body wasn't found for three days. He'd taken vacation time, so nobody was looking for him. She had plenty of time to get gone. Plenty of time to track Tosha and plan the rest."

Eve took out her signaling 'link again. "Contact Jenkinson, let him and Reineke know we're setting up here."

"Eve." Mira came on. "I was able to reach out to the head of the institution in Stockholm. He believes Maj Borgstrom may be responsible for the deaths of two psychiatrists, father and son, who treated her."

"I got the second one, stabbed during

burglary, with a heavy suspicion the suspect vamped — Peabody's term — the doctor."

"The term's likely accurate. The senior doctor treated her for nearly eighteen years, with limited success. Though during her first few years she displayed violent behavior, had to be restrained or given sedation, she learned to control the behavior. The key is control," Mira stressed. "And to use that control for gain. More privileges. Though she expressed remorse for her actions, the senior doctor considered this a mask. His son began to assist in her treatment about five years ago, and disagreed with his father's analysis."

Mira paused. "We'll make a long story short. Less than thirty minutes after a session with the suspect — which was recorded — the senior doctor died of an apparent cardiac arrest. He was alive when she left his office, but there are a number of medications or combination of medications on site that could induce a heart attack. The suspect had spent considerable time in the infirmary, and in fact, had studied alternative medicine while confined."

"Not enough to lay it on her."

"No, there wasn't enough. The younger doctor took over her case and her treatment."

"And had her released to a halfway facility. Six months later, he's dead, she's gone."

"Yes. Eve, there were two more deaths at the institution during her last ten years there. One patient, one medical. There wasn't enough evidence to charge her."

"Stabbings?"

"The patient, yes. The medical initially looked like an accidental overdose, but was ruled homicide."

"And still she gets a pass to a halfway house?"

"I'll send you the case files. In talking with the head of psychiatry, and with his permission reading some of the first Dr. Edquist's findings, I can tell you she's paranoid delusional. She believes her sister's very existence diminishes her, threatens her. Where most healthy twins form a bond, she sees her sister as an opposing force. She needs to eradicate her in order to be completely whole, to reach her true potential."

"Then why not just kill the sister? Why take the kids?"

"It may be to punish, to torture. She has strong sadistic tendencies. She may delude herself into replacing her sister as their mother. Taking what belongs to her sister, as she might a doll or an outfit. *This is mine now.*"

"So they'd likely be safe, unharmed."

"For now. But her sister still exists, and from her sister came the children."

"Yeah. I got that."

"I want to review all the data I have. It may help us see her, and her purposes and actions, more clearly."

"Get back to me whenever you have more."

She went back to the living room to see Baxter and Trueheart working with Peabody to set up a temporary HQ.

Baxter, a solid detective despite looking like a model for an upscale men's fashion designer, muscled the murder board in place with Trueheart's assistance.

Trueheart, with his young hero's face and squared-away uniform, had come a long way under Baxter's training, Eve thought. She liked the contrast of them, in looks — and the dynamics in how they worked as a team.

"Nearly got the comps set up," Peabody told her as she worked. "I should be able to rig it so we can use the wall screen there."

"If she can't, the geek squad's on its way." Baxter lifted a bag. "Disc bag, laser pointers, and anything else we could think of. Nice digs," he commented. "But why the remote HQ?"

"Our strongest lead is that toy," Eve began.

"The Jamboree." Curious, Trueheart picked one up. "Cassie's little brother has one," he said referring to his current girlfriend. "Fun stuff."

"It may end up saving those kids. How far is Feeney behind you?"

As if in answer, Feeney, his suit rumpled, his hair a small ginger and silver explosion over his droopy face, walked in just ahead of the colorfully clad McNab and Callender.

McNab sent Peabody a wink, which Eve chose to ignore. She might never get used to the intimate byplay between those lovebirds, but she didn't have time to rag on them.

Besides, he carried a tote she assumed held tools of the e-trade.

This would be her core team, she thought. Peabody, Baxter, Trueheart, Feeney — McNab in his screaming orange baggies and shirt of daffodil and kiwi stripes — and Callender, her curvy body snugged into red skin-pants, and her pockets crowding over a long, sleeveless vest covered with silver stars.

Peabody straightened in her pink cowgirl boots and ordered the comp to print the various ID shots for the murder board.

They might resemble a motley crew, Eve

thought, but they were some of the best cops in the department.

"Start setting up the board, Peabody, while I brief the team."

Gala sat on the floor between the beds playing with her doll. It wasn't her favorite doll. The evil witch hadn't brought Princess Elsa. But it was good to have Miss Zelda with her.

She was so scared, and she wanted Mommy. She wanted to be home having a tea party with Darcia.

But Darcia had gone to heaven. She hoped they had tea parties in heaven.

Behind her Henry played with blocks. But he wasn't really playing, just as she wasn't really playing. He built a fort, and in it he tried very hard to call the good witch.

Daddy said good beat the pants off evil, so they needed the good witch to come beat the pants off the evil witch.

Gala told Henry they should pretend to be good until the good witch came. Then maybe the evil witch wouldn't make them drink any more of the stuff that made them feel sick and tired.

And she would be brave, like Henry, and sit in front of the fort so the bad witch saw her playing when she came in again. And

Henry could hide the Jamboree.

But when the door opened she wanted to cry. She wanted Mommy and the bad witch looked like Mommy.

She's not Mommy! Henry shouted in her head.

Crying now, Gala hugged Miss Zelda close.

"Cry baby, cry baby." Maj sang it. "Keep it up and I'll give you something to cry about, you stupid, ungrateful baby. Didn't I give you cookies? Didn't I give you cakes?"

Reaching down, she yanked the doll out of Gala's hands. Smiling, she took a knife out of her pocket, held it to the doll's throat. "If you cry, I'll cut her head off. Do you want me to do that? Do you want to *kill* her?"

"No! Please, don't hurt Miss Zelda! I won't cry. I won't, I won't."

"Miss Zelda. That's a stupid name for a stupid doll." Maj hurled it across the room, and zeroed in on Henry.

He jumped to his feet behind his fort, and stood quivering, hands balled into little fists.

"I don't like the look on your face, *pojke.* Maybe I'll cut your sister's head off." She grabbed Gala, waved the knife. "How about that? You'd better show me some *respect* or I'll cut her throat just like I did your precious nanny's."

"Yes, ma'am." He choked it out, could hardly get his breath.

"What? What did you say? Stop mumbling."

"Yes, ma'am!"

"That's better." She shoved Gala aside so the little girl fell. But she didn't cry. She trembled, but she didn't cry.

The evil witch smiled as she circled the knife in the air. "What are you doing there, Henry?"

"We . . . we've been playing. I built a fort."

"Is that what you call it?" Lunging forward, she kicked at the blocks, sent them tumbling and flying. "It doesn't look much like a fort to me. You don't know how to build anything. You don't know how to do anything. You're stupid."

Her eyes burned when she saw his gaze shift to the knife. She waved it again. "Would you like to get your hands on this, *pojke*? Would you like to hurt me with this?"

Yes, yes! he said in his head, and hearing him, Gala crawled over to him.

Don't, Henry. Don't, don't, don't.

He swallowed hard. "We're not allowed to play with knives."

"Is that right?" Deliberately, Maj flicked the knife against his arm, laughing, laughing when he jolted back in shock, when tears of fear and pain sprang into his eyes. "I am! I can play with knives all I want. You remember that, little boy. Remember that, little girl."

And the most horrible thing happened. They watched her as she licked Henry's blood off the knife, and smiled.

"Delicious! Now, I have things to do. I'm a very busy woman. Later I'll bring you something to eat. Maybe more cakes and cookies. Or maybe worms and bugs. Whatever I bring, you'll eat or I'll slice off your piggy fingers and toes and fry them up in a pan."

She went out, shut the door, turned the locks.

Henry looked down at the hand he'd pressed to his arm, and saw the blood. His stomach rolled; his head swam. His legs gave way so he sat hard on the floor.

"It's all right, Henry." Though the tears came now, Gala kissed his white cheek. "I'll take care of you, just like Mommy and Daddy and Darcia take care of us when we get hurt. I know how."

The little bathroom only had a sink and a toilet, but she ran water over the rough paper towel, scrubbed soap into it — because of germs. And she promised she would eat worms and bugs. She would do anything so the evil witch didn't hurt Henry again.

Chapter Five

Eve had to block the e-speak out of her head. The EDD team huddled in its corner with the toys, tools, and other equipment she didn't want or need to understand.

At one point, McNab went racing out of the house with one of the handhelds. She didn't ask why, but continued to circle her board.

More than a murder board this time, she reminded herself. She couldn't stand for the dead until she brought the living to safety.

"Money's not her motive," Baxter commented. "It's a by-product. She scammed and killed the doctor not just for money, but to get out. She couldn't get to the sister when she was locked up, so she needed a key, and that was this Edquist. The money she got from him. By-product."

"Agreed. She needs funds to hide, to eat, to travel, to have the time to find the sister.

But getting out was primary. Killing him," Eve continued, "means he can't talk, confess his duplicity, and give the name on her new ID. But I'd say that was another by-product. Killing him was purpose and reward in itself."

"She doesn't have a motive to kill the kids," Trueheart began. "It doesn't gain her anything. If the sister is her focus, the kids are a way to get to her. Dead, she's alive and there's nothing to use as bait."

"Kill the kids, cut out the sister's heart," Peabody disagreed. "That's as good as dead."

"That's a point, but as good as dead isn't enough." Eve stopped, studied Maj's ID, rocked on her heels. "She can't win, can't have or be everything she wants as long as Tosha's breathing. But those kids are a living, breathing piece of the sister. The one who crowded her in the womb, who shares her face, her body, who she likes to blame for the death of the mother, who sucked up too much of the father's attention. There can only be one. Now there's not just the sister, but . . . by-products."

"That's one way to put it," Baxter agreed. "I don't know if we're going to logic this out, LT. She's bat-shit crazy."

"Even bat-shit has routines, patterns,

goals. We have to figure hers out."

She wanted the case files, police reports. Wanted data.

"She waited until the sister and husband were out of town," Eve continued. "That says she didn't go directly for the sister. She had the element of concealment, of surprise. But instead of going at the sister when she was, say, taking a walk, doing some shopping, heading to work, she waits, then takes the kids."

"So she wanted the kids more than she wanted the sister dead?" Peabody suggested.

Too simple, Eve thought. And too rational. "No. She wants them all dead."

"We got damn near a mile," Feeney called out. "McNab's out eleven blocks, and we're getting a weak signal. That's more than triple the standard range."

"She could be farther out, but the probability is she's within a mile." Eve crossed to their workstation. "She needed the car. She couldn't stroll along even a couple blocks with two drugged kids and their stuff. Too much to handle, too big a chance to be seen, remembered. What are a couple of kids doing walking around after midnight?

"And she brought the car back." Eve paced away, paced back. "The time line presents she drove the kids to her secure location, locked them up, drove the car back to the garage, logging in roughly twenty-three minutes after she exited the house with the kids."

"I'd put the drive time between five and eight minutes. She'd need the rest of the time to haul the kids inside, secure them."

Eve nodded at Feeney. "So close, most likely within that mile. How do you find the kid's signal?"

Feeney rubbed his face, the back of his neck. "We're going to open up. We'll pick up a lot of signals from anybody using one of these things, but we'll filter it out. The problem is, we've got the booster, so we can pick up. But the kid's unit doesn't have it, so its signal is limited. It's just a toy, Dallas," he continued. "Enhancing on this end's going to help us pick him up, but he's still just got a toy in his hand."

She turned her circle, tried to think. And asked herself if she was putting too much time and effort, too much hope into a damn toy. "What if we could trace the exact unit. We find out when and where it was purchased, see if we can get the schematics on the exact unit."

"They're all pretty much the same. They're mass-produced. It is what it is,

Dallas." Feeney pulled a wrinkled bag of candied almonds out of his pocket, popped a couple. "We took this one apart, so we know how it works, how it's put together. Maybe if we talked to the designer, I don't know, we'd have a brainstorm, but —"

"Why not? We can try it. Who makes it?"

"It's Kidware. That's Roarke's." His ginger eyebrows arched. "I figured you knew."

"How would I know?" She pulled out her 'link, then paused as the door opened. McNab stepped in. And HSO Agent Teasdale and a whip-thin man in a bad black suit came in behind him.

"Tag him," she snapped to Feeney. "Agent Teasdale."

"Lieutenant." In her calm, precise way, Teasdale gestured to the man beside her. "This is Agent Slattery with the FBI. We've been fully briefed on the situation, and will be conducting a joint agency investigation."

Eve kept her tone and gaze even. "Okay."

"The priority of our part of the investigation will be the kidnapping. I'm sure we agree the safety of the children, and their quick return, is the most vital goal."

"No argument. Our e-team has boosted the range of the toy — the same toy we believe Henry MacDermit has in his possession — to nearly a mile radius. We'll attempt to intercept any transmissions or communications he makes, and use that to triangulate his and his sister's location."

"That's excellent, though we can't know if he still has his unit, or the opportunity and wherewithal to attempt a transmission."

"He was smart enough to make a recording when he was drugged and being kidnapped, after he saw the nanny who was part of his family dead on the floor. I think he's smart enough to keep the unit hidden, and to keep trying."

"To reach the good witch." Teasdale nodded. "Fully briefed, as I said. He's just a child, but yes, I agree, a smart one."

"There's still been no communication or demand for ransom from the abductor?" Slattery asked.

"None. I have two men with the MacDermits, in a safe house downtown. I . . . Can I have a moment, Agent Teasdale?"

"Of course."

Eve led the way into the kitchen, paused to assess the woman she'd learned to trust during another investigation. Deceptively slight in build, cool, enigmatic Asian eyes. "Listen, I'm not trying to shut you out."

"I think we understand each other, and should, given our past collaboration."

"Good. Is he solid, Slattery?"

"Very, and he has considerably more experience than I with kidnappings, particularly with minors."

"I don't know if she's going to try for ransom, but at some point she has to communicate with her sister. She'd need to gloat, to twist the knife."

"I agree."

"I could use my men here, Teasdale, that's a fact. And another is, I think you and Slattery are better suited to deal with parents, to be on top of it when the sister contacts them. She will. She has to. She may try to lure the sister out."

Teasdale inclined her head in the slightest nod. "Because she doesn't just want all of them dead, she needs all of them dead."

"That's how I see it, yeah. My men are good, and if you weren't on tap, I'd trust them to see that end through. But you are, and I think you'd do better. Constant communication, complete open line. My word on it."

"I don't doubt your word, and don't need it. I understand your priorities, and shutting out valuable assistance isn't one of them. We'll take the parents, but we'll move them to one of the federal safe houses, locate them back uptown. I want to be closer, geographically."

"Good enough."

"The director is in contact with the Swedish authorities, and Global. It's obvious the investigation into Maj Borgstrom's escape, and the murder of Dr. Filip Edquist — the possible foul play in the death of Dr. Dolph Edquist — were badly bungled. We'll find out why."

"Even better."

"She won't keep them alive long."

"Why do you say that?"

"Children are . . . work. Even frightened children who may be cowed into obedience take time and effort. She may kill one. It's how I would handle it."

Eve jammed her hands in her pockets, nodded. "Yeah, I was thinking the same."

"Kill one — halving the time and effort — and allowing her to send proof of life and death to her sister. Bring grief, panic, and a desperation to save the remaining child."

"And it's a hell of a scenario."

"It's also a logical one."

"From my take, too. Let's hope she isn't logical."

But the idea weighed on her.

She thought of Stella, the woman who'd given birth to her. If she'd been left alone with Stella, she'd never have survived. Too much time and effort, as Teasdale said. Richard Troy, her biological father, had kept her alive. It hadn't stopped him from hurting her, raping her, torturing her — but he'd kept her alive because he'd seen her as an investment.

Which direction would Maj Borgstrom take?

She went back into the living area. "Listen up. Teasdale and Slattery will take over for Jenkinson and Reineke. Peabody, contact them, let them know — and tell them to pick up two more of those toys on their way here. We'll keep communication open and complete between our team and the agents. Everything we know, they know."

"Agent Slattery and I will afford your team the same cooperation," Teasdale added. "We'll move the MacDermits to a safe house in this area, to aid in that cooperation. We are, even now, in contact with Global re the suspect, and any and all information gleaned from that will be shared."

"I'd like to have one of those boosted units," Slattery said. "Our location will mean we may be able to pick up a signal."

"Feeney, show Agent Slattery how that thing works. Peabody, have Jenkinson pick up four of those things. We'll get a second one to you," she told Teasdale.

"Callender will show you," Feeney told Slattery, as he rose and moved over to Eve. "Roarke's going to get us more data. I don't know if it'll add much, but we'll have it. And he's coming in."

"I don't —"

"I can use him," Feeney interrupted. "Another big brain wired for e-work. And it's his toy, Dallas. She's had those kids better than fifteen hours now, and not a peep out of her."

"Okay. You need him, you've got him. Right now, Baxter, take the unit we have left, take a walk. We're going to cover the mile radius continually. The kid's going to try to reach out sometime."

He already had, once from inside the fort, and again after Gala tended to his cut. They didn't have medicine or bandages like at home, but he'd remembered playing war with Daddy. Daddy had been wounded in a battle and showed Henry how to tie a cloth around his arm. He said it was a field dress. It didn't make sense because it didn't look like a dress. But the cut felt better when Gala tied a towel around it.

He was afraid she'd cut him with the knife again, or cut Gala. He was more afraid maybe she was an evil witch vampire because she'd licked his blood right off the knife. He'd snuck out of bed one night and seen part of a vid his daddy watched about vampires. And had nightmares after it.

Maybe she'd make him and Gala vampires, too.

They had to get away.

But no one answered when he called out for help.

Chapter Six

Not an apartment, Eve thought as she hammered away at possible locations. Not a condo. Possibly a small building, lower-level unit, but most probably a detached unit, a house.

Somewhere she could get two kids inside without showing up on building security, without worrying about neighbors.

Would she keep the kids restrained? That didn't seem practical, and wouldn't explain why she'd taken clothes and toys.

If she bound them, she'd have to let them loose for the bathroom, for food.

"She wouldn't see a couple of seven-year-olds as a risk, right? She's bigger, stronger, and kids tend to do what an authority figure tells them. Especially if they're scared."

She had, until the end, until the pain and the terror he meant to kill her overcame everything else. But Eve wasn't sure it applied for all or most, so she glanced at

Peabody for confirmation.

"I've got a couple cousins who could have taken an adult down and left him begging for mercy when they were seven, but generally? Yeah. The adult's in charge, in control."

"So she probably doesn't have them restrained — or if she has, they're still free enough to play — or why take stuff? A room, a locked room, closed off — and she couldn't put a couple of kids in a room near where other people live and work. Windows," she added. "You could use privacy shields, but it's risky."

"A basement?"

"Maybe. A tightly sealed room, probably without windows or boarded and shielded windows. One door's the smartest. She has to have easy access to it. And it has to be somewhere some bystander couldn't wander into. We recanvass, a mile radius from the garage. I want officers paying attention to any single residences, any vacant buildings.

"She could, and likely did, walk around this neighborhood. People were used to seeing the sister, and wouldn't think twice. She probably shopped around here, ate around here. On the recording, the kid said, 'It says second.' Second Avenue? He could've seen a street sign out the window. Let's focus there."

"I might have something."

Eve shoved up from her jerry-rigged workstation, hurried to Callender.

"We're getting a lot of little communications. Kids are out of school. In the listening area, we've probably got at least a dozen or more playing around with this thing. But I think . . ." She shook her head. "I can't hold it. It's weak . . . and it's gone. I just can't triangulate, Captain, it's wavery, and there's too much interference."

"Clean it up, boost it," Feeney ordered. "Let's see if we can hear the transmission."

"Working on it. It's through Trueheart's boosted unit. Yeah, I got that, cutie," she said, Eve assumed, to Trueheart. "Hold your position. We might pick it up again. Let me work some magic here."

Patience straining, Eve waited while Callender worked a keyboard manually. Behind her, Peabody rose to answer a brisk knock on the door. "Keep the nosy out," Eve snapped. "Come on, Callender."

"I'm getting it. It's like trying to pull a whisper out of a hurricane."

Then Eve heard it, indeed hardly more than a whisper. *A knife . . . licked blood . . . make us vampires . . . hurry.*

Eve whipped out her comm. "Trueheart, answer him. Keep him calm. Tell him we're looking for him, but ask him if he can tell you anything about where they are. Anything. How it looks, sounds, smells. Make it fast."

She heard Trueheart, his easy voice, call the boy by name.

"Hey, Henry, we're going to find you. It's going to be okay. Can you tell me where you are? What do you see, Henry, what do you hear? What —"

With her comm open, Eve heard the wavery response.

A room . . . two beds, no windows . . . make us eat cookies. Cake. Cut me. Hurts. Send good witch, hurry . . . .

"Henry," Trueheart began, but even the hum of the transmission dropped away. "He's gone, Lieutenant. I'm sorry."

"His battery's low."

Eve turned, saw Roarke behind her.

"Yeah." Feeney hissed through his teeth. "I was afraid of that."

"It'll hold a charge for about twenty hours, depending on usage, but he's just a boy, isn't he, and might not have charged it up recently."

In his elegant business suit, his mane of black hair sweeping nearly to his shoulders, Roarke shifted to study the board. "I've seen their faces all over the reports, through the day. And hers." He looked back at Eve. "I've brought some equipment that may add to what you have here, but the problem will remain, I think, the limitations of the toy he has, and the battery life of it."

"He got through once. He's going to get through again."

"He seemed a smart and steady one for his age." Roarke smiled a little. "We'll bet on him then. I've brought some other supplies. Coffee."

"Oh thank God."

"And food's on its way — pizza," he added before Eve could object. "We'll work better with food in us."

"Everything's better with pizza," McNab claimed. "Hey, Baxter, let's go out and haul in the new toys."

Roarke took Eve's hand briefly, squeezed it. "Well then, let's see what we have." And shedding the jacket of his suit, moved to join the e-team.

Eve switched off with Trueheart, took the boosted unit. She needed the air, needed to walk.

Cold, she thought as the wind kicked at her. The days were colder now, and shorter. This one would be ending soon.

She knew what it was to be a child, alone

and afraid in the dark, in the cold.

Using her earbud, she contacted Teasdale to check in.

"No communication as yet."

"How are they holding up?"

"By a thin thread now. It helped to be able to tell them you'd captured a transmission from Henry. I . . . Yes, Tosha, it's Lieutenant Dallas. She'd like to speak with you, Lieutenant."

"All right. Put her on."

"Lieutenant, please, have you heard any more?"

"Not yet. But I'm out right now, scanning for another transmission. We're all working on this."

"Gala. Did he say she was all right? Did he —"

"He didn't say she wasn't. We've got cops canvassing a mile radius. We strongly believe the children are inside that area, and they're both alive and well."

"If Ross and I could come home, if we could try to reach them ourselves —"

"You're better where you are. Agents Teasdale and Slattery are experienced." Terrified parents shuddering over her shoulder was the last thing she needed. "Your sister's going to contact you at some point. You need to be ready. You need to do and say exactly what they tell you. And you need to trust us."

"They're just babies. They still believe in fairy tales, and that their daddy can keep the monsters away. Don't let her hurt them. Please, don't let her hurt them."

"Nothing's more important than getting your kids back safely. Believe it. I promise you, when we have more, you'll know it. We won't stop looking for them."

Eve slipped the comm back in her pocket, covered ground, circled, backtracked. And stood scanning buildings as the day ended and the long night began.

When she rejoined the team she passed off to Reineke. The home, turned crime scene, turned temporary HQ, smelled of coffee and pizza and the carnival lacing of sugar from the donuts Jenkinson had brought in.

It smelled like cop, she thought.

"Peabody, let's try what worked on the Reinhold case. We'll generate a map, using the target area. Eliminate high-rises to start. Let's look for single homes, or smaller buildings with basements."

"I'll get it going." Peabody took a slug of coffee. Sometime while Eve had been walking she'd pulled her dark hair back in a stubby tail. "With Reinhold we knew he'd had only a couple days to secure a location. She's had a year or better."

"And Reinhold was days ahead of us," Eve reminded her partner. "She's only had hours. The kid said there were two beds in the room, no windows. Not that the windows were shut or boarded or shielded. No windows. And goddamn it, I know he's just a kid and the intel could be wrong, but we're going with it."

"Okay. I got it."

Roarke walked over, held out a slice of pizza. "Eat."

"In a minute."

"You've been at this all day. Eat. Take a break."

"Those kids aren't getting a break." But she took the slice. "She knew they were away, the parents. She knew the nanny would let her in, thinking she was Tosha. She didn't have to kill the nanny. Knock her out, restrain her, get the kids, get out. She killed the nanny because it would hurt the sister more, and because she likes killing."

She bit into the pizza, thinking, thinking. "The symbol — she carved the pentagram into the nanny, like she did with her father, and later with the doctor she killed. It means something."

Eve circled around. "Tosha — the mother — said the kids still believed in fairy tales. In her way, so does Maj Borgstrom. Her sign, on her kills. Her need to eliminate her sister so she . . . gains power? I think it's that as much as the obsession with being the only one.

"She'd had enough time to observe the household, the dynamics of it. I say she knew her sister and the nanny had a strong relationship. Maybe . . . sisterly? I don't know. I haven't had time to give the dead nanny any attention. It's not right. It's disrespectful."

"Bollocks."

"It's not —"

"It is," he interrupted. "How long had she tended the children?"

"Over six years. Almost as long as they've been alive."

"And you say she and the mother — and I assume the father as well — had a strong and personal relationship."

"Yeah, that's my take from their reaction to her death. It hit hard."

"Is it your take the nanny — what was her name?"

"Darcia Jordan. She was twenty-nine. She had parents, grandparents, great-grandparents. Two sisters. A niece and two nephews."

And she berated herself for not giving the dead her attention? Roarke thought.

"Would you say Darcia loved the children, or was it just a job?"

"She loved them. The wit — her friend — her statement, the next-of-kin's statement, the parents.' Yeah, she loved the kids."

Because he could see the frustration and worry, he skimmed a hand over her hair. "And wouldn't she want you to focus all your time and energy, your skill, on bringing them home safe?"

"I know that in my head, but —"

Before she could evade, and knowing she'd object, Roarke pressed his lips to hers. "You're standing for her, Eve. And you'll bring her justice when you bring the children she loved home again."

"No kissing on duty."

"I'm not on duty. I'm a civilian." He smiled at her. "But I do see how shocked the badges in the room are at such a display."

Since work went on without a hitch — or a smirk — she didn't have much ground to stand on. But the principal remained. "Aren't you supposed to be doing some geek work?"

"I have done, and will do. We're on shifts

at the moment, waiting for the boy to transmit again. We should be able to amplify the transmission, and clean out any noise."

"Can't we home in on it, like we could on a standard 'link?"

"But it isn't a standard 'link, is it?" Roarke dealt with some frustration of his own. "He's just the age group, Henry is, it's targeted for. Too young for a 'link, too old to settle for a unit that just makes noise, just sets off a recording. He can talk, real time, to his mates down the block, or play games — play games with those friends as well, in real time, or run up his own scores, wait for them to have a go."

"I know Feeney took one of them apart, but maybe you should. It's your thing."

"I didn't design the bloody toy. I manufacture it. He's more than capable of sussing out the workings, and I've put him together with the design team. All I can do is lend a hand, and a bit more high-powered equipment."

Frustrated, she thought. He was every bit as frustrated as she. They were combing the area, scouting it foot by foot. Generating maps, poring over data and time lines.

But their biggest lead was a seven-year-old with a toy.

"What else does it do? It records, right?

He left that disc."

"It does, yes. Again in a limited way. He could do a bit of schoolwork on it, checking math and letters, playing match games and simple brain teasers, adventure games and the like. He can photograph or —"

"It takes pictures?"

"It does. Rather decent ones considering."

"Can he transmit them?"

"Ah." Realization dawned in his eyes. "If he's learned how, he could."

"Okay, okay, we can work with that. Peabody, how's that map coming?"

"It's coming."

"Trueheart, work with Peabody." She turned to Roarke, lowered her voice. "Can you and McNab handle that hardware for a while?"

"Of course."

"Good. Feeney, Callender, you need to take a shift on the canvass."

"It's been nearly two hours since he transmitted." Callender rubbed her eyes. "He could try again any minute."

"McNab and Roarke will handle it from here. Geeks walk, too. There's a twenty-four/seven market near the southwest corner of this block." She dug in her pocket for credits and cash. Frowned at the amount.

Roarke barely sighed. "How much?"

"I don't know. Enough for bottled water, tubes —"

"Cherry fizzy!" McNab called out.

"I wouldn't mind one of those," Trueheart added.

"Fine, fine, fizzies galore. Show the photos again. Do a sweep, bring back supplies." When her 'link signaled, she pulled it out, glanced at Roarke. "Thanks. Put in an expense chit."

"I'll be sure to do that," he said dryly, and handed Callender cash.

She glanced at the readout on her 'link, saw Mira's name. "Dallas."

"Eve, I've had time to read over more of Maj Borgstrom's records, and speak to some of the staff at the institution and halfway house." The concern in Mira's tone tightened Eve's belly.

"And?"

"Needless to say, she should never have been released from high-level security. Several members of the staff reported her for violent behavior, lodged complaints. She was twice caught in intimate situations, once with a guard, once with a medical. Both times she claimed coercion. It couldn't be disproved, and the staff involved were fired."

"Bartering sex for privilege. That's nothing new in or out of a cage."

"In the second instance, security was alerted when the medical began to scream, when he ran out of the infirmary, bleeding. According to reports she had been performing oral sex, and bit him."

"Okay."

"Bit through, Eve. Bit off the tip of his penis, and consumed it."

"Ouch, and yuck."

"The report states they found her, face smeared with blood, laughing. Later she claimed she'd been forced, had panicked, tried to defend herself. I can't say the institution covered it up, altogether. They terminated the medical, and negated Borgstrom's privileges, confined her to solitary for a week, increased her meds and her therapy. She never wavered from her story. And engaged counsel, threatened to sue."

"So they closed it down," Eve surmised. "If she'd been able to get her hands on a sharp or a shiv, the blow job boy would've lost more than the tip of his dick."

"I tend to agree. In altercations with other patients she was known to bite — viciously."

To let out some steam, Eve kicked a chair. "How the hell did Edquist get away with letting her out?"

"For a period of nearly three years she appeared to respond to treatment. She became less volatile, more cooperative. There were incidents, but in each case it proved difficult to be certain she instigated or was at fault. Even after she was transferred she appeared to have balanced. She showed remorse, and an eagerness to make amends. However, after she'd escaped, another resident stated she'd seen Borgstrom sneak out at night, or had seen her sneak back in, with blood on her face, her hands. The resident claimed she was afraid to speak up as Borgstrom threatened to kill her. And eat her."

"The kid said something like that. A vampire thing. You don't actually believe she's a cannibal."

"She believes her sister consumes her space, her life, her being, by existing. She may have twisted that to mean she must consume in order to be whole and free."

"Dr. Mira, I don't want to tell these parents the lunatic sister killed their kids and ate them for breakfast."

Licked the knife, she remembered. Licked the kid's blood off the knife. Licked and lapped her father's blood.

"Send me everything you've got. Every report, every conversation. Anything you can think of," Eve demanded.

"I'm already putting it together for you. I don't know how much time they have, Eve."

"It's going to be enough."

CHAPTER SEVEN

Eve pored over Mira's data, she picked apart the case files from the investigation into Edquist's murder, and reviewed the reports on the incidents involving Maj Borgstrom at the institution.

Mira's data and analyses were detailed, insightful, offered a clearer picture of the subject. Bat-shit crazy pretty well summed it up, but with the seriously dicey element of cannibalistic tendencies.

The police reports might have lost a bit in the translation, but she couldn't see where the Swedish cops hadn't done a reasonably thorough job.

On the other hand, the institute's internal and external reports came off spotty and smelled ever so lightly of cover-up.

Still, they all contributed to the whole.

She added key elements into her own notes, reorganized them. Borgstrom had worked in the prison library, laundry, kitchen, infirmary. She'd studied alternative medicine and had bartered sex for gain.

Could she have used any of those experiences or predilections to establish her identity, her location, her revenue stream?

Had she worked in medicine, education, food or domestic services to establish identity, to earn enough to pay for a place to live? A place she could hold two young kids?

"There's an interest in the occult, of the dark and nasty variety," Eve said to Roarke while Peabody continued to slave away on the map. "And her violence doesn't seem random or impulsive, but planned and purposeful."

On a short break from e-work, Roarke downed water and studied Eve's data on screen. "The medical area might be her choice. Access to drugs, a chance to give pain or withhold it."

"Yeah, I'm looking at that. Or one of those wicca-whatever shops. Herbals, rituals. Maybe a combo of traditional and nontraditional. Peabody! Do a search in the working area for small clinics and witchy places. Maybe alternative medicals. Like that."

"I'll add it in."

"I wonder . . ."

Eve looked up, over at Roarke. "Wonder

out loud. We can use anything."

"If it is shadowed by the occult, and touching on ritual, would the knife she used to kill the nanny be a ritual knife?"

"It's a thought. It's an angle. Trueheart! Do a search for any occult retail in the working area, and see if any are open this late."

"On it, Lieutenant."

"She used sex for gain. Maybe she's continued that pattern. An LC license? It would give her unlimited opportunities. Or she may have an accomplice, bound by sex — willing and informed or not. Or may have used one then disposed of him."

"I'll take that angle," Feeney called out. "IRCCA's my baby. I'll dig in, look for like crimes."

"Okay. Okay. Baxter, take it from Callender when she gets back. McNab, keep scanning for a transmission from the boy. He's going to try again."

She moved off, into the kitchen. She needed some quiet, some space to think. She couldn't just put her boots up on her desk and study her board, let her mind shift from point to point, not with this setup.

But she could program coffee, let it all circle around, and try to find a new starting point.

Roarke came in, got coffee of his own. "I could set you up somewhere else in the house."

"No, I just need to think a minute without all the chatter. And the bopping and jiggling. What is it with e-geeks and that constant —" She bopped and jiggled to demonstrate, made Roarke laugh.

"Even Feeney, a little. He bobs his head around, bops his shoulders once he really gets going." She got the coffee, frowned at Roarke. "You don't. Why don't you do the geek boogie when you're working?"

"It's heroic control," he told her, and skimmed a finger down the shallow dent in her chin. "Inside I'm a dancing fool."

"Hmm," she said, and veered back on track. "She plans, and though she's bat-shit as previously stated, she thinks things through. She has an agenda, a goal, a purpose, and apparently a taste for human flesh and blood."

"Always a bonus."

"She may have bought things to outfit some sort of confined space for the kids. Beds — he said there were two beds. She may have hired someone to put in locks or doors, or to outfit a bathroom. She'd have to know without an accessible bathroom she'd have a big mess on her hands. She thinks, she plans, she acts. We can check on a lot of that tomorrow."

He glanced around the kitchen, the family feel of it, the wall board covered with bright, childish drawings. "She plans to kill those children."

"Oh yeah. She's not going to let them go. But she may plan to torture her sister for a while, try to extort money, more at some point, lure her. Then she'd have it all. The sister she's convinced is sucking up her power, and the progeny from said sister who would, in her logic, do the same. I don't worry about her killing them tonight. Much."

"Then what?"

She stared down into her coffee a moment, into the black depth of it. "You can do a lot to the human mind and body without destroying it. We both know just how much you can hurt a kid without killing."

"What will she do next? You're trying to put yourself in her head," Roarke said before she could respond. "You're asking yourself what the next steps are. What do you think she'll do next?"

"Torture them — hopefully just mentally, emotionally right now. That's bad enough, and she'd enjoy it. She has to contact the sister at some point. Sooner is better. Rub it in, hear the fear and distress. It's not enough to project it. Maybe she starts the deal making then, but . . . I'd string it out for maximum pain. And I'd want to get some sleep, or at least relaxation time, so I'd drug the kids. Wouldn't want them trying to pull anything while I was sleeping. Better to put them out, start again tomorrow. Early. Get some sleep knowing her sister won't. So she has to make that contact."

He followed the line of logic, nodded. "They'll demand proof of life, the feds."

"Yeah. If she doesn't expect that, she's stupid. I don't think she's stupid. She'll have something."

"We can, and will, track any transmission she makes."

"Yeah, and if she doesn't know that, she's stupid. She'll have a plan there. She won't be at the location where the kids are when she contacts. Why be an idiot? But we'll use whatever tracking we've got, correlate. Everything we get adds in."

Even as she started out, Peabody raced to her. "They're getting something from Henry."

"Are you doing okay, Henry?" Feeney asked as Eve dashed in.

"We wanna go home. You're not the good witch."

"No, I'm a friend of hers. She's right here."

He signaled Eve while both Callender and McNab worked frantically to boost and stabilize the signal.

"Hey, Henry, where are you?"

"I'm hiding . . . bathroom. Gala's watching for . . . witch."

"Henry, do you know how to take pictures with your Jamboree?"

"Yeah . . ." Static buzzed in, his voice faded, wavered back. ". . . pictures good."

"Okay, why don't you take some pictures of the bathroom, and if you can of the door of the room where she's got you? Of the walls. It's going to help me find you."

"It's going to take battery power," Roarke murmured in her ear.

"Just of the door, Henry, and of the bathroom, like from right outside. Just those two pictures right now. Have Gala stand next to the door, and take one. Hurry up, okay?"

" 'Kay."

"Tell me what the walls look like?"

"Like . . . sidewalk."

"The floor?"

"Like . . . walls. A rug. Toys."

"Do you remember anything about how you got where you are? Anything at all."

"It was cold, and there . . ." He dropped out, chopped back. ". . . window. We didn't have our boosters . . . stopped and made us drink. It wasn't good . . . sleepy."

"Where did she stop? Do you remember anything about where?"

". . . towers and a star."

"A building with towers and a star?"

"Uh-huh . . . didn't go there. She said drink . . . drove more, and I fell asleep. I . . . pictures."

"Good. Do you know how to send them?"

"I send pictures to . . . and to Granddad and Grandma, and —"

"Okay, good. Here's where you should send them." She gave Henry her 'link number, slowly.

"Not yet," Roarke told her.

"But don't do it yet. Why?" she hissed at Roarke.

"He needs to shut down, better to delete some of the other functions. It may help give him enough of a boost."

"Shit. Henry, I'm going to have you talk to somebody else, and he's going to tell you what to do."

She shoved the comm at Roarke, shifted to lean over McNab's shoulder. "Have you got him?"

"It's not enough of a signal, Dallas. It slips and slides."

"I can hear him fine. Mostly."

"We're boosting audio here, and filtering out all the noise we can. It's the source that's the problem."

"She's back!" Henry's frantic whisper seemed to boom into the room. "She's right outside . . . bathroom. I —"

"Henry! What . . . doing in there . . . fat little pig?"

"I'm going . . . bathroom. I . . . wash my hands. I . . . hide my Jamboree," he whispered.

"I . . . you're playing with yourself, you ugly . . ."

Eve heard the girl screaming: *Don't hurt him. Don't you hurt my brother.* Then the sound of a crash, a wail a second before the transmission went dead.

"It's off," Callender told her. "He shut it off, and that was smart. We'll hope he got it hidden in time."

"Upper East Side building with towers and a star." Eve started to turn, give the order.

"I'm already looking," Roarke told her, standing hunched over a portable comp.

"I found two occult shops, Lieutenant."

Trueheart tapped his screen. "One of them's open until two A.M."

"Baxter."

He grabbed his coat. "We're on our way. Let's go, Trueheart."

"There has to be a way to track his damn signal."

Feeney rubbed at his eyes before swiveling around to Eve. "It's a damn toy, Dallas. A nice, well-made toy, but just a toy. It's got severe limits. And his batt's weak. Shutting down the other functions was a good call. It'll help prolong the batt. And if he transmits when we're closer, we could track better."

"It looks like it's south of Seventy-second," McNab put in. "Most likely north of Sixty-first. Probably west of Second. East of Fifth — that's ninety-nine percent."

"Okay. Peabody, let's go with the looks like, maybe, probably. Highlight that area."

"I have a strong possible, a synagogue on Sixty-eighth, between Third and Lex."

Eve strode over to Roarke, studied the image. Two towers, and the Jewish Star on the building. "Yeah, that could be it. From here, she would've crossed Second Avenue — Henry's second. And she would've gone south on Third. Stopped near that building to give them the booster drug, put them out so they'd wake up inside, secured and disoriented. Peabody, put the map on the wall screen."

"I haven't finished —"

"As it is," Eve ordered. "You can keep working on it. See, there's her route." Eve grabbed a laser pointer, traced it. "Going with McNab's perimeters, we lock in above Sixty-first, and with this stop, we'll focus south of Sixty-eighth. West of Second, east of Fifth. What have we got there?"

"A hell of a lot of brownstones, townhomes, upscale retail."

Eve strained at Peabody's assessment, but couldn't argue with it. "If we could get those pictures, we may be able to work out if they're in a basement, some sort of attic, a utility room, something. We might be able to judge the age of the building. Still, we're narrowing the area."

Eve raked her fingers through her hair, squeezed her hands on her skull as if to wake up fresh thoughts.

"She has to eat, shop, probably work. After all those years of confinement, she's not going to close herself in. I still think closer is better for her. The kid said he got sleepy pretty quick, we'll figure she wanted that. She's at Sixty-eighth, so let's start with above Sixty-fifth. She's probably east of

Madison. Park's possible, but Lex or Third keeps her easy walking to this place. Let's play with that. Look on Lexington, look on Third."

"It's like following bread crumbs," Roarke muttered as he sat to assist Peabody. "From point to point, and never being sure if some bloody bird hasn't pecked a few up."

"Jesus, it is." Peabody shuddered. "Two lost kids, evil witch. Henry and Gala. Hansel and Gretel. Bread crumbs," she repeated at Eve's blank look.

"Is that where that came from? What happened to those kids?"

"They outwitted her," Roarke told her, "and the witch ended up in the oven, burned alive."

"Nice story for the toddler set."

"Folktales were often brutal."

"But . . ." Peabody stared at both of them, dark eyes stunned. "I thought they escaped, and came back with their parents, brought healthy food to the witch. Their kindness transformed her into a kind grandmotherly type, and she opened a bakery."

Eve smirked at Roarke. "Free-Ager version. Sap."

"But —" Peabody just sighed when Roarke patted her shoulder.

"The tale has another disturbing cross-reference," he added. "The evil witch in the gingerbread house planned to fatten them up and cook them for dinner."

"Christ." Eve dragged her hands through her hair. "Well, this ain't no fairy tale."

Eve dragged out her signaling 'link. "Dallas."

"Teasdale. She's contacting now."

Feeney shot a thumb up in the air. "We're locked in here, too. It's go."

Tosha answered, the fear in her voice as palpable as a heartbeat. "Hello."

"It's been a long time, *syster.*"

"Maj, please, Maj, don't hurt the children. I'll do anything you want."

"Oh yes, you will. His blood tastes like yours, weak and thin. I'll sample hers soon."

"Please, please, don't . . . How do I know they're all right? How do I know they're still alive?"

The room filled with screams — the boy, the girl, calling for their mother to come, to help them. A video, brutally close to those terrified faces, snapped off and on, with the time stamp hitting only minutes after Eve and Henry's transmission.

"Mommy, Mommy!" Maj taunted. "You don't even teach them your own language. You don't deserve to live. Neither do they."

"They've done nothing to you. Tell me

what you want, and I'll do it."

"Will you die for them?"

"Yes! Yes! Let them go and take me. I'm begging you."

"Much, much too easy. You'll pay five million American dollars?"

"Yes, yes, yes. Please. Anything."

"Here is anything. Choose one."

"What? I don't understand."

"One dies, one lives. You choose. Your son or your daughter? Which little piggie comes home?"

"Maj, dear God, Maj —"

"Five million dollars. I'll tell you where to send it the next time I talk to you. And you'll tell me which lives, which dies. Choose, or I kill them both. There can never be two, *syster*. You know it. Choose, or both are lost."

"Have you got her, have you got her?" Eve demanded when Borgstrom's line went dead.

"Got her, already dispatching. Feds, too. She was moving, probably on foot from the speed," Feeney relayed. "Tagged her at Madison and Sixty-first. Locked on there, and it's stationary."

"She tossed the 'link," Eve said.

"Yeah, my guess, too."

She grabbed Feeney's comm since it was

handy and open. "I want officers fanned out from the last location, west to Third, north to Sixty-eighth."

She tossed the comm back, began to pace. "It's a good plan. A damn good plan. Torment, torture. Pick one or lose both. She won't do either of them until she contacts again. That buys some time."

"Those screams were recorded," Roarke told her. "She could have altered the video, the time stamp."

Logically yes, Eve thought, but shook her head. "They're alive. She needs her sister to pick one. She figures she will, she's *sure* Tosha will pick one, sacrifice the other. She'll likely still kill them both, but she'll have destroyed her sister with the choice. That's genius. She's crazy, but she's brilliant."

She pulled out her 'link again. "Dallas."

"We hit," Baxter told her. "Four Elements, woo-woo shop, Seventy-first, between Lex and Third. She's a regular. And she was in two days ago, bought some herbs, a sleep aid, candles. She previously purchased a ritual knife. The shopkeeper insists it's used symbolically, but it's plenty capable of slicing up a nanny."

"Do they have an address?"

"No. She always paid cash, but as far as

this one knows, was always on foot. We've got to be close, Dallas."

"See if you can dig any more out, then come back in. Walk along Lex, down about six blocks, cross over to Third, walk back up. She made contact. I'll fill you in. But keep your eyes open."

Chapter Eight

The minute she was inside, Maj pulled off the gray wig, peeled out of the big, padded coat with its frayed hem and torn pockets. She took the time to remove every trace of the carefully applied makeup, and watched the years fall away. Within ten minutes she transformed from a plump, poor, slightly hunchbacked old woman to young, vital. Beautiful.

She spent some time admiring her face. *Her* face, she reminded herself. Tosha was nothing but a pale, weak copy — one that had to be completely destroyed.

She herself was The One. There could be no other. Tosha was responsible, by her very existence, for the death of the woman who'd created them. Maj had no doubt that had the mother lived, she would have smothered the weak, pale copy in her crib and lavished love, attention, and *power* on her true and only daughter.

Tosha was responsible for the death of the father. With her wiles, her lies, her mewling ways, she'd corrupted him, turned him against his true and only daughter. The copy had tried to make her less while she connived to make herself more.

Who else but that pale, weak copy held responsibility for all the years of confinement, of boring, useless, maddening talk, talk, talk, medications, restriction?

Now the reckoning.

Humming to herself, she unlocked the door to the basement, all but floated down the stairs. At the base she unlocked the reinforced door she'd had installed when she'd acquired the property more than six months before.

Inside, the ugly little piggies slept, taken deep into nightmares by the potion she'd mixed into the fizzies she'd made them drink. Yummy, yummy, bubbles and sugar. She'd made them sweet, sweet, sweet, like the frosted cupcakes, the glossy tarts.

Sugar, white and pure, to sweeten their pale blood.

She could poison those cakes and tarts, she considered. Stuff all those sweet sweets down the little piggies' throats.

But she'd rather slit them. Their blood might be weak, but it would be warm.

Anyone could see they were monsters, tucked into one bed together like a creature with two heads. Monsters to be destroyed, consumed.

Once consumed, their youth, their energy, the power they didn't yet understand would be inside her.

Then, finally then, she would spill her sister's blood and drink of it. Drink deep.

But tonight she needed her beauty sleep. Tomorrow, she thought as she locked the door, Tosha would choose.

Which would it be? she wondered. The girl pig or the boy pig? Whichever the copy chose, Maj decided as she climbed the stairs, she would kill that one first.

They worked the map, the data, the probabilities. They scanned, ears pricked for any sound, with the electronics. They walked, covering the streets, showing the ID photos to any passerby who happened along.

Hours passed with no contact, no movement, no change.

"Eve." When Roarke found her in the kitchen about to program more coffee, he laid a hand on her arm. "Henry won't contact us again tonight. You were right before. She's given them something to make them sleep, and likely did it before she went out to contact her sister. It's past one in the morning. The children are sleeping, and so is she."

"I know it." Her mind circled; her eyes burned with fatigue. "I know it."

"Your team, including you, needs some sleep as well. Feeney's fagged out. You can see it. He won't be sharp unless he has a couple hours down."

She sat a moment, just sat where she imagined the once happy family gathered for breakfast on sunny mornings. Took a breath.

"You're right. We need to move to shifts. I was just working it out. I'm going to move half to our place, leave half here, then switch out. Three hours, I think. Three and a half," she amended. "Okay." She pushed up, started out.

They'd work all night and through the next, she thought as she scanned the room. Cops would. But they'd work better with the break.

"We're going to shifts," she announced. "Feeney, Jenkinson, Reineke, head to my place, grab a bunk. Report back here at oh-five hundred. Roarke and I will head out shortly, do the same. McNab, Callender, stay on the e-work. Peabody, Trueheart, Baxter, work the data and the streets. We'll switch off at five hundred hours."

"Summerset will see to your rooms," Roarke added. "I've spoken to him."

"Move out now, get some sleep. You relieve the first shift at five hundred sharp. Anything comes in, anything, while we're down, I know when you know."

"You got that, boss," Baxter assured her.

"I can bunk here," Feeney began.

"You won't sleep if you're here. Neither would I. Odds of anything breaking before morning are slim. Let's take a couple hours while we can. I'm going to stop by, check in with Teasdale," Eve told him. "Then we're right behind you."

The night held a deep cold and stillness that felt like waiting. Was she abandoning those kids by taking the time to grab sleep in her own bed? She could be back in ten minutes, but . . .

"Stop," Roarke ordered, and took the wheel of the car. "You could take a booster and stay on it, but there's no point. You divided it well — sending the three oldest cops down first, leaving the youngest under Baxter, who you know can deal with it. And you're taking second shift because that's when you believe something might break."

"That's about right." And still.

A light burned on the main level in the

trim town house where Teasdale had secured the MacDermits. Eve used her 'link first, alerting Teasdale so the agent opened the door as Eve and Roarke crossed the sidewalk.

"Nothing since the first contact," Teasdale told them, leading them through to a living area where equipment covered two tables, and a tall coffeepot stood half full. "Slattery's grabbing a couple hours' sleep. He's the expert on child abductions, so we decided he'd go down now while we expect it to stay quiet."

"We're taking shifts. How are the parents holding up?"

"By their fingernails. Tosha melted down after she talked to the sister, and Ross wasn't much better. Hard to blame them. But Slattery's good. He settled them down, finally convinced Tosha to take a mild soother and try to sleep. I could hear them pacing up there till about an hour ago, so maybe they're both down."

Teasdale gestured toward the wall screen. "I've been working with your map. The narrowed area seems most plausible."

"I want to recanvass that area in the morning, knock on every door."

"I can get you some foot soldiers for that."

"It would help. Did she give you anything

else on the sister? Any more details?"

"Not much. I got her talking a little earlier in the evening, just prodding her memories. What was her sister into, what did she like, what didn't she, and so on. But they haven't been together since they were twelve, so that was limited to things like dolls, sneaking on makeup, baking cookies and tarts, listening to music."

Teasdale lowered to the arm of a chair, rubbed at the back of her neck. "That's the normal. There was plenty of abnormal. Putting bugs in her sister's bed, locking her in the basement, killing the neighbor's pet rabbit and cooking it. She never told her father that one because her sister said she'd kill her and cook her next if she did."

"Nice."

"And it slides in with Dr. Mira's assessment of cannibalistic tendencies. She cut Tosha a few times, so it seems she's always enjoyed knives. And she'd sneak in vids and discs on witchcraft — the dark variety — began practicing rituals as a child."

"Fits, too."

"She claimed the birthmark was a sign of power and legitimacy. It proved she was The One — that's capped, like a title. Overall, Tosha's memories are general and unpleasant. I don't know if she can give us any specifics that will help find the children."

"We work with what we've got." And, Eve thought, wait for the boy and the bread crumbs. "I'll be back on at oh-five hundred. Baxter's in charge at the temp HQ, but I'm on if anything happens."

"She plans to kill them both, but she won't move forward until she contacts Tosha again, gets her answer."

"Does she have one?"

"Of course not." A hint of pity eked through Teasdale's voice. "So we'd better find the children before the next contact."

"We hit the streets again, full force, first light."

"I'll have men here, ready to assist."

And that, Eve thought, was the best they could do.

She didn't speak on the short drive home, and Roarke let her be. The house he'd built stood silhouetted against the black sky, as still as the night around it.

But he took her hand when they got out of the car. "You're going to find them."

"We could use some more bread crumbs."

"We'll hunt for them as well. He's a clever boy, Eve, and his sister seems brave and true. You heard her voice when she shouted not to hurt her brother. There was fear there, but fierceness as well."

She nodded as they went in, started up the stairs. She'd heard Maj Borgstrom's voice, too, she thought. There she'd heard madness, and a horrible kind of glee.

The fat cat sprawled snoring across the wide bed, and that was a kind of welcome. She'd stretch out, Eve told herself. Clear her mind, and circle back to the beginning. Somewhere from start to now, had to be answers. But when she slid into bed, when Galahad moved his considerable weight to lie across her feet, when Roarke's arm curled around her, she dropped instantly into sleep.

And quickly into dreams.

The room in Dallas that lived in her nightmares had windows. She could see out if she wanted, to the dirty red light that flashed on, off, on, off. It was a cold and hungry place, a place of fear and pain.

The children with their bright red hair and pale faces sat at a table full of cookies and cakes and bubbling drinks. And they watched her with frightened eyes.

"Don't eat any of that," she told them.

"She makes us. She'll make you eat, too, before she eats you."

"We're going to get out. I'm going to get you out."

"The door's locked."

She tried to break it down, but she was just a child herself, only eight, and cold, hungry, scared.

"We have to have a tea party," the little girl told her. "She said. And if we don't eat it all she'll make us sorry. She made Darcia sorry. She made her dead. See?"

The nanny lay on the floor, soaked in her own blood. "She's not paying any attention to me." Darcia sighed and bled. "I'm not important enough."

"That's not true. But I can't help you until I help them."

"I'm too dead to help. We'll all be dead soon if you don't *do* something."

"I'm trying. I don't know where they are. Pigeons must've eaten the bread crumbs."

"You only have to look in the right place." And Darcia turned her head and sightless eyes away.

"The good witch is supposed to fight the bad witch and win. We're supposed to go home to Mommy and Daddy and live happily ever after. You're supposed to protect us."

"I will. I'm going to. I'm trying."

Something banged on the door. Something huge.

"She's coming." Tears running free, both

children stuffed their mouths with cakes and cookies. "You have to eat or she'll hurt us."

Monster at the door, Eve thought. But which monster? Hers or theirs? And did it matter. Either brought death.

But she stepped forward, shivering in the cold, to shield the other children and make her stand.

"Here now, here, Eve, you're freezing."

She shuddered her way out of the dream, into his enfolding arms. "It's cold in the room. I can never get warm."

"Just a dream, baby. Only a dream. I'll get the fire on."

"No, no, just hold on. I don't know which. Troy or Borgstrom. I have to fight the monster."

"Shh. A dream. It's done now. I'm right here. You're safe."

"Not me. The kids. How come I can't find them when they're right there?" She gripped him hard. "Hold on to me, will you?"

"Always."

"I'm not going to be afraid. I can't be."

When she lifted her mouth to his, he met the kiss gently while he ran soothing hands up and down her back. And murmured to her words of comfort.

She wouldn't be afraid, she thought again. She wouldn't let the torments of her childhood damage what she'd become or stop her from doing what she had to do. What she would do.

And here, with him, she knew the ease of his faith in her, his love, and his unwavering trust.

She warmed, degree by degree, and the room — her prison, the prison of two innocent children — faded away.

She was home.

She needed, he knew, the human touch. His touch. It humbled him that she found strength there. That what they found in each other steadied them both. Soft here, and tender, to reaffirm who they were, what they'd beaten back. And would always beat back together.

She rose to him on a sigh, quiet as the night. He filled her, murmuring of love, of promise.

They held tight, moving in the dark toward solace.

When they were still again, when she could count the beats of his heart against hers, she had no fear of what stood behind the door.

"I only have to look in one place. The nanny said that, in my dream."

"True, but not simple."

"Henry said the walls and floor were like

sidewalk. So some sort of concrete? That says basement to me. She couldn't lock them up anywhere someone else could access, so it takes it back to her having the building, or at least the only access to that area. It's going to be a smallish building, a limited or no tenant situation."

He raised his head. "You're not going back to sleep."

"Sorry."

"You've more than an hour yet before you need to get ready to take your shift."

"I need to go back, Roarke. Grab a shower, some coffee, go back, walk around. I want to believe I'll know the place when I see it. I know that's stupid, but I want to believe it. So I have to go back, walk around, look for the damn bread crumbs."

"Then that's what we'll do."

Chapter Nine

Streetlamps pooled light on sidewalks, and a single cab rumbled down the street. The rest stayed quiet, with that almost eerie stillness playing along Eve's skin like a tripped nerve.

"Midnight may be the witching hour," Roarke said as they got out of the car in front of the MacDermit house, "but I think it's the hour between three and four — that slice that's neither day nor night — that's the darkest and deepest."

"All I know is she's had those kids more than twenty-four hours. They're trapped in the darkest and deepest."

She stepped inside, into the lights, into the hub of cops at work. Peabody slumped over her computer, and Callender broke from an enormous yawn and stretch to blink.

"Is it change of shift already?"

"We're early."

Baxter stepped out of the kitchen area with a large pot of coffee. "What?" he said. "No donuts?"

"That and more on the way," Roarke told him, then merely lifted his eyebrows at Eve's puzzled frown. "I took care of it."

"You're the man." Baxter, in wrinkled shirtsleeves, his usually meticulously groomed hair mussed, his eyes shadowed, pulled out a smile.

"Anything break loose?" Eve demanded.

At his station, McNab shook his head. "All quiet on our front. Nothing from the kids or EW. Evil witch," he said before Eve could ask. "Callender and I've been playing around with a scan program that picks up — kind of hit and miss there — the standard signal from the toy then translates it to our code for a satellite bounce. We've been working on filtering out similar signals from the scan. A lot of kid-comms out there."

"That's a good thought," Roarke commented.

"Hit and miss," McNab repeated. "And the toy has to be on, and the translation has to mesh. We picked up a handful, but did a search run on the locations. Not our kids — established homes with offspring types."

"We might correlate the sister's unit," Roarke began, moving to e-territory linguistically and geographically. "They were purchased at the same time, same place, manufactured at the same time, place, same lot. We could try a splice and lock, then push through a de-babble."

"Tricky," McNab decided, but his tired eyes glinted. "And frosty."

Eve left him to it, turned to Peabody. "Report?"

"We've been refining the map, and following it with search and scans on buildings in each separate sector. I'm starting to feel she could be in here, this run between Sixty-sixth and Sixty-eighth, Lex or Third."

"Why?"

"Just, I don't know, I keep coming back there, but the probability runs aren't any better there than the rest of the area." Peabody rubbed the heels of her hands over her eyes. "I just keep coming back to it."

"We've been able to narrow it a little, Lieutenant," Trueheart put in. "Eliminate some of the buildings — established families, long-term owners or tenants. Unless . . . the data could've been compromised. She could've covered herself on it."

"It feels like spinning wheels," Peabody admitted. "Except I keep coming back to that more narrow area."

"Okay, I'll work it. Baxter, go catch some

sleep. Peabody, Trueheart, you're relieved as soon as Jenkinson and Reineke get in. One of you can go," she told Callender and McNab.

"I've got it," McNab said.

"I've got it," Callender disagreed.

They eyed each other. "Winner stays," McNab suggested, held out his fist.

"Fair enough."

After three shakes of fists, McNab held out two fingers, Callender the flat of her hand. "Damn it," she muttered. "I figured you for rock. I've never done a de-babble on a splice and lock."

"Go," Eve ordered. "Grab some food and a rack. Be back by . . ." She checked the time. "Make it seven thirty. Let me see what we've got here. Get some coffee," she told Peabody. "Take a walk."

Grabbing coffee herself, Eve sat, read over Peabody's notes, studied the probabilities. Reran them with some slight variations."

Then she sat back, drinking coffee, studying the map on screen, adjusting highlighted areas in her head.

She read over Borgstrom's data again, and Mira's profile and assessments. Rose to study the board, and the map.

When the other men came in, followed by three delivery guys and a boatload of food, more coffee, she stayed hunched over her computer, trying to finesse those angles and probabilities.

"Trueheart," she said without looking up, "call Peabody in. Grab some fuel, then the two of you go get some sleep. Report back, eight thirty."

"I can stay, Lieutenant. I've got my second wind. Maybe it's my third."

She flicked a glance at him. Lack of sleep had leached color from his face, highlighted smudges of fatigue under his eyes. He probably could and would stick it out, but a few hours down would keep him sharper.

"We've got it for now. Take the rack, be back by eight thirty."

"Got some data from IRCCA." Feeney shoveled eggs in his mouth. "Checked for the results on the way in. Couple may be our girl, but the closest I got is a dead guy in Paris, eight months ago. Sliced and diced — and missing his liver and heart — some evidence it was cooked up, sautéed like with wine and shit, right on site." He crunched into bacon. "Cops looked for a woman — person of interest —" He paused to inhale more eggs. "Wit statements indicate he maybe had a lady on the side. Wife swears he did, but they never ID'd her."

"Who was he?"

"Big-deal pastry chef. Did cakes and stuff for the rich set, gave private lessons if you had the money to buy the time. Took him out in the kitchen of his fancy shop on the Chomps de Leezay," he added, mangling the French over a mouthful of hash browns. "Pulled out half a mill, in cash, the day he bought it."

"The money, the internal organs. Was he marked?"

"Yeah, that's how we caught it. Pentagram-type symbol, just over his heart — postmortem."

"That's her work," Eve said, firmly.

"Don't get how people eat liver, no matter where it comes from. One wit claims she saw him with a brunette, so the hair's off. But the rest of the description jibes. Five-eight, mid to late thirties, white. I'll talk to France, see if I can pull out any more."

"Good. If we factor it in, it narrows her time here. That may help on the location." She took the slice of bacon Feeney offered her, chewed thoughtfully.

"Reineke, narrow the location search to the last eight months — rent or purchase. I'm going to take a unit, walk around."

"I'm with you," Roarke told her.

"You're probably more useful in here."

"McNab has this, and Feeney's here. Two

units, more coverage." He tossed Eve her coat, grabbed his own.

Eve pulled it on, then frowned at the bread pocket he held out.

"What's that?"

"Breakfast." He handed her a unit as well, picked up another, and a second bread pocket. "Let's have a walk, Lieutenant."

"Feeney, keep it covered," she said, and biting into the sandwich — warm eggs, crisp bacon, a bit of peppery cheese — headed out the door.

"We're a couple hours from sunrise," Eve began. "I looked it up. I don't see her starting on those kids until morning. Just trying to factor in Mira's profile, the little else we know, she's more likely to string this out a few more hours, make her sister sweat through the morning. Or maybe I'm just hoping she will."

Eve looked down at the silent unit in her hand. "We don't even know, not for certain, she put them under last night. We're guessing that, going with the odds. She's fucking crazy, Roarke. And kids are scary anyway. She could've killed them both just to shut them up."

"You don't think that, and neither do I. To shut them up she locks them in, drugs them, or just leaves them alone. Alive they're more exciting. And she wants her sister to choose one of them. One to live, one to die."

"Whichever one Tosha picks to live? She'll kill that one first. She'll figure that's the one more powerful, more important, and take that one out."

"The mother won't pick. They'll stall." He took her free hand to warm it in his. "The agents have the experience here, and they'll have a way to stall it. Buy more time."

"How much battery life do you figure Henry's got left on this thing?"

That had been a worry niggling in his brain since the evening before. "At this point, I think no more than an hour, likely less. He won't have many more chances there, especially if he tries to send those photos."

"Was I wrong there? To have him use the time left to take a couple pictures he may not even be able to send?"

"Not if it helps you find him."

"We should separate, focus on Peabody's hunch." She paused at the corner. Which way, which way? Where were the goddamn bread crumbs?

"Bread crumbs," she said out loud. Liked baking cookies, prison kitchen, dead pastry chef. "What if we're looking for cookie crumbs. She's making them eat cakes and cookies."

"Pushing childhood fantasy — all the sweets you can eat?"

"The sweeter to eat you, my dear."

"You're mixing your folktales, Lieutenant, but that's a grim thought. Evil witch, gingerbread house, plump them up to eat."

"Maybe, and maybe it's cookies. Bakery. Lives in or works in. Dead baker in Paris, and she doesn't do anything without purpose. He gave private lessons. Maybe she took lessons, did the vamp thing, killed him and ate his liver."

"With fava beans and a nice Chianti."

"What?" She blinked for a beat. *"What?"*

"An old classic line from an exceptional vid. Hold on a minute." He pulled out his PPC, began to work. "There's a bakery on Third, between Sixty-sixth and -seventh. Indulge Yourself. And a little pastry shop on Lex and Sixty-fifth — Magic Sweets."

"Take the first one," Eve said immediately. "I'll take the second."

"You think it's the second. Magic — pastries instead of a standard bakery. That's your instinct."

"We need to cover both, and the whole thing may be wrong." She pulled out her comm, intending to tell Reineke to pull data on the two buildings, but switched it to her signaling 'link. Grabbed Roarke's arm.

"It's the photos, Henry's sending the photos."

"Hello?" The voice piped onto her unit, and Roarke's. "Is anybody there? I don't . . . good. Gala won't . . . up. I don't feel good."

"We're here, Henry. I got the pictures — the door, the bathroom. You did really good."

"I feel sick. I want to throw up, but I can't. Ga . . . won't wake up."

"Keep him talking," Roarke murmured, tapped his earpiece. "Yeah, we've got the signal."

He circled his finger at Eve, stepped a foot away, and began to talk geek in a rapid, quiet voice.

"Henry, can you hear anything besides me?"

"Uh-uh."

"What do you smell?"

"The bathroom doesn't . . . good."

"Anything else?" Eve demanded as she studied the picture of a tiny john, narrow, wall-hung sink. Cheap, but new, she decided. And the door — new again, reinforced — and standing out against the rough gray walls.

Basement, goddamn it. Basement.

"Cookies. She made . . . eat cookies. I don't want . . . cookies . . . Mommy."

"Okay, Henry, just hang on. I'm losing him," she hissed to Roarke. "He's starting to break up more, and for longer."

Roarke shot up a finger to silence her, continued his rapid conversation even as he worked the little toy and his own PPC.

"Henry, look at the walls. You said no windows, but does it look like there were windows and they got covered over?"

"No, I don't . . . I don't know. It smells wet and . . . Grandma's basement."

There! Eve thought, and considered it confirmed. "Good, that's good. That's helping."

"South, move south," Roarke said under his breath. "Keep him talking."

She didn't question, just began to jog beside Roarke. "Henry, can you hear the evil witch before she opens the door? Do you hear her coming?"

"Gala . . . Daddy says . . . ears like a bat. Gala listens for her . . . talk to you . . . won't wake up!" His voice broke on a shaky sob. "Did . . . kill . . ."

"West," Roarke snapped, turning the corner.

"You hold on, Henry. I'm losing him, Roarke."

"Not yet," Roarke murmured. "Not yet."

She glanced up at the street sign. "It's the pastry shop."

"Maybe. The trace is fragile, barely there. A bit stronger when he's talking."

"Henry, tell me your full name, your date of birth, your sister's."

Roarke spared her a glance while Henry recited, shook his head at her shrug.

"Talk to him," she ordered Roarke, then pulled out her comm.

"Magic Sweets, Lexington at Sixty-fifth. Get me back up, call the rest of the team in, relate to the feds. I'm not waiting."

She kicked up her pace, listening to the boy's voice talk about a magic spell and a brave prince, a talking dragon. Listening to the voice fade, fade, fade.

"His battery's dead. Bugger it."

"It doesn't matter." She stopped, and she drew her weapon as she studied the trim, three-story building. The storefront pastry shop's display window was empty and dark, as was what she assumed was an apartment above.

But she saw a faint backwash of light spilling out of the back of the shop.

"We're going in, and going fast and quiet. Maybe she's upstairs, sleeping. Or maybe she's in the back there, baking up something to force on those kids."

"Closed for remodeling," Roarke said, reading the sign on the door. "You know what you say about coincidences."

"They're crap."

"Alarm? Cam?"

"Both. Let's see what I can do."

"Whatever it is, hurry."

Chapter Ten

"Feeney," she hissed into her comm. "Can you pull up blueprints on this building? Do we have a basement?"

"Let me work on it."

"No time. Roarke's through the security. We're going in."

"Reineke, Jenkinson, McNab on their way to you. Feds sending men in. Full team heading back."

"We're not waiting. I don't know the status of the girl. Clear?" she asked Roarke.

"You're clear."

"Straight through to the back," she told him. "Clear as we go. Look for a door. She'd have it secured. And if we're wrong and some nice grandmother type is back there, we'll apologize."

"It works for me. On three?"

"One, two —" She went low and left. He went high and right. Skirting a couple of tiny tables, then a long display counter, she moved straight toward the rear and that light. And music, she realized.

The bitch was singing.

She smelled the sugar — the warm, comforting scent of fresh baking.

A moment before Eve reached the door, Roarke grabbed her arm, pointed up.

She saw the internal cam, the tiny red eye of it. Cursing, she started to ease back out of range.

Too late.

The door between the kitchen and showroom slammed.

Eve reared back, kicked it, reared back again. And she and Roarke kicked it together. She caught a glimpse — just the shoulder, a bounce of a blonde ponytail, before the door to the right shut, clicked.

She started to kick again.

"Wait. A minute, a minute." Roarke bent to the lock. "It's reinforced. You'll just break your foot on the bastard."

"Hurry, hurry, hurry."

"Does it look like I'm taking my bloody time with it? There."

He yanked it open, and together they ran down the steps. She swept out with her weapon.

Damp, chilly, dark, but the faintest hint of light at the door at the base of the steps.

She went carefully, mindful of booby traps, and continued to sweep when they reached the bottom. Roarke went to work on the next door.

"I can hear them." Straining, Eve caught the muffled sounds through the thick walls and doors. Screaming.

It was their monster, not hers, that came through the door.

She remembered being too late before — a child, just a little girl and the man hyped-on Zeus with a knife. Seconds too late to stop him from slicing up that tender flesh.

Not this time, not this time. Please, God, hurry.

And at Roarke's nod, they hit the door together.

She had the ritual knife at the girl's throat, her arm clamped around the boy's.

She'd trapped herself, Eve thought, in a room with no way out, because spilling blood was what she wanted most.

"Stun me. My hand jerks, she's dead. Pretty little girl with her pretty little throat slit wide."

Identical but for the birthmark, Tosha had said. Yet Eve saw subtle differences. This face was leaner, a little longer, and these ice blue eyes held a wild glitter.

"We're going to hold back here." Eve spoke with her eyes on Maj, but the words were for her Roarke. "Just hold. Your back's to the wall here, Maj. If you cut her, I take you down."

"If you take me down, I cut her. I kill her. And maybe have just enough time to wring this little bastard's neck. Drop the stunners, both of you. Drop them and move aside. I'm walking out of here."

"Not going to happen." She could take the head shot, Eve calculated, but the jolt would slice the knife right across Gala's throat. No way around it.

"Maybe you take the kids out, maybe not. But there's no doubt you're down." Eve flicked a glance at the kids, hoping the calm in her voice would reassure them, keep them still. She saw the way their eyes tracked to each other's, held. The fear, yes, fear with the shine of tears, but something more, something intense.

Were they . . . communicating?

"I'll trade them both for Tosha, my *syster.* Bring her here, and I'll let them both go. Fast, fast, or I bleed her like a little piggie."

"Why her?" Distract, Eve thought. If she could distract, just enough to move the knife a fraction away, she could take the risk, take the shot. "Why not him?"

"Girls are more tender. Sugar and spice." She smiled as she said it, smiled madly. "Sugar and spice and blood. Snakes and snails for him."

"Don't you want to know which one she chose?"

"She chose." Maj's face illuminated, a fanatical joy. "Tell me, tell me! Which does she love best?"

"How bad do you want to know? You've made your choice." Eve glanced deliberately at Gala. "But is it the same as Tosha's?"

"Tell me!" In the split second, as Maj's body shifted forward, as the knife eased a fraction, angling toward Eve in threat, Eve prepared to take the risk.

But the children beat her to it.

Both of them clamped down, fierce little teeth into the exposed flesh of Maj's forearms. She howled in shock and pain. The knife nicked the side of Gala's throat before it jerked away.

Eve took the shot, and as Maj's body jittered, the knife wavered in her shuddering hand.

"Drop!" Eve shouted to the kids, and sprang forward. She led with her left, plowing her fist into Maj's face, pivoted, grabbed the knife hand, twisting it as Maj slammed the wall and slid, shuddering, to the floor.

"Suspect's down! Suspect's down. Move in!" Eve kicked the knife away, put a boot on the now unconscious woman's back. And turning, saw Roarke had both kids, one tucked under each arm as he crouched to their level.

"How bad's she cut?"

"It's just a scratch. Isn't that right, sweetheart? You're all safe and sound now."

Gala pressed her face into Roarke's shoulder, wrapped her arm tight around her brother.

"I'll take them up and out of here, all right with that?"

"Yeah. Tell Peabody to contact their parents."

Eve started to reach for her restraints, but Baxter moved in.

"We'll clean this up, boss." He bent over Maj, pulled her arms back to cuff, saw the bloody teeth marks in both forearms. "Jesus, what, did you bite her?"

"Not me, them." She nodded toward the kids as Roarke hefted Gala into his arms, held out a hand for Henry's.

"Good for them. Damn good for them."

"Have her transported to Central, then go get some sleep — you and Trueheart. You, too," she said to Peabody as her partner came in.

"I really hear that."

"Reineke, you and Jenkinson take her through Booking once she's conscious. Make sure she's Mirandized as soon as she's lucid. I'll be in to interview her."

"I can go in with you, Dallas," Peabody said.

"I can handle it. Go hit the sheets. You can call in the sweepers before you do. Let's get this place processed. Everything neat and tidy."

She looked around first, as men moved in, moved out. The tiny, windowless room with its open closet of a bathroom. Bright toys, the table full of sugary crumbs.

Not like the room in Dallas, she thought, but the same purpose. Terrorize, torture, and confine.

She walked out of it, walked away from it — and wondered how long nightmares would plague the two children who'd been taken and trapped.

She saw them in the stillness and cold, in the murk before day dawned, huddled beside Roarke in blankets some cop had pulled out of a trunk.

She started to speak to one of the officers, but caught Henry's eye, watched him break away from Roarke and walk to her.

"Is she dead?"

"No, but she can't hurt you anymore. She'll be locked up now. How's that arm?"

"Gala fixed it for me." He held out a hand, and though they hadn't spoken, though his sister had her face pressed to Roarke's chest, she stepped away, went to Henry. And taking his hand, looked up at Eve.

"You're the good witch," Gala said.

"Kid, I'm a cop."

"You saved us."

"You did a lot of that yourselves. You were really smart — smarter than her. And really tough."

Henry pressed his lips together where they trembled. "Who did she pick? Who did Mommy pick?"

"She didn't. I lied." Was this the bigger fear? Eve wondered. Even bigger and deeper than any blade? She crouched down again. "I lied to make her think of something else. Your mother didn't choose, and she never would."

"You're not supposed to lie." But Henry smiled. His eyes filled, but he smiled, and Eve thought: That's courage. The real deal. "But it's okay that you did. I'm Henry, and this is Gala."

"Yeah, I know. I'm Dallas."

"You're the Good Witch Dallas."

Henry let out a little sound, a sob choked off, then shocked Eve to her toes by flinging himself at her, wrapping his trembling body around her. Then Gala did the same.

"Okay, okay." She wasn't sure if she should pat them, or where. "It's all over now. We'll get you home, get you something to eat."

"We don't want cookies." Gala's voice was muffled against Eve's shoulder.

"Yeah, no cookies for you." She tried to stand again, but the little girl gripped her around the neck so she ended up lifting her while Henry clung to her leg.

"Ah . . ." She looked toward Roarke for help, but he just smiled, shook his head.

A car screamed up. Before it fully stopped, Tosha shoved out of one door, Ross the other.

"Henry! Gala!"

The girl all but leaped down, and the boy raced toward his parents, his blanket flying back like a cape.

Eve let out a heartfelt sigh of relief, but didn't object when Roarke stepped over, slid an arm around her shoulders.

"It's a pretty sight on a cold morning," he murmured.

It was, the four of them tangled together to form one unit.

"They're going to be all right," Eve decided. "She had them for what, about thirty hours, and it feels like a lifetime, but they're going to be okay. And they had each other, the kids, through the worst of it. I think . . . I think they can talk to each other, without, you know, talking."

"Perhaps. The twin bond, and a little magic — of the good kind, thrown in."

Teasdale crossed to her. "Slattery and I will meet you at Central. We'll let the brass wrangle where she lives out the rest of her life, but we'll make sure — the three of us — we wrap her tight."

"That works for me."

Teasdale glanced back at the family. "A pretty picture. The kind that can help get you through the long, troubling nights. Good work, all of us."

With a satisfied nod, Teasdale moved off. Eve started to turn to Roarke, then paused when the family walked to her. Ross held his son, Tosha her daughter.

"This is the Good Witch Dallas," Henry began.

"Lieutenant."

"Lieutenant Good Witch Dallas."

And he smiled, so sweetly, Eve let it go.

"Thank you. Thank you for our children," Ross said in a voice thick and shaky. "We'll never forget. We can never repay . . ."

"Vanquishing the bad is the job of cops and good witches, isn't it, Henry?" Roarke asked.

Tosha leaned forward, left Eve no choice but to accept the light kiss on each cheek. "Every day, for the rest of my life, I'll say a prayer for your safety, and for your happiness. Every day, when I look in my children's eyes, I'll remember you. All of you."

Eve slipped her hands in her pockets as they walked away. Together, Henry and Gala lifted their heads, smiled at her over their parents' shoulders, and waved in unison.

"Oh yeah, they've got some internal conversation going. Weird. Anyway." She blew out a breath. "I need to go in and nail this bitch in hard and tight." Energized by the prospect, Eve rolled her shoulders. "And you need to get back to universal financial domination."

"It should be a fine day for it. You'll be making a stop before you go in. I'll go with you, then be on my way."

She blew out a breath. "Are we having an internal conversation?"

"I know how you think, what you feel. It comes to the same on some things. I'll drive you there, then get my own transpo back."

"Okay." She touched her fingertips to his.

"Thanks."

So he stood with her in the chilly air in the morgue, over the body of Darcia Jordan.

"I barely had time to do more than look at her, have her bagged and tagged. It doesn't sit well."

"You couldn't save her, but you stood for her, Eve, by standing for the children, by working to get them back."

"It's what we had to do."

"Say what you need to say to her."

It felt strange, even with him, but she had to get it out, get it said. "The kids are safe, they're home. I'm going to do everything I can — and I've got plenty of backing — to see the bitch lives out her crazy life in a cage. Off-planet, if we can work it. The farther away the better. I didn't forget you. I just had to put them first. So . . . that's it."

She looked at Roarke, shrugged. "That's it."

"Then go do that." He took her hand to lead her out of the room, down the long white tunnel. "Go see she lives out her crazy life in a cage."

She stepped outside where the sun had risen to lighten the sky, and the stillness had lifted with the faintest wind that smelled ever so lightly of snow.

She took a deep breath of New York. "You know, you're right. It looks like it's going to be a fine day."

Since no one was around, and what the hell, she'd earned it, she leaned into him for a quick kiss. "See you around, pal."

"Take care of my cop — Lieutenant Good Witch."

Laughing — yeah, a pretty fine day — she climbed into her car to finish the job.

■ ■ ■ ■

If Wishes Were Horses

MARY BLAYNEY

■ ■ ■ ■

For Tom Langan

PROLOGUE

Craig's Hill Castle
Derbyshire
May 1816

"This stupid coin is worthless." Martha Stepp tossed the coin to Ellen. The younger maid caught it in pure self-defense.

"But, Martha," Ellen said, as she rubbed her rounding stomach, "its magic worked for me and Johnny. We have a babe coming."

"Dear girl, I do not think the origin of your much-hoped-for babe had anything to do with magic."

Ellen blushed and Martha patted her arm. "The coin *is* magical," Martha admitted. "I misspoke. I've seen it work. Once, a man and woman's minds switched bodies so that the man had to live as a woman and the woman was husband. And I saw a boy cured of a dreadful fever. Both happened with a wish on this very coin."

Ellen shook her head in amazement. "If it had not worked for us I would think you mad."

"The truth is that I am upset because it has never worked for me." Martha picked up the coin from the table where Ellen had placed it.

Its black face and gold rim with foreign writing was unlike any coin she had ever seen.

"It's not worthless, even without its magic quality," Ellen ventured. "It has the number ten on its face. So it's worth ten of something somewhere."

They had finished dusting the books at least a quarter hour ago and, at Martha's insistence, had tried out the chairs nearest the fireplace to see if they were as comfortable as the ones in the green salon.

Ellen had balked at Martha's temerity but Martha knew her friend tired easily these days and so would not actually refuse the chance to rest.

"Yes, it is worth ten of something somewhere, but not at any market in this country. So, for me, at least, it's worthless."

"Unless you find out where it's from and try to go there." Ellen made a face even as she suggested it.

"I've thought of that. I've always wanted a

bit of adventure. But, Ellen, even if the coin is worth as much as ten guineas, that would not be enough to establish myself in some foreign place where it seems they do not even speak English. I want a bit of adventure, not a boatload."

"It's never turned gold and bright for you the way it did for me when I made my wish?"

"No, never." Martha sighed. "I can give it to people and invite them to wish and it always seems to work."

Ellen nodded as though she had heard this before.

"You know I've even tried to leave it behind," Martha went on. "I've tried twice. But it's always been back in my pocket by evening."

"I doubt you can abandon it. I expect you must find the right person to pass it on to."

"Do you think so?" Martha asked as though the idea had never occurred to her.

Ellen answered with an unconvincing shrug.

They both stared at the coin for a bit.

Stop feeling sorry for yourself, Martha thought. *You have work to do, a roof over your head, and food to eat. Embrace that and stop wanting more.*

"So what do you think of these chairs?"

Martha asked.

"They are comfortable enough." Ellen wiggled a little deeper into the seat as she spoke.

"But not perfect," Martha decided. "They need a higher back to catch the warmth from the fire." That placed them significantly lower in comfort than the chairs in the green salon but much higher than the chairs in the servants' gathering room. Martha was convinced that those chairs, long ago rejects from the grander rooms, were the least comfortable in the entire castle.

Before Ellen could do more than nod, the bell announcing supper sounded.

"You go on, Ellen, and I'll finish here. Can you take these three books that need repair to the housekeeper?" Martha gathered the cleaning cloths as she spoke.

The dust tickled her nose and Martha pressed her finger between her eyebrows to stop the sneeze that gathering the dirty cloths had instigated.

Ellen did not bother to stifle her sneeze, but then hers was a delicate sound and not at all embarrassing.

"Go on now," Martha urged. "I know you've not seen your man all morning. You take the books and I'll take the basket to the laundry and be at the table in five minutes. Save some of that Cotswold cheddar for me, will you?"

With a nod and a smile Ellen hurried out.

Martha glanced at the coin on the table. She grabbed it, holding the coin in the palm of the hand that also held the basket handle. It wasn't that her wish was unrealistic, Martha was sure of that. The coin did not deem anything impossible. She pulled the door open with the basket resting on her hip, and wondered what was so impossible about finding love with a man who would take her away from the servant's life and share his bed and his world with her forever.

If she could not have that, then she wished someone else would be named the coin's keeper and free her from a hope that plagued her whenever she looked at it. The coin bit into her hand and she let it fall on the carpet. No doubt the coin would find its way back into her pocket. Martha Stepp pulled the door closed behind her and hurried toward the back stairs.

In the library, resting on the fine old rug where Martha had dropped it, the coin turned gold and for the briefest of moments lit the room with a glow of promise. Then it disappeared.

Chapter One

Craig's Hill Castle
Derbyshire
One week later

"Martha, you cannot keep on doing this!"

Martha Stepp gathered the blanket from her bed and moved to the door of the tiny attic bedchamber.

"Wanda, I've been doing this for months without anyone noticing. This place has dozens of bedchambers and I am going to sleep in each bed until I find the most comfortable."

"But why?" Wanda wailed as if Martha was venturing into some foreign country without money or papers.

"Because this room is too hot in the summer and too cold in the winter. I'm looking for a room that is just right."

"Then what will you do?"

"Sleep there whenever I can. And start looking for the best of something else. Did you know I discovered the chairs in the west attic rooms are the most comfortable in the house? It's where I am going to start spending my half day. I even bought a candle so I can read there if I wish."

"You could fall asleep and start a fire."

That was Wanda. Always worried about what horror could befall them. The last time they walked to the village for the countess's maid Wanda was sure they would be attacked by a wolf. Never mind that Derbyshire had no wolves. As a matter of fact, there were no wolves in all of England.

Martha felt guilty but Wanda was one of the few of her friends to whom she had never offered the magic coin for fear that Wanda would have her named a witch and have her dismissed. Martha patted her pocket where the coin settled, feeling much heavier than its slight size should warrant.

"Good night, Wanda," Martha said firmly.

"Do not forget your prayers, Martha!" Wanda called after her.

Her prayers? Martha slipped down the stairs, smiling at the thought that her prayers were heard by God. How could He make sense of the millions of people sending prayers to Him, some of them far more urgent than the health and happiness of her friends and family? But yes, she would pray, and hope that someday her needs would move to the front of the queue.

For now she had more amusing concerns. She was going to sleep in the room she liked the best, though that was no guarantee that the bed would be the softest or firmest or whatever a bed needed to be for perfection.

It belonged to the countess's youngest son, the one who had gone off to fight Napoleon. The war was over so he should be coming home. But he had been wounded at Quatre Bras just before Waterloo and his recovery had slowed his return. Still, rumors ran rife now that Napoleon was a prisoner once again, the major was on his way, and would arrive any day now.

Then again the war had been over before and Napoleon imprisoned before and all had started up anew when old Boney had escaped.

Just in case the major was truly on his way home, Mrs. Belweather had insisted that Martha and a chosen few others ready his room for whenever he should arrive, freshening it every other day. There was no doubt that the housekeeper was right to have the room as perfectly prepared as possible. For her part Martha would believe Major Craig was home when she heard his boots hit the floor.

Martha made her way along the darkened passage. When she had first come to Craig's Hill, she had avoided walking the house at night. Surely the old castle was filled with ghosts and the darkened passages seemed like their natural milieu. After six months and no night visitors, Martha decided that she was not the type to whom ghosts appeared. Which was just as well since the magic coin was quite enough for one woman to handle.

The castle was square, with an open center courtyard, which made for good light during the day and when the moon was full. Tonight was such a night and Martha had no trouble finding her way along the third-level passage and into Major Craig's room.

It was not too big but that made it all the more appealing. Two tall windows looked out on the kitchen garden, outbuildings, and beyond to the parkland at the back of the castle. For now the curtains were drawn closed to protect the rugs from too much of the strong afternoon sun.

Lighting her stub of a candle, Martha considered the bed. Larger than most that she had tried, she could not decide whether to sleep in the middle or on one edge. She decided to try the half closest to the window, made herself comfortable atop the coverlet, settled her head on the pillow, and pulled her own blanket up to her shoulders.

Sleep came quickly even as she realized that the firmness of the mattress was not completely to her liking.

Jack Tresbere followed the night porter down the passage. It was just like the major to time his arrival for the middle of the night. "The easiest way to avoid being soaked with tears by my mother," he'd insisted. The major well knew he would still be soaked with tears but at least he would have a decent night's sleep first. And in his own bed.

His own bed. Jack could not even imagine what it was like to have your own bed, in your own room, in the house in which you were raised. His life had been army centered from birth.

They reached a door, but instead of opening what Jack assumed was the major's bedchamber, the night porter turned to him.

"Have you been with the major long, Sergeant?"

Jack could not tell if the question was from curiosity or civility. "Since Badajoz."

The night porter looked blank and Jack closed his eyes as he explained. "Since April sixth, eighteen twelve." The date was burned into his heart and mind and soul, a date that was a nightmare memory he would never forget.

"Aha, the battle where the major was promoted."

So the man did know a little about the earl's third son.

"Yes." Jack hoped the terse response would end the conversation.

"You were in the battle where he was wounded most recently?"

"Yes." He'd stood right next to him, been spattered with his blood.

"The countess will be so happy to know he is home. She refused to believe that he would be healed enough to travel any time before fall. Her physician son said that it's a wonder the major can even walk."

"She will see for herself soon enough." The major did use a cane and would probably always limp, but his brother was wrong. It had not been a miracle that he could walk but a testament to his brother's dogged determination and one more thing less easily explained.

Jack nodded at the door. "Is this his room?"

Taking the cue, the porter opened the door and stepped back, allowing Jack first entry, which was pointless since the night porter was the one with the candle.

Jack stopped short. "This room is occupied."

The night porter came in behind him and the candle lit the room enough to show them an empty bed.

"No, sir, it's not. A ghost, for sure. There are ghosts aplenty in this place. That would be it."

Jack shrugged even though he did not agree. He'd heard someone, saw some movement in the dark.

Major Alistair Craig came up behind them and all but stumbled into the room, encumbered by two insanely happy dogs determined to play with their long-gone master. It seemed they thought his cane a toy brought just for them.

A manservant followed with a plateful of ham and cheese on a tray along with two mugs.

"They remember me, Sergeant. How can that be? It's been years. How many years has it been, Jack?" The major laughed as the dogs nudged his legs.

"At least six, sir. You bought your commission just after the Battle of Corunna and that was early in oh-nine."

"They seem to have aged better than I have, haven't they?" None of the three answered the major as he bent to scratch the bigger dog at the base of his neck.

The truth was the major looked like hell, Jack thought. Absurdly gaunt, his eyes sunken into his face.

The porter gasped and raised his hand to his own cheek when the major turned into the light.

The major looked up and waved away his shock. "The scar will fade." He rubbed the red mark on his face. "It's not a month old. Though I guess I do look more like a prisoner of war left for dead than a conquering hero."

Ah, Jack thought, and were they not all prisoners of war? Even if none of them had ever been held behind enemy lines. "Major, let's rid you of that uniform and get you into something more comfortable. Like your bed."

"Right." The major hobbled over to the giant canopied piece of furniture and then looked over his shoulder. "Who's been sleeping in my bed?"

"Why, no one, Major," the night porter assured him. "The countess had it made up when she had word you were coming." They all looked at the rumpled cover. "Mayhap the dogs came up to see if you had arrived."

Even as he spoke the smaller dog jumped

up onto the cover, circled three times, and settled at the foot of the bed. The bigger dog was sniffing the floor along the edge of the bed and trying to work his too-large frame underneath it.

"Enough of dogs." Jack scooped up the smaller one, who was still a good thirty pounds, and with his foot urged the bigger dog away from his attempted exploration under the bed. Rousting both dogs out the door, something he knew the major did not have the heart to do, Jack thanked the night porter and the kitchen servant at the same time and closed the door on them all.

"Thank you, Jack. I wish for nothing more than one night in my own bed and then I will be ready for the mixed blessing of a Craig's Hill homecoming and all the company the dogs want to share. Just one night," he repeated on a yawn.

Having the man eat the food and ale was no more than a fond thought as Jack helped the major undress and fall into bed without even buttoning his nightshirt or bothering with a nightcap.

The major was asleep that fast and Jack held his hand over the major's forehead, close, but not touching, and prayed for a serene night's sleep, and that all the man's darker dreams would be given to his sergeant. Tresbere felt the frisson that accompanied the healing touch that had been his gift and his burden since he was fifteen.

Certain that the major was sleeping peacefully, Jack stepped back, took his mug and downed the ale in one swallow, placed some of the ham between two pieces of cheese, and called it supper.

Then Jack Tresbere sat in a chair close to the cold fireplace and waited to see who was hiding under the bed.

Chapter Two

Martha wanted to scramble out from under the bed and race from the room. *No, no,* she thought, trying to calm her panic. *My only chance of escaping is to wait until they are both asleep.*

Thank goodness the sergeant insisted the dogs leave the room. The small dog did not like women and tended to ignore them, but the bigger dog, the one they called Midge, loved everyone and had been well on his way to calling attention to her. Martha drew a deep breath and let it out as soundlessly as she could. Her heart was still racing but not at the mad, burst-from-her-chest gallop it had broken into when she heard someone at the door.

She'd barely had time to slip from the bed and under it, thinking clearly enough to drag her blanket with her.

Shoes were all she could see from her hiding spot. She had never realized how much shoes could tell you about a man.

The sergeant, the one the major called Jack Tresbere, stood with authority, his feet planted slightly apart. He seemed to occupy more space than the other three men and not because he was bigger than they were, though he probably was, given the size of his shoes.

The major's boots were well kept but worn and he stood as though using the wall for support, clearly still recovering from a wound as well as exhausted from travel.

The servant from the kitchen was wearing an old broken-down pair of shoes that were too big for his feet. A boy, she thought, probably one of the gardener's sons, who slept in the kitchen when he could convince his father to allow him away from their crowded cottage.

As for the night porter, his stance was tentative, as though he could not wait to go back to the door and his regular routine.

Everyone knew Pegwell was ill suited to the role of night protector of the great castle but it was a testament to the earl's easy ways that he never considered finding someone more suited to the post. It was also what made it so easy for her to sample beds and chairs and the occasional glass of wine at night. He never wandered from his spot by the front door.

From the way the sergeant sounded, the way he so easily sent the servants and the dogs away, if he was in charge no one would consider wandering the halls much less storming the castle. Martha shivered as she wondered what would happen if he caught her about the house at night. The shiver was fear, she insisted to herself, but a little bit of that shiver settled lower than her belly and left her somewhat distracted.

A snore startled her. Martha pressed her hand to her mouth to hold back a threatened squeak. Pulling herself to the edge of the bed as slowly and quietly as she could, Martha saw that the sergeant was in a chair facing the fireplace, his head back, his eyes closed. At least she hoped his eyes were closed. It was hard to see much at all with the curtains drawn as they were. The candle had guttered its last, and even with eyes adjusted to the dark it was difficult to make out any detail.

As the major gave out another snore, Martha prayed to the God who did not seem inclined to listen, a prayer for a successful end to this disaster, and then pulled herself out from under the bed.

With her eyes glued to the sergeant she stood up and tiptoed across the room. She counted her steps, seven in all, and when she reached for the door allowed herself the slightest hope of success.

With a stroke of genius and immense self-control, Martha waited until the major snored again to turn the latch, the quiet click lost in the snuffling sound of the major's snoring.

The door was well-oiled. She had done it herself a week ago, just one on her regular list of duties, so she knew it wouldn't creak. She slipped though the smallest of openings.

Her elation was overwhelmed by terror as a huge arm clasped her around the waist and a hand covered her mouth just as she was about to scream.

He pulled her a few feet down the hall and then whispered, "If you scream and wake the major there will be hell to pay."

There would be hell to pay in a dozen other ways, not the least of which was losing her position here. As the sergeant loosened his grip she did the only thing she could think of and bit his hand as hard as she could. She felt the skin break. The taste of his blood in her mouth made her feel sick to her stomach.

Martha wanted to tell him, "I'm sorry, really I am," but instead of saying it aloud she used the breath she gasped to make good her escape. Dashing into one of the unused bedrooms, she used a connecting door that led into another room. The door from this sitting room opened on a different corridor. She leaned against the wall and waited for her breathing to even out. The sergeant could not possibly know the layout of the castle. She was sure she had successfully escaped.

Damn the little witch, Jack thought as he shook his hand and then glared at the blood welling from the bite marks. He stood stock-still in the passageway. No point in running after her. She obviously knew the house better than he did, and he would look beyond a dolt if he lost his way and had to wait until daylight to ask someone how to find his way back to the major.

No, he was not running after her, but he knew how tall she was, how neatly she fit under his chin, that she had good, strong teeth, and amazingly curly golden hair. He would find the girl with the gold locks, he had no doubt about that. The question was: What would he do with her once he found her?

Wrapping his handkerchief around his embarrassing wound, the sergeant slipped back into the bedchamber and made his way to the dressing room off it. The cot there looked about as comfortable as the camp cots in Portugal. He toed off his boots, stripped down to his small clothes, lay down, and smiled. It might look like a camp cot but the mattress on it soothed his weary body as only down and feathers could. He reached for the blanket he had pulled from under the major's bed and tucked it in around him. It smelled of oranges and soap, which was a guarantee that despite the comfortable arrangement, a certain mischief maker would haunt his dreams.

Martha barely slept a wink and it was not because the room she shared with Wanda was stuffy or because her roommate had a disconcerting way of talking aloud in her sleep. Reliving her escape over and over, and the feel of the man's arms wrapped tight around her, kept her from resting, and she had only just fallen asleep, or at least it felt like that, when the wake-up bell sounded.

Wanda popped out of bed as though forced by a spring. Martha envied her ability to wake quickly. Even on the best of days Martha was much slower.

"Hurry, Martha, you do not want to be

late for breakfast or you will be given the worst chores for the day."

"Yes, yes," Martha mumbled. They did each other's stays. Martha had to do Wanda's stays twice. The two of them hurried down the five flights of steps to the lowest level and the great cavern of a kitchen where the cooks and kitchen staff had been up for hours.

The usual hush prevailed. At the housekeeper's insistence there was no more than essential conversation until they were all seated for breakfast. It was a peculiarity that Martha appreciated.

Like Mrs. Belweather, Martha needed that first sip of tea, weak as it was, before her ears would work, much less her brain.

They all took their seats, the dogs weaving around them waiting for food to fall. One of them sat on Martha's feet. She reached down and stroked his head.

Everyone settled and looked to Jenny, who would announce any news of the night. Jenny was the first to work in the morning, to rouse the banked fires to life, to carry water, to prepare the tables for baking, and as such was always privy to what might have happened overnight. It was her one moment as the center of attention and it was to her credit that she never kept them waiting.

"The major is home! He arrived late last night with his sergeant. The night porter says he still looks very ill, must still be recovering from his wounds, and has a nasty scar on his cheek, but is in good spirits nonetheless. He was very tired and went right to sleep despite the fact he was sure that someone had been sleeping in his bed."

Mrs. Belweather thumped her cup on the table, putting a sudden stop to the outpouring of conversation at such welcome news. "What did you say?"

When Jenny made to repeat it, Mrs. B. waved her to silence. "Martha!"

"Yes, ma'am," Martha gulped, wondering how the housekeeper knew.

"You were in charge of preparing his room. I chose you because you are so attentive to detail and fast as well. Would you care to explain how you could have left the bed in less than perfect condition?"

Relieved despite the censure, Martha nodded. "It was perfectly ready, Mrs. Belweather. If you will pardon my forwardness, you inspected it yourself."

Mrs. Belweather sniffed and sipped her tea.

"It could have been one of the dogs, Mrs. B.," Jenny suggested. "The night porter said that they were all excited about seeing the major and ran up to his room and were underfoot until the sergeant chased them out."

The housekeeper nodded and took a spoon to her porridge. That gesture always marked the end of conversation.

They all were nearly done with their porridge when the majordomo came out of his office. He did not eat breakfast with them, being too busy with his responsibilities to take the time.

There was a man with him and Martha felt her heart quicken. She tried for a casual glance, then busied herself with toast and the wee bit of butter they were allowed.

"Attention, please," the majordomo called, a request that was not at all necessary since every one of the twenty pairs of eyes, all except Martha's, were fixed on the impressive figure next to him.

Martha realized her mistake and looked up to find the man regarding her with close inspection. She could feel her cheeks redden. It took all of her willpower not to look at his bandaged hand.

"This is Sergeant Tresbere. He was with Major Craig in Spain and will continue as his valet until a suitable one is found. The sergeant tells me that the major is making a good recovery but needs several weeks of peace and quiet before he is ready to resume his duties."

The sergeant nodded to them without a smile or change of expression.

"The sergeant will be treated as one of the upper servants and take his place at table when the major does not require his help. He will sit at the place reserved for his valet."

The seat was empty, but the sergeant made no move to take it.

"The sergeant has asked for a tour of the castle. Is that not right, Sergeant?"

"Yes, with an emphasis on the places that the major is most likely to frequent."

Everyone nodded. Martha liked the sound of his voice. Well spoken, but not presumptuous, as if he'd had an education but was not going to try to impress them with it the way the countess's lady's maid did.

"Martha Stepp."

She gave a jerky nod and stood up as was expected when addressed directly by someone as important as the majordomo. The dog at her feet snuffled his disapproval but did not trip her up.

"You will accompany the sergeant. Show him the ground-floor parlors, the library, the long hall, and the bathing chamber. Show him the location of the countess's wing. But do not disturb her. Her ladyship's maid can show him that suite of rooms later."

The countess's maid nodded with that supercilious disdain that Martha actively loathed. It distracted her for a moment. Distracted her from the thought of spending any time at all with the sergeant. That could only prove disastrous. She fingered the magic coin, which had once again found its way to the pocket of her apron, and wished with all her heart. *Please let me not be found out.*

She did not feel the coin warm and as she stood up she thought, *This must be what the aristocrats who went to the guillotine felt like.*

Chapter Three

"This is Martha Stepp, Sergeant. She has been here for almost a year and has learned quickly. She is one of our best."

Flattered by the compliment, Martha tried not to preen like the countess's maid did, but instead stayed solemn, curtsying slightly to the sergeant, an honor befitting his position, somewhat more than servant but not a guest.

He nodded to her, not a bow, as befitted her position as servant.

"This way, if you please, Sergeant."

At least his rank spared her the need to figure out what to call him. Again, that nebulous position between stairs, that is neither above nor below, made it difficult to work out the etiquette.

Martha could feel everyone's eyes on them and the spontaneous burst of conversation as they passed from sight.

She turned abruptly and almost ran into

his chest, he was following that close. Espying a quirk of a smile on his lips, she dreaded the thought that he was one of those who would try to take advantage of her.

Thank goodness Mrs. Belweather had no tolerance for such behavior. Mrs. B., the butler, and the majordomo were ardent in their protection of the staff. It was an order direct from the countess with a story behind it that every servant knew. Who would tell the sergeant?

And how would she handle it until then?

"These steps lead up to the entrance hall." She led the way and they walked to the main level as another thought occurred to her. What if he knew she was the bedchamber interloper and used it to blackmail her into wicked behavior? She almost ran up the last few steps and into the entry hall, quiet now but occupied, thank heaven, by two of her favorite footmen.

Martha introduced the sergeant to them, as they had not been at the early breakfast but would break their fast as soon as the others were about.

As the footman opened the door, Martha resumed her comments. "This is the receiving salon where guests wait to find out if the countess, or in your case, the major is receiving. Depending on how welcome they are, the major may prefer to deal with them here, or even have you deal with them. Or he can have them brought to the study or the blue or square salon, which is on the first floor, right up these stairs."

All the time she talked he watched her, not so much listening as studying her.

"Tell me, Miss Stepp, are these chairs comfortable?"

"Erp" was all she could manage.

"The general used to have the most uncomfortable chairs in front of his field desk to discourage anyone from spending more time there than absolutely necessary. I was wondering if that was something all gentlemen did."

"Oh, well, these are comfortable enough." Martha was grateful for his long explanation. It gave her a chance to recover her composure. "These chairs are certainly more comfortable than anything in the servants' day room."

She moved toward the door, trying for a sedate pace, when what she really wanted to do was run full speed away from this man. Did he know or not? Was he baiting her or was she just too sensitive to him?

Her sensibilities were askew, she had no doubt of that. Not from guilt. She had nothing to feel guilty about, though hiding under the bed did imply some sense of wrong.

Mrs. Belweather had never told her not to sleep in the bedchambers or try out chairs for comfort or sneak a taste of the best brandy. Hmm, the list was growing in length and the God-fearing part of her, small as it was, did have some trouble with that.

"Miss Stepp?" the sergeant asked with a hint of concern in his voice.

"Oh! I'm sorry." Martha began to move toward the stair. "I was trying to decide which way to take you."

Now she could add lying to her misdeeds.

"I found my way through countryside where most landmarks were in ruins, I think I will be able to find my way around the castle soon enough."

The war, she thought. He had been through war and her greatest adventure was stealing a few hours of sleep in a comfortable bed.

"All the major's letters made it sound like an adventure."

"You read his letters?"

He sounded personally affronted by the idea.

"Oh, you see the countess would invite all those who wished to hear them into the entry hall. She would read them aloud to us."

The sergeant nodded.

"I think it was a way for her to relive them herself, that is, to feel the major closer to her. He was very good about writing, though sometimes there were long weeks between, which made all of us worry." She wondered if the sergeant had anyone to write to and why he had not figured in the major's letters.

"It turns out our worry was not misplaced when we received word the major was injured that first time and his friend Debarth killed." She remembered the moment vividly. The water in the countess's eyes, the way even the footmen had sniffed away tears. "We were heartsick. Debarth had figured in so many of the major's letters about their gaming and how they would wager the buttons on their jackets when nothing else was at hand."

As they paused at the top of the steps, she looked up at Sergeant Tresbere. His face was wooden as if he was doing his best not to cry. Which was absurd. It was hard to imagine a man of his size in tears.

"That was just after Vitoria at the end of June in 1813," the sergeant said, as if to prove he remembered it as well.

She reached out and touched his arm, then withdrew it as quickly. Even though she knew nothing of it, she understood that war was awful, not an adventure at all, but a kind of hell on earth. As much as she knew it, Martha could not bring herself to say it aloud.

"This way, if you please, Sergeant. This is the library."

And so it went. They worked their way through the three floors that housed the rooms that the major would frequent. Sergeant Tresbere listened intently but rarely made comments.

The last stop was outside the dressing room that was part of the major's suite of rooms.

"Very efficient, Miss Stepp. The major would be pleased with your competence."

But you are not? she wondered. It seemed that in the hours they had been together he had grown more distant.

"Good day to you." He bowed slightly,

"Sergeant?" she began, his name a question.

"Yes, miss?" His face was tense.

"Please let me know if you want anything else from me." It was not what she meant to say at all. She wanted to know if he knew she was the one under the bed. If that was why he was so cold to her.

"If I want anything else from you, Miss Stepp?" he repeated her question, a note of incredulity in his voice.

"Yes." The single word was doubtful.

"If you must ask then you cannot begin to imagine what I want." The anger that tinged the words made her move back and with a curt nod, he closed the door in her face.

"Martha, for a bright girl you can be very stupid."

Martha whirled around to find Joseph, the second footman, coming down the passage with a bucket of hot water. He tapped on the major's door and made his delivery with dispatch. Martha waited. Joseph was a particular friend of hers. If he had been at all ambitious she might have taken more of an interest in him, but he was content here at Craig's Castle with no thought of a future beyond senior footman. He was too complacent.

"Why did you say that?" she asked. She fell into step beside him as they made their way back toward the kitchen.

"Because I think you offered him more than you intended. Or is it just me to whom you are cool?"

"Joseph Smith! You insult me."

"Martha Stepp, do you recall what you

said to him?"

"Yes, of course I do. I told him that he could ask if he needed anything else."

"Not exactly, Martha. You know I have an excellent memory."

She nodded.

"You said, 'Please let me know if you want anything else from me.' That is exactly how you phrased it."

"Oh dear goodness." Martha put her hand over her mouth. They continued on down the stairs, Joseph rattling on about how many ways that statement could be interpreted.

"Joseph, I don't need any help. My mind is quite capable of thinking of any number of embarrassing ways he could have answered that."

Joseph laughed, the big oaf, and waved good-bye as he headed back to the kitchen while she went on to Mrs. Belweather's office.

What she did need help with was understanding why she had used such a suggestive phrase.

Chapter Four

"So how does the castle strike you, Sergeant?" The major rubbed his thigh and then stretched it out in front of him.

Jack could tell it pained him and wished he could convince the major to take some exercise. It would help ease the stiffness or at least distract him from it.

"Do you see it as a great moldering pile or — ?" The major left the comparison incomplete, as he often did.

"If I compared it to our unit, Major, I would say it is better run than most, with a competent command structure and the usual run of men, and women, in the ranks. Odd to see a woman in such a role of authority as is Mrs. Belweather."

"Who is Mrs. Belweather?"

"The housekeeper." At first Jack was surprised that the major did not know her name but then he realized that the man had been from home for nigh onto ten years.

"Not to put too fine a point on it, Jack, but my lady mother is also part of the command structure. At least she is when my father, the earl, is in London."

"Yes, I liken the earl to our Wellington. I imagine everyone is on their toes when he is in residence and aims for a notch above their usual excellence."

The major nodded as he made to stand up. The dogs jumped to their feet, ready to accompany him. Jack did not offer him help, but let the man reach for his stick and lever himself out of the chair. "Speaking of the countess. I am off to her wing to present myself to her. I will spare you that, Sergeant, for there will be the usual tears and such."

On both sides, Jack thought. Despite his tone, the major and his mother shared a special bond. Martha Stepp was not the only one who had heard letters.

As the major brushed dog hair from his trousers and reached for a comb one more time, Jack heard shouting and moved toward the window to see what caused it.

The sunlight hinted at a perfect summer day. Ideal for fishing if there was stream nearby and he would be allowed. *Aha,* he thought, stopping halfway across the room, struck by an idea that would give him that information and solve another problem.

"Major, I know the house well enough now but would it be possible, after noon perhaps, for us to make a reconnaissance of the grounds?" He waited for the major to say no, but when he looked interested, Jack went on. "I could go to the stables now and see if your horse can be readied and find another that might need exercise."

"A fine idea, Sergeant. It will be a pleasure to ride without fear of attack, will it not?"

"Yes, sir."

"That will take care of today." The major waited while Jack opened the door. "Now we only have to decide what to do with the rest of our lives."

Jack watched the major move down the hall, his dogs trailing behind though he was fairly certain the dogs would not be included in the welcome-home meeting with the countess.

Now that he had some time to himself, Jack closed himself in his dressing room and took stock. It was small, but fitted out with various built-in elements so that there was room for a bed in an alcove, which could double as a window seat.

His belongings fit in the chest that slid under the bed. All but his pistol, which he wrapped in stout cotton and tucked under his pillow. Old habits die hard, he thought and wondered what could threaten him in this house, in this shire, in this world as far from the fields of Quatre Bras as it was possible to be.

He stood with his knees nudging the end of the bed, and watched the day unfold beyond his window. The gardener's boys made noise attacking every weed in sight while their father pruned and trimmed the plants nearby. Apparently the boys needed supervision.

Even as he had the thought, two of them began a tussle that involved rolling in the grass and punching each other. Jack watched the gardener break up the fight and box the boys' ears before setting them back to work as far from each other as possible.

Keeping this house running and presentable was as demanding as keeping a battalion housed and fed. Perhaps somewhat easier as the house did not rise up and move on a sometimes daily basis.

He knew the moment Martha Stepp came into the major's room. He could sense her presence as if the air around him shifted to accommodate her and brushed up against him with the scent of soap and oranges.

Jack heard her talking with someone else as they freshened the bed and reset fuel in the fireplace. Martha sent the other maid for fresh water and Jack stepped away from his window to speak with her.

He came into the major's bedchamber just as she was replacing the toweling on the washstand.

"Miss Stepp?" he began and she all but shrieked as she turned to face him. Apparently she was not as sensitive to his presence as he was to hers.

"What are you doing here?" she demanded.

"I live here now."

"Yes, I do beg your pardon. You startled me. I thought you would be with the major."

"I am acting as his valet, miss. I am not his shadow. He went to see his mother."

"I'm here to make up his bed," she told him quite unnecessarily as she was tucking in the sheets as she spoke.

He watched her work, both of them in silence, for a minute at least. A minute in which she grew more and more graceless. *Ah,* he thought, *I make her nervous.*

Finally she stopped her fussing. "Why are you watching me? Do you not have something better to do?"

"I cannot imagine what could be better than watching a pretty woman."

She looked insulted rather than flattered by the comment. Turning her back, she lifted the dirty bedsheets and a length of towel and went to the door.

He moved ahead of her but did not open it.

"Was that rude of me?" he asked.

She shrugged.

"You have the strangest hold on me. I know when you come into the room, when you leave, when you look at me, and when you look away. And I have known you less than twelve hours."

She nodded, which was better than a shrug, and he went on. "I do not know many women. No man who makes the army his life does. I can count on my fingers the number of social conversations I have had with a woman, and now I find I am surrounded by them and fascinated by one in particular."

She said nothing but swallowed hard, her eyes growing large. Her eyes invited him closer, at least he thought they did. Not wanting to insult her, or, to be honest, ruin his chances, he did not move but waited for her to do so.

"Martha, open the door for me, if you please," said a voice that came from the other side of the door. "Stupid of me, but I need both hands to hold this can."

Each watching the other, Martha Stepp

moved back and Jack opened the door. When the other servant came into the room the spell between them was broken. Jack took the can of water from the girl and Martha Stepp hurried from the room. He could feel the air shifting back, less compressed, less fragrant.

The other maid was inclined to chat, flirt, Jack decided, but he felt he'd used up his quota of words for now and he excused himself and went into his room, closing the door firmly behind him.

Jack wandered to the window again and for the fifth time wondered why he had not confronted Martha Stepp last night. He had no doubt that she had been the one hiding beneath the bed. Indeed, she had been sleeping on it before they arrived.

He had walked close, almost into her, when she had been assigned to show him the house, and her bright gold hair had smelled of soap and oranges, as had the woman's hair from the night before.

Beyond his failure to expose her, the question was, what had kept her from her own bed? An argument with the girl with whom she shared a room? Was she hiding from a discarded suitor? Or lover?

And what did it matter? Would any woman be willing to tolerate, much less accept, his gift of healing? More like they would see him as a servant of the devil and avoid him at all costs.

He looked up at the sky, not seeing the bright blue or the sharp white of the clouds but imagining a world where he had no gift to complicate his life and the love of a good woman to complete it. By the time he abandoned that fantasy, the boys were gone from the garden.

He saw a woman come out of the house carrying a full armload of something. It was Martha Stepp with the bedding she had taken away, and he watched her, kneeling on the cot so he was a few inches closer to her.

She stopped at the door to the outbuilding, a laundry perhaps, juggled her load to one arm, took something from her pocket, and set it on the lintel of the door before entering.

Her disappearance inside left the garden empty and Jack stared at the blue door to the laundry waiting for her to come out again. She did, not a minute later, hurrying toward the garden and then stopping abruptly.

With what he judged to be a huff of anger she pulled something from her pocket and dropped it on the ground. She stomped on it and then picked it up and threw it toward the pond a few feet away. The object rippled as it broke the surface. Martha watched for a minute and then, with a firm nod, continued back to her work.

Martha sat on the edge of her bed, fingering the coin that had found its way back into her pocket yet again. Was this to be her lot in life? To have this coin to offer people their fondest wish, but never to be granted one herself? With a sigh she buffed it and considered whether the sergeant would be interested in making a wish.

"Stop dawdling, Martha," Wanda called. "We will be late for the major's homecoming party."

Martha pocketed the coin and hurried out. Wanda was long gone, but Ellen was headed toward the stairs. "Do you think the major would like to make a wish?"

"Or think you crazy?"

"That is always a concern," Martha admitted. "However, I would think that someone who has come as close to death as he has would know there is more in the world than we can see or even imagine."

They found Ellen's John and his brother, James, waiting at the bottom of the stairs to the kitchen.

Before James could ask her whatever he was looking so anxious to ask, Mrs. Belweather called him.

"You and John take these pitchers up and fill the punch bowl."

Martha and Wanda were sent to the entry hall to take wraps and help the ladies.

"I think James is sweet on you, Martha." Wanda raised her eyebrows, all curious and coy.

Martha shrugged but mentally agreed. It had seemed to her that James was seeking her out more of late. She'd hoped it was only her vanity.

"Do you want me to pass on any message from you?"

"No!" Martha tried to control her panic. "He is very nice but he is too young."

"Too young? He is a year older than you are."

"And that is too young for me. I prefer a more experienced man." Mostly she preferred one who did not breathe through his mouth.

"He is loyal and devoted to his mother."

"That's true." As a matter of fact, his hangdog look was in keeping with his admirable loyalty, for he was as loyal as the major's dog.

"So you do admit that you admire him."

"Wanda, I do not want you to pass any message to him. Let me make it perfectly clear to you that I want to kiss him about as much as I want the major's dog to lick my face."

"All right, Martha." Wanda's tone implied that Martha had been a little too insistent. "There is no need to be disgusting about it."

"I just wish I could find a man with the qualities I admire in men like James, and the footman Joseph, who also appealed to me in his person."

"You find a man and, I tell you, he might seem perfect, but then once you are married you will find out the truth."

"And what truth would that be?" Martha asked.

"I don't know," Wanda said irritably, "but there is always something that transforms the perfect man into an idiot."

"Which explains why you will never find a man. I am not looking for perfection, Wanda. I want a man who is perfect for me, like the ideal bowl of porridge. Neither too hot nor too cold but just right."

Chapter Five

Before Martha and Wanda could bicker anymore, the first of the guests arrived. The staff was kept busy for the next hour. After all the ladies had refreshed themselves and joined the party, Mrs. Belweather had one last commission for her.

"Find Sergeant Tresbere, Martha. The countess wants him to join the guests this evening."

Martha nodded and hurried off, not at all sure where to find the sergeant but thought to start in the obvious places. He was not in the suite of rooms he and the major used. He was not in the kitchen or the servants' dayroom. She even looked in the library and the bathing room.

Martha reported to Mrs. Belweather, who accepted her failure with good enough grace and sent word to the countess via Joseph that "the sergeant was not available at the moment."

Taking that phrasing as a mandate, Martha insisted that she would keep on looking. "He must be here somewhere."

"That's a good girl, Martha."

The stables, she thought, and ran around from the front of the house to the block of buildings where the horses were kept. There was some game of chance underway; the usual way to pass time among the coachmen and drivers when there was a party, but no Sergeant Tresbere was among the men gathered there.

Martha was walking slowly back to the house, ready to admit defeat, when she smelled tobacco. With the scent came a wash of memories. Her father favored a pipe. She could see him, in front of the fire, smoking while he read or talked with Mama.

She fingered the coin in her pocket. Oh how she wished she could find a man as wonderful as her papa. She sighed and ignored the way her eyes filled. That was entirely too much to wish for.

No one smoked a pipe at the castle. Of course it could be one of the guests but they would be lingering on the terrace closer to the ballroom, not off the path through the kitchen garden that connected the back of the house with the stables.

She rounded the corner and there sat the

sergeant on the bench that was left out for the occasional traveler who came to seek food or shelter, the dogs curled around his feet. He stood up when he saw her.

"Miss Stepp," he said with some surprise.

"Mrs. Belweather sent me to find you and I have been looking for forever." It was not very gracious of her to sound petulant and she had no idea why she was being rude. "The countess would like you to join the major."

He shook his head. "No, I am not ready to go in yet."

Martha was silent a moment, then ventured, "I do not think it was a suggestion, sir."

"Neither Mrs. Belweather nor the countess are my employer, Miss Stepp. To be precise, the major is my employer and he understands my wishes in this."

Was it something they had discussed? she wondered. And why did he not want to join the celebration? Wanda might think her bold but Martha was not so bold as to ask such personal questions.

She nodded instead. "Very well." She gave a vague curtsylike bob. She really had no idea what this man's position was in the household hierarchy, but if he was able to defy the countess and Mrs. Belweather, then his station was definitely above hers. She began to turn away.

"Sit a moment, Miss Stepp," he invited, though it sounded more like a command.

It wasn't a particularly nice evening. The air was heavy with the threat of rain and too cool for that damp to be welcome, but Martha found herself accepting his suggestion and seated herself at the end of the bench.

They were quiet together and it was a pleasant silence. Martha stroked Midge, who had put her doggie head in her lap, and the sergeant puffed on his pipe with, Martha noticed, something like a nervous sensibility.

"Is your work finished for the day?" he asked.

"Not quite. Mrs. Belweather already knows I have not been able to locate your whereabouts and when I return she will probably have another task for me."

"So I am keeping you from your work?"

"Only for a few minutes." She pressed her lips together to keep from smiling. "I am a conscientious maid, mind you, but I like to think that the occasional moment of rest is what makes me so good at my work."

The sergeant laughed. "Your mind is as devious as the colonel's." He went on in a hurry. "That is a compliment, Miss Stepp. Perhaps I should have said clever, not devious. The colonel was a brilliant man, always able to make his request sound as though it was the only sensible option. A fine leader he was."

Martha nodded. "Where is he now?"

"Dead at Quatre Bras, the same battle where the major was injured last."

"Oh, I'm sorry." She was embarrassed and had no idea what else to say.

"The cost of war, Miss Stepp." He breathed in the night air without the aid of his pipe. "It is worth it. To be able to breathe the scent of rain and to know when the daylight comes we will be free to make our own way on our own terms. It is worth it. Though perhaps the colonel would not see it that way."

She wasn't sure if he was trying to convince her or himself. They were silent again. This time there was pain in the silence and Martha tried to think of a new subject.

"My father smoked a pipe. He might have even used the same tobacco."

"It's Spanish," he said.

"Yes." Martha turned to him with a smile. "He did favor Spanish blends."

"What did your father do?"

"He was a silversmith."

Which probably made him wonder why she was in service. It was too sad a story to tell. It would ruin her evening, if not his.

"My father was an army man all his life."

"So you followed him." She liked it when he volunteered these little bits of information.

"I had little choice. I thought of the navy for a bit but a ship would have felt too confining. No, the army it was for me and my brothers."

"How many brothers?"

"Five."

"I was an only child." She wanted to ask how many had survived the war but was afraid of the answer.

"You had a much quieter life than I did, no doubt of that."

"Too quiet." She smiled into the darkness. "Much too quiet. How I longed for adventure." She looked around her, fingering the coin in her pocket. "And now I have it."

"You consider working as a serving girl an adventure?" She could hear a whisper of surprise in his voice.

"Compared to life in York, yes, I do. I have not always been here, you know. I worked in London for a time. That was fascinating."

"You prefer cities?"

"I suppose so, but a house as large as Craig's Castle is a small city unto itself. All in all, the earl employs several hundred men and women."

"Several hundred?" The sergeant's surprise was gratifying.

"Yes, it's amazing, is it not? Of course most of them work in the fields and on the home farm but the household staff is one of the largest I have ever seen."

"Do you count them friends?"

"Yes. Some of them are dear friends. Ellen and her husband, John, and Wanda, who I share a bedchamber with. Mrs. Belweather is one of the finest housekeepers I have ever met. If I could manage an estate house as well as she does I would consider my life a success."

"That is your goal, then?"

"I suppose it must seem trivial to someone like you who has fought for the country, has done something truly fine, but for me it is ambition enough."

"As I said, you are free to live your life as you choose."

It seemed the perfect opening to mention her interest in wishes. "If you could wish for anything what would it be?"

"No more wars."

"Oh," Martha said, momentarily taken

aback. "I am not sure even the finest magic coin in the world could grant that wish. Something more personal," she suggested with a voice made tentative by her boldness.

"Martha Stepp, if wishes were horses, beggars would ride."

"What does that mean?" It was a phrase she had never heard before.

"Do you see beggars riding horses, Martha?"

"No." Was this some sort of trick?

"What it means is that wishing is not the same as working to win it or else every beggar in the world would be astride."

"So you do not believe in making wishes?" Martha tried to hide the profound disappointment she felt.

"Indeed, I am fool enough to wish as often as the next but not fool enough to believe that wishing is all it takes to make a dream come true."

Martha brightened at that and pulled the coin from her pocket, holding it so tight in her palm that she could feel the edges cut into the fingers. "If I could offer you a magic coin to wish on would you be willing to test it?"

The sergeant turned on the bench and looked at her directly. The movement roused the dogs who wandered off and left the two of them quite alone. *Oh, dear,* she thought, *he thinks I am flirting.* But before she could explain he shook his head.

"No, Miss Stepp."

He'd used her Christian name a moment ago.

"If I want something from someone, I ask for it. I have no need of wishes."

And no need of an imagination either. How disappointing. Pushing the coin back into the pocket of her apron, Martha ignored the threat of tears and tried to think of a good excuse to end the conversation.

He puffed on his pipe again and then asked, "Do you not consider marriage and a family?"

Well that certainly was direct. Or perhaps not. She was girl enough to wonder why he asked and woman enough to want to know his answer. "Do you, Sergeant?"

He grinned around his pipe stem. "No, marriage would not work for such a man as I am." He spoke with a conviction that told her he had given it some thought. "But if my world was different I would look for a woman who did not mind a pipe and longed for adventure." He took the pipe from his mouth and watched her.

She found she could not hold his gaze but

watched the smoke curling up from the pipe while she tried to find a way to answer him that was less than shouting "Me! Let it be me!" and jumping into his arms.

The sensible part of her screamed "too soon" and "no imagination." Sensible won, rare as that was. Standing up, abruptly she gave him a clumsy curtsy. "Mrs. Belweather will be suspicious if I am gone any longer. Good night, Sergeant."

The sergeant stood and bowed slightly in return and Martha hurried through the door into the kitchen.

So not quite that adventurous, Jack decided, as he repacked the tobacco in his pipe and sat down again. Or had he been too ham-handed in his flirtation? If that's what that was. Or was it his inconsistency, to say on one hand he would never marry and then talk about his ideal in the next breath? How would he go about telling her of his gift, of what it would mean to them as couple? Not that he knew, but he could guess.

The dogs wandered back to his side and he thought them cowards for leaving him to face her alone. They circled and settled at his feet, unaware and uncaring of his censure.

He wished he knew proper women better.

The camp followers were generous with their favors and those needs were easily met. Sex as a function of the body and not part of the heart or soul. It's what he was used to. All he had known.

He thought he'd been circumspect enough when he'd asked the major how a gentleman, that is a gentleman in action if not in name, would court a virtuous woman. The major had surprised him in more ways than one, Jack recalled.

"You do not want to head off to the Canadas without a companion, eh?" the major surmised.

Jack had not even realized that the major had an inkling of his not-quite-a-plan.

"Sir, I am thinking that my days here are numbered. You will be wanting —" He rethought his wording at the major's scowl. "Or your father will insist you find a proper valet."

"So you are looking for someone else to take care of, is that it then?"

"I'm not sure what I want. Before we arrived here I could not imagine a woman who would want to spend her life with me, with what I am. But now I am not so sure."

He shrugged away the implication, true as it was, that there was someone here at the castle who had made him rethink his conviction. "The thing is, Major, I want to do it right and not offend. The world beyond the army is a strange place for a man who has spent his whole life there."

"You could have stayed on. Your skills are so highly valued there are any number of men, of far higher rank than major, who would wish to have you at their side."

"Sir?" Exactly what was the major referring to?

"Yes, I think you have what it takes to be an officer, Sergeant Tresbere."

"There is no more war left to fight, Major," Jack said, shaking his head.

"Even so. When you were injured at Badajoz I thought I was doing you a favor to ask you to stay with me. Now I think it was a disservice."

"No, sir, I did not have the heart for fighting after the way the English soldiers entered the city with nothing but rape and pillage in mind."

"You are a natural-born leader. You recovered, yes, but you should have recovered somewhere behind the lines. With time to put Badajoz out of your mind you would have come back, found a way to lead men and, more important, to keep something like what happened there from ever happening again."

Jack just shook his head. He wanted to say that the cost would have been too great but there were so many who had given far more than their sanity.

"Which is why your healing skills are a blessing and a curse."

Jack sank into the chair, even though the major was still standing.

"Do you not think it is time we talked about that? I have pretended ignorance long enough."

"If you say so, Major," Jack said, still shocked by the realization that the major had kept his knowledge of Jack's healing skills to himself for so long.

"I remember wondering," the major went on, "how it could be that the number of casualties in our company was so much less than in the others? The way you insisted on helping the surgeons after battle or how much time you spent in the sick tent. No wonder you so often looked like death yourself."

"Nothing that a good sleep couldn't cure." Jack felt for his pipe but did not draw it out. "Did any others know?"

"The surgeons thought you a damn good nurse."

"And when did you know for sure, Major?

When did your wondering become certainty?"

"For sure when I was injured myself. I felt you pour your life into me and force the devil death out of me. I don't know how you did it but most days I am grateful for it."

"My mother had the gift. I'm the only one of my brothers to have it. And I'm the only one still alive. Is that odd or another sort of gift?"

"I think you are still among us because you have more to share, more people who need your touch."

"How is it that you are willing to believe something so strange?"

It was the major's turn to fidget uncomfortably. He let his stick drop and closed his eyes. When he did speak his eyes were still closed.

"Because I have always felt, always known, that I was intended for something out of the ordinary myself. I've known from my youngest years that I did not truly belong here at Craig's Castle."

Having made this confession he waited a moment.

Jack was the last man in the world to question such a sensibility.

The major must have sensed that, for he

opened his eyes and went on. "I wished constantly to be someplace else, anyplace else. As a matter of fact, it's why my father agreed to let me have this set of rooms at the back of the castle. I wanted to live out in the stables but finally we compromised on these rooms."

"I see. I did wonder, sir, how it was that a member of the family could have rooms so far from the rest."

"My choice, and the gift of an understanding mother and a frustrated father." He shook his head with a fond smile, rubbed his leg and went on. "Which is why I bought my commission. Thinking that was my 'out of the ordinary' path in life. But no, whatever I am meant to do has not appeared yet, and when it does I want to be open to it. Which, Sergeant Tresbere, is a very roundabout way of saying that I am open to all manner of nature's oddities. Do you see?"

"Yes, indeed, sir."

The major picked up his walking stick and tapped it on the floor. "But your skills are best suited to military life, are they not?"

"Major, that has been decided for me." Jack spoke with finality and the major nodded. "I think the frontier of Canada will have need of healing as much as any battlefield even if the Indian savages are largely defeated."

Jack stood up. This baring of the souls was as exhausting as any healing he had ever done. "I will leave the army when you do. That is decided. Where and when I go next is still unknown. If I go alone is even more uncertain." For a moment he considered asking the major if he thought a woman could deal with his gift without calling him a devil but decided he had poured out enough of his thoughts for one day. That worry was not the highest on this list anyway. "For now my biggest challenge is finding a way to talk to a lady without offending her."

The major had suggested that all he had to do was ask questions, any questions, and a woman would be only too happy to prose on about herself, her life, her family.

He'd failed to mention that she would ask questions herself, and that sort of conversation was far more intimate than an hour with a prostitute.

Chapter Six

Within a fortnight the earl came up from London, the return of his son and the summer weather making a country sojourn irresistible. The castle came alive when he was in residence, not only because Earl Craigson was the master of the place but at least as much because of his charm and enthusiasm for every pleasure life had to offer.

The number of guests that came and went was endless, keeping everyone on the staff busy from morning until night and sometimes far into it. The major's recovery continued and he and the sergeant were off on their horses most mornings.

Martha would see them now and again but even in the two quiet weeks before the earl had arrived she and the sergeant had not seen each other.

Except for that one time.

Martha was putting the major's bedchamber, sitting room, and dressing room to rights as was her usual chore.

The dressing room where the sergeant slept smelled of the sergeant's pipe and she went to the window, and knelt on the bed, so she could reach over and open the window in order to air the room.

She loved the way the scent echoed in the room but knew that Mrs. Belweather preferred no more than the scent of flowers.

Just as it occurred to her that someday she must try this bed, she heard voices in the other room.

"Oh, Sergeant Tresbere!" It was a woman's voice, one of the other maids, Martha was sure. "I thought you were out with the major. I do beg your pardon."

As she slid off the cot, Martha recognized the voice of Sally Lipton, the senior housemaid. What was she doing here? Her duties kept her in the earl's wing.

"That's quite all right, Miss Lipton. I only came to collect my hat. The sun is blinding today."

"I think we are well met, Sergeant. I have been hoping to find a moment or two to talk with you."

Martha heard the change in Sally's tone and blushed for her. The flirt!

Martha was staring at the sergeant's

broad-brimmed hat, resting on the top of a shaving stand. How embarrassing to be caught listening in on this conversation. She wondered if she could make it into the clothespress before the sergeant came into the room.

"How can I be of service, Miss Lipton?"

Martha could hear the stiffness in the sergeant's voice and wondered if Sally would accept the rebuff or press on.

"Oh," she said, and Martha could picture her moving closer to him. "Oh, Sergeant, I think you could make me a very happy woman."

No. No. No, Martha wanted to shout at Sally. Leave the man alone. She fingered the coin in her pocket. *I wish someone would interrupt them right now.* She waited a moment but no one came. It is up to me, she decided. With a spurt of action she gathered her basket of cleaning supplies. Humming as loud as she could, Martha opened the door and stepped into the bedchamber as though she had no idea the room was occupied.

The sergeant turned to her, his expression so incensed that she wondered if he thought she was part of this game.

"Sally! Were you looking for me? I'm sorry to be so long." She offered no excuse for her supposed tardiness but moved toward the door. "Good day to you, Sergeant Tresbere."

Sally had no choice but to follow her. When they were out in the passage, the sergeant called after them. "Miss Stepp. A word with you."

For a sergeant he was very good at giving commands.

"Wait for me here, will you, Sally?" she asked as she walked back to where he waited.

Sally nodded, all curiosity.

He had his hat in his hand and he worried the brim for a moment. "I do not know why the beds in this suite so fascinate you."

Holy mother, she'd forgotten to straighten the bedding! "I was only —"

He cut off her explanation with a raised hand. "If I ever find you in, or under, any bed again, I will take steps to convince you to give up that hobby."

Steps? Exactly what did he mean by that? she wondered. But his obvious anger was so unusual that she thought now was not the time for debate. "I'm sorry, Sergeant."

"I'm sure you are. But only sorry to have been discovered."

"It is a perfectly innocent hobby, sir." She could not resist the defense. "As Sally said, we thought you out with the major."

"Ah, yes." He put his hat down and shook his head. "Tell me, Martha, why is every woman here so hell-bent on marriage?"

Hell-bent? Did he think she was trying to trap him?

"I do not have marriage on my mind." Anger simmered to a boil. "I have a position here and the respect of my peers."

"Martha, listen to me."

Now she raised her hand to stop his words.

"If I was interested in marriage with any man I would expect a proper courtship and a proper proposal."

"Martha," he began, again.

"And I would not marry you if you were the last man on earth." Martha turned her back to him not wanting him to see the tears that filled her eyes and began to stream uncontrollably down her cheeks.

As she made her way to the passage she called back, "Wanda is right. All men are idiots."

Sally heard the last phrase, her expression switching from curiosity to awe.

The sergeant swept by them and down the passage at something close to a run as she whispered to Sally between her tearful gasps, "If you dare say a word about this I will tell them about your oh-so-bold offer to the sergeant."

Sally nodded and the two of them went down the back stairs to the kitchen, where Martha made a detour out to the garden to compose herself.

Later that evening she walked down to Ellen and John's cottage where she unburdened herself. It was a huge relief to have someone else express indignation at his arrogance even if it was support she only partly deserved. That's what friends were for, were they not?

Over a mug of ale the three of them sat in the front room of the two-room cottage, with the door open to the evening air. It was John who put an end to his wife's rant about how rude men could be.

"I think his question was sincerely meant, Martha. I know he thinks of you as a friend."

"He does?" She wanted to ask John what men meant when they thought of a woman as a friend, but John did no more than nod in answer to her question and speak on.

"The sergeant has been importuned a good bit lately. We were walking back from town together just yesterday and he asked me if all women were as bold as the women hereabouts."

Martha and Ellen looked at each other

and nodded encouragement.

"It seems that any number of the women from the village and the girls on the staff here at the castle have been inviting his attention."

"So you are saying he could have his pick of company but has no use for any of us."

Was she at fault? Martha did not think she had been particularly forward. Indeed, she had been almost shy around him since that night of the major's welcome-home ball, but now she could see how he had misconstrued his mussed bed. "But I wasn't flirting! I had only kneeled on his bed to open the window."

"Yes, but he is overly sensitive right now and he is not used to virtuous women and has no idea what their flirtation means."

"So you instructed him?" his wife asked with raised eyebrows.

John took her hand, kissed it, and held it tight. "I told him not to trifle with any of the servants and to go to the Cog and Crown if he was wanting more than flirtation."

Martha and Ellen exchanged another glance, this one of complete understanding. For her part Martha wondered if the sergeant ever did venture to that den of iniquity.

John offered to walk Martha back to the castle but she waved off the suggestion that she needed protection. Both John and Ellen watched until she was out of sight.

Just then the major appeared along a path that met the same lane she was turning onto. The dogs ran ahead and then back to greet Martha.

"Took the dogs out for a walk," he explained. "Good for the leg, don't you see."

"Yes, sir, I can see that you are much improved already. No more stick and almost no limp."

"Feels good and right to be whole again."

"I'm sure it does, Major."

Midge, the big dog, nudged her hand and she pulled it out of her apron pocket to give him some of the attention he craved. The coin fell to the ground.

She would have not missed it at all, but it was the major who called her attention to it, and gentleman that he was, bent to retrieve it for her.

"Unusual coin that," he said. "Do you carry it for luck?"

"Not really," she said with honesty induced by the night and moon. "It's a coin from a shipment that was lost at sea more than fifteen years ago in the early eighteen hundreds. Some say it has magical properties, but it's never granted any of my wishes."

The major laughed. "Perhaps the coin is waiting for you to wish for the right thing."

Martha stopped short and looked at the major. "Why did you say that?"

"It's the way of magic," he explained with a matter-of-fact air that belied the word *magic.* "It's as whimsical as any of nature's oddities."

They walked on in silence as Martha puzzled over what the major could know of nature's oddities. When they reached the side door that everyone used when coming from the grounds to the west, the major opened the door for her.

"Does your silence mean you are wondering if I suffered a brain injury when my face was scarred?"

"No, not at all, Major. It is only that too few people are willing to accept them. Nature's oddities, that is."

"Ah, yes." He examined the coin as well as one could in the dim candlelight of the passageway. "Does this one grant wishes?"

"I have seen it do so," Martha answered with caution and prayed to the God who might or might not be listening that such honesty would not mean her dismissal.

The major was still holding on to the coin

as he made his way to the stairs that led to the wing where his rooms were situated. Martha followed.

When they reached his floor he held the coin up but instead of handing it back to her he said, "Do I speak the wish aloud or merely think it?"

"Whichever you prefer, Major. I must warn you that the coin grants wishes in its own sometimes rather odd way."

The major considered that caveat and then straightened. "Very well then, I will trust in the coin's wisdom."

Oh, Martha thought, she had never considered that the coin's wisdom would exceed a person's. They walked to his suite in silence. At the door, he turned to her and with the coin held between them announced, "My wish is that I find work that will be fulfilling for as long as I live."

Martha reached for the coin, but before she could take it, such a bright light burst from the coin that she gasped and the major stepped back, though he did not release it.

"I do believe your wish will be granted, Major." Martha's awe was evident she was sure.

The major nodded. "I've always known that, but the question is, when will it be granted? There's the rub."

CHAPTER SEVEN

Martha did not notice the coin was missing until just before noon. It was not in her pocket. For the first time in years it was not where it always was, no matter how she tried to rid herself of it. And now without the slightest effort it was gone.

She was so overcome that she fell into the nearest chair, this one a wingback near a fireplace, which she knew from past experience was not nearly as comfortable as it appeared. Twisting the dusting cloth in her hand, she tried to recall the last time she had held it, seen it, or felt its presence.

Last night when the major had wished on it.

She would go to his suite now to see if somehow she had left it behind. The figurines she had been sent to dust were too fragile and valuable to do while so distracted.

Moving at a purposeful pace, so no one would suspect that she was shirking her duties, Martha made her way up a flight and halfway around the castle. She was making the last turn when she ran into the sergeant, quite literally.

She had been lost in thought, wondering what the missing coin could mean, but the sergeant must have had some idea of the pending collision as he had his arms out to stop the impact.

Enfolded in his arms, her head tucked under his chin, she could feel his heart gallop, or maybe it was hers.

"I'm sorry. I do beg your pardon," she blustered as she stumbled back, necessitating a helping hand from the sergeant yet again. They were not on the best of terms ever since he had accused her of attempting to entrap him, and she hoped this did not further convince him of something else awful about her.

"I was on my way to speak with the major and was not watching where I was going."

The sergeant nodded but said nothing, and Martha went on in a rush.

"Is he still in his suite or has he gone out for the day? I need only speak with him for a moment. You see, we had a conversation yesterday evening —"

Before she could finish her sentence the sergeant held up the coin. "Is this what you are looking for?"

"Yes," Martha said on a great breath of relief. How odd that she had wanted nothing but to be rid of it but was almost panicked at the thought of it missing.

"The major asked me to bring it back to you." He handed it to her and she slipped it into her pocket. The sergeant did not say another word but turned on his heel.

"I did not leave it there on purpose. I didn't," Martha insisted.

The sergeant turned back slowly. "But of course you didn't."

"Oh!" Martha stamped her foot. "Are you doubting my word?"

He said nothing, but stood with his arms folded across his chest as though blocking her way when all she had to do was turn around and leave.

She did so, and over her shoulder tossed her final shot. "You are impossible."

"Impossible to trick, you mean?" He seemed amused by her temper.

"No, that is not what I mean." She turned to face him again, her own arms folded, unconsciously imitating him. "Sergeant Tresbere, I told you before and I will tell you again that I have a sterling reputation here at Craig's Castle and I resent your implication that I am trying to trick you into anything." She could not quite bring herself to say "marriage," which was proof of how ridiculous that was.

"You misunderstood me that day, Miss Stepp. Which I would have made clear if you had listened instead of storming off as you are about to do again now."

"Then you accept that I am an honest, honorable woman not given to trickery?"

"Indeed," he said, and then spoiled it by laughing. "Except for that one flaw of sleeping in beds that are not your own."

"Empty beds," she clarified, wondering if he intended another insult.

"Aha, so you admit that you do it."

Caught by her own admission, Martha nodded, a tiny little nod but a confession nonetheless. "But, Sergeant, it does not harm anyone. I am only looking for the most comfortable bed in the castle. One that suits me. One that is just right."

"And what was it before the beds?"

"Chairs," she muttered.

"And will it be the wine, next?"

She blushed and looked away.

"My God, you've started on that already." Now he sounded more shocked than amused.

"Well, yes."

The admission did not seem to appease him.

"I do not even like the taste of wine. I had a sip when John and Ellen were married."

The sergeant shook his head. "You need someone more than Mrs. Belweather to keep you out of trouble."

"I do not need anyone and I am not in trouble."

"Do you not see that you would be if someone finds out and tells the housekeeper. Martha, discovery is inevitable."

She was embarrassed before; now she was just a little afraid. What would it take to guarantee his silence? "Are you trying to blackmail me? I would sooner lose my position."

"Blackmail? Who said anything about blackmail?" The sergeant looked away from her and shook his head. When he looked at her again his expression was as aghast as hers had been. "Did you think I would threaten you with exposure unless you meet my demands?" As he spoke his eyes fell to her mouth and she felt a tingle there as if he had actually touched her lips.

Yes, that was what she had feared but she was not going to admit that aloud.

"It seems that neither of us trusts the intentions of the other, Miss Stepp —"

"Tresbere, you forgot the coin!" The major made his way down the hall to them, the coin in his fingers and held out to the sergeant.

"No, sir, I gave it to Miss Stepp just this minute."

"I put it in my pocket." She felt for it. "It's gone!"

The three of them stared at the coin in the major's hand.

"How can that be?" the sergeant asked. Confusion colored his voice.

"Oh! Oh!" Martha said, almost dancing with excitement. "I know what happened. I know what it means." Martha nodded vigorously at the major, who seemed to consider her words.

After a long moment and with a decisive nod of his own, more like a jerk of his head, it was clear the major had made a decision. "We will not discuss this in the passage." As he spoke, the sergeant acted on the statement and pushed open the door to the nearest room, some sort of sitting room, and waited for the other two to go in before he followed them and closed the door.

"Sit," the major ordered. Both gentlemen waited for her to take a seat. None of these chairs had made the top of her list but Martha chose the least comfortable one and waited while the other two seated themselves.

The major stretched his leg out and rubbed it with some effort. Was his pain that constant, Martha wondered? How interesting that he had not used his wish to end it.

The sergeant rose quickly and found a footstool for his major. With a grunt of thanks the major rested his leg on it.

"Now, if you would explain your coin's odd behavior, Miss Stepp."

"It is not my coin anymore, Major, sir. It is now yours." The certainty and joy that the magic coin was in the right hands, and, yes, the relief, made her giddy with pleasure.

"How does a coin choose who owns it?"

Martha closed her eyes and willed herself to start at the beginning, or at least start at some point earlier than ten minutes ago.

"I came into possession of the coin quite by accident when I was employed by the Earl Weston. Actually, the coin came to me right after I had been dismissed." She started at her lap, hating the truth but determined to be honest.

"It was in someone else's hands before that?"

"Oh, Major, I can only assume so. I found it on a table where I was employed and I picked it up to examine it because it was so unusual, and from that moment on it has been as much a part of me as my beating heart. I did not steal it," she insisted.

Both the sergeant and the major nodded apparent understanding and Martha relaxed some.

"In the years I have had it, nine years, I have traveled all over England, been employed in numerous households, and seen the coin grant wishes that would amaze. I once worked for a couple whose minds switched from one body to the other in response to a wish that they could understand each other better. There was a woman who was given a shawl that granted the wish of invisibility so she could understand what people really thought of her."

"There can be no doubt that this coin is truly one of nature's oddities." The major examined the coin and clutched it tight in his fist.

The sergeant was listening with interest. Martha saw no doubt in his face and was relieved. The idea that he did not trust her was upsetting. She trusted him, she was sure of that, just doubted his good judgment when it came to women. She brought herself back to the moment.

"There were many more conventional wishes granted, but I tell you those so that you will see what a responsibility it is to have the safety of the coin in your hands."

The major nodded again. Martha could see the coin glowing ever so slightly as he held it, conveying just enough magic to convince him.

"Why did it choose me?" the major asked.

"I do believe it was what you wished for." Martha waited for the major to recall his words.

"But I wished for fulfilling work."

"The coin does interpret the wish in its own unique way. I warned you of that."

"You are telling me that my work is to care for the coin?"

"I promise you it is very fulfilling." *At first,* she added to herself. She wondered if the major would tire of the responsibility, not the least of which was the need to judge who would accept the coin's magic and who to avoid lest they think the one who offered it quite mad. "Though, in all honesty, I must tell you that I am happy to be done with it and will run away as fast as I can if I ever come upon another of nature's oddities."

The major smiled. "I do suspect that you only need a respite, dear girl. For my part I should like very much to assume the role of the coin's keeper." His smile grew into a grin. "I should like it very much, indeed."

Turning to the sergeant, he held out the coin. "You first, Jack." He glanced from Martha to the sergeant. "Or have you made your wish already?"

There was an uncomfortable pause as Martha avoided looking at the sergeant. He stared at the coin. "Martha offered it to me and I declined."

"Will you reconsider then?"

The sergeant took the coin and folded it tightly in his palm. He looked off into the middle distance, then shook his head, handing the coin back to the major.

"No." The sergeant looked at Martha, his expression solemn. "No, sir. As I told Martha, I have no need of wishes, but ask directly for what I want. It is how I judge whether it is an honorable want or not."

The major nodded but Martha noticed that the coin glowed a moment, not the burst of light that had validated the major's wish but a brief glimmer only she seemed aware of. She was almost positive that the sergeant had thought a wish and the coin had heard, even though he seemed to have thought better of it.

The bell rang for the servants' dinner and Martha started. "Oh, dear, I have not finished my morning chores!"

She gathered up her basket and hurried for the stairs. "Good luck to you, Major. I shall be near if you have any more questions."

Jack sat on the bench near the kitchen door, considering his day, the highs and the lows. He was relieved that the major had something to do, even if the care of the coin and the distribution of wishes seemed a fanciful way to spend one's days.

He had thought of a wish to make if he had been so inclined. He had wished silently that he would find someone in his bed. Thank God he had not declared it his wish, for that someone had a name and he had no desire to compromise Martha Stepp in any way except, perhaps, in his dreams.

Chapter Eight

The house settled into a quieter rhythm once the earl returned to London. The countess went with him and the plan was for the major to join them after he had found a valet.

"Why is he not going to London to find one?" Martha asked Ellen as the two of them made up the beds and tidied the major's suite.

"John tells me that the major is not going to stay in London for long and wants someone who will be willing to move around the country with him for a few years before he finds a place to settle."

Martha wondered how much his possession of the coin had to do with that decision.

"John says he has asked some of the footmen if they are interested."

"Oh, I see," Martha said. "He could send the footman to London and the earl's man could train him properly. He could wait for the major or come back for some practice so that he will be less nervous."

"That's a good idea, Martha. I'll tell John to suggest he come back for a bit."

Where will the sergeant go and what will he do? Martha wondered. "Which of the footmen?" she asked instead.

"Joseph, Melvin, and Hasbro," Ellen answered promptly.

"What an adventure it will be for one of them."

"Yes, though why one needs adventure to make life complete is beyond my ken."

It was a familiar comment and the source of some discussion between them. For her part Martha thought that having a child was the greatest of adventures, but Ellen insisted it was what women were made for. Anyway, there was no point in talking it through yet again.

Martha gathered last night's tea tray. "I am going down to see if the linen is ready. Will you check the dressing room to be sure that nothing else is needed there?"

"Of course."

Martha made her way down the stairs and out the garden door. The boys were supposed to be weeding but it looked to her like they were more actively engaged in playing with the dogs that were usually the major's constant companions.

Looking around she saw the major heading up from the stables with the sergeant at his side, absorbed in conversation and not noticing the chaos his dogs were causing.

Martha loved watching the sergeant in unguarded moments. He gave his complete attention to whomever was speaking. You could see it in the way his head was bent and his eyes narrowed slightly as though he were taking in more than words. She loved that about him. The way he seemed to care about everyone in his world from the countess to the gardener's boys.

With the final detail arranged, the major turned to take the path to the front of the house. The sergeant headed toward the kitchen and smiled at the boys and the dogs now tumbling over some vegetable seedlings. Their father would be furious. And there was Martha Stepp making one of her endless trips from the laundry with her basket of clean linen. He looked up to see Martha's friend Ellen closing the window over his bed. He'd forgotten to do that this morning.

The focus of Craig's Castle might be the earl and his family but the lifeblood was the staff he had come to know and watch from the very spot where Ellen stood now. Though he'd been a part of it a short time, even he had found a place for himself here.

There was no doubt in his mind that this next adventure would have been far more appealing in the company of a good woman. Where had he gone wrong with Martha? She was more than a good woman. She was full of life and energy and had a kind of joy in living that made even the mundane fun. His happiest time these past months had been sitting on the bench outside the kitchen talking with her. So innocent and yet filled with such possibility.

It had all changed that day he had found her in the dressing room, where she had so obviously been lying on his bed. He wondered if it was possible to start again with her or at least go back to those comfortable days when they shared the bench by the garden door and talked of the past, the present, and hinted at their future.

And the final nail in the coffin that held his hopes was that comment to the major that now that he had the coin she would run from any other display of nature's oddities. He might not have explained his gift to her but he had her answer to her willingness to share it with him.

As he approached the boys saw him, abandoned the dogs, and ran for him. The dogs were not about to be left behind, and in a flash the innocent scene changed dramatically.

The boy in the lead looked back over his shoulder to see if the others were gaining on him just as Martha came around a corner. The boy ran into her at full speed.

Martha fell back and her basket went flying. She landed with what Jack knew would be a bone-jarring thump. The boy fared worse. He flew back, bouncing off the basket, and landed flat on his back, his head hitting one of the paving stones that marked the path to the kitchen door.

Martha sat for a minute, gathering the laundry and stuffing it back into the basket. But the boy did not move. The other boys gathered around him and Jack could feel fear radiating from them even from yards away.

With no thought but for Martha and the hurt child, Jack raced toward them. It took him no time to reach them but Martha was already on her feet, the basket forgotten. She gave the boys orders as if born to the task.

"Robbie, run and find your pa."

"Lester, do not hover over Edward. Let

him have some air. Mickey, you go find your ma and tell her that your brother needs her."

Lester looked up, his eyes large with terror. "I'm not sure he's breathing, miss."

"He's breathing," Martha told him, and Jack knew she was willing it to be so.

"Martha," he said, speaking gently so as not to frighten her.

She whirled to face him. "Oh, Jack," she said, the relief in her voice evident. "Edward," she began, but the sergeant stopped her with a hand on her arm, willing calm and comfort through it.

"I saw from the path. Are you all right?"

"Yes." She drew a deep breath. "Better now that you're here."

He nodded and turned to the boy, so still on the ground, his face chalk white. "I have some experience with this kind of injury. May I examine him?"

"Of course. I'm not in charge. I was going to see if the earl's physician son would be willing to examine him, but you probably know as much about this sort of injury as he does. We should move him off the cold ground."

She made to do so but Jack stopped her. "No, let me see him as he is."

Jack knelt beside the boy as Martha drew Lester away from his brother. He resisted.

"Move aside so I can help your brother," Jack ordered.

"You're a surgeon then?" the boy asked.

"No, but I have been at war for years and am adept at helping the wounded."

The boy nodded with some reluctance.

"The best help you could be right now is to go find me a cloth wet with water. Martha will help me until you come back." Martha of the magic coin would have no trouble understanding what she was about to see even if she did not wish it to be part of her world.

With Lester out of sight, Jack bent over the still form and put his hands on the boy's cheek and then on his head. With one hand hovering over Edward's heart, and the other a scant inch from the top of his head, Jack Tresbere closed his eyes and called on the healing power deep inside. He could feel the warmth of it move through his body and radiate from the palm of his hand.

He stayed that way for as long as the heat poured from him, even though it weakened him more than he would have liked. Finally, as color returned to the boy's cheeks, he realized how close the child had been to death. Jack moved his hands away and sat on the pavement.

He did not look at Martha and the silence

stretched between them. When they could hear the others returning, she moved away from him, but not before he heard her say, "Dear God in heaven. How do you stand it?"

He looked up at her, too tired to do more than try to breathe. Now she would turn and leave, run from him. As far from this "nature's oddity" as she could.

A crowd of people burst on the scene just as Edward moaned.

Jack stumbled out of the way and found the bench near the door. He collapsed onto it and — with his head in his hands — tried to shut out the sounds around him and concentrated on regaining enough strength to stand, walk, climb the stairs, and find a bed.

"Do you need help?" Martha sat next to him while she waited for his answer.

He almost stopped breathing altogether when he realized that she had not abandoned him.

"Your arm?" He could barely speak the words but she stood up and offered him her arm.

Leaning on her, he let her pull him through the empty kitchen and up one flight of stairs. She pushed open a door into a room he had never been in before.

He fell onto the sofa despite her warning. "It's not very comfortable."

It didn't matter. He needed only rest and quiet. And her.

When he was stretched out on the thankfully long sofa, Martha leaned close. "Do you want me to find the major?"

"No. Sleep" was all he said before he slipped off into what she hoped was a restful repose and not some prelude to a brain fever.

Martha watched him for a few minutes, or longer. She really had lost track of time and assumed at the moment that none of the usual rules applied.

With his eyes closed and his breathing deep and even, she saw something in him that she had never seen before. He might be a tall, well-built man but he was as vulnerable as the boy he had saved or the women he seemed to have no use for. He was used to being dependent on no one. It had been his way for so long she wondered if he could change. Did he even want to change?

Apparently not, she decided, as she covered him with a blanket that she found in a cupboard along the wall.

Martha tiptoed out of the room and went to tell the major what the sergeant had done. If there was any man Sergeant Tresbere would accept help from, it was Major Alistair Craig.

The major listened to her story with apparent equanimity.

"He let you watch him?" was the first question the major asked.

It was not what she'd expected. "Yes, but he had little choice. Edward was in desperate need."

"You may say so but I have never known him to allow anyone near while he worked with someone injured."

I can think about what that means later, she thought. "But you knew of his skill."

"Yes, because he is why I am alive even with a scar and a bad leg."

"I see," she said, a whole new insight passing to her with those words. He had spent his years in the army saving lives, saving many more lives than he had ever taken she guessed. "But does he not need you now, sir?"

The major shook his head. "No, he needs only to sleep to regain his strength. It may take the better part of the day but he will be right as rain once he has awakened and eaten."

"But that's incredible."

"No more incredible than a magic coin,

Martha. Now you see why I am more than willing to accept nature's oddities."

"Have you seen others, then, besides the coin and the sergeant's ability to heal?" She was almost afraid of his answer.

"Yes, I knew a colonel's wife who could tell if one was lying or not. And there have always been gypsies who could see into the future."

Martha nodded. She'd always thought gypsies were making up stories, but now that the major presented it so matter-of-factly, why should the English be the only ones to have these unexpected gifts?

The major patted her on the arm. "Thank you for taking care of the sergeant, my dear. I will see to him now."

Martha accepted the gentle dismissal. He bowed to her curtsy, which was very flattering, and then added one more thought as she left the room.

"I would not be surprised if the sergeant avoids you for a day or two."

Martha gave him a nod that was a little uncertain but did not press for details. Their conversation had left her with a head full of questions to which she strongly suspected there were no certain answers. This last comment just added one more.

Chapter Nine

The major either counted mind reading as one of his unrevealed skills or he knew Jack Tresbere very well. The sergeant was not in his usual haunts for the next two days.

Martha and Ellen were polishing the brass wall sconces in rare silence, each lost in her own thoughts at first.

Martha rubbed the sconce vehemently. Was the sergeant embarrassed about his weakness after healing Edward? Was he afraid she would ask too many questions? Did he regret letting someone see him use his magic?

Finally Martha could not stand it any longer.

"Where could he be?"

"I am guessing you have looked in all his usual spots?"

"Yes, the bench outside the kitchen, in the north-facing window seat in the library. In the stables even. And I must say the groom thought it odd for a housemaid to be asking when the animals were fed."

"When the animals were fed?" Ellen echoed with some confusion.

"I pretended the major sent me to ask." She grimaced. "It was the only thing I could think of."

"Yes, well, the fact the senior groom has run off with that buxom dairy maid will have made him forget your visit."

Martha nodded. It had shocked them all, the senior groom having been engaged for two years to a girl from the village.

Perhaps it was not about her at all. It could be he was looking for work now that the major had chosen Hasbro as his new valet. The former footman had gone up to London to learn the finer details of his work from the earl's valet. When Hasbro returned his would be the bed in the dressing room, the cot tucked under the window. It remained one of the few beds that Martha had not sampled.

"His tobacco is very distinctive," Ellen suggested.

"Then he has given up smoking or left the castle because I have not been able to detect a hint of it."

Any more discussion of the sergeant's whereabouts was stopped by the sound of

Mrs. Belweather making her way up the stairs, each step followed by a pause and a grunt. It was as ladylike as a grunt could be but a grunt nonetheless.

"Good girls. When you are done here, please go to the major's suite and change the major's bed linen and prepare the dressing room for Hasbro. That way it will be ready whenever he returns."

Martha felt her heart lurch. "Has the sergeant left?"

"Without saying good-bye?" Ellen added. "He and John were such good friends."

"He and the major have gone fishing today and will not be back until dark. After that the sergeant will be off."

"Will we be giving him a proper farewell, then?" Ellen asked after a pleading look from Martha.

"The major said the sergeant wanted no fuss."

Mrs. Belweather made her way down the passage, leaving Martha stunned and Ellen disappointed.

"Why?" Martha knew she sounded near tears. "I wish I could understand why he would leave so suddenly." She knew why. He was afraid that once people found out about his healing skills he would either be shunned or, much more likely, called upon for every real or imagined hurt.

"He may come yet," Ellen said with an encouraging pat on Martha's back. "Let's go on about our work. There is nothing we can do now but find a way to make the time go by."

Martha could think of something she would rather do. Walk, or even run, down to the river, find the sergeant, and confront him. Why was he leaving so suddenly? Why was he leaving without saying good-bye? Where was he going? And the biggest question of all, and the hardest to ask, if things had been just a little different, would he have asked her to go with him?

"You do the dressing room, Martha. I'll fetch the fresh linen."

Ellen trotted off and Martha went through to the dressing room. The sergeant was a very tidy sort and there really was nothing to be done. She knelt on his bed and ran a dust cloth over the window ledge.

Tucked against the window as it was, this bed looked more like a window seat, and the curtains that were tied back at the side added to the effect.

She sat on the mattress and then lifted her legs to stretch out fully on the bed. There, she was sharing his bed, or as close as she would ever come. Ignoring the way her eyes watered, she concentrated on the mattress and closed her eyes. Oh. It was wonderful. Who would have thought that a little bed in a dressing room would be so perfect? The pad must be stuffed with down, she thought, and wondered who had judged a servant fine enough to warrant having the special mattress made for this space.

There was no doubt that it was the best of all the beds she had tried.

Martha did not really fall asleep but realized later that she must have been in that strange half-waking trance that could be as restful as a nap. She woke with a start as the door opened.

"It is in the dressing room." It was Mrs. Belweather's voice. Martha had no trouble recognizing it. The door opened and she came into the room, the butler right behind her.

"I am not sure whether it is a leak or —" She broke off when she saw Martha and her expression changed from practical to shock and then outrage.

"Martha Stepp! What are you doing in the sergeant's bed?"

"He is not here, Mrs. Belweather. He and the major have gone fishing for the day. I fell asleep."

"Or you are awaiting his return. When you should be about your duties."

"Which is the least of your transgressions," the majordomo added.

"Go to my rooms, Miss Stepp, and do not expect any sort of leniency, just because you are one of our best. You will be dismissed immediately and without a reference."

"But, please, Mrs. Belweather, I only fell asleep. I was not waiting for anyone. Truly."

At that very moment the worst possible thing happened. The sergeant himself came into the room, adding weight to the worst of the housekeeper's suspicions.

The sergeant looked from one to the other and the rumpled window bed. He closed his eyes and actually moaned, "No, no," sounding so much like a man caught in the throes of some terrible anguish that Martha forgot her own misfortune. Finally his gaze settled on Martha. "Not this way. This is not what I wished!"

"What you wished!" Mrs. Belweather grabbed Martha by the arm. "Out, out at once!" She paused at the door to the passageway and called back to the sergeant. "The major will hear of this."

The major heard of it. Everyone in the household did before dinner was over. Sally Lipton saw to that. Martha was sent off that very day with a month's pay and fare for the post to London.

John was given permission to take her to the village in the cart the staff used to transport goods. Only Ellen came to say good-bye. It was as though they feared her supposed depravity was contagious.

"Write me, write me," Martha begged, "and tell me if it is a boy or girl."

Ellen nodded, unable to speak through her tears. Martha was still too much in shock for any sensibility but confusion. How could her whole life have changed so quickly? To be sent away without a reference was not the worst thing in the world. It had happened before. She had enough other good references and she had been at Craig's Castle less than a year — so perhaps that small gap would not be noticed. She could say she had been nursing her sick mother or dying father. Yes, that would work. All the way to town she sat silent next to John.

The worst of it was to leave with her reputation compromised for which she truly could not blame Sally Lipton entirely. Martha had made the misguided choice to sample the sergeant's bed when she should have heeded his warning.

By the time they reached the market town,

five miles beyond the nearest village, Martha was outwardly composed, if pale. She bid John a fond farewell and sought out the inn that serviced the mail. Mr. Morris was known to Craig's Castle and he knew them, but the news was not good.

"I'm sorry, Miss Stepp, but the post is delayed overnight. The driver took ill and the carriage was damaged when he could not control the horses. No one was injured but that's because there weren't but three passengers and all of them drunk as lords."

It was not an auspicious beginning to the next chapter of her life. "Please tell me you have a room I can have for the night."

"Of course, miss. We are at sixes and sevens what with the surgeon coming and going and the extra customers but I will insist two of the men share a room and give you the one that looks out the back. It be quieter."

It was obvious that Craig's Castle gossip had not reached the inn yet, for which Martha muttered a prayer of thanks to God, Saint Peter, or whoever was listening today.

The room was as nice as a room at an inn could be. Mrs. Morris had been a housekeeper herself until her late-in-life marriage to Mr. Morris, and her skills had been put to good use here. It had been years since

Martha had a bedchamber to herself and she thought she might actually enjoy the little adventure.

No sooner had she allowed that "enjoying this adventure" was an out and out lie even she did not believe, then sobs erupted from her throat and she buried her face in the pillow and cried for all that might have been.

Jack hoisted his travel bag from the bed and gave a last look around the room. It had never felt like home, but it was the most comfortable camp he'd ever had and probably the nicest for a long time to come.

He could hear one of the footmen in the other room, helping the major out of his riding clothes, and hoped that when the newly trained Hasbro returned he would have some understanding of the difference between a military uniform and the type of clothes most gentlemen wore. The day was moving on and tomorrow looked to be a good day for traveling. Now that his future was in the present it wasn't as appealing as he'd thought it would be.

He'd done his best to redeem Martha's good name. But Mrs. Belweather would have none of it. The truth was too clear to her and altogether wrong. Jack's only hope was that he could track Martha down at the inn to which they were both headed and find a way to make amends for his poorly timed arrival and badly chosen words.

He made his good-byes to the major, who argued once again that he did not have to leave under such a shadow.

"No, sir, if Miss Stepp has been let go then I must find her and do my gentlemanly best to see that she is not without support."

The major rubbed the smile off his mouth with one hand and gave Jack a hearty handshake with the other.

"Are you sure you will not make a wish, Jack?"

"Never ever again, Major. That coin has near ruined more than one life. I warn you, sir, to be careful who you share it with."

The major nodded, his smile now completely gone. "God bless you, Jack. I have no doubt that your future is as blessed as you are." It was a lovely thought if Jack had felt blessed. But at the moment he felt his gift was a burden beyond bearing.

At the Hare and Hound he found the place more resembled a camp after a battle than a quiet country inn.

He knew the coach west was not due in until the next morning and had planned on an overnight stay, mostly in hopes of finding Martha before she claimed a seat on the coach to London. At least that is what Ellen and John had told him she planned to do. He needed to make sure that she had resources and a plan.

The wife of the innkeeper handed him off to one of the maids, which showed him exactly how important his custom was now that he was not connected to an officer in his majesty's service. "Take him to the room at the top of the second stairway. Mr. Morris moved a man out of that room and in with another gent."

Jack trudged up the narrow stairs, watching the provocatively swaying hips in front of him. Not that he was even interested enough to wonder if she was. She showed him the door to the room and was about to open it for him when they both heard Mrs. Morris calling her back to the kitchen.

"Maybe later, sir," the girl said with a wink, and Jack did not even bother to shake his head.

Pushing open the door to the dimly lit room, he was pleased that the hinges did not creak, an element of housekeeping that Martha Stepp had told him was a simple way to judge how well a house was kept.

He had second thoughts about that judgment when he saw what a jumble the bed was, as though someone had slept there and the bedding had not been changed or even smoothed. He was about to turn and leave when he realized who the person on the bed was.

Martha Stepp.

He almost laughed aloud at the sight of her snuggled under a blanket that must have been folded at the bottom of the bed.

Instead he tiptoed across the floor, with only one or two squeaks, and took the chair next to where she was so sound asleep. This bed must be to her liking, he thought. Or more realistically, the woman was probably exhausted. He watched her breathe, studying the way her eyelashes shadowed her cheeks, then noticed the tear tracks down the side of her face. Had she cried herself to sleep?

He could use his gift to ease her pain, but hesitated, sure it would be wrong to influence in any way someone whose feelings mattered so much to him.

There, he thought, *I've at least admitted it to myself. I could have loved Martha Stepp.* Her reaction to his gift of healing was as painful as any injury he had ever took on the field of battle. Her "How do you stand it?" made him realize how much of an outcast he was in the world beyond war.

Still, that punch to his heart had awakened

him to the truth — that this woman meant something to him. That he had wanted to try to explain his gift and beg her to take a chance on making a life with him even if he was one of nature's oddities. As he watched her sleeping he wondered if he was being given a second chance.

Martha opened her eyes.

"Jack Tresbere," she said in a wondering tone that said she was still half asleep. "Am I dreaming?"

"No, you are testing my bed," he said, smiling as he reached out to smooth her hair. He stayed his hand, deciding that touching her while she was in bed was much too intimate a gesture.

"It's very comfortable," she said. "But it is my bed. I paid for it and have it until the coach leaves tomorrow. You will have to find another bed, sir."

"Do you really think there is another room to be had with the London coach so delayed?" He leaned back in the chair, and waking ever more, Martha pulled the blanket up to her chin.

"I will go sleep in the common room, Martha, but first I want to tell you how sorry I am for the way my wish was fulfilled."

"But you told both the major and me that

you had no need of wishes. That whatever you want you ask for directly."

"That's true. It's what I believed then." Jack felt for his pipe but did not take it out. "However," he said, and paused before continuing. "I did think that *if,*" and he gave the word sharp emphasis, "*if* I was going to make a wish, I would hope to find a woman, a very specific woman, in my bed."

"And you did," Martha said with understanding. "Why do people refuse to heed me when I tell them that the coin has its own way of making a wish come true?"

"I am convinced now, and at great cost to you, for which I cannot apologize enough." He leaned a bit closer. "I want to be sure that you are provided for and will have resources until you find a new position."

Her smile disappeared and he knew he had said the wrong thing. Again.

The silence stretched and she looked away even as she spoke. "Thank you. I have enough money and friends in London who will help me."

"Good," he said, though convinced that somehow he was in her ill graces again. He had made so many mistakes with this woman. Clearly the direct approach did not work with her. He was beginning to wonder if that only worked with men. So he decided to try a different way.

"Tell me, Martha Stepp, what sort of adventure are you looking for next?"

Now Martha struggled to sit up in bed, to sit with her back against the headboard so that she looked like the queen receiving guests in her bedchamber as he had been told some royalty did.

"I only want another position so that I am not destined for the workhouse."

"Your adventuring days are over?"

"I think passing the coin on to the major marks a change. It's time for me to accept that my life is not destined to be one of adventure but rather one of refined service."

Jack laughed and then bit his lip. "I am sorry to laugh, Martha, but the idea of you not seeking adventure wherever you land is quite beyond my imagination."

Why did he always laugh at her? It was a cross between annoying and endearing. Even though she was intrigued by the thought that he had "imagined" her adventures, she pushed the vain thought aside and asked a question of her own. "Why have you been avoiding me since Edward's accident?"

Nothing for it but the truth, he decided. "Because I wanted you more than the sun, the moon, and the stars, and knew that after you learned of my healing skill you would want nothing to do with me."

"Why would you think that?"

"Because you told the major you would run as far and as fast as you could from any other of nature's oddities, and then when you saw me heal Edward you asked me how I could stand it. I did not take that as a ringing endorsement of my healing talent."

Oh dear, she had said that; she recalled it as well as he did. But how to explain the first had been the statement of a woman with no imagination and the second was grounded in awe and not revulsion? "You wanted me more than the stars and you let that rash statement stop you?"

With a move so unexpected it took her breath away, Jack threw back the blanket and scooped her from the bed, standing her on her feet directly in front of him.

"Martha, I doubt I will ever understand you but I know I will never stop loving you."

He did not wait for any protestation from her before he touched his lips to hers. It was her first glimpse of heaven, if heaven welcomed such human pleasures. Their bodies blended together as though it was exactly what God intended. Martha wound her arms around Jack's neck and did her best to convince him that his touch was the answer to her fondest wish.

When they drew apart, she did not step away but rested her head on his chest, and slid her hand down to rest there as well. After a moment, she leaned back and looked into his eyes. "Jack, let there be no doubt that your healing ability is a gift straight from heaven, not an oddity at all."

She welcomed his kiss again. After a long moment, Jack stepped back, breaking contact. He took her hands and they stood apart but thus connected.

"Martha, let me go request the private parlor so we can have a meal and talk."

"If that is what you want." It sounded so prosaic.

With a glance at the bed he nodded. "I know exactly what I want but we both need time to think it through in a place where we are not so sorely tempted."

Martha's blush convinced him she knew exactly what he meant. "Yes, I see. I would not be at all happy if my next adventure" — she paused and corrected herself — "*our* next adventure, started out in the wrong bed."

He laughed and grabbed his bag as they went through the door together.

Martha followed Jack Tresbere down the

stairs. There was no private parlor available; no magic could make that happen with the inn so crowded. They found a space in the corner of the common room, ate whatever was served, and talked most of the night. First she explained his misunderstanding of her comment after Edward's healing. From then on they seemed to understand each other perfectly, speaking as they were with hearts overflowing with love.

As the evening progressed, Martha Stepp was more and more convinced she had found the man she would spend her life with. The turning point was when she voiced her biggest concern. "I love you, Jack, but I do not know you as well as I would like."

"I understand." Jack nodded. "But if we continue to talk this much we will know each other better tomorrow than we do today and even better the day after." He was silent a moment. "But *I* worry that you are so bent on finding perfection. In the beds you test and the chairs. You have to know that I am not perfect and can never be."

Martha stood up and moved to sit beside him rather than across from him. She took his hand. "Jack, I was never looking for perfection, not in beds, chairs, or people."

Jack nodded, which she took as encouragement. "I was only ever hoping to find what was just right for me." Martha leaned close and dared a quick kiss on his cheek. "And that is exactly what you are."

"Just right for you," he whispered, his lips against her mouth.

Someone cleared his throat and whether it was aimed at them or not, Jack and Martha drew away from each other a little.

They talked about his gift of healing and soon Martha was sure Jack understood that she was ready and more than willing to embrace his gift as part of their life together.

He broached his idea of traveling to the Canadas and seeing what that world had to offer them.

Martha's eyes grew wide with interest and she bit her lip to keep from grinning.

Jack nodded as though that was all the answer he needed. They sat together in silence awhile, watching the fire. Eventually Jack spoke again. "Martha, I wonder if you can ever truly know someone you love until you have been married near forever." It was Martha's turn for an encouraging nod.

"Loving someone and coming to know them better," Jack went on, "I think that will be an adventure all its own."

"Oh, yes," Martha said as if Jack had just given her a great gift, which, in a way he had. At that moment she realized fully that loving and learning about the other was the heart and soul of what their marriage would be.

The innkeeper kept the fire fueled all night, the common room filled as it was by delayed travelers. It was close to dawn though not yet light when Martha fell asleep against Jack's chest, his arm holding her close. He rested his cheek on the top of her head and fell asleep with the smell of oranges and soap in the air. Jack Tresbere hoped it would be the last scent he knew every night of his life.

■ ■ ■ ■

Beauty, Sleeping

ELAINE FOX

■ ■ ■ ■

For Tom and Ruth, a true love story.
And for my wonderful mother.

Prologue

"Who is that man, Daddy?" Cassandra pointed her five-year-old finger toward the screen, the corner of her blanket scrunched in her palm.

"That's the man who disappeared, honey."

She studied him. He looked like the hero in her favorite book, *The Night Prince,* the one her father read to her when she awoke scared from one of her many terrible dreams. The Night Prince understood as no one else did what frightened her.

Some nights, however, reading Cassandra the book wasn't enough, and her father, face creased with worry, would lift her from her bed, carry her downstairs, and let her fall asleep on his lap while he watched an old broadcast of *The Odd Couple* or *M*A*S*H.* Sometimes he'd even watch *Bewitched,* which was her favorite. The songs the shows started with and the canned laughter soothed her, making her feel like the world was safe again, even if only temporarily.

But this night she'd had a particularly menacing dream. A monster had stolen someone she dearly loved and wouldn't give him back. So her father brought her downstairs with him while he watched the eleven o'clock news. Normally she fell right back to sleep in his arms, but this time — maybe because there was no music or canned laughter — the monster in her dream had followed her into the waking world, and she kept her eyes peeled for peril in the shadows, alert to every movement in the corners of her eyes.

Just when she was certain the dream ogre had morphed into the slithering shadow behind her, the one creeping so silently only she could tell it was there, a man's face appeared on the television screen.

He had a smile that knew her, and eyes that gazed with confidence into hers. He was the Night Prince, and for a moment she felt impossibly happy to see him.

Then fear grabbed her as she remembered that the people on TV were saying the Night Prince had disappeared.

"Is he coming back, Daddy?" She looked up at the side of his face.

"Who, honey?"

"That man. The man who disappeared."

She looked back at the screen. A woman was on, talking without moving anything but her lips.

"I don't know. I hope so." Her father squeezed her tight.

They showed the prince's smiling face again and, despite her fears, she calmed. Cassandra smiled back and felt his presence banish the evil. Fear leapt away, as if scalded by boiling water, and the ogre was sent hissing into obscurity.

Suddenly she knew where he was. He hadn't disappeared, he'd gone into the dream world and chased off her ogre.

She turned her head, looking bravely around the room with both eyes. It was bright from her father's reading lamp. Friendly. The living room of the daytime, when coloring books and chocolate milk held sway.

She put her thumb back into her mouth as the screen changed to a picture of a house, the most beautiful house she'd ever seen. Tall and white with a round turret on one side and black iron railings by the stairs and at the windows.

She pointed again at the TV. "What's that place?"

"That's where he lived."

She smiled. It was perfect, the perfect

castle for her prince to live in. "He'll come back, Daddy. He'll go home, to that place." She gazed with great certainty at the house on the TV. "I'm going to live with him there when I grow up."

"Really, honey? He'll be an old man by then."

"No he won't. He'll wait for me. That's what princes do."

Her father laughed, and all was right with the world.

She never had nightmares again.

Chapter One

Fairies are a petty bunch. I know, because I've had the misfortune to associate with a number of them. My only friend — and I use the term loosely — is a fairy named Astrid, which she tells me means "godlike beauty and strength."

I call her Asta, which I tell her means "annoying little dog from *The Thin Man* movies."

She calls me Michael, because that's my name. Or it was. Michael Prince. If she's pissed at me she calls me Mike. If she wants me to be pissed at her, Mickey.

We have that kind of relationship.

Pissing off women is — *was* — something I was good at. Most of the time it was unintentional, but often enough I knew what I was doing. Now, though, since I'm down to just the one friend, I've rethought things and most of the time I try not to make Asta mad.

See, I'm a ghost. Or something. People can't see me, and time comes and goes. But I'm not *dead.* I'm just not *here.*

Yeah, yeah, I hear you laughing. Fairies? Ghosts? This guy is batshit crazy.

Maybe. I'm heading in that direction anyway. Regardless, here I am in all my spectral glory. So argue with that.

The weird part is that I didn't die. At least not in the conventional sense. I was turned into a ghost — *poof!* — by a malicious fairy. You see where I'm coming from here. Fairies — not what they're cracked up to be.

You hear a lot about "fairy tales" referring to some idyllic scenario that people *wish* would come true. But I'm here to tell you, you don't want to go anywhere *near* a fairy tale, let alone a fairy.

Here's what happened. I was a basically good guy — and by "basically" I mean that my intentions were never to hurt anyone — just taking care of myself, which every self-help book in the world will tell you to do. I was nice to waitstaff and homeless people, never kicked a dog in my life, occasionally made people laugh, and got on with the business of living without asking a lot from other people.

And I was single, so I dated. Sure, I was looking for that *one special woman* who would, I don't know, complete me, have me walking on buttercups, talking to daisies, singing in the rain, that sort of thing. But I also enjoyed the not-so-special dates I had in the meantime.

Until I met a woman who turned out to be my undoing.

You see, *unbeknownst to me* — I'd like to stress that, Your Honor, because in my defense this story began when I was an infant and had zero control over things — I'd been cursed by an angry fairy to meet up with a poisoned spindle and die.

My mother had this aunt — Aunt Malva, for whom the phrase "crazy old bat" was invented. Case in point, she called herself a fairy and warned people not to piss her off. In any case, nobody could stand Malva because she had a tendency to wreck every event she was invited to by getting mad at somebody or other and causing a scene. So when my parents had a christening party for me, they decided not to invite her. She was about two hundred years old by then, or okay, maybe ninety, so they didn't think she'd care even if she managed to hear about it somehow.

Well, turns out she *did* hear about it and threw one helluva fit. Cursed me in my cradle. Can you imagine? A little baby?

Nobody took her seriously except my other great-aunt, Amelia, who then claimed to have altered the curse so that I wouldn't die from the spindle, I'd just go into a kind of waking sleep.

I heard about all of this later, when I was a teenager. I think we were at Malva's funeral when Amelia decided to warn me that I was cursed to die, or sleep, or something, from being pricked by a poisoned spindle.

The problem with this warning was threefold. A) I didn't know what the hell a spindle was, let alone a poisoned one. B) It was way too ridiculous to take seriously — though it did prove useful in high school to convince cheerleaders that I was a Tragic Figure who they might want to, ah, console in some way. And C) It wouldn't have mattered if I had known what a spindle was and took the curse seriously, because all of this was *metaphor.*

Fucking semantics.

So there I was, your average basically good guy, who happened not to be able to communicate very well and didn't feel the need to fix that not-inconvenient condition, when I met up with Deirdra.

Asta tells me *Deirdra* means "anger," so I should have known. I told her *Deirdra* means "black-thong-under-white-pants" and *she* should have known.

But anyway.

Deirdra and I went on a few dates and she, like so many others, tried to crack my head open like a pecan to see what was inside. She asked lots of questions like, "What are you thinking?" or "What do you like best about me?" or "Why don't you talk to your parents anymore?" Stuff I either A) didn't know; B) didn't care to know; or C) didn't want to think about.

Is that so wrong?

YES.

Ah, okay, here is Asta now, flickering like the mini aurora borealis she is.

Tell them what you did.

I'm sure they already know.

Tell them anyway.

Okay. I slept with Deirdra. Of course I did. I'm a guy. We'd gone on two, maybe three dates and the opportunity arose, so. Show me one other man who wouldn't have done the same thing.

Tell. Them. What. You did.

It's more what *she* did, but all right. One day she stops by — the dreaded "drop by." I don't know why women persist in doing this when it almost never yields a good result — and she finds me with another woman. Now, we'd never said we were exclusive —

Did you ever say anything? Anything at all?

We had perfectly nice conversations. That's not the point. I was not caught in flagrante or anything. The other woman and I were simply having dinner on my patio. And Deirdra flew into a rage.

I don't mean she just got mad and started yelling. I mean she literally took flight around the patio, spitting sparks and dropping microburst tornados like hand grenades until the patio table overturned and hot coals burst into flame and my date ran screaming for her car. (Her shoes are still in the bushes by the patio fence, blown there by fairy fury. Go ahead, check.)

Turns out her name was — *is*? I'm still not sure she was real — Deirdra Spindle. A poisoned *Spindle,* get it? I don't know about you, but I don't think that kind of wordplay should be allowed in curses.

But I don't make the rules.

Or follow them.

You know, a lot of people would consider that a good thing. Very American. Thinking outside the box.

Which is all you can do outside the box these days. Considering you're trapped in this house. [snickering] You can't even retrieve that woman's shoes from the bushes! [fairy laughter, making plaster dust rain from the ceiling]

Fairies, you might be noticing, are not like angels. They don't have to do good, or be nice, or help you see God, or even be on your side; nothing like that. They just do what they feel like, and most of the time they feel like messing with human beings. It amuses them.

Hey, I'm trying to help.

Don't roll your eyes.

How are you helping?

I've sold your house.

[stunned silence]

Pay attention now, because this is important. People are coming, and one of them could change your life.

I don't have a life. I'm dead. Or something.

Already with the arguing.

Okay, okay, sorry. What's important? How can these people change my life? Nobody can see or hear me, right? Wait. Are you going to let them see me? *Hear me?* Can they change me from being a ghost?

Tell me what to do, Asta. I'll do anything. Just tell me how not to blow this.

[more fairy laughter]

■ ■ ■ ■

"That can't be good," the guy says.

The woman looks up as plaster dust floats down onto the skin of her arms. She brushes at it, her brows knit.

Suddenly I'm in my dining room, looking at the most riveting woman I've ever seen.

Jesus, that sounds asinine. But it's true. It's not that she's beautiful, though she's pretty, but we're not talking magazine covers and movie stardom here. No, she's more complex than that. She's . . . a Shakespearian sonnet. An elegantly constructed math equation. She arrests the eye, then captivates the mind.

I am a lot of things, but I do not exaggerate. Especially not about women.

"And you're going to have to kill those rosebushes. Holy crap, they've shredded my shirt just coming in the front door. It's a wonder we could even get in the house." The guy fingers some minuscule snag in his pink — that's right, *pink* — polo shirt. (The pony emblem is lavender.) I hope he's not the one important to me.

He has dark hair that I'm sure he dyes. Nobody has hair all the same color, and besides, his face is older than that coif. He's wearing pressed, factory-faded jeans, a Rolex watch, and worst of all, Italian leather shoes with no socks.

You used to wear shoes with no socks.

They were boat shoes, Asta. They'd have looked stupid with socks.

"I like the rosebushes. They just need to be trimmed back a bit." The woman turns toward him, her eyes speculative.

You're going to think this is a line — and God knows I've used lines like it — but the moment I hear her voice I know. *She's the important one.*

I don't know how to tell you what it is, but there's something about her. Something . . . significant.

"Cass, we could barely open the door. You're going to have to do something — the damn roses have taken over the house. It's like a frickin' flower fortress."

She laughs. "A flower fortress! I love it."

It's a sexy laugh, low with just that little bit of huskiness to it that makes you think about mornings in bed.

Unbelievable.

It's a description, Asta, not a pickup line. Besides, she can't hear me, remember?

She's pretty in an utterly unpretentious way, with long brown hair in a thick braid and dark, watchful eyes. She has on a tank top under overalls — do women really wear overalls these days? How long have I been gone? — and an over-sized cardigan.

I'm certain I've never met her before. How could I? I've been trapped here for years. But I feel like I recognize her. Like *my soul* recognizes her.

And I get that sounds hokey as hell, but that's the best I can do.

I move close to her and examine her face, her soft cheeks, her thick eyelashes, the unruly curl escaping her braid. She can't be more than twenty-eight, thirty if she's got great genes. But I know her, I swear I do. It's not just that I want to.

She also gazes at my house as if she approves of it, and that makes me warm with pleasure.

The guy looks up sharply. "Did the lights just get brighter? I hope you had the electrical system checked because that could be a huge expense. And messy. Maybe you shouldn't move in right away."

"Of course I had it checked. It's old, but fine." She runs a hand over the burnished chair rail in the dining room. Her fingers leave three trails in the dust.

The place had looked better, once upon a time.

"Salt on the roots will do it." He fiddles

with the dimmer switch, pulls his hand back, frowns at his fingers, and wipes them on the fake-faded jeans. "Then I can get someone to bring in a backhoe and pull them out by the roots so they never come back. You'll get more light in here, too, and with fall coming that'll be important. Those things have damn near taken over the house. Who knew rosebushes could grow so thick, or so high?"

"Stephen, I love the way they look. They must be fifty years old, at least. How could you kill something that old?"

She's close, they're seventy-five. My mother planted them when she was a girl.

Stephen sighs, and frowns at her, his mind obviously working for a way to convince her he's right. "Just because something's old doesn't mean it's good. They've probably grown into the mortar and ruined the brick. I'm surprised your inspector didn't catch that either. I'm telling you, Cass, the place is a money pit, just like your mother said. I don't know why you bought it."

"You know why I bought it." She scrubs away the film on one of the windows and bends her head to look out the clear spot, down the side of the house. "I love it. And you will, too, once I'm finished with it."

"I know you think that." He rubs a hand

across his forehead.

She glances at him over her shoulder. Her face wears that look of pity women get when they know they've got a guy in their back pocket. "I'll trim them away from the doors and windows. It'll look pretty. And imagine how it'll *smell* when they're all in bloom."

"Like my grandmother's closet. That rose-water she used to wear gave me an instant headache." He drills a finger into his temple.

She looks away, lets a breath out very slowly.

It's clear to me that Stephen not only doesn't understand her, he doesn't deserve her. I hope to God they're not married or anything close to that.

She turns back toward the room. "You know what I'm going to get? One of those big farmhouse tables from that place out in Sperryville. You know the ones? Made from old barn wood?"

"Oh no. Not for in here. This room's way too formal for that. I'll get you the name of my decorator." He puts his hands on his hips and looks up at the ceiling. "You've got cracks in your plaster."

You, your. Good. The place must be hers, not theirs. Or worse, his.

She strolls up behind him and puts a hand on each shoulder as if to calm him. "Stop worrying. I'll take care of it all. I've got weeks before the move, and I've got money now, remember?"

She can't see his face, but he looks pained. "Yeah, I remember. You won the lottery and don't need me anymore."

She gasps. "Stephen. Stop that. You know that's not the reason we broke up. And if you say it again I'm going to —"

She stops herself, shakes her head, pressing her lips together.

He knows he's screwed up, though I'm pretty sure he didn't say anything he didn't mean, and turns around all abashed and says, "I'm sorry. But you used to let me buy you things. Now . . ." He shrugs.

I get it. I don't particularly like the guy, but I understand him. He doesn't know what to do for her. And he's desperate to do *something* for her.

She looks at him a long minute, then pushes her hands into her pockets and heads toward the kitchen. "Come look at the kitchen. You'll like this."

He watches her go, two deep lines forming between his brows. The guy's at sea. He wants her, but doesn't know how to woo her now that she doesn't need him. All he has is himself.

■ ■ ■ ■

My mother died when I was seventeen. She'd been sick, but not for long. Near the end, she talked about a lot of things, one of which was old Aunt Malva's curse. She said to be kind to Amelia because she saved me, but to beware of spindles nonetheless.

(*No,* I didn't ask what a spindle was even then. I'm a guy, what can I say? I didn't ask a lot of questions.)

But all of this was around the time she was getting delirious with the pain meds, so again, I didn't take it seriously. They were her aunts, Malva and Amelia, so I figured recounting this story was just part of her reliving old family stuff. Because at the same time she talked a lot about where she'd grown up, how much she'd loved the place, how happy the family had been.

The house was a big, old, end unit row house in Georgetown, up the hill from the river, far from the freak show that was M Street. The place backed onto a cemetery, which might have been creepy but was peaceful instead. When it came up for sale I didn't think twice. Offered full price and got it.

I'd owned the place for three or four years

when I "died." They thought I'd been murdered, since they never found a body, but they never found evidence of a crime either. So then they thought I'd killed myself. My dad had to wait seven years before the courts would legally consider me dead. That was the hardest, watching Dad waiting for me to return, even though he knew I'd never just disappear on him like that. Not if I was still alive.

Watching Dad weather the media storm was no fun either. I'd been a small-time celebrity, a local TV newsperson who people would recognize on the streets and in grocery stores. An up-and-comer at the network, though not yet nationally known, so they were able to use me for one last big ratings surge, examining my disappearance from every angle, interviewing everyone from my seventh-grade teacher to my dog trainer, then acknowledging every anniversary of my mysterious disappearance until I was proclaimed deceased.

Now they've forgotten all about me. It's been about twenty years, I'd guess, but since I can't leave the house and nobody's lived here since I did, I have little way of knowing what's gone on in all that time.

Dad used to come by and visit the place every now and then. He'd talk to me, in a way. The conversations seemed to be more developed in his mind but what came out of his mouth as he shuffled through the house were fragments like, "Just like I told you." And, "You remember her." And, "I don't know what you were thinking, there."

What I wouldn't have given to be able to answer him. Or even to just say, "What the heck are you talking about, Dad?"

He'd have been startled if he'd heard me, and not just because I was supposed to be dead. I never used to talk to him, barely listened, and never asked him questions, not even stupid ones like, "What the heck are you talking about, Dad?"

Nope, he'd be the one to ask me questions, because I was the interesting one. I thought I knew everything about the old man, thought his life was boring, thought his prying into mine was just a way of looking for stuff to disapprove of. Never occurred to me that he might be interested in what I was doing.

Not 'til he started saying things like, "I bet you'd have been national by now." And, "You'd have been thirty-nine today, son." And, nodding at some stray creative thought, "I think you'd have liked that," in a tone more questioning than certain.

I wished I could have hugged him, and

told him how much I loved him. A thousand times I wished it. He'd have dropped over in shock if he'd known, but it was true. Instead, all I could do was wander along behind him like a penitent dog: unseen, unheard, unknown.

It's funny, I was always a pretty reticent guy. Didn't like to open up or talk about myself. Never asked people questions and certainly never answered any if I could help it. In a way, I think that's what the women liked. At least at first.

But now . . . now that nobody can see or hear me, I'm desperate for it. Desperate to be heard, to be able to ask other people about themselves and tell them how interested I am in the answers. Hell, I'd tell anybody anything, if only they'd let me, but I've missed my chance.

Anyway, I'm glad Dad sold the house. It was time. Getting rid of the personal effects was hardest, I think. For both of us. All that baseball stuff I'd collected, a lot of it from when I was a kid, from Dad, like the cards, an old mitt, a baseball signed by Willie Mays. A lot of it from the years I was a local celeb, Orioles paraphernalia mostly, but some from visiting teams. A Ken Griffey, Jr., jersey. Autographs from Mark McGwire and Barry Bonds when they were rookies.

Once the furniture was gone, the place empty, it didn't feel like me anymore. Dad came a couple more times, then stopped altogether. One of the last times he came, though, he went through every single room, from the basement to the attic. When he got to the little room under the eaves in the attic, I saw his eyes well up as he placed his fingertips on an old TWA sticker on the aged wall. It looked like it was from the forties — a smiling stewardess in a light blue uniform — and I knew that my mother must have put it there as a girl because Dad sighed and said, "Rosemund," as he touched it.

How he would have known that, I'm not sure, but I believed him.

After that the house sat empty for years until Asta somehow arranged to have my father sell the place to this girl. This Cassandra. Cassandra Carlisle, I know from the mail that's started to drop onto the floor in the front hall from the mail slot. I don't know what happened to Dad and I don't ask.

No, I don't ask those questions, even of the one being in all the universe who can hear me. But now it's not because I'm not interested; it's because I don't think I could bear the answers.

Chapter Two

"And the plaster, Cassandra, just look at the cracks!" Her mother's voice echoed down the hallway as her sensible heels fell like hammer strikes on the hardwood flooring.

Tuning her mother out, Cassandra turned her gaze to the ceiling, to the crown molding and decorative plaster medallion anchoring the overhead light. The details in the house charmed her over and over again.

Cracks in the plaster be damned. They were hairline and easily fixable, according to the inspector.

"See?" Stephen echoed, entering the room from the front hall. "I'm not the only one who noticed."

Cassandra sighed, and wished again that he hadn't come today. Her sister was coming later — one of the only people on earth who could satisfy her mother — and while that might balance the scales, she still didn't need Stephen validating every fault her mother found.

"She agrees with me about the bathroom, too," he continued, a bit too jovially. "Take out that old tub and put in a Jacuzzi. It'll increase the value of the house. Speaking of which, I should check out that upstairs bathroom, make sure the plumber caught that leak."

Cassandra moved to the window, hooking her fingertips over the rail between the upper and lower sashes, and searched for the moving van. She wouldn't relax until she knew the truck could make it down the narrow street. They'd assured her it could, but she had her doubts. Revery Street was narrow, with parking on both sides. If one car parked a little too far from the curb . . .

Her mother's footfalls sounded in the hallway, this time coming toward her.

"I thought you were getting a new stove in that kitchen," she said, even before entering the front parlor where Cassandra awaited the moving van. "You're going to have a hard time with that old thing that's in there now."

"It's a Chambers C-90, Mother. Rachael Ray has one just like it. Turns out it's worth thousands!" She took a deep breath, turned and gave her mother a bright smile. "Isn't that cool?"

As unlikely as it was that her mother would find anything "cool," this gave her pause. She would deny it to her dying day, but her mother had a fondness for celebrities.

Elegantly dressed, as usual, in Chanel, with her soft white hair cut to her shoulders and smoothly turning under, she looked like Catherine Deneuve, only not quite as old. Except for the two frown lines permanently etched in the space between her brows.

"Cassandra," she said, lowering her voice and joining her daughter at the window. "I hope Stephen's presence here means you've decided to give him another chance."

Cassandra let her eyes trail back down the street. She could not stop the sigh that passed her lips. "I know you're disappointed we broke up, Mother, and that he's a favorite of yours —"

"Because he loves you to bits and you just tossed him away. I honestly don't know what else you think you can ask for in a man. It's not about *my* disappointment, it's about yours."

"Mine?" She laughed lightly and met her mother's gaze. "I'm happy, not disappointed. Stephen and I do much better as friends."

"A husband who is your friend is the very best thing you can find," she insisted. "I know you're twenty-nine, but if you weren't so naïve you would understand that. And you know Stephen is a good man. He's also successful *and* he loved you *before* you won the lottery. You may never know what the next guy loves you for, you or your money."

Anxiety stabbed Cassandra in the gut and her eyes jerked back to the street. "Is that what you think, Mother? That nobody else could ever love me except for my money?"

It was *exactly* her fear. Not just because of her sudden wealth, though that added an extra level of paranoia. But also because she'd *never* felt loved for herself — maybe because she'd never figured out who "herself" was. All her adult life she'd had boyfriends she'd strived to please, and she *had* pleased them. She was the ultimate chameleon. But every time she would end up displeased. Every relationship she'd had, she had ended because she didn't feel seen, or understood, or loved for the right reasons.

And that was on her. She knew it. Because she'd always been somebody else in a relationship, whoever the guy wanted.

"Of course not." Her mother waved the accusation off with a hand. "*I* don't think that, but I worry that *you'll* never believe otherwise. And you're too young to realize what a rare find Stephen is."

Steeling herself, Cassandra raised her chin. She wasn't quite up to looking her mother in the eye, not today, but she said in a firm voice, "Look, I'm just not ready. And Stephen is not the one. Is it so bad that I want to be alone for a while?"

She felt her mother's gaze on the side of her face for a long moment, before she said in an ominous tone, "Be careful what you wish for."

Cassandra winced.

"Besides, you love Stephen, don't you?" Her mother asked in a way that said she knew the answer already. "I've heard you say it to him a dozen times over the last two years."

Cassandra looked down at her fingers on the edge of the window, *her* window, in *her* house. "Of course I do. He's a wonderful person."

"Then I don't know what you're waiting for." Her mother turned and threw her hands gracefully out to her sides, looking at her with brows raised. "Some kind of cosmic message?"

Cassandra shoved her hands into the pockets of her overalls and turned, too, with a short laugh. "That would be good."

Her mother smiled smugly. "Then look at this house. If anything is a cosmic message, it's *this* place. You need help with it. You need a partner, a *husband.*"

Cassandra looked around the front room and an ethereal calm overtook her again, the same way it had the very first time she'd walked into the place.

She shook her head, breathing deep. "No," she said. "No, I don't need any help here. If anything, this place will take care of me."

She had wanted this place since the first time she'd seen it, all those years ago on television when that poor man had disappeared. The story had been heartbreaking, but the moment she'd seen the house she'd known it belonged to her in some predestined way.

Of course it had been impossible to do anything more than dream of it until two years ago, when she'd won the lottery. What a weird, wild whirlwind that had been. Thank God it was calming down now. Somebody in Rockville had recently won the Powerball lottery — nearly ten times the money she'd won — so she was old news. Thank all the powers that be.

But if her mother wanted to talk about cosmic messages, Cassandra could bring up how this place suddenly came on the market right when she — miraculously and unexpectedly — had the money to buy it. After being empty for twenty-four years!

"Listen, I know you think I'm browbeating you," her mother said in her reasonable voice. "I'm just worried you're going to lose Stephen completely and not know how much you wanted him until he's gone."

A gust of cold air washed through the room. Cassandra looked up, but her mother didn't seem to notice.

Stephen's footsteps sounded on the stairs, and a moment later he walked into the front room with a bunch of greasy old pipes in his hands. "It looks like they found the leak all right."

Cassandra beelined across the room toward him. "What's all that? What did you do? Did you take something out?"

"Sweetheart!" her mother objected.

Stephen looked up, startled at her tone. "No. These are the old parts they left. See, here's the split pipe."

Cassandra exhaled, laid her hands on his forearm. "I'm sorry. Thank you for checking on that."

He shook his head mournfully at the broken pipe. "Bet it froze; there's probably no insulation in these walls. It may only be

September now, but the weather will be turning before you know it."

"You see, there was no need to jump down his throat about it," her mother chided. "Aren't you glad you have Stephen here to help you with that?"

Cassandra blushed. "I'm sorry. I'm just on edge. I don't know how in the world they're going to get that moving truck down this street."

Stephen patted her hands, then glanced at her mother and they shared a look. "It'll be all right. I'll make sure of it. Now let me call these plumbers for you and ask them why the pipe split. If it did freeze we'd better get someone to check the insulation."

Stephen pulled his cell phone from his pocket, placed all but the one pipe on the mantel, and went out to the front stoop to make the call. Her mother raised a smug brow at her, said something about inspecting the bathroom, and left.

Exhaling, Cassandra turned back to the room, biting her bottom lip. She sat in the window seat and gazed across the hardwood floors, trying to imagine her tattered, mismatched but well-loved furniture in the empty space. Her mother had probably been right about that; she should have bought new instead of moving the old stuff.

She just didn't want to get here, to this spectacular new place, and not feel like there was anything left of her old self.

Something shimmered by the fireplace and she jerked her head to look directly at it, fearing something had caught fire. But whatever it had been was gone. Must have been something in her eye, a floater. But it did draw her attention to the hearth, and the pretty purple tiles that lined either side of the opening. They were the first thing she'd noticed on entering the house; she'd immediately pictured how they'd gleam and glow when a fire burned in the grate.

The mantelpiece was also one of her favorite details in the house: carved, painted wood, with delicate rosettes on each corner. As she studied them, she noticed that one looked askew.

She rose from her seat, approached the fireplace, and touched the flower, pushing it back into place. It slid easily, revealing vague scratch marks where it had drifted off to the side. She gazed at it a minute, then pushed the rosette aside again. It moved as if on a pin, slipping up and to the right. She pushed it farther and found a dark hollow beneath the ornament. A secret hiding place!

Heart thrumming, she bent forward, looking close. There was dust but no spiders that she could see. She poked two fingers inside — about all that would fit — and could tell something was there. Gently, she pulled what felt like a thick piece of paper from the space.

It wasn't a note, or even a full sheet of paper. It was something with shape that had been rolled. As carefully as she could, she unrolled the piece, placed it flat on the top of the mantel, and gasped.

Something shifted deep inside of her, recognition and memory coming together like two well-oiled pieces of machinery. It was *The Night Prince.* Somebody had painstakingly cut a picture of the prince from the storybook — her *favorite* picture, with the prince in his dress uniform, his blue eyes calm and smiling, epaulettes rich with gold glitter and his sword topped with a deep red tassel, one strong hand resting on the hilt — then rolled it up and put it into this hiding place.

It was like running into a long-lost friend on the street, one you thought had died or disappeared. Suddenly Cassandra was transported back to the most magical time of her childhood.

Smiling, she pressed its yellowed edges flat with her fingers. For some reason, tears stung the back of her eyes. The prince gazed up at her with his calm, confident expression, looking as if he were as happy and relieved to see her as she was him.

"Hello," she said softly.

A mass of cold air blew by her side and she jumped. The picture snapped back into a roll and bounced off the mantel.

Cassandra's eyes scanned the room. It hadn't really been a breeze, not this time. It was more like something cold had pressed up against her. And when she'd jumped it had leapt away.

Great, she thought. *The place is haunted.*

Then she sighed, smiling, and picked up the rolled prince. "Good thing you showed up when you did," she said, feeling stupidly reassured by the prince's presence.

Eyes scanning the empty room, she gently straightened the picture once again and went out onto the front stoop to show Stephen. But he was not as amazed as she was at the prince's sudden appearance.

"Huh," he said, then pointed. "Look, here comes the truck. And just like I said, there's plenty of room. I better go tell them where to stop."

As Cassandra turned away she noticed that inside the house the lights brightened, a long glowing surge, then went back to normal.

CHAPTER THREE

She felt me. She nearly *saw* me. I know she did. I was standing by the fireplace and her eyes nearly met mine.

She *is* the one who's important.

It's lucky I'm here today, because terrifyingly I feel as if I drifted away somewhere for a time. When I first saw Cassandra she said she had weeks before the move, but now suddenly today's the day and where the hell have I been in the meantime?

Never mind. I'm here now, and she very nearly saw me. There's hope! I can sense it, and the urgency I feel is overwhelming.

It's hard to describe how I move, what I can do, so I'll put it in terms that'll sound right to you and it'll be close enough. Yeah, I do kind of float, but I still act like I walk and have limbs, and all that.

Just in case anyone's watching.

Something like that.

Once on TV, always on TV, right, Mickey?

No, not like that. I mean, yeah, I want to be seen. Jesus, I want to be seen like I've never wanted anything else in my life. But not for fame, Asta. Give me a break, who the hell cares about fame anymore? You have no idea what it's like to be *nonexistent. No* idea. It's hell, Asta. This is *hell.* I can't *do* anything — I can't — *dammit.*

[She's lifting her flipping eyebrow, pompous freaking fairy.]

All right. Proceed.

A raft of curse words bubble in my consciousness but with a Herculean effort I hold them back. It'll do no good to turn her against me. But still. I hate it when she winds me up like that. And if I could do something about it . . .

Anyway, I go up to the attic and start looking around. There's stuff up here from long ago. Maybe some of it was my mother's but there have been several families in the house since she lived there and they've all left behind some detritus. Just little stuff, things nobody felt like moving out of an attic four stories up and one narrow staircase away from a broken neck.

So there's a bassinet, a broken rocker, a large old wooden crate with the words "McNally's Extra Aged, McNally Ltd., Cheshire, England" burned into the sides. What Mc-

Nally's was and why it was "extra aged" is a mystery, but the box is cool. And it's filled with long rolls of thick paper, some of which have building plans on them, some hand-drawn maps, some unidentifiable sketches of geographic patterns.

I tear a corner off of one blank page and dig down deep where I know some old grease pencils live. I was a passable artist in my day, often sketching people or scenes when I needed a break at work. It was a form of meditation for me, I guess, and it was also a great way to pick up women. If you could sketch a woman's face on a bar napkin you could pretty much get laid.

I sit down on the floor and start drawing. I haven't looked in a mirror in two decades — well, I have, but I haven't seen anything — but I remember what I look like well enough and the desire to have her see me, even in grease-pencil form, is overwhelming. All of a sudden I sense a path to communication.

So I draw myself in the uniform of that cutout soldier — no, she called him a prince, the Night Prince, when she told Stephen about it — and I have to say it looks not only like me, but like the original drawing. Then, next to me, I draw her.

She's fun to draw, with her big doe eyes

and long braid, her willowy body and those funny overalls. We look silly, disjointed, next to one another, but there we are, and for a long moment I can't look away from my own drawing.

There's something about it, about the two of us together . . . as if I've seen it before, lived it before. I'm mesmerized, spellbound, and struggling to retrieve what feels like a memory that's just out of reach.

Then I have to break away. The feeling borders on painful.

Though I can't cut our figures out like the picture she found, I tear the paper as close to the edges of the figures as I can, then roll us up and place us in the hole behind the rosette.

Will she look there again? I move the rosette off center the way it had been.

This is important. *She* is important. Even though Asta tipped me off, I'm pretty sure I'd have known it anyway. And now it feels imperative that she know I'm here.

I settle down and wait for her to find me.

Asta, where do I go?

What do you mean?

I mean, where do I go, when I'm not here?

You're always here.

No I'm not. The seasons have changed

since I was last here. And that girl, Cassandra, she must have come and looked at the house at some point. She said she had an inspector come. She didn't just buy the place sight unseen. But I've never seen her before. So where was I when she came looking? I thought I couldn't leave the house.

It's complicated.

Try me.

[sighs] Remember that dream you had?

I sleep?

That memory, then. You were remembering your prom. With Jody Williamson? You remembered the whole night, almost as if you were reliving it.

It's creepy that you know that. But go on.

You were reliving it. You were there. It was happening.

The prom was happening.

Right.

You're saying I was at my high school prom when Cassandra Carlisle looked at the house.

Right.

I don't know what to say to that.

It's a space-time continuum thing.

But it already happened. If I was *re*living it, it had to be a memory. So I was immersed in a memory to the point where I didn't notice people coming and going in the house? I was — what? — comatose or something? A ghost in a coma. That's rich.

No, it wasn't that you were sitting here indulging a memory; that's not how it works. Everything is happening all the time, just not always in the same plane. And because you're a ghost you have access to a bunch of different planes.

You're saying I caught a plane to the past. [snort]

Funny.

I thought so.

You know that old adage about living in the moment, because that's all you have? The present moment? Well, it turns out that's true. They're all present moments, and if your present moment is thinking about the future, then that's the present moment that's going to live on for eternity, you thinking about the future. In the present. Doesn't have anything at all to do with any future. Which naturally doesn't exist.

It doesn't? All that planning?

No. There is no future. There's only now. There's only ever now. So you visited a now on another plane.

Another now? So there's no future — and I'm assuming no past — but a whole bunch of nows? Is that why I don't feel like I've gotten any older, even though I've been here for God knows how long?

You haven't gotten any older. You're still thirty, just like the day you died.

I didn't die, Asta, and you know it.

Whatever.

This whole thing's ridiculous.

Not my idea.

So what was the me on this plane doing while I was in the now on the other plane?

Whatever it is you're doing right now. Because that's happening now, Cassandra Carlisle looking at the house, you being at your prom, even as you're here now, talking to me. See?

No, I don't see. None of that makes sense.

Yes it does, you just can't understand it.

You're giving me a headache.

Technically you don't have a head.

Then I'm reliving a headache.

It's no good. As you can see, talking to Asta is like, well, talking to Asta from *The Thin Man* movies. Fairies, like dogs, have a different sense of time and reality. Fairies have a bunch of nows, evidently, and that works for them. Dogs pee on things they like, and that works for them. Asking them to explain these things to non-dogs, or non-fairies, won't make us like them any better.

But see, it's not enough to throw up my

ghostly hands and say, "That's just Asta!" anymore. I can't maintain my near-human perspective and sense of humor in the face of the fact that *I could disappear at any moment.*

What if Cassandra finds the drawing of us and I'm not here? I won't be able to see her reaction. I won't be able to make myself real to her. What if I'm off reliving, I don't know, my driving test at the DMV when she lays eyes on me for the first time? How will that help me?

The panic rising in my incorporeal chest is the most human I've felt since I was phantomized. I have to reach her. I have to make myself known.

I pace the bare wooden floors in the front room even as she directs movers and peers in boxes and steals a bite or two from her fried chicken. I run behind her as she trots upstairs and down, shoves books onto bookcases, unearths sheets and towels from Hefty bags and tosses them on the bed Stephen assembles.

I want *him* to leave. Almost more than I've ever wanted anything else in my life I want him gone. His presence is like a loud piercing noise, scrambling my senses. The sister, Pamela, is all right, though she watches Cassandra and Stephen like a psychologist on the other side of a two-way mirror.

And thank God the mother left before the heavy lifting began. If she'd praised that know-it-all Stephen one more time I was going to hurl a ghostly snowball in her face. She obviously doesn't know it, but every word out of her mouth puts another dent in her daughter's self-esteem.

Finally, *finally,* the movers leave and the bucket of KFC is finished. The beer is drunk and the bed is made and Pamela is yawning.

"I can't thank you both enough for helping me," Cassandra says. "I don't know how I would have done this without you. Truly." She reaches out her hands, one to each of them, and squeezes their forearms. They sit at a dainty kitchen table in the middle of my cavernous dining room, the chandelier overhead dimmed to a candle-flame glow.

"Cass, the place is wonderful. You're going to be so happy here." Pamela lays a hand on hers and smiles sleepily.

Stephen wears a face that could grace the sourest elementary school teacher. "This is a lot of house to handle. There's no way you could have done it yourself, so I was happy to help."

Prick. She could have done it without leaving her seat if she'd wanted to. The movers did the hard stuff. All Stephen did was complain about them scratching the floors and bumping the walls as they hauled items as awkward as pregnant livestock up a nineteenth-century staircase. I'd like to have seen him do it.

"I'll come back tomorrow, if you want," the blowhard continues, "and touch up those places they hit in the hallway with the headboard. They also chipped one of the doorknobs. There's a salvage place on Sixteenth Street; I can check to see if they have another one like it."

He casts beady eyes around the room, probably looking for marks on these walls as examples.

"No, Stephen," Cassandra says firmly. He looks at her. "You've done enough. Now it's up to me to get settled."

"But there's stuff still sitting in the middle of the floor!" He waves a hand, as if the furniture's having an unsanctioned party in the unattended rooms. "You can't move that by yourself. How are you going to settle in if you can't move that stuff?"

Cassandra and Pamela glance at each other — Cassandra annoyed, Pamela concerned.

"If I run into trouble I'll call you, but for now you've done enough." She smiles grimly. "Now go home, both of you, and get some sleep."

Pamela's eyes look momentarily wistful. "Stephen, could you give me a ride home? I took the Metro here but I'm so tired . . ."

Cassandra shoots her a grateful glance as I have an a-ha moment. Pamela, I think . . . she's the answer to getting rid of Stephen once and for all.

Meantime, though, Stephen's cornered into leaving and that makes me happy. No kiss good-night for you, buckaroo.

The chandelier brightens incrementally.

I watch Cassandra clean up. Her expression goes from tense and guarded to soft and sure. And I feel something almost physical. Like a heartbeat, which I haven't felt for a score; or a breath, deep and satisfying. Funny, I'd forgotten all about breathing.

She cleans up after them, taking the dishes into the kitchen and washing them by hand, but it doesn't look like she's going back into the front room. She isn't going to look behind that rosette tonight — why would she? In fact, why would she ever? She's already looked in there. Even if she sees the rosette off center she'll just center it again, won't she?

My calm diminishes and I feel myself once

again nearly vibrating with anxiety. I have to reach her. Somehow I have to let her know I'm here.

"Hey!" I jump up and down, waving my arms, more to release a sudden excess of energy than with any hope that she'll see or hear me. Nothing happens but some plaster dust falls from the ceiling and the lights flicker.

I fully expect Asta to appear by my side with a snarky comment and a sarcastic face, but she stays away, maybe to save us both embarrassment. I begin hopping on one foot and turning in circles.

Cassandra starts to hum.

The song stops me. I know it, from somewhere long ago. There are no words, I don't think, just da-dah . . . da-dah, more of a rhythm. Then Dah-da-da-da daDAH . . . I sing it along with her for a full minute before realizing it's the theme song from that old TV show *Bewitched.*

I lean a hip against the stove and laugh, my arms crossed over my chest, and her head shoots up. She whirls to face me and I straighten, then freeze, stock-still.

"Cassandra." Her name flies off my lips like a wind.

Her eyes seem to be looking right at me. Then she's looking right through me. And then she walks toward me.

I remain motionless. I want to touch her. I'm *desperate* to touch her. If I were alive I'd reach out and cup that dewy soft cheek, I'd move the curled tendril of hair behind her ear, and I'd lower my mouth to hers, to those tender lips . . .

And then she's walking through me. I moan. She gasps. For a long moment I feel as if I've been suffused with sunshine — the feeling you get when you lie on a beach with the sun beating hard into your body, when your insides stretch luxuriously in the heat and you feel like a cat on a windowsill.

I can't believe I'm feeling this. It's heady, enveloping, and *tactile* in a way I haven't felt since I was alive.

She pulls her arms around herself and spins out of my sphere.

"Is somebody there?" she whispers. Her eyes bounce off the walls and appliances like pinballs.

She can't see me.

I swear in frustration and run a hand through my hair.

She jumps again.

"Cassandra!" I say, too loud, but she doesn't react. *"Cassandra,"* I whisper, but the thread seems to have been cut. She looks again around the room, shakes her head as if ridding it of foolishness, and turns for the stairs.

I am suddenly furious. The unfairness, the burden, the *silence* of the last twenty years threaten to split open my illusory head. I yell Asta's name — I even call her Astrid — but nothing happens. Nothing but more silence. More isolation. More loneliness.

I marshal my masculinity and decide to break something. I look around the room, and it's all her stuff. I don't want to break her stuff.

So instead I follow her up the stairs like the starved, abandoned dog that I am.

Chapter Four

Cassandra stretched languidly in her bed, her eyes opening to the new day, and immediately remembered the strange flashes of light she'd seen last month in the kitchen. She'd thought about the experience every day since it had happened, and she walked the rooms and hallways of the house with her eyes wide and the hairs on the back of her neck standing up, waiting for something similar to happen again. But nothing did.

It had first been a mere flash. Then several flashes of shimmering light appeared in the kitchen as she was cleaning up after the move. For a split second she'd thought she'd seen a person leaning against the stove, but that must have been something she'd conjured from the corner of her eye.

Then an even stranger thing had happened. When she'd walked in the direction of the flash, she reached a spot — around where her imaginary intruder had been standing — where she felt as if she'd walked through a bubble of frigidly cold air. It wasn't a draft. Nothing was blowing. It was more of a thick, icy area that chilled her straight through, then released her back into the warmth of the house after a step or two.

She hadn't told anybody about it, but she'd dwelled on it constantly, and every time she turned on the stove, she waved a hand around the area where she'd felt it, or stepped tentatively into it, as if expecting to feel the chill again. Only to feel nothing. Just the same air as everywhere else in the room.

She got up out of bed, pushed her feet into her slippers, and grabbed her robe off the back of the door. She was waiting to get her first heating bill before turning the thermostat up higher, but it was getting harder to get out of bed in the mornings as the October temperatures dropped at night.

She headed for the kitchen, put the kettle on to boil, and sat down at the table with her decorating magazines. They were full of so many gorgeous rooms and color schemes she knew she'd never be able to decide what to do with the place. She'd probably end up with a mishmash of wildly divergent styles that startled people as they moved from one room to the next.

Then again, she told herself for the umpteenth time, it was her house and she could do whatever she wanted to it. Her mother, Stephen, even Pamela, could hang if they didn't like it.

The kettle whistled and she rose to pour boiling water over her tea bag. As the steam billowed in the chilly room, she extended her hand out to that once-icy area again. Nothing.

She took her tea and pushed through the swinging door into the dining room. As she passed her "new" farmhouse table — a gorgeous heavy country table made from old barn wood polished to a high sheen — she ran her fingers along the varnished top and smiled. Of all the things she'd bought to furnish the house, the table was her favorite. Not just because it was beautiful and unique and unusual, but because everyone had told her not to buy it, that it wouldn't work in the room. But here it was, and it was *perfect.* Even Stephen admitted it.

She passed the table to sit in the front room on the sofa and peruse her magazine. But she gazed back into the dining room from her perch and smiled again. She'd have to have a dinner party soon. She wanted to see her table piled with steaming dishes of savory food and surrounded by her closest friends.

She sighed, cupping her hands around her mug, and turned her gaze to the fireplace, magazine open facedown on her lap.

She should get some of those fake logs, she thought, so she could have an easy fire when she got up in the morning. She wanted to see those tiles glowing in the light from the flames. After a second she noticed that the rosette behind which she'd found the Night Prince had moved again.

Setting her tea and magazine on the coffee table, she rose and moved to the mantel. She pushed the rosette back into place, then, on second thought, pushed it far to the right and poked a finger inside again.

Her mouth dropped open and she inhaled sharply as she felt something. Another piece of paper. Had she missed it the first time? Another page from the book perhaps?

As she dragged the paper out she could tell it was of a different weight than the page from the book, but nothing could have prepared her for what she saw when she unfurled it.

The Night Prince, drawn in some kind of crayon, looked out at her once again, but *next* to him was a figure — a woman — and there was no mistaking that it was *her.*

Cassandra yanked her hands back as if the

picture were poisoned, then gripped them together in front of her as the paper rerolled itself. A chill shot up her spine and her heartbeat accelerated in her chest. She raised her head, looking around as if someone might be watching.

The last picture was old, brittle, and dusty. It had obviously been there for years, she would swear it. But this one was new. This one showed her in the same clothes she'd worn on moving day. Standing next to the Night Prince.

She gingerly unrolled the picture again and peered at it. So simple, yet so provocative.

Who on earth could have done this? Pamela? She couldn't draw at all, though she would probably remember Cassandra's obsession with the Night Prince. Stephen? He wasn't this creative, nor would he have reason to draw her with a character she'd once fancied herself in love with.

It crossed her mind that this could be the work of some kind of stalker. But how would a stalker know about the picture? Or *The Night Prince*? No, this had to be from somebody who knew her.

She had told her mother. Would her *mother* do something like this, in some misguided attempt to scare Cassandra into moving? She hadn't been thrilled at Cassandra's choice of houses, but then she was never thrilled with anything Cassandra did and she'd never resorted to this kind of tactic. No, it would be completely uncharacteristic.

Not to mention that drawing her with the Night Prince was more likely to make her *stay* than anything else. It almost felt like a gift from the house. A welcome.

She smiled, and looked around the room. "Are you here?" she asked aloud, as if her prince might magically appear if she just believed in him enough.

Then she blushed at her silliness and re-rolled the picture. She gently inserted it back into the hole and straightened the rosette into place. Taking a step back, she gazed at the mantel. She'd leave it there. A secret between herself, the house, and the Night Prince.

"Winning the lottery is enough luck for any lifetime," she said decisively. "Expecting to find a real prince is asking too much."

After a second she moved the rosette off center again, to remind herself how lucky she was to have found even this Night Prince here, in her new home.

I'm getting worried. I seem to be missing

more and more time. I don't know where I go or what I do, but when I reappear in my house I find it completely furnished and looking thoroughly lived in. If this woman is supposed to be "important" to me, I need to know how, and the only way to find out is to *be* here. So why am I not?

I don't know. And Asta is no help.

But now that I'm here I'm going to do everything I can to stay and try to make contact.

It's the middle of the night and I've got an idea. I've been sitting by the bed, watching her sleep. Watching the way her eyes flicker with some dream, her dark lashes twitching against her skin. I imagine running a finger along those lashes and know they will feel soft as pussy willows.

Her hair is loose on the pillow, and for as long as I've been a phantom my sense of touch was the least missed of sensations until now. I want to feel that glossy thickness in my palms, clutch the silken strands in my fingers, and pull her close. Put my lips on hers, touch her tongue with mine.

And I want to feel her hands on me. Feel her skin on mine. Body to body, flesh to flesh. But most of all I want her eyes, those fathomless dark eyes, to rest upon me, drink me in, *see* me.

I am here! I want to shout. *Feel me here.*

No, I think. Asta was wrong. I don't need to be seen — not on TV and not here. Most of all I want her to *hear* me. Hear my voice. Hear my thoughts. My *questions.* The realization staggers me. It might be the most selfish thing I've ever wished, but I want this girl to know me. And I want to know her.

Which is a helluva big surprise to me, guy voted most likely to dump you for no discernible reason by all of my ex-girlfriends. (I'm not kidding. This actually happened at my memorial service.)

It's not an option anymore, however. I've missed my chance to be heard, understood, loved. All I can do now is watch. And yearn.

I bend over Cassandra, with my insubstantial body, and I draw myself close. With nothing but the most softhearted feeling, I lean in to kiss her, but just before my lips meet hers, her eyes open.

I freeze, stunned, because this time I know with everything I am that she's looking at me, *seeing* me.

"It's you," she says, her voice soft and languid.

Stunned, I say back, "It's me."

The heart I recently remembered hammers in my spectral chest. It's unclear if she heard me, but I *know* she sees me.

Her lips curve and her eyelids drop again. "The man who disappeared."

"It's the strangest thing," Cassandra told Pamela on the phone, as she pushed pieces of cantaloupe around in her bowl with a fork. "I found that picture, and then I dreamed of that guy, the one who used to live here. And it was *so real.*"

"What was the dream?"

"It was simple, really, he just leaned over me, and for a moment I thought he would kiss me. And when I opened my eyes I knew exactly who he was."

"Where were you, in the dream? Was something else going on? Like, were there other people around or were you someplace from your childhood?"

Pamela loved analyzing dreams. And because Cassandra was so close to her she usually did a pretty good job of unraveling her subconscious.

"That was the strangest part, that's what was so real. I was here, in my bed. And it was like he woke me up, his breath on my cheek. I felt as if I knew him, like it was a memory of somebody I've loved forever. But then I opened my eyes from the dream, and I saw him still, and I knew this would be the first kiss he'd ever given me. Unfortunately I really woke up before he could."

She shivered, remembering it. The thing she'd felt most strongly when she opened her eyes was *relief.* As if she'd been waiting for him, and worried, and now she knew he was okay.

She *still* felt that way.

The Night Prince was here waiting for her, just as, on some level, she'd always believed he would be. But she couldn't tell Pamela that, could she? Her sister would think she'd cracked.

"Sometimes those dreams that feel so real happen because you've been sleeping with your eyes open. So you're incorporating the actual room around you with the fantasy stuff your head's making up. I think this is a coming-home dream. You're feeling like you made the right decision about the house."

Cassandra laughed. "He's a welcome-home gift from the house?"

She got up from the table, put her bowl in the sink, and wandered through the dining room into the front parlor. She loved that she had a house with a "parlor."

"Exactly!" Pamela laughed. "Listen, I have to go. I've got a meeting and I'm already late, but let me know if you want me to stop by tonight and help with the unpacking."

"Oh no." Cassandra waved a hand, casting a smile around the room. "I'll be fine. I'm enjoying doing it myself."

Her eye caught on the rosette by the fireplace. It was still off center.

"Okay, then. I'll talk to you later!" Pamela hung up and Cassandra let her arm drop, turning the phone off with her thumb as she approached the fireplace.

Every time she thought about this secret cubbyhole, the warmer it made her feel. It was as if the Night Prince really was trying to reach her.

She pushed the rosette back into place. It slid easily. She didn't need the reminder anymore, and she liked knowing no one else would find the hiding place. She'd leave the picture where it was, a secret between herself and the Night Prince, her dream prince.

Smiling, she went back to the kitchen to clean up her dishes.

Dammit! Asta, where the hell are you?

Cassandra hasn't taken my picture out. Hasn't she looked in the hiding place?

I move the rosette again. Perhaps she'll look next time, but I have the unnerving feeling that I don't have much time left. I don't have a body, I technically don't have a brain, but I do have intuitions and they are lit up and flashing like the dashboard on a nosediving airplane right now.

Because apparently days have passed. Maybe more. Weeks? The place is furnished, put together. She's bought new things. There are pictures on the walls, knickknacks on the tables, a small bit of clutter from everyday living.

Where have I been?

Asta! This isn't fair. Shit, I know you don't care about fair. But it isn't *right.* I have to know the rules here. Am I stuck here forever? Hell, I'm not even a ghost. Nobody sees me, I can't haunt anyone. Or at least I haven't been able to in the past. Then again, I've never felt this way about anyone who's been in the house before . . .

Asta! This girl is important, you said it yourself, and I can feel it. But *why?* How? What the hell am I supposed to do?

Suddenly a wind blows up, swirling around the house. Trees bend and sway and I feel it buffeting against my non-existent body. My hair seems to be moving. I'm cold. I'm crushed by a tremendous feeling of gravity, something pressing down from overhead. I can't breathe — but I don't breathe, so what *is* this?

Then I remember. It comes back like an

electric shock, the night that this all began, out on the patio, my last night alive —

Suddenly, here is Deirdra.

She stands before me in the front room wearing spiked heels and tight white jeans, a tiny red top showing her midriff, her curly hair wild around her head.

I remember how I once found her sexy. Now she's as sexy as an asp with a fang in my femoral artery.

Michael Prince, how lovely to see you again.

She purrs in a way that turns the meaning of every word to its opposite.

"Deirdra," I say, and my voice comes out like peanut butter, blobby and thick with disuse.

God's gift to women.

She strolls toward me, one long fingernail dragging along my cheek. Oddly, I feel this. Pain. It's not a feeling I've missed, but any feeling is amazing.

Handsome, smart, successful, a prince among men! Everything a woman could ever want.

This is not flattery.

How the fuck have you been?

She asks this with a curl of her lip, then she slaps me across the face.

You look like shit.

I take a moment to gather myself, then

say, "Well, I've been dead twenty years. It's not a good look for me."

It doesn't feel like twenty years, though. It feels like yesterday that she blew into my life and destroyed all that I was.

She sneers.

I'll say. Look at you, in your twenty-year-old suit and your ridiculous hairstyle. Nobody'd want you now, I can tell you. You have passed your expiration date. You're stale. Your stock has tanked. You are not even yesterday's news anymore, Mike. You're a loooooser.

She forms her fingers into an *L* and puts it to her forehead.

In all the years I've been gone I haven't felt the rage I do now.

"That's right, Deirdra. I'll give you that. I am a loser. I was a loser when you met me and I haven't changed since. You spotted it and you could not have been more right. But you know what? I never did an intentionally mean thing to anybody in my life. I never once did something I knew would hurt someone, or took revenge on anyone for anything. And believe me, there were times I wanted to."

Well, aren't you just a perfect fucking saint.

Her eyes glitter like road ice in the glare of an oncoming semi.

Maybe that was because everybody fawned

over you, flattered you, told you that you were actually going somewhere — on television!

She laughs wickedly.

Like television means shit. I took care of that. Me. The woman who you chose to toy with and throw away like she was garbage. You had no idea what it felt like to be treated that way until I came along and put you in your place. She calms suddenly and smiles. *Because who cares about you now, huh, Michael Prince? Michael "The Money" Prince?*

She's right, nobody cares. A few people might remember — for example that stupid moniker, *The Money,* I had for a while — but nobody *cares* about me. They have no idea there's a "me" left to care for. I have become what all people who are gone become — forgotten.

"People have done me wrong, too, you know," I say, my voice shaking with rage. "But I never cursed someone out of my own injured pride. I never got my feelings hurt and blew apart somebody else's life." I stride toward her, hot as a blowtorch.

Her eyes shimmer and I half expect her to start flying around setting things on fire like she did last time. But instead she is preternaturally calm, looking at me with all the passion of a shark settling on dinner.

I stop moving.

You think that's what this is about?

Her voice is chillingly amused.

My feelings? Your pathetic little love life?

"That's the thing, Deirdra," I say, struggling to keep from throwing what would end up an impotent punch. Never let them see you sweat. Not that I could sweat if I wanted to. "I don't have a clue what this is about. Never have. I don't know whose authority you're acting on, if you have some kind of contract with God or Satan or whoever, or if you're just a spoiled fucking fairy who didn't get what she wanted. But if there's a point to this purgatory, I want to know what it is. *Now.*"

My outrage flares again, and perhaps foolishly on the last word I fling a hand out toward a blue flowered vase of Cassandra's. To my astonishment it flies across the room, shattering into a thousand pieces against the opposite wall.

I stare at it, mouth agog.

I've moved things before — the grease pencil, the rosette, just to give two examples — but never like this. This time, *I felt it.* It was hard and cool against my fingers, the pads of my palm. It almost hurt.

Deirdra begins to laugh. It starts low, then grows high and hysterical.

Look at you! So shocked! You never knew

what power there was in feeling something, did you?

I look at my hand. "I did feel it. I touched it and I *felt* it." I stare at my fingers, half expecting to see a bruise, a cut, actual blood. Have I got form now? A body?

Not the vase, you imbecile.

Her lip curls again and she whirls. A tiny, fiery cyclone erupts, then disappears behind her.

I told you he didn't get it, Astrid. What am I doing here?

She flings up her hands and stalks away on spiked heels.

Asta's sparkling form appears by the mantel.

Give him a chance.

Deirdra turns back, hands on her hips, red fingernails stark against her white jeans, and looks at me in disgust.

A chance for what? To do something unpredictable? To act against his own deplorable little nature? I don't know why you still believe in this cretin, Astrid, but he seems to have his hooks in you, too, just like all those other bimbos.

Asta's sparkling grows brighter, bathing the room in light.

You're not getting it, Deirdra. Give him a minute.

She scoffs.

He's not getting it. That much is obvious. But all right. I'll humor you and give him another chance. Go ahead, Mikey, touch something else.

She says it sweetly, raising her eyebrows and looking exaggeratedly expectant.

See how it feeeeeels. Show us you have feelings at all, because frankly I find it doubtful. You didn't in life and I'd sure as hell be surprised if you found some in death.

Like a kid on a high dive being taunted for cowardice, I run headlong into uncertainty. Cassandra's farmhouse table is the closest thing to me and I grab the edge, feeling with my newly functional fingers the icy-slick top, the substantial heft and weight of it.

Behind me Deirdra hisses. It's like fingernails on a blackboard.

I boil over. With my hands under the long edge, I flip it up and over like it's made of foam. The thing crashes through the chandelier, glass flies everywhere, and hits the wall next to the kitchen. But it's so damn solid there's barely a mark on it, despite the broken light and a dent in the wall.

I grab it by the legs, imagining myself whirling the whole thing in a circle and taking off Deirdra's head with it, and the truss-like legs break off in my hands with a sharp crack. I twist, hurling the pieces at her.

She sidesteps them neatly, her eyes narrowing.

Oooh . . . She coos, but she's flushed and angry and that makes me feel good. *He's so strong!* She adds this in the voice of the bimbo I once knew her to be.

I turn back to the table, thinking to grab the other legs to continue my assault, but I'm stopped cold by the carnage before me.

The table isn't new, in fact it's mostly old, made from repurposed barn wood and solid workbench trusses. It's heavy and rustic and beautiful, in its way.

Or it was.

The middle plank of the table's surface is split down the middle. The raw inner wood of the plank shows through, stark white as it meets air for the first time in history. Long splinters jut out at lethal angles. It looks like someone has taken a hatchet to the thing.

Deirdra laughs.

You hated that table, didn't you? That horrible country-bumpkin table in your fancy formal dining room. It didn't belong. Just as she doesn't belong. I bet she leaves now!

I look from the table to Deirdra, gloating, her arms over her chest. My tormentor, my captor, my jailer.

I look at Asta, her sparkling form turning multicolored, trying to cheer me, trying to lessen my shock at what I've just done. But it's no use.

I think about Cassandra's face when she talked about getting that table. Nobody else thought it was a good idea, but she wanted it. It meant something to her — it meant believing in herself. I bet when it arrived she circled it again and again, looking happy and satisfied and sure.

I glance at the paint samples on the wall behind it. A half-dozen rectangles of color painted near the table for her to decide what goes best. Something that isn't my decorator-inspired gold-leaf wallpaper that she obviously had steamed off at some point.

Vaguely, from somewhere behind me, I hear Deirdra chastising Asta for being fooled by me, but they are both unimportant to me now. Because what's suddenly obvious is what I've done. I've destroyed something important to another human being — a woman I actually care about. I've done exactly what I bragged to Deirdra that I'd never do: I hurt someone for my own ends.

I didn't just break Cassandra's table. I did something that's going to frighten and dishearten her. And Deirdra's right, she might actually move. She's going to take this as a message, a sign, a threat. She's going to think somebody did this *to her. On purpose.* So that she won't live here, won't do what she wants, have what she loves.

My suddenly somatic knees give out and I sink to the floor next to the ruined table. I picture Cassandra's face, the fear and heartbreak it'll wear when she gets back from wherever she is to see this: what *I* have done to her.

Regret falls on me like an anvil. I am flattened by it. Devastated. As if I've killed someone I loved.

It doesn't matter that I felt the damn table, that the release of all that rage and energy felt good. It doesn't matter that I was goaded into it by Deirdra, that I didn't *mean* to do it. All that matters is that what I've done is suddenly, clearly a mistake. A horrible, hurtful mistake.

And because of it I might lose Cassandra altogether.

Asta says something gentle that I don't catch. But Deirdra's voice, dripping with incredulity, penetrates.

Is he crying?

Chapter Five

Cassandra unlocked the front door of the house and stepped inside, flipping the light switches for the front porch and foyer lights at the same time. She stood for a minute in the lit hallway, inhaling the scent of her home — a combination of old wood, furniture polish, and scented candles.

Every time she walked through the door she smiled, feeling as if she were returning to a cocoon, the safest place on earth, the place she'd been destined for since childhood.

It was a peculiarly satisfying thing to feel that she was exactly where she should be.

She looped her purse over the newel post at the base of the stairs and unzipped her jacket. The house felt chilly, with November bringing the first real cold of the season, so she headed toward the dining room thermostat.

As she neared the room something glittered on the hallway floor and trepidation blossomed in her gut. Something was wrong. Her eye caught first one glint, then several, and after a frozen second her mind put together that what she was seeing was broken glass.

Her steps slowed until she stood just outside the entry to the dining room, one hand on the high-gloss paint of the molding. Her gaze ran from the few silvery shards of glass in the hall light to the multitude scattered on the dining room floor. Then her eyes took in the table, standing tall on one end, leaning against the far wall and split down the middle. One half skewed outward as if someone had plunged an ax down the center of it.

She gasped. The legs on one side were still attached, holding the lower end of the table together, but the other legs were . . .

She shrieked.

The figure on the floor looked up, startled.

Their eyes met. Cassandra's world tilted. Her fingers scrabbled for purchase on the molding by the door, but it was too narrow. She felt her fingernail break as she stumbled backward, her head spinning.

Her back hit the wall underneath the rising staircase behind her, but her eyes remained riveted on the man who knelt in her dining room. In his hands were the other set of legs from the table, as if he had been trying vainly to press them back together.

Now, though, he was looking at her, and as his arms lowered, the pieces of wood hit the ground with a thud.

He moved his lips as if speaking, but no sound emerged.

A wave of recognition washed over her. He was the Night Prince — he was the man who disappeared — he was the man who'd tried to kiss her in her dream. He was a man who did not exist.

But he was more. He was someone she *knew.* She felt it clear down into her bones, and in the back of her mind the echo of distant music played. A waltz, or a minuet. Something archaic, and impossibly familiar. She knew the feel of this man's arms around her waist; she knew the heat of his gaze looking into hers, piercing her soul.

"Who *are* you?" Her voice was high and shrill.

A sane person would have run for the phone to call 911, but she couldn't. She *knew* him. At least a part of her did. It was like she was two people simultaneously: the woman she'd been for twenty-nine years who wouldn't hesitate to call the police; and another woman, a shadowy memory, who'd been secure and well-loved by the spirit that inhabited this man.

His mouth moved again, his eyes anxious and pleading, but she heard nothing.

"Stop that!" she cried, panic warring with excitement within her.

He couldn't be who she thought. He was here in her house. An intruder. Maybe he was a crazy person. Maybe *she* was a crazy person.

"What did you do? Why? Wh-why?" It was all she could get out, so she thrust her hands in the direction of the table. Her beautiful, unique table, reduced to kindling.

The man rose slowly to his feet, and if she'd thought he was frightening before by virtue of his being in her house and looking like the Night Prince, she now realized that something else was dreadfully wrong.

He wasn't . . . quite . . . solid. Rather, he shimmered, appearing intermittently insubstantial. Though he was tall and well built, he seemed to fade and blur, then come back into focus, like a hologram.

And he made no sound. It wasn't just that he wasn't talking, but as he rose his clothes didn't rustle, his knees didn't crack, his shoes made no shuffling sound on the floor as he moved his feet apart.

He looked around himself, as if searching for something. Then patted his suit pockets like he was looking for his wallet. His expression went frustrated and he strode to the sideboard — again, making absolutely no sound. He opened a drawer. Inside was Cassandra's grandmother's silver.

The twenty-first-century woman took over.

"No!" She held a hand out and he spun back toward her. She recoiled. "Never mind. Take what you want. Whatever you want, just take it and go. *Please* go. I won't call the police, I promise."

But even as she promised she knew that the statement was ridiculous. This was no regular burglar. This was no regular *man.*

He held his hands palms-up, extended toward her, like a magician saying, *Nothing up my sleeve.* His brows were raised, his eyes still anxious. She paused, licked her lips, wondered how incredibly stupid she was for not just grabbing the phone and dialing 911. But she stilled, and after a moment he gave a grim smile, his eyes still holding hers, and mimed writing on his palm.

She stared at him dumbly for a moment — a mute, transparent trespasser wanted to write her a note? — then she sidled out of the room, backed up the hall to the newel post where her purse hung, and dug her hand inside. Her fingers scrabbled frantically as she kept one eye on the door to the dining room, ignoring the checkbook and hairbrush and lipstick that fell out of her bag to the floor, until she found her pad with the pen stuck inside.

With a deep breath, she crept back down the hall to the dining room, unsure whether she hoped the man was still there or that he was gone. If he were gone it could mean she was crazy, that he'd never been there, the shimmering, intangible man. Or it could mean that she was a fool and he'd escaped through the kitchen and out the back door.

That was what she *should* have been hoping for, but when she got back to the dining room doorway she was relieved to see he was standing where she left him, his anxious eyes looking for her.

He smiled when she reappeared and her heart gave a flip. She had a momentary impulse to throw herself into his arms. But she didn't. That would be truly absurd.

There was an appealing array of light crow's-feet by his eyes, and deep dimples. His eyes were blue — very blue. Just exactly like those of the Night Prince. The man who'd nearly kissed her.

Before she could dwell further on this, he moved toward her, holding out a translucent hand.

For the pen, she realized. She shoved it toward him, letting go before he could take it. It, at least, made a reassuring clatter as it fell to the floor. She watched, fascinated, as he bent down and the pen — ten times denser and more corporeal than he was — rose in his implausible grip. He looked up at her expectantly. She slapped the pad of paper down on the sideboard and stepped back, nodding toward it as if she couldn't speak either.

He inclined his head in thanks, and pulled the pad toward him, flipping the pen into writing position in his hand. Then he stared at the page a long moment, two lines of consternation between his brows.

His gaze flicked toward her — self-consciously, she thought — then he started writing. A moment later he turned the pad toward her and stepped back.

My name is Michael Prince. I'm sorry about your table. I'm not here to scare you.

She looked up at him. He was *introducing himself*? This was not exactly the information she'd expected, but then, what had she thought he'd say?

"Prince?" she asked, incredulity bathing

the word.

He appeared to laugh, wryly. *Yes, like the singer. Or the Fresh Prince. Or whatever other joke you care to make. I've heard them all.*

She noted that he didn't mention *The Night Prince.*

"Did you break it?" She once again gestured toward the table.

His shoulders sank as he read what she wrote. Then he glanced up, made a rueful face, and shrugged.

Anger shot through her. *"Why?"*

He wrote, *It's a long story.*

On the heels of confusion, she registered amazement that she was not feeling sheer terror. What was wrong with her? She was conducting a conversation, of sorts, with a transparent man.

"What *are* you?" she breathed.

She thought he might have sighed — his chest rose and fell once — then he wrote again. *I'm sort of a ghost. Don't ask me why. I didn't die, I was . . . taken. Turned into this. You are the first person ever to see me.*

He turned the pad toward her, tapping the pen point at the end of the last sentence a few times imperatively. He watched her read, then swiftly turned it back and wrote, *What do I look like to you?*

"You look . . ." She swallowed. "Kind of

halfway invisible. A little shimmery. Glittery."

He frowned. *Do I look like a person? A man?*

She laughed, then pressed her fingers to her lips. She had to be cracking up. This was bad.

"Yes." Her voice shook. At his look of alarm, she added, "You look like the Night Prince. From the storybook."

He appeared momentarily stunned, then a smile broke onto his face. She caught her breath at the brightness of it.

He wrote, *You did find the picture!*

She nodded. He nodded back, smiling eagerly, as if they'd just found friends in common.

He's called the Night Prince?

"Yes, it's an old book. From the thirties, I think. You don't know it?"

He shook his head. Then wrote, *I saw the picture you found. The first one.*

"He . . . he looks like you," she said, realizing that it wasn't just the picture he'd drawn, but the *original* that looked like Michael Prince.

The coincidence unnerved her. She took a step back. "I'm afraid I'm going crazy. This . . . this isn't . . . how . . . ?"

He stepped toward her, hands out again

as if telling her to calm down, be quiet. He looked so alarmed that she stopped.

He turned back to the pad and wrote furiously, *PLEASE DON'T GO.*

The insistence of it — the capital letters, the blackness of the pen — frightened her. He seemed to see this and wrote something more.

I've been so lonely.

She read the words, taking in the sudden unsteadiness of the hand, and to her surprise felt tears well in her eyes. She raised her gaze back to his and something passed between them, a shiver of comprehension and a surge of emotion.

She inhaled sharply, and his hands jerked as if he might reach for her.

Shaken, more by her own feelings than his movement, she took another small step back. "Have you . . . have you been here . . . long?"

He nodded slowly. Then wrote, *Years.*

She took a deep breath. "Are you the man who disappeared? The newscaster? From the nineties?"

His eyes widened. He looked enlivened, and tragic, and she worried that exciting a ghost was not a good thing at all.

The pen flew quickly. *Yes!*

She nodded, keeping her eyes on his, on

those blue relieved eyes. "I remember. I saw you. On the news. And I saw this house. I knew then I was going to live here someday."

He regarded her with interest, head slightly tilted. *You knew?*

She nodded again.

How old were you?

"About five."

He looked sad. *You must think I'm old. But I'm only thirty.*

She smiled. "I'm twenty-nine." She shrugged.

He smiled in return, looking enthralled as he gazed at her. His lips moved and she frowned in incomprehension.

He turned back toward the paper. *You have a beautiful smile. You are a beautiful woman.*

Despite herself, her eyes narrowed. She had always mistrusted compliments, and while she didn't exactly think she was being hit on by a ghost, she did suspect him of flattery for ulterior motives.

He appeared to laugh.

I seem to have lost my touch, he wrote.

"You almost kissed me. The other night, you tried to kiss me while I slept," she said, a slow realization dawning. "Do you watch me? Can you see me . . . ? *All the time?*"

The implications of this reverberated in

her one at a time, like gongs from a clock. He might watch her undress. He could have seen her in the bath. What if he were —

He scribbled so furiously that her attention was caught by the sound of the pen on the page.

I don't. I can't. I come and go — it's not under my control. I never — he crossed that out — *I watched you sleep that one night, because I wanted to communicate, to figure out how to communicate. And then I thought of kissing you. I'm sorry. I am not here to scare you!*

This last, which he'd said before, he underlined several times before spinning the pad back to her.

Her eyes went from the pad, to his face, to the broken table behind him. "Tell me why you did this."

He took the pad back, flipped to a new page, and stood a long minute staring at the blank sheet. *I thought the one who did this to me, who turned me into a ghost, would* — He crossed that out and wrote, *wanted me to.* Then he paused, crossed that out, and with a frustrated expression wrote, *I thought it might change things.*

She slumped. "You thought God wanted you to break my table?"

The dry tone of her voice obviously registered with him, because he looked upset. Then he shook his head and wrote, *Not God. Definitely not God.*

She crossed her arms over her chest and rubbed her shoulders. "And did anything change?"

He didn't meet her eyes at first, and she felt sorry for him. He looked bleak.

Then his expression turned pensive, and lightened. *I don't know. Maybe.* He looked up at her, gesturing with his hands between them, as if saying, "You and I."

He turned back to the pad. *You can see me.* He shrugged again, palms up, eyebrows raised, hopeful.

She pushed her fingers into her hair, then rubbed her eyes with the heels of her hands. This was nuts. The guy was *sparkling,* for pity's sake. He was next to invisible. He made no sounds.

And yet . . . She looked again at the table. That wood was definitely split. And there was nothing imaginary about the shards of glass on the floor. On an impulse, she bent and picked up a broken crystal drop from the chandelier. She pressed her finger against the sharp edge and watched as a drop of blood appeared on her fingertip.

She heard the pen on the paper and

looked over.

That's real.

Her eyes snapped up to his. He nodded knowingly.

Something cold clutched her stomach. Could he read her mind?

He smiled sadly and shook his head.

"What?" she asked, unable to suppress the challenging tone.

I understand. You.

She frowned again, looked at him askance, and put her bleeding finger to her mouth.

Don't ever play poker.

It took a split second, then she laughed. Her father used to say that to her all the time. Her face was as easy to read as a stop sign.

She looked at her fingertip again, at the fresh drop of blood oozing out of the cut. The man moved and she looked up to see him brandishing a handkerchief, an ironic smile on his face, one eyebrow lifted.

She laughed. On impulse, she reached for it.

There was a whisper of cold on her fingers, and then, like the bursting of a soap bubble, Michael Prince disappeared.

Chapter Six

I have seen nothing of Deirdra. Asta has also been MIA. I've been wandering around the house looking for Cassandra for days, but she doesn't seem to be here. And I can't tell if I'm coming and going in time, if I've missed a week and she's just out, or if three years have passed and I am nothing but the fading memory of a dream to her.

The dining room has been painted, but there is no table. This gives me hope. Maybe it's only been a short time and she's getting a new one.

The problem with hope is that even if Cassandra shows up, even if she sees me and I see her, what can I change? Will I be able to talk to her this time? Will she even be able to see me again?

And what about that feeling that passed between us? That wave of knowledge and desire? It was so palpable it damn near knocked me over. And I *know* she felt it, too.

But this is the thing. There is just too much I don't know. Like what's going to happen and what I'm supposed to do to become whole again. Or maybe it's to become whole for the first time.

Cassandra makes me feel things I've never felt before. I want to care for her and give her things and make her as happy as she can possibly be — whatever that takes. She doesn't need to love me, but I'm desperate to be able to love her completely, to take care of her, be there *for her,* in whatever way she will have me.

My inability to stay with her, to be all she needs, makes me feel like I'm going crazy. Most of the time I'm half-mad with it, but there seems to be nothing I can do.

I can touch things, feel things, I could break something again if I wanted, but where would that get me? *Us?*

If I ever do find my way back — to where? to when? — I am afraid I'll have been rendered deranged by this situation, insensible of the change, a phantom in my mind forever.

But right now, all I want to do is see her. Cassandra. What I felt with her wasn't just the burnished pine of her table. As insane as it sounds, I know I am in love with her. Hopelessly and completely in love with her.

But I can't find her!

And I must.

"Mother, I told you I don't *want* another table. The one I had was perfect and I'm getting it fixed."

Cassandra stabbed the lock with her key and twisted it so hard she wrenched her wrist. Rubbing it absently, she opened the door. Just as she had every day, every *minute,* for a month, she scanned the hallway for Michael, her heart breaking all over again when she did not see him.

Behind her, her mother followed her into the house in a cloud of Dior perfume, her jet-black mink softly brushing Cassandra's arm as she passed.

"Regardless," her mother said with an airy wave, "the gentlemen from Roche Bobois are here and they've got a classic, formal dining table for you."

"But you didn't even *see* my table." Cassandra heard the plea in her voice and despised herself for it. And besides, she knew that even if her mother had seen her table she would have hated it.

Not that it mattered. Nothing really mattered, she felt, because she'd been abandoned by her prince.

Which was *insane.* Literally.

She turned her attention back to her mother, who had strode straight to the near-empty dining room.

Where the table argument was concerned Cassandra knew she was on weak ground to begin with, because she'd had to tell everyone that *she'd* broken the table. She'd concocted an elaborate story about changing a bulb in the chandelier, slipping, and grabbing onto the light, only to have it fall onto the table, breaking everything.

People seemed to buy it, even if they did now regard her as incompetent. But she couldn't very well have told them the truth. She could barely believe it herself. In fact, she probably didn't believe it, except she had the pad of paper on which the Night Prince — Michael Prince — had written to her. She'd read and reread it dozens of time in the weeks since she'd seen him, simultaneously scared she'd never see him again, and worried that she'd seen him in the first place.

Had he gone forever? Had she sent him into some new dimension just by trying to touch him? What did it mean that she felt so sure she *knew* him? Or had known him . . . once upon a time?

"I'm sure your table was lovely, dear, but this one is spectacular. And perfect for the space." She stepped toward the hall, waving the deliverymen back. "In here, boys!"

Two large Italian-looking men who could not be further from "boys" wrestled a brown-paper-wrapped table through the doorway.

Just as she was feeling her heart rate slow in defeat, Cassandra's gaze was caught by a shimmer over her mother's right shoulder. Her eyes flicked involuntarily and she gasped as the Night Prince appeared in the room.

Her mother whirled, looked in Michael's direction, and Cassandra's heart flew to her throat. "For heaven's sake, Cassandra, what is it?" She turned back around directly. "You act as if you've seen a ghost."

Crazily, Cassandra nearly laughed — both at her mother's accurate description and her relief that Michael Prince had returned. After a full month without him, he was *back*. The fear and worry she'd associated with his last visit evaporated, and her heart sang as if one of her dearest friends had returned.

They gazed hungrily at each other for a very long moment. If anyone had been able to see them both they'd have looked like lovesick teenagers, goggling at each other with pure joy.

But while she could see Michael, her mother couldn't!

She frowned, looking back at her mother. Was that proof that she herself was crazy? That this vision was hers alone? She comforted herself with the pad of paper upstairs, the masculine handwriting decidedly not her own.

Fortunately her mother did not witness the wave of expressions on Cassandra's face, as she was busy directing the deliverymen on placement and how to gently — *GENTly!* — remove the paper from the furniture.

From the periphery of her sight line, Cassandra saw Michael Prince look at her with concern. She turned her eyes to him and he put his hands out, pressing his palms downward slowly a couple of times.

Calm down, she understood, the kindness in his eyes warming her.

"Now, I may not have won the lottery, dear, but I hope I still have my good taste. Tell me what you think of this."

Cassandra turned to see her mother spreading her arms wide to encompass a gorgeous mahogany table with an inlaid top. Cassandra actually gasped when she saw it.

"Oh, Mother," she breathed. She looked up to see her mother beaming — actually *beaming* — at Cassandra's reaction. "It's stunning."

Her mother gave her the broadest, most natural smile Cassandra had seen on her face in years. Maybe since her father had died ten years ago. "There, you see? Your mother knows a thing or two about decor, doesn't she?"

Michael Prince tilted his head, considering her mother, a kind expression on his handsome face.

He glanced at her and nodded, mouthing something she didn't understand.

"I will never doubt you again." Cassandra ran her fingers over the marquetry top, admiring the precise lines of the inlay. She looked up at Michael, who raised his brows appreciatively, then gestured in her mother's direction.

She understood then the words that he'd mouthed. *Include her.*

She straightened. "Maybe you could help me choose a bureau for the bedroom. I think it's time I got rid of that old college dresser I have."

To her surprise, her mother actually flushed. "Well, of course, darling. I'll call you this week and set up a day we can go look."

A gentle smile formed on Cassandra's face

as she looked at her mother — really looked — for the first time in years. She'd never gotten over Cassandra's father's death. Both of her girls had been closer to him than to her, but he had loved her unconditionally. And Cassandra could see now how much she'd relied on that, needed it, and did not know how to ask for it. Instead she pushed and demanded and generally made herself a nuisance in an effort to be present for them — her and Pamela. Cassandra resolved to change that, to appreciate all her mother tried to do, even when she was her most trying.

"That would be perfect." Cassandra reached out and squeezed her mother's arm.

"Well," her mother said, obviously flustered. "Let me just tip those deliverymen and I'll be on my way. Here they come with the chairs now. I'll call you tomorrow!"

Fifteen minutes later, it was all delivered and done, and Cassandra turned to Michael Prince.

"Where have you *been*?"

He gave an elaborate shrug, eyebrows up, but she saw relief in his eyes, too, as he gazed at her.

She glanced from Michael toward the hall, where her mother had just closed the door behind her. "You understand women pretty well, don't you?"

His expression went dark with what appeared to be regret. He shook his head, placing a fist against his forehead and gently pounding a couple of times. His chin dropped in a gesture of shame, and he lifted his eyes toward hers. *Stupid,* he mouthed. *Stupid, bad man.*

His pain was palpable. Did he truly believe he was a bad man?

"I don't believe that's true. I don't even think that's possible." Automatically she reached out a hand to touch his arm, to reassure him, but he pulled back, alarm on his face.

Because of course that's how he disappeared the last time.

"I'm sorry!" She gripped her hands together at her waist. "I forgot. I'm so sorry!"

He shook his head dismissively.

"I'm so afraid of losing you again." She stepped toward him but didn't dare to reach out.

He nodded appreciatively, as if to say, "Me, too."

"What are we going to do?" she asked. "I mean . . . I just feel . . . I wish . . ."

This was ridiculous. Could she tell a man she barely knew she didn't want to live without him? No, not even a man — a mere shade of one! For what would become of her if she fell in love with a man who wasn't really there? She'd become Miss Havisham living in a cobwebbed house of memories.

I know, he mouthed, reaching toward her, then jerking his hands back and grabbing his hair in frustration. He turned and marched several paces away. Then he went to her purse on the newel post, got out her pad and pen, and started writing.

Do you feel it, too? Do you remember another time? Another life? Together? he wrote.

She read the words and looked up at him, mouth agape. "I . . . think so. I hear music sometimes."

He nodded vigorously. *Yes! Classical. Some kind of dance music.*

He wrote so fast it was hard to make out all the words. "What is — Oh yes, classical music. And I feel like I remember us . . . dancing."

Their eyes met, and all of her insides lifted as if inflated with helium.

And do you feel it? Feel —

He stood for a long time over the pad, then looked up at her bashfully.

She smiled, blushing. "I feel it," she whispered. "I feel . . ."

LOVE.

They both looked at the word.

His left hand lay on the sideboard. She moved her right hand next to it, not touching, but close.

He looked over at her, and the expression in his eyes crushed her. Yearning, frustration, tragedy.

"We'll figure it out," she whispered. "We will. We *have* to."

CHAPTER SEVEN

God, I want to touch her. I want to touch her more than I've ever wanted anything.

We stare at each other. *We'll figure it out.*

I'd give anything to believe that.

I feel as if I suddenly have a heart, and it's expanding and reaching out to hers. The look in her eyes says she feels it, too. It's almost as if I can see inside of her, as if our joined gazes create a physical strand, a tangible connection.

Sensations assail me. My hand is on the sideboard and I feel the polished wood under my palm. And there is her hand, right next to mine. I want to take it, touch it, skin to skin, feel her warmth.

And then I want to turn, cup her face with my palm, let my fingers linger on that soft, smooth cheek, run my thumb along the pillow of her lips. I want to grab her, slide my hand into her hair, pull her close, and kiss her like she's never been kissed before . . .

our souls meeting in our breaths.

Except I have no breath. I have no skin. I do not actually have hands.

What I have, however, is emotion. Emotion moving inside me like a tidal wave.

I. Have. *Never.* Felt this way.

Finally I close my eyes and tear myself away. I can't take it. The agony of our separation might kill me, I truly believe it.

"I don't know what to do," I mutter.

She gasps. I think for a moment that her mother has returned, but when I turn, she's got me pinned with those wide dark eyes.

"I *heard* you," she whispers. "Like a real man. Not a . . . specter."

I stare, my mouth agog. A long moment passes.

"*Say* something." She issues a slightly hysterical giggle.

"Cassandra."

Her eyes melt and she lets out a gentle, "Oh . . . You have a *lovely* voice."

I am so stunned I'm frozen. What do I do? What does this mean? Am I still a specter? I look at my hand. It looks as it always does to me. Remote. Familiar but not solid.

Cassandra's eyes grow concerned. "You're still . . . transparent." Her brows lower. "But you can speak normally, and I can hear you."

"Something has changed," I say. "Something is changing."

Her smile is tremulous.

I step toward her. "Cassandra, I know you. I think I've always known you. But I want to know who you are *now.*" I laugh at the absurdity. "Does that make sense? I want to know Cassandra Carlisle. I want to know . . ." I lift my hand, hold it close to her face, then raise it as if I can stroke her hair, but I stay one inch from contact. "I want to know everything about you."

"I know," she says, wonder in her voice. "I want to know you, too. Not because you're the Night Prince, though you are. But because something inside of me recognizes you. Something inside has known you since I was born." She gives a trembling laugh. "Isn't that crazy?"

I smile. "Yes! But there's nothing wrong with crazy sometimes."

We laugh together.

Then something changes in her face. She gets serious — deadly serious.

"Michael," she says urgently. "Forgive me if this is wrong, forgive me for this, for what I have to do, but . . ."

Her eyes are so scared the smile melts off

my face.

"Cass —"

But the word is cut short, because before I can even ask what she means, she pushes forward, takes my face in her hands, and puts her lips on mine.

I feel heat first, the heat of her body, the warmth of her aura, then the press of her lips. I am overcome with awareness, perception, *touch!*

My hands rise and feel her arms, the coarseness of her sweater. My mouth moves under hers and . . . and it's as if the whole world has opened up to me, a magical garden of light and air and the bliss of sweet sensation.

And the scent that clings to her — flowers! I haven't smelled anything for a score and it hits me like a breaking wave.

My senses are *alive,* and they drown in everything that is Cassandra.

We pull back, staring at each other. Breathing hard. *Breathing!*

My hands rise to her face, I cup her cheeks, and they're petal soft. I slide my fingers into her hair, my eyes scanning her face, the arched brows, the light freckles on her nose, the trickle of tears down her cheek, and the blessed curve of her lips as she smiles up at me.

"I'm real," I marvel. "*Am* I real?"

Laughing, she says, "Yes!"

"My God . . . Cassandra . . ." I hold her face in my hands, feel her arms around me, and look at her as if doing so is drinking the magic elixir of life.

"I love you." We both say it at once. And we both laugh.

A split second later an electric shock hits me.

It's so unexpected and so powerful I stagger backward, away from her. She cries my name as I hit the floor, banging my head on the hardwood so forcefully that I see stars. It *hurts,* but the pain is so sweet I revel in it.

My breath — the breath I haven't felt in decades — is knocked from my long-unused lungs and I struggle to gasp.

Cassandra flies to my side, landing on her knees with a clatter, her hands on my chest. "Michael!"

I close my eyes, willing myself to recover. Could I be brought back to life only to suffocate and die in the presence of the woman I love?

"Michael, no! *Come back to me!*"

I panic when I open my eyes, fearing it had all been a dream. But I immediately feel

Cassandra's hand on my cheek, her tears on my face.

"Are you back?" she asks in a trembling voice.

I answer her by reaching up, into her hair, and pulling her lips to mine. My body — my *physical body* — responds in a way I had nearly forgotten about. My heart thrums, my nerves stand up and reach for contact, and my manhood . . . well, let's just say I have never been as stimulated as I am now. Every cell in my body is quivering, hungry for her touch, her taste, her skin.

She pulls back, light shining in her eyes.

I begin to unbutton her sweater but she pushes my hands aside and pulls everything, sweater and shirt, off over her head. My palms reach for her skin and the softness of it nearly undoes me. She is everything I've missed, everything I've ever wanted.

She leans toward me and kisses me while my hand loops around her back, and with one snap of my fingers I unfasten her bra.

She pulls back an inch and laughs. "Wow."

"Some things I guess you never forget." I chuckle even as my cheeks burn.

She begins to unbutton my shirt — my twenty-year-old Brooks Brothers button-down — and I am so certain I never want to see it again I rip the front open. Then, hands around her waist, I lift her to the side, push myself up and land her gently on her back beneath me.

"Smoooooth." She grins.

But I have no words, because my hands are cupping her perfect breasts, and her nipples are standing hard and her body is about the most beautiful thing I have ever laid eyes on.

I undress her slowly, reveling in the feel of everything from her belt buckle, to the tender flesh of her inner thighs, to the socks she wears with her clogs.

She pushes my shirt off my shoulders and the feel of her fingers down my naked chest nearly makes me lose it right then and there.

"Michael," she sighs, her gaze as tangible as kisses on my skin.

I slip out of my clothes for the first time in twenty years, flinging them across the room, and lower myself onto her. The sensation of my chest against hers, my hips meeting her hips, our legs entwined, is the most beautiful thing I've ever felt.

This is not just because it's been a score of years since I've touched anyone, though that's part of it. This is, unquestionably, because I have never made love to a woman I loved.

My soul reaches out to Cassandra through

my skin, and I feel hers reaching back.

I push myself up on my arms and look down at her. Her face is glowing, her hair spread like an aura around her, and I look into her eyes — eyes as familiar yet fresh as my newly found body — as I push deeply into her.

Her lips part, her breath catches, and she exhales with a gentle sound. Her eyes crinkle as her legs wrap around my hips.

"My love," I whisper, moving my lips to her face and kissing her cheeks, her chin, her nose, her forehead.

Then nature surges back into my limbs. I thrust deeply, then ever faster, inside of her. She meets me surge for surge and we couple like animals free in the wild, meeting essence to essence, body to body, and soul to soul.

She cries out, shuddering with pleasure, her body gripping mine and I come, hard as a geyser, emptying my entire being inside of her.

"I will love you forever," she says.

And I laugh, thinking of Asta's space-time continuum. "I have already loved you forever, and I will love you forevermore."

One year later they were standing in her parlor, next to the mantelpiece, upon which a garland of pine ran between pictures of Cassandra and Michael together everywhere from Aspen to Paris to their very own kitchen, where they'd taken a picture of themselves having coffee at their newly restored farmhouse table.

Around them the guests at their engagement party mingled, everybody as happy as the holiday season.

"So how did you two meet?"

It was Michael's great-aunt Amelia asking for the third or fourth time that evening. She was holding on to what had to be her fourth glass of champagne.

"Amelia, you remember." Michael's father put an arm around her shoulders and gently took the glass from her hands. "They met when Michael got back from his assignment overseas."

It was the story they'd told everyone. That Michael had been overseas for a year, on assignment, and had just moved back to Georgetown when he met Cassandra on the street in front of her house.

But the truth was that by the same unbelievable magic that had sent Michael into obscurity, he was brought back to life — to a life that included everything he'd had before, as if he'd never left.

His father hadn't aged, nor his aunts, and

his career was taking off just as it had been when he'd disappeared back in the nineties. But it was a new century now and everything was as it had ever been for Cassandra, except for the magical appearance of her Night Prince.

It was mind-boggling to think about — Cassandra and Michael had tried to wrap their heads around it nightly when they first got together — but now they just accepted it. If a fairy could turn him into an apparition for twenty years, then a fairy could make those twenty years disappear for him, yet stay the same for Cassandra.

Michael had told Cassandra about Aunt Malva's curse that he die, and Aunt Amelia's amendment that he only "sleep," but it was difficult for Cassandra to fully comprehend how such a thing could happen — even though she'd only known him as a ghostlike presence for their first few months together.

It wasn't until they escaped into the kitchen during the party, on the pretext of refilling a tray of canapés, that Cassandra got her own taste of the dark side of that magic.

By chance — or perhaps by someone's magical design — the caterers were all out serving and they had the kitchen to themselves for a moment. Michael took the opportunity of grabbing her and pulling her toward him. As she reached up for his kiss, his hands slid under her shirt, and just as she did every time he touched her she reveled in the feel of his warm, solid hands on her body.

Suddenly a tornadolike breeze blew into the kitchen and Cassandra gasped as a woman with wild red hair and an outlandishly sexy outfit appeared in the middle of the room.

Don't let him do it, sweetheart. He was doing the exact same thing to another woman the night I caught him. He doesn't stick to just one woman, you know.

Her voice was slick as oil and caustic as battery acid.

Cassandra turned in Michael's arms, and felt them tighten around her as she said, "You must be Deirdra."

The fairy looked shocked, then quickly composed herself and put her hands on her hips.

Don't believe a word he's told you about me. He's a lying dog who deserves to pay for what he does to women.

"Great," Cassandra said. "Then let him pay for making me the happiest woman on earth."

Behind her, Michael chuckled before

releasing his hold on her waist and stepping beside her.

"Go back to wherever it is you came from, Deirdra. I've learned my lesson. There's nothing you can do to me now."

What do you mean, nothing I can do? Have you forgotten what I did to you for twenty years? Have you forgotten how it felt to be nonexistent?

Michael laughed grimly. "Hardly."

Do you doubt that I could do it again?

Her voice got shrill, almost ear splitting, and Cassandra had her first moment of doubt before spotting something shimmering near the farmhouse table.

"There she is," Cassandra whispered to him, pointing toward the sparkling glow. "Tell her, Astrid. Tell her she can leave us alone now."

Astrid spoke. *You're powerless here, Deirdra. And do you know why?*

Michael took Cassandra's hand in his and kissed her fingers, his eyes not leaving Deirdra. "She knows."

What? Deirdra actually shrieked. *What do I know??*

Astrid's sparkle warmed to a fiery glow.

He loves. Deirdra, he truly loves. Cassandra has saved him.

"No." Cassandra shook her head, and

turned to smile at Michael. "He saved me."

Oh for God's sake — Deirdra spun in a circle and flung a tiny twister at the floor, where it sputtered and died out.

So it's real then? He's woken up?

Deirdra cast a skeptical eye at Astrid, who shot beams of pure white light out in every direction.

She woke him up.

It's real.

Deirdra crossed her arms over her chest and stomped one foot.

And I suppose they're going to live frickin' happily ever after now?

Her voice carried the sulk of a ten-year-old.

That's right. The curse is broken.

After a second of frowning, Deirdra flung her head back, shook out her hair, then put her hands on her hips and took a deep breath. Giving Astrid a broad smile, she said cheerfully, *Then I guess my work here is done!*

Cassandra had barely registered her words, let alone her sudden change of demeanor, when the evil fairy whirled into a tornado and disappeared.

Astrid glowed brightly another moment, warming them both, then popped off like a lightbulb.

But her voice echoed throughout the kitchen:

And they did live . . .
Happily . . .
Ever . . .
After!

▪ ▪ ▪ ▪

The Christmas Comet

MARY KAY MCCOMAS

▪ ▪ ▪ ▪

For Ruth and Tom Langan —
and their own special fairy tale

Chapter One

"Hope you're right about all that magic Christmas Comet stuff." The mix of hope and doubt in the young woman's voice was a distraction. Natalie watched her most recent cell mate shrink herself into a men's wool dress coat like a turtle in its shell. Her street name was Paisley but everyone in the police station called her Cindy-something. "I could use a little magic right now."

Natalie's lips tipped upward and her brown eyes warmed. "They call it a once-in-a-civilization occurrence — a comet fifteen times brighter than a full moon with a glorious tail that will cover half the sky. That's *something.* That's special. I feel good things coming. I do."

Cindy-Paisley looked her up and down and then gave her a short, considering nod before she turned to the man who'd posted her bail and headed for the exit.

Natalie's smile sagged — the young woman's legs were bare; her cheap flats were no protection against the biting cold outside. There were lots of labels for and opinions about people like her . . . Natalie's was *human being.*

A throat cleared deeply to reclaim her attention.

"So? Where are my matches?" Natalie scowled at the officer behind the booking desk at the city jail, her possessions scattered out between them. "My box of matches? I always carry stick matches and they aren't here."

The tall, thin, and laced-up-proper-looking young man appeared to be exhausted from a long night of admitting and releasing lawbreakers who were — one could only hope — far more monstrous than her. But at the moment she wasn't inclined to have mercy on him.

Last night one of his brothers in blue deliberately spilled seventeen quarts of beef stew — that cost her $33.76 to make — into a Dumpster behind Danny's Den of Drag downtown. And then he arrested her for trespassing. Again.

"*And* I wasn't trespassing, Officer . . . J. Reese," she read off his name tag. He was new and clearly unaware of her circumstances. "I had Danny's permission to use the alley behind his club. He lets me use it all the time because I'm always done and gone before dark." She sliced air with her hand, then let it drop on the counter and added in a more doting tone, "Usually. But even if I'm there a bit longer than expected, none of the artists care, and they're the only ones who use the back door. They're great people. Some of them bring me their old clothes. Not their costumes, of course. Warm clothes. In fact, most of the nice suits I keep for the men to use on job interviews are from them. They're snappy dressers on and offstage." She gave a half-laugh at her amusing comment on the drag queens and waited for Officer J. Reese to do the same. His eyes had glazed over.

She made a disapproving noise. "Fine. But I wasn't trespassing."

"Streets and alleys are public property, ma'am, and not exclusive to building owners or leaseholders and are, therefore, subject to city rules and regulations — including those that pertain to the ban on the outdoor feeding of homeless people."

"A ban that is a clear violation of the First Amendment, by the way. And I would love to feed them inside — somewhere out of the wind, somewhere warm. Unfortunately, I don't have those kinds of resources . . .

yet. But I have been through the food safety program and I do have a permit, so I was not breaking any laws."

"Except for trespassing on public property that isn't zoned for outdoor meals."

"Hardly a meal. How long would you last on twelve ounces of soup and two slices of bread?" He stared at her. "And where are we supposed to go? All the way over to the other end of Dover Street to the Takes-a-Village shelter that, in case you are totally oblivious to the displaced population in this town, has a strict policy on families with children under sixteen only." She reconsidered her overcritical tone. "They're great about opening up to everyone on holidays though. And if they could afford to do more I know they would but . . ." She looked up and into the officer's eyes. She'd seen apathy before; it challenged her. She started gathering up her stuff. "Do you know that eight out of ten homeless people would sell their souls for your job? Do you know that one in four is a veteran of the United States military? Do you know that —"

"Do you know that you're holding up the line?" asked a man standing in the open doorway that led out of the building, to freedom. It was another uniformed policeman; he wasn't as tall as J. Reese but he was bulked up and thick with muscles that he used more for intimidation, she knew, than for serving and protecting.

He struck a wooden match to light the cigarette he held between his narrow lips — blew the smoke out the door. He smirked, looked down at the little red matchbox, and shook it to show it was empty before tossing it in a nearby trash can. She didn't need to see this one's name tag. Officer P. Morgan had arrested her . . . and stolen her matchsticks.

"You're the only reason I'm in this line, Poo—"

For the record: His mother called him Paul, not Poophead — for which Natalie received a summons for disturbing the peace last year.

Still, noting the three people waiting on the benches between them, she raised her voice conspicuously. "Do your superiors know how you spend your work hours, Officer Morgan? Do they understand that you seem to have nothing better to do than drum up false charges against me? Has anyone in your psych department explored your irrational aggression toward the indigent?"

She had no intention of mentioning the matches; he was getting too much satisfaction as it was. Tucking a file folder into her hobo bag, she turned to walk his way. She was not immune to his bullying but she knew as well as he did that she was a wall of defense for the down-and-out in their town — albeit a thin one. Sadly, however, she had nothing to fight back with but tenacity and a sharp tongue.

"Frankly," she said, staring into his mean green eyes. "That's where I'd start if I were them, with your psych evaluation. There's something seriously askew with a police officer who has no empathy for those less fortunate than himself — especially at Christmas. Please move aside. *You're* holding up the line," she added, hearing footsteps behind her.

She didn't need to see Paul Morgan's gaze dart away briefly, then come back bold and defiant and aimed above her shoulders, to know whose step it was. And it wasn't as much a step as the rhythm of the distinctive creak-and-rub noise a policeman's thick leather utility belt made when he walked. It belonged to a tall, lean man with a heart as warm as his eyes were cool blue. The early frost at his temples was a tribute to his wisdom, and it belied his boundless strength and verve. Miles Richardson was her friend — her protector, her ally, her hero. He was her beacon in the dark, her cavalry on its way and . . . Well, she was afraid that calling him anything more would be presumptuous.

"Hey, Morgan, how's it goin'?" His deep, throaty voice soothed her like a warm blanket . . . but his affable tone was irksome. "Missed you at Remmy's for the Army-Navy game last Saturday." He chuckled. "Army's bound to get it right eventually," he said, and at the same time his fingers curled around her upper arm and squeezed gently. "I heard about your troubles; hell of a time for the heat in your cruiser to go."

Morgan flicked the remains of his cigarette out the door and shrugged. "I got a loaner. Mine'll be back tomorrow."

"Good. Another perk to having a motor pool, huh?" Miles began steering her sideways around Morgan's cumbersome form in the doorway, past him, out onto the slush-covered sidewalk beyond the heavy security doors, and into the dull morning light. She hunched her shoulders and shivered against the cold. "Crank 'er up and stay warm out there, man."

Both Morgan and Natalie made telltale noises in their upper chest — passive acknowledgment and active contempt. Only the second sound concerned Miles so, still grasping her arm, he quickly guided her up the sidewalk while she sputtered for words.

The metal door closed and she spoke.

"Stay warm? In his car? With the heater on? While women and children and . . . and real men with real honor and true character freeze . . . and go hungry because *he* threw more than four gallons of stew in a Dumpster? Then he threatened to arrest anyone standing in the alley after he put me in the back of his car." Her soft snort was derisive as she walked and angled backward to look into his face — the angry flush in her cheeks warding off any chance of frostbite. "A couple of the older guys actually stayed. They were willing to be arrested on whatever trumped-up charge that . . . that *person* could dream up just for a warm bed and a cold breakfast. And do you know what? He *knew* that and didn't arrest them, and now they're out there and . . . You know, I don't know how you can keep a civil tongue in your head when he's around."

He looked down at her, noticed he was still holding her arm, and let go. "Because if I take him on and draw a line in the dirt, it'll only get worse for you and your friends. This way, he's not fighting with kids his own size; he's bullying good, kind people who can't really fight back. And everyone sees it. All his misdemeanor charges are legitimate infractions but so innocuous, and frequent, they've become a waste of everyone else's time." He laughed quietly. "Calling a public defender every time was a stroke of genius, by the way. They hate him."

She shook her head. "I don't get it. We're not hurting anyone. Why does he hate us so much? Me, especially. It feels like everything I do is against the law, and it isn't." She hesitated. "Better me than the Posers, I guess. They're too old . . . and poor Lynie would take it as an act of terrorism but . . . but why at all? Why does he go out of his way to be mean to us?"

This was not the first time she'd asked him. Nor was it the first time Miles had no answer — a sporadic suspicion perhaps, but nothing concrete, and nothing he wanted to dig into.

He sighed, and with a voice filled with caution, he said, "Just so you know, I'm pretty sure those old fellas weren't hanging around to get arrested last night. One of them flagged me down to give me a heads-up. They're keeping an eye on you, especially when the Posers aren't around." He cast a stern look. "And they're putting themselves at risk to do it. I'm not the only one who worries. You're not safe out there alone."

"I'm careful now, I promise. I never unlock the doors or get out of the car until I see someone familiar. Everyone knows I don't carry cash or credit cards or even a bottle of aspirin with me . . . Plus that magnetic sign you got me lets all the new folks know . . . *Plus* I'm done, packed up, and halfway home before dark." She took a breath. "I'm careful."

He was unconvinced. One of her two trips to the ER after being mugged was in the back of his squad car. That's how they met three years earlier. That's what flashed through his mind whenever he had cause to worry about her, which was often.

The first time he laid eyes on her, she came staggering from the shadows of a dark alley onto the street in front of his cruiser. He nearly killed her. At first, with only the glow of the streetlights for backup, it was hard to make out her age. Young, he'd decided; too young. Her short dark hair was scruffy and wet from the rain and motor oil on the alley floor where she'd fallen; her hands were scraped and bleeding. Her big brown eyes were wide with shock and fear as she denied a sexual assault. Mechanically, she lamented the tear in the knee of her jeans . . . She cried understandably and seemed quite normal under the circumstances until he assured her that an ambulance was on its way.

That's when the world seemed to tip a bit and he was forced to admit that he simply didn't have as much control of it as he thought. He watched while she used her split lips and swollen, deeply discolored jaw to announce that the prohibitive cost of an ambulance, where unneeded, was unnecessary and wasteful. Then she emphatically declared herself to be a clear-thinking adult woman who was capable of and adamant about refusing the assistance of one. Period. Although she wouldn't mind a quick ride to the ER in the back of his car; she was concerned about her ribs. Also, she promised not to bleed on anything.

He never recovered. Since that night she'd been a constant source of wonder and awareness, understanding and appreciation, and a deep, searing pain . . . in his ass, who tugged at his heart like no one else before.

Natalie was the product of a foster system that actually worked more often than it failed, truth be told. Raised off and on the streets by her birth mother, by her mother's friends, and by complete strangers from time to time, she was six years old when

DCFS stepped in to protect her. She was taken in by a family who loved her and taught her to not only count her blessings, but that if she shared them, they would be returned to her tenfold.

Miles was not unfamiliar with the philosophy; he simply didn't think it always worked the way it was advertised. And in Natalie's case he was certain it was being carried out to an extreme and that *tenfold* was a gross overstatement.

Okay, to be fair, most of her flock of displaced people considered her and her friends to be compassionate souls willing to help when they could, and they were grateful. But were there people who knowingly took advantage of her? You bet. People who unintentionally abused her kindness? Absolutely. Was she aware of it? She firmly denied it, but she wasn't gullible. Could he stop her? No.

They'd come to a T in the walk. Turning right would take them to the police parking lot and the impound yard on the next block; turn left and they'd end up in public parking. She automatically turned right. Impounding their cars was another game Paul Morgan liked to play.

"I called in a favor," he said, and she stopped. "It's in the parking lot."

Her smile was uneasy. "Truth: Did you call one in or do you owe one now?" A short wag of his head said he'd never tell, but she had long suspected he wasted most of his favors on her. She walked back to him. "Thank you, Miles. Someday —"

She stopped. It was always the same promise: Someday I'll find a way to repay your kindness to me. But she'd said it so often it was hard to believe anymore. She'd been working on a new one.

"Someday, after we open our soup kitchen, I'll be less of a bother. And you can come eat whenever you want. Also, you will have your own special chair at the head of any table you choose."

He nodded, yeah, yeah, sure, and motioned her away with his head — she was getting cold. A moment later he called after her. "I want a special bowl with my name on it, too." He heard her laugh — and tried not to enjoy it too much.

"Definitely. No problem. A mug, too," she said, not turning around.

"And a soup named after me."

"Clear or thick?"

"Doesn't matter." All her soups were good. "Surprise me." Then, as he thought about it: "Do you work today?" His panic was irrational, he knew it; so was the thought of giving her a police escort to the hospital where she worked.

She stopped short, consulted her mental calendar, and visibly relaxed. "No. I work the weekend." She looked back at him, smiled fondly, and delivered the two safest and most sincere words she knew: "Thank you."

"Try to stay out of trouble."

His admonition sounded more parental than friend-like . . . and light-years from beloved. They both cringed and kept moving — it had become an unsettling habit with them.

The security door opened to release another wrongdoer and Miles hurried back to go inside.

Chapter Two

She could have let spending the night in jail ruin the rest of her day. Many people would have taken it as a dark omen and locked themselves in a padded closet.

Not Natalie. Either fate or her own DNA, possibly both, had determined that her life be busy and full. And significant — to *her,* at the very least. However, staring into the back of her Cavalier wagon with her hands on her hips, it was difficult to recall *why.*

Frustrated didn't come close to covering the sweep of emotions she felt taking in the culinary carnage before her. Stew from the night before, that hadn't made it into the Dumpster, had splattered throughout her car when Officer Morgan pitched the pots inside. All the way to the driver's seat, she noted with an angry huff. To that, he'd added open bags of bread, unwrapped packages of paper bowls, her precious propane camp stove, and its stand to top it all off.

And then he'd called for a tow truck.

She worked as a lab tech at the hospital — microbial contamination and sterility were a part her business; cleanliness was her nature. The wanton waste in the back of her wagon made her lip curl in disgust.

Sighing, she plucked out three unopened boxes of plastic spoons. The coffee urn Miles gave her two years ago for her birthday had been tipped and tossed but upon inspection didn't appear to be damaged.

She was no Pollyanna, but she was glad of one thing: She was a quick learner. And so, because this wasn't the first time her car had been Morganized, most of the mess was contained on the cheery plastic tablecloth she'd taken to draping her cargo area and tailgate with.

Parked near the basement entrance of her apartment building, she began the cleanup process that today would take twice as long as usual — denying her the warmth of her bed that much longer.

The stove and the urn and anything else that was salvageable were set aside while she gathered everything else up in the reusable table cover, tramped through several inches of old crusty snow, and shook it into the trash receptacle — most was frozen solid and came off in chunks. She wadded up the plastic — which was not as stiff as it once was, due to repeated washings — as if it were a bedsheet, grabbed the urn and whatever else she could carry for her first trip down the basement steps into the super's service area.

Say what you will, but it was Natalie's experience that most people were not like Officer Morgan. Henry Fish, her building's manager/maintenance man, had graciously offered her the convenience of the deep multipurpose sink in his utility room to clean her equipment.

She put the cloth into warm soapy water to soak and went to fetch the rest of her stuff. Washing and drying it all, she scowled and added the dented scratch on her camp stove to Paul Morgan's ever-growing list of offenses — then shuffled it back to a five-by-eight-foot cage that was her storage unit.

She paid Mr. Fish a tiny bit extra every month to keep a small chest freezer plugged into an extension cord inside. And where most of the other units were crammed with boxes, bikes, bassinets, and tennis rackets, hers was lined with metal, paint-covered shelves she'd salvaged a few years back. On them she placed her valued supplies and paraphernalia — from adhesive strips to cheap toothbrushes; free samples to thrillingly cheap bargains; shoe boxes to banana crates she was always watching for and gathering because to people who live on the streets it was generally the smallest, simplest things that mattered the most.

Her eyes felt dry and heavy when she finally snapped the lock closed and shook the wire door to make sure it was secure. With a slow step and muscles stinging with exhaustion, she climbed the stairs to her fourth-floor apartment — the elevator being too far and too unreliable to bother with.

She thought at first that the door to her place was jammed — the key fit, the knob turned, but it wouldn't budge. Old buildings were like that, the walls shrinking and expanding with the weather as if they were breathing. Slamming against it with her shoulder caused it to bounce, first open and then closed, and that's when she realized that something was blocking it — that something was wrong.

"Aldene?" She knocked. "Aldene? Are you there? Hello? It's Natalie." Apprehension stirred. Her voice rose. "Aldene. It's Natalie. Open the door." She tried Spanish. *"Abra la puerta. Aldene? Estas ahi?"*

Knocking again, harder this time, she was prepared to scream the door down when she heard movement and muffled voices on the other side of the door. A baby started crying and she muttered a soft, "Thank God," and then waited patiently for the door to open.

"You are here." Aldene's expression was a vivid array of emotions: fear, relief, joy, concern. "I have been worried. All night, I worried. I did not know what happened to you. Come in. Come in now." Natalie obeyed, taking note of three Hispanic men standing to one side — two teens and a man much older than everyone else in the room. She recognized them, but not by name, from the soup lines. Aldene hurried to explain their presence. "This is my uncle Luis and my cousins Pirro and Feo. I sent Arturo to get them when you did not come home. I waited too long and was very afraid. I asked them to go find you . . . to all the places you go."

"Oh," Natalie said. The situation was becoming clear to her. "I got arrested."

"Yes, yes. I know this now. They saw. When they came to say, I made them stay. To be warm. To be here with me. Please do not be angry."

She was shaking her head, denying any annoyance, when Arturo, Aldene's ten-year-old son, appeared in the bedroom doorway — his sisters, Crista and Deina, five and three respectively, at his heels. She smiled at the sweetness of their sleepy eyes and bed-heads and said, "Good morning. Are we making too much noise?"

They shook their heads in unison and stood watching . . . and worrying.

There it was, the crack in Natalie's armor — the one thing she had no defense against and no way of dispelling, not even temporarily. The always-silent disquiet in the eyes of the children who lived on the streets remained even after they were fed and made warm and sheltered in a safe place with the people they loved. Once the uncertainty and foreboding touched their souls it stayed. No matter how much their conditions improved, they knew tomorrow had no guarantees.

Natalie knew. She'd walked in those small shabby shoes once upon a time — until her mom and dad arrived and gave her the greatest gifts of all: hope and love.

"Good," she said, clutching her big purse and striving to keep her smile cheerful and optimistic despite the fog of fatigue that was rolling in quickly and numbing everything in its path — mind and body. "Well then, we should probably think about breakfast. I know there's oatmeal and milk and, oh" — she grinned at the children — "maybe raisins to put in it. Bread for toast and maybe a few eggs and —" She stopped suddenly and made a quick U-turn decision. "Actually, you know what? I'm beat. Aldene, you know your way around here. There isn't much but you can help yourself to whatever food you can find. I'll get more groceries later." Making her way over the blankets and backpacks, the sparse furniture and large boxes of used clothing in the overcrowded two-room apartment she rented, all she could think of was quiet and sleep, and neither seemed likely where she was.

By the time she reached the bedroom door she was saying, "*I* am going to take a peek at little Franco to put some sunshine in this dreary day, grab a couple things, and find myself a place to sleep for a few hours."

Looking down into the blanket-lined bottom drawer of her bureau at the beautiful little cherub warmed her to the marrow — and validated what she was doing with her life . . . *and* how she'd spent her night. She grazed the back of his chubby fist with her index finger, lingered for a moment in her heart's yearning, and then quickly plucked her personal pillow and comforter from the closet and a flat bedsheet from a storage hamper.

"Don't forget to get to the free clinic as

early as you can," she continued. "The baby at least needs his vaccinations and they all need flu shots." Aldene had mentioned having a visa more than once, but Natalie never asked to see it. So just in case, she added, "They don't ask questions. It's important. And Mr. . . . ?" Emerging from the small bedroom, she made eye contact with Aldene's uncle Luis.

"Pena. Luis Pena." When she smiled and nodded acknowledgment, he added, "Thank you. For the night here. For what you do for Aldene and the little ones."

"You're welcome. But I'm afraid you and your sons have to leave as soon as you've eaten something." She was heading for the door again. "Mr. Fish is a good guy but my lease has a maximum occupancy of three, and while he and I have agreed to squish all the kids together to make one large adult, I do, unfortunately, have a couple of neighbors who are sticklers for district ordinances and feel it's their civic duty to complain," she said, explaining their bigotry as kindly as possible. "And I'm already in a little trouble with my —"

"But no. Do not leave," Aldene interrupted, emerging from the kitchenette, moving quickly, pushing at the children to get dressed. "We will go. You will sleep here.

This place belongs to you."

"No, no. I'll be fine. Eat. Go to the clinic." She opened the door and looked back at the family of eight as they stood watching her, saying little, asking for nothing. "Good things are coming our way, you'll see. There's a women's shelter with transitional housing and free child care that might have room for you soon." Closing the door, she added, "We can talk later."

Back in her storage unit in the basement, she locked the gate from the inside and used clothespins to hang the bedsheet on the outer wire wall. She unrolled an old yoga mat, covered that with a well-worn runner rug, and covered *that* with two of the Mylar blankets she'd bought in bulk — or salvaged from stretchers at the hospital. She hated waste. Wrapping herself in another shiny blanket, she then tucked herself into a lovely warm cocoon with her comforter, put her head on the pillow, and turned off her mind.

This was not her first sojourn at Chateau de Cage.

Chapter Three

She heard a voice but didn't open her eyes until the gate of her coop rattled.

"Come on now," said Henry Fish. "Your friends have gone out. Go upstairs to your bed. You'll rest better."

"Hey, Mr. Fish." Natalie's voice was hoarse with too little sleep. Clinging to her blankets, she struggled to a sitting position, contorting her back to work out a kink. "What time is it?"

"Half past one."

"And they just left?" Hours had passed. Aldene and the children would be in line at the clinic for hours, she thought, climbing slowly to her feet.

"No, they've been gone for some time now. I just didn't know you were down here until I came for my ladder to change the lightbulb in ol' Ms. Lenty's kitchen."

She smiled. Henry Fish was maybe fifty-five and just a little chubby, but he wasn't five foot four unless he stretched out his spine as far as he could and stood on his monkey wrench. Where a more average-sized man could have managed with a chair, the high ceilings in the old building were a challenge for him.

"It seems to me that you help Ms. Lenty a lot. I think she's got a little thing for you," she said, grinning as she unpinned one corner of her sheet to see him.

He harrumphed and pointed a finger at her. Ms. Lenty wasn't a day less than eighty years old. "It's the old ones that keep me busy, not to mention employed. Besides, blue is not the color of my true love's hair . . . This month she's trying a rusty brown with sulfur-colored stripes, streaks she calls 'em. The top of her head is . . . is a . . . well, she's like some dazzlin' exotic bird, that one. And she promised long ago that she'd peck my eyes out if I strayed, and I don't trust her not to."

Natalie chuckled, her eyes twinkling with humor. She unlocked the wire gate and stepped out, clutching all her linens close, holding them high off the dirty concrete floor. She started fumbling with the latch. "How's she feeling? Is that chest cold passing on its own? So many people at the hospital have ended up on antibiotics."

"Here." He reached forward to snap the padlock closed for her. "She's better, but you're not thinking all this chitchat is distracting me from the rent you still owe, are you?"

She grimaced. "Not entirely. I mean, I am glad your wife is feeling better." She smiled. "And I do think Ms. Lenty has a little thing for you."

"And . . ."

She sobered and sighed. "And my whole paycheck will go to rent next Friday. I swear."

"That will cover the month before last. What about last month and this month and next?"

"No, no. I have some overtime coming. Enough to cover half of last month," she said brightly, dimming when the disparity between what she would have and what was still overdue roared and reverberated in the air between them.

"And when I am forced to turn off your electricity and you must eat cold food in your cold apartment? These things are not in my hands, dear girl. I must answer to others same as you."

"I know. I know." And she did know. Henry approved of her undertakings and admired her devotion to those less fortunate. It pained him to have to enforce the rules she'd contracted to obey, simply to do his job. Over and over he'd pushed the limits to breaking for her. It wasn't fair. It was not her intention to help some people at the expense of others. "And you shouldn't have to be answering any questions about me. I'm sorry. And I *will* pay you — before the New Year. All of it. I promise." Her intent was sincere, but perhaps not feasible.

The small inheritance her parents had left her was gone — but gone in a way in which they would have approved, she believed. She'd either sold or consigned nearly everything of any real value that she owned and had pressed her foster brother's charitable nature to its limit — or so it would seem by the annoyed impatience in his voice whenever she called him lately.

"I'll get the money, Mr. Fish. It's flu season, there'll be lots of extra shifts at work and —"

"And you must give to yourself before you give to others, young lady," he broke in, trying to sound stern. "You'll soon become one of them, and then how will you help?" He nodded sagely.

"I know." Her shoulders drooped in defeat. "That's what Miles says, and deep down I know it's true, but I don't know what else to do. I . . . The people at my church are great, you know? They do so much — the food and clothing drives, hot meals three days a week, raffles to make money for the free clinic — *so* much. But there are still so many holes left open. I can't sit in my nice warm apartment without wondering what those people are eating the other four days of the week . . . or wondering about the ones who don't know or can't get to the church or the clinic. I'm awake all night in my nice clean bed worrying about the parents who might not know about the Takes-a-Village shelter, about the children."

Her gaze caught on his; on the hazel-green eyes filled with understanding and sympathy even as his more personal concerns loomed large and heavy before him. She smiled at him fondly and snaked a hand from her layers of warmth to pat his arm.

"Don't worry, Mr. Fish. It'll be fine. And you're right. I won't have anywhere to freeze and store my soup if I don't pay my rent. First things first, right? I'll get you the money. There isn't a better time in the year to make extra money. Flu season *and* Christmas." She started shuffling backward toward the metal door protecting the stairwell. "Everyone's looking to take on temporary help — I was a pretty good waitress in high school, you know, and . . ." And for years she'd given every job she'd come across, temporary or otherwise, to those who hadn't seen a paycheck in quite a while, who needed to feed their families and put a tiny patch on their pride. "I'll figure something out. I can cook more than soup, you know. I'll have the extra money in no time."

She let the heavy fire door close before he had a chance to say anything more and took a moment to lean against the inner wall, discouraged. There was never enough money to go around — and goodwill did have its limits. Even her old friend at the service center wanted cash now to replace the battery and alternator in her car because she'd used up all his patience months earlier on the repairs to someone else's car that had been more dire, more expensive, and more of a necessity for his new, hard-won job — just another unexpected, unavoidable, and overriding circumstance that seemed always to be lying in wait for her.

Truth be told, they weren't that unexpected anymore.

Reluctantly, she rearranged her mental budget to put off the repairs on her car for another month or two — three months if she wanted service for her cell phone sooner rather than later. She was missing the luxury of instant communication.

Putting one tired, lead-footed step in front of the other, she started up the stairs, weary with the fact that life was always so . . . *complicated.* Oh, she knew if it was perfect or easy it would have no meaning or purpose or value. But couldn't there be a happy medium in there somewhere?

A few nights later, as a light rain turned to a freezing drizzle, Miles got wind that Natalie's soup was being served under the bypass bridge off Market. But not by Natalie.

It was his custom to make a drive-by whenever he heard she was out — usually twice, three times if he had the time — until he was certain she'd packed up and gone home for the night. Nights he didn't hear about her, nights he knew there was no meal being served at her church . . . those nights he worried and almost always found some lame excuse to drive past her apartment building to see if her car was parked in the back.

He was pathetic. He admitted it freely. He'd tried dating women his own age: ambitious women, interesting women who weren't constantly throwing themselves into danger's path — he'd found them ordinary and boring. Natalie, on the other hand, was impulsive, reckless, unpredictable, contradictory; too good, too young, and too trusting . . . not to mention a freaking fiscal disaster, and she was constantly on his mind.

"No, she's fine and dandy," said Jack Poser, who, along with his wife and a deceptively timid young woman named Lynie Morris, were Natalie's most frequent partners in crime — breaking zoning laws right and left and flouting town ordinances every other night by feeding large numbers of people outdoors. Miles knew him to be dependable, banked on him to look out for her, and yet hadn't exchanged more than several dozen words with him at a time, ever.

"She's taking a few extra shifts at work. Helping out," he said, and then reconsidered, rubbing his near hairless head beneath his cap. "Probably more than a few because I haven't seen hide nor hair of her in more than a week." He smiled at Miles's frown. "No worries. She calls Janice near every day from the hospital to check on her stragglers . . . the folks who take a little longer to find us; she frets about them."

Miles nodded absently, observing and

cataloging every face in the crowd — male, female, and child — lined up peaceably around the two women and a second man he'd seen before who came to assist sometimes. The children all seemed to be attached to an adult, not nervous runaways he was going to have to chase down.

He tipped his head at the weary gathering, saying, "Tell those with the kids that I'll come back around later if they want a ride over to the family shelter."

"They get under your skin, don't they?"

"The kids? Yeah."

"No. The women. Our women. The ones we love." Miles turned his head slowly and looked at Jack more directly, his expression as guarded as it was tolerant. "They dig in and get under your skin so deep they can make you do any number of things you'd never think to do on your own. Me? I used to think being out in a cold rain feeding strangers when I could be warm and dry at home in front of my television was crazy . . . Well, technically I still think that. And when my wife did her charity work at the church for all those years, and let me be a couple nights a week to watch my programs . . . well, hell, it was worth every penny she shaved off our budget — *which* she didn't think I knew about — to use for this good reason or that good deed." He barely took a breath. "Still doesn't know, I bet. But it doesn't matter, never did. I could see the peace it gave her, doing what she could for others. It made her happy. And you want that for them, don't you? To be happy. So I was fine with it, until she took up with Natalie and headed out into the streets . . . out here in the heat and the blizzards . . . with God knew who, doing God knew what. And all you know about it is what you read and hear, isn't that right?" He paused. "Worried me sick. Of course, we'd been married a thousand years by then so I knew better than to forbid her to come out here, so there you go . . . I had to drag my ass up off the couch and out the door to keep an eye on her — protect her like I promised on our wedding day."

"Oh." Jack made such a production of looking suddenly shocked and confused it could have been a Broadway play. "I forgot. You're not married to her."

"Who?" Jack smiled, his eyes dancing with intelligence and awareness — and Miles looked away. He bounced a little to keep his blood moving, to stay warm, and hunched his shoulders against the rain-damp chill in the air. "Protecting is my job. I took the oath."

"Mmm. Doesn't matter. Even if you were married to her, you wouldn't be able to keep her from doing exactly what she wanted to do. In the beginning, before I knew what was what, I tried telling my Janice not to do something, and for my efforts I got burned breakfasts, dirty clothes folded up nice and put back in my drawers, no gas in the car . . . not a drop. I'll give her credit though, she didn't hold back on the sex, not once — but there was a certain lack of enthusiasm that was disturbing. Very disturbing."

Miles's composure broke and he laughed out loud; then slowly he sobered and accepted that old Jack Poser had him nailed to the mat. Still, he was tentative. "Yes, she's gotten under my skin."

"Like a bad rash."

He nodded. "An itchy one."

"So stop your suffering, man. Scratch it."

He looked directly at Jack, took a deep breath, and let it out. He'd never talked to anyone about Natalie before, not about his feelings for her anyway, and not about his reasons for keeping her at arm's length . . . Well, he'd always intended to keep her at a distance, but the fact was she'd never come too close.

"We're friends."

"That's good. That's where most of the love comes from. That's what makes everything else work right."

"We've been friends a long time. So long she doesn't suspect anything. She trusts me. Taking a run at her now would probably feel like an ambush. I don't want to scare her off."

"That young woman doesn't scare easily, you know that. And women like surprises."

Miles scoffed. "They do not. They can handle flowers and candy and gifts, maybe, but nothing that's going to alter their lives in any monumental way."

"That so? It's been my experience that any time a man puts himself out there, puts everything he's got on the line, especially his heart and including his pride, it's generally taken kindly and held with great care."

"Generally."

The gray-haired man gave him a hard look. "You see that girl doing it different, do you?"

Knowing *kindly* and *with great care* defined Natalie, his shame had him lowering his eyes away. However Natalie received the news of his passion for her, she would be gentle with it.

Still, there was one more obstacle for which the old man would be hard-pressed to find an antidote: "I'm almost ten years older than she is."

"Ah. I don't just watch TV, you know. Sometimes I read. Samuel Langhorne Clemens, Mark Twain, one of the wisest men to ever live, once said: 'Age is an issue of mind over matter. If you don't mind, it doesn't matter.' "

"It does matter. I was in the army before she went to middle school. I told her once that I was ten years old before my mom got a microwave — she thought that was why I related so well to the poor." He glared at Jack when he snorted. "I'm serious. *Nobody* could afford one before then — my mom was one of the first on our block to have one. Natalie has no perception of time; she never thinks about the future, *her* future . . . and her music makes my ears bleed. We have nothing in common. We're practically from different generations."

"You make it sound like you're old enough to be her father. Yes, dating her when you were in the army would have been very wrong. But you're both adults now. You have the safety and care of these people in common. Your history and your tastes in music are what you share, how you get to know and appreciate each other." He bumped his shoulder to Miles's. "She lives in the present, the now. How good are you at that?"

Maybe it wasn't his best grammatical tense — present. He loved history. Not necessarily his own, but as a subject in general, it fascinated him. Natalie loved to cook and focused on what she saw and knew to be true in the moment.

And he was concerned about the future, nothing wrong with that. Not overly so, but he did spend time planning and preparing for something that might never happen — a reality for her that she'd faced and lived with every day of her life.

They *were* different, more like opposites. Not like magnets that attract one way and repel in another, but like interlocking puzzle pieces that fit.

"Compromise, too . . ." Jack was still talking. He talked a lot, actually — an odd thing to realize after all this time. Miles's gaze traveled in the direction of the old man's wife who, if they, too, were puzzle pieces, would be the quieter, less chatty of the two — like he would be if he and Natalie ever . . . "That's the key to it. You have to compromise on everything. Let her have her creamy peanut butter if she keeps plenty of grape jam on hand. Let her have the bed when she's sick and she'll take the couch when you are, *plus* she'll bring you soup and water and cold cloths for your forehead and give you backrubs with baby lotion —"

"Yeah, okay, thanks . . . for the pep talk. I should get going before —"

"Pep talk?" They faced one another square on. "If I haven't made it clear that this is *me* kicking *you* in the ass, then I'd better start over from the beginning." Miles opened his mouth to stop him, too late. "The wife and I are tired of watching the two of you, year after year, mooning and pining over each other and then walking away like strangers. It's depressing . . . and annoying . . . and stupid." Miles quickly decided the man was just too old to clock. "Damnedest thing we ever saw, the two of you. So now is the time. Step up like a man and tell her how you feel. Grab her up and kiss her. On the mouth. Kiss 'er till her toes curl. Hang on to her. Take her home. Chew her clothes off —"

"Jesus. Okay." He stepped away. "I get it. My ass is kicked."

Chapter Four

"It's been too cloudy to see it the past few nights, but as its orbit draws it closer and closer to the earth, it gets bigger and brighter and more powerful." Natalie watched the eyes of the children grow large with wonder. She'd mentioned the comet to their parents in passing and caught the young people's attention. She was glad they hadn't yet seen the cosmic phenomenon — it meant they spent their nights indoors. "It's called Comet ISON and astronomers say it is the brightest comet anyone alive has ever seen, that there hasn't been one even close to it since 1680."

The older boy fingered the edges of his food tray as he tried to figure the time lapse. The other four didn't seem to care . . . the tone of her voice declared it to be a really, really long time.

"That's over three hundred years," she said to their delight. "And it's shooting through *our* skies, now, for us. That's something. That's special."

She glanced back and forth at the set of parents and the single mother looking on and smiling as their children took a short excursion back into their childhoods — until her attention was reclaimed.

"Can you wish on comets? Like wishing on stars?" This came from a girl with braids and no front teeth.

"I don't know," Natalie said, wondering as well. "I don't see why not. They are leftover pieces of stars . . . stars that exploded thousands of years ago . . . That should count, right? It works for me."

Excitedly, the younger ones began to divulge several specific and detailed wishes they planned to make . . . most involving their upcoming Christmas gifts. Santa *and* a magic comet — it was a double whammy for sure.

Natalie glanced up, and in that lovely sort of unspoken language adults use to maintain the enchantment of Christmas, ascertained if they were aware of the Christmas Eve party there at the church. And with a slightly different expression she reminded them to submit requests for special gifts, if need be.

The members of Natalie's church dedicated and donated so much of who they were and what they had all year long, but the holidays were different. A true joy crept into their endeavors to create a Christmas spirit that was as much for themselves as for others — and especially for the children. It wasn't enough to simply share food and warmth and kindness; it was a time for the celebration of peace and love and goodwill toward all mankind. The air fairly vibrated with it.

She'd missed the last three meals served at the church since she'd taken an off-the-books job six days a week as an evening maid at the Doze Off Hotel and Lounge where she knew the manager. He would, from time to time, need cheap temporary help . . . not usually *her,* but he wasn't overly particular or nosy.

On this, her one night off, she'd stopped by only to pass out a short list of other jobs she'd heard about that might still be available.

"I remembered that you have a lot of experience with computers. This one might actually turn into something," she told a man named Parker. He appeared to be in his forties, but often stress and depression made people look older. And because jobs were few and too important not to be brutally honest about them, she looked him up and down and added, "I have a few suits, if you need to borrow one for the interview. And I have a barber friend who cuts hair for free sometimes — I'll give him a call. Do you need a voucher for the showers at the men's shelter? You'll need to scurry around tonight and then go in tomorrow, first thing. There might not be a lot of people around because of Christmas, but you need to get your application in soon. Can you do that?"

He first shook his head and then began nodding vigorously. He assured her he had a suit — clean and pressed at his cousin's house, a phone call away — and that he and his family were still paying by the week to stay at a motel she knew to be a little more than rundown. But he would be grateful for the haircut and, in fact, he didn't know how he could ever thank her enough.

"Get the job and come back when you're on your feet again. I'll have a whole list of ways you can help." She grinned at him. "Good luck, Parker. Bring your family back for Christmas Eve and tell me how it went."

The fellowship hall could squeeze in one hundred people at a time, a few more if parents held a child on their lap — more than double that number were fed every

Monday, Wednesday, and Thursday night when the space wasn't needed for other church activities. The needy came and went in unorganized shifts; those with homes or warm places to go came and went early, seeming to know there were others who would appreciate the heat more as the evening grew colder. Even so, strict hours needed to be kept. The doors opened at four o'clock and closed promptly at eight P.M. — when every nook and cranny and bathroom stall was inspected for stragglers who, along with those left eating in the hall, were locked out by 8:30 when the cleanup began.

"Oh, no, you don't." Janice Poser was small and delicate, elderly, full of energy, and really, really bossy. She plucked the wet towel and spray bottle of disinfectant from Natalie's hands and passed them off to one of the irregular volunteers they were always so happy to have. "This is the first night you've had off in two weeks. Go home. Go out with your friends. Enjoy it."

"I am." Natalie looped her arm lightly over her friend's shoulders. "I am out with friends and I am enjoying it. I hear that you and Jack and Lynie are handling the soup nights perfectly fine without me, so I'm feeling a little insignificant at the moment. I thought I'd come over to remind you that

I'm still around and make sure you haven't given my job away yet."

"You must have heard that I'm taking applications," said Janice, her eyes twinkling behind pink-framed glasses. "It hasn't been easy sorting them out, let me tell you. Smart young women who can cook like Gordon Ramsay and have no social life are few and far between."

"I'm not all that young." She couldn't debate the rest.

The older woman made a scornful noise before she pushed on the swinging door that led into the kitchen and announced, "This one says she's not all that young."

Three men and eight women in aprons stopped what they were doing, turned toward them, and burst out laughing.

Natalie simpered at them. "Very funny."

Smiling fondly up at her, Janice reached out with fingers bent from arthritis to touch her cheek. "Dear girl, the point I'm trying to make is that as young as you are, or as old as I am, there is more to our lives than just this."

"I know that."

"Do you? When was the last time you went out on a date?"

"A date?"

"Yes. That's when two people agree to

spend time together, both hoping to establish a lasting relationship . . . or score some mediocre sex."

Again there was laughter.

"I know what a date is. I just . . . I haven't . . . I don't know. No one's asked me."

Immediately, she thought of Miles — and immediately her heart sank. She knew his personal history contained a messy and painful divorce, and while he didn't seem immune to women in general — she knew he dated from time to time — he'd never shown any interest in dating *her.*

Tamping down on her disappointment, she let herself be distracted with the kind offers from sweet gentlemen who wished they were forty years younger and, of course, the convenient offer of an ambitious young nephew of one who, at present, was a sweat collector for a deodorant company with nowhere to go but up . . . She chuckled and nodded appropriately, knowing full well that she wasn't really treading water if she could feel the bottom of the barrel with her toes.

But Janice, knowing her too well, simply took her hand and led her to the exit at the rear of the room. Pushing her out into the cold, quiet evening, she said, "Go get him. Go make him a pie or a cake — put a heart on top with your initials in it. Go after him. You're a pretty girl. You've got plenty of color in your cheeks . . . but you could use a bit more than mascara to help him see that you're batting your eyes at him. A little lipstick to let him know you're willing to be kissed." She harrumphed and scanned Natalie's bulky winter attire. "Nothing we can do about that ridiculous coat at the moment, I suppose, but come summer . . . Oh. Stop being so logical and practical all the time — get crazy! Be bold, girl. Ask *him* for a date."

"Who?" She saw immediately that playing stupid wouldn't work. She shook her head. "We're friends. He's not interested in me that way. Don't you think I'd know if he was?"

"Not unless you've asked him face-to-face. Have you ever asked him?"

Natalie's face twisted into an *as-if* expression, then melted into an *okay-I'm-a-coward* frown. "But if I do and he doesn't, I won't be able to take it back," she said, voicing what she'd thought so often. "What if it damages our friendship?"

"Then it isn't much of a friendship, is it?"

Stunned by her response, Natalie was only vaguely aware of Janice leaning in to kiss her cheek, looking about the lot, and asking about her car.

"What?"

"Your car, dear, where'd you park?"

"Oh. Out front."

"Drive safely, then, and don't forget to get tomorrow night's soup out to thaw. I'll have Jack pick it up in the afternoon."

Last week Jack Poser had come too close to being arrested for breaking in and removing several bags of the frozen soup she had stored in her freezer in the basement of her apartment building. She nodded and turned to walk away.

"I'll warn Mr. Fish that he's coming."

The floodlights in the parking lot provided pool after pool of brightness as she walked through and then veered off, away from the front of the church. Gas cost money and she was only eight blocks up a busy street from home — and she was not above a small fib to keep her friends from worrying about her.

Lifting her eyes heavenward, she was foiled once again by the overcast skies — no stars, no moon, no comet. Obviously, there were crystal-clear nights when the harsh winds blew the thick clouds across the skies, out of the way, to reveal the magnificent Christmas Comet . . . she simply hadn't been out in one. Although, if she strained her imagination, she thought the night sky had a certain . . . glow, like lamplight behind a curtain.

She coughed. She sniffed. She became fully aware that her throat was sore and scratchy and groaned aloud. Great. It was the last thing she needed — but it was also an unspoken proviso that when you spent as much time in the general population as she did, a winter cold was as unavoidable as time passing.

Inescapable, like so many things in her life. A *happenstance,* like so many others.

Her destiny wasn't something she questioned very often. If it truly was the inevitable, predetermined course of her life, it didn't seem worth worrying about. It was what it was, would be what it would be — it was enough of a challenge getting from one day to the next without examining the impact of every little thing that crossed her path.

Except for Miles.

Trudging across the plowed but slippery asphalt toward the sidewalk, she noticed it was one of those times when she had a great many reservations about the wisdom of living willy-nilly to the whims of . . . well, God knew what . . . Some hidden power, an ultimate force, simple luck?

Did she really have so little control of her life, as some philosophers claimed? Did Miles have to remain always out of her reach or was it up to her to step forward and take hold of him, like Janice said?

Or — a really big OR — was it Miles's celestial mission to determine their future? Was it his lot to never know her better than he did right now? But then, in the same way, if her will was stronger than fate, then it stood to reason Miles's was, too. He could step forward and take hold of *her,* if he wanted to, if he was interested — unless she was meant to step forward first . . . and then —

And *this* was exactly why she didn't question her destiny very often, she thought wearily. Much better to put one foot in front of the next in the direction of her warm apartment and sleep, and let tomorrow be what tomorrow would be.

At least that's what she was thinking before she realized she was hearing a voice. She had the impression it was far away so she was surprised when she turned to find a young woman only two or three yards away, running after her.

"Please." Her voice was softer than the wind — her face was pale as the snow on the walk and almost as dirty. "Please stop.

I'm sorry. Please. I need —"

She stopped, panting for air, and that's when Natalie saw she was shivering . . . and hugely pregnant.

"Oh, my gosh! Did you come for dinner? Come on, come on. We'll go back. You're not that late. It'll be all right." Natalie unzipped her big coat and tried to stuff the girl inside with her, under her arm, but gave up quickly. Removing her coat and pushing the girl back in the direction of the church, she wrapped it around her saying, "Have you come far? Where are you staying? Do you have a place to stay?" The girl's quiver was a yes-no. "Do you know about the women's shelter? What about Takes-a-Village over on Dover Street? Have you tried them? I don't think I know you," she said absently. She gave a feeble half-laugh and encouraged the reluctant girl to move on. "Doesn't matter. We'll get to know each other. Let's get inside and warm you up; get some food in you. I'll call both places. We'll find you a place to stay."

"Please. They said you would help me. I can't stay here. I want to go home. Please. Help me." She came to a full stop. "I need to go home. My baby can't be born here. Please help me."

Only the warm clouds from her rapid

breathing kept her tears from freezing.

"No, no. Now don't cry. That never helps. Let's get inside. We'll figure something out."

"He'll find me."

"Who?"

"People know this place. And he knows I need to eat." She glanced at her belly and held it tighter. "He's smart. Really smart, you know? He'll look everywhere there's free food. Please. People know about this place. He'll come for me. I need a safe place. I need to go home. They said you would help me. I don't know anyone who —" She was getting quite frantic in her fear. "I have some money. I just need help. We aren't safe."

"Okay, okay." They put their backs to the church and started up the street, the girl scanning constantly, shrinking from every car that drew near and then passed them. "Whoever it is won't hurt you. I know a policeman who —"

"No!" She balked. "No cops."

"Stop it." Using her arm to get the girl going again, she became stern. "Listen to me . . . what's your name?"

"Caroline."

"Listen to me, Caroline. I'm happy to help you but not if you're going to be stupid. If someone is after you we need the police . . .

unless you've committed a crime . . ." She thought about it briefly. "No. Even if you're in trouble with the cops he's still our best bet. He's a friend. He'll help us. Come on. I'm cold."

Huddled together, she kept the girl moving forward, fielding every piece of panic and protest with a positive pledge of a solution and wishing for the millionth time that she'd paid for the cell phone service that would make it so much easier . . . and safer.

It wasn't as if she didn't understand when she was doing something impulsive and ill-advised — she did, every move along the way. And it wasn't as if she didn't feel the peril and fear — she did, the whole time. But too often her choices were too limited: act or walk away. In this case it was take the girl to the closest safe haven she knew — her home — until arrangements for her trip could be made . . . or leave her in the cold. Seemed like a no-brainer to Natalie.

There was no way they could avoid going in the front door of her apartment building; all the other doors were locked by nine o'clock. That meant a pass by the security camera on the first floor, a ride in the elevator, and a walk down a hall of snoopy neighbors with a whimpering girl. Assuming that Aldene and the children were still there — and she hoped they were — Mr. Fish wasn't going to be pleased.

But once they were inside her apartment, their reception was as she expected. Aldene took over. She wrapped Caroline in all the blankets she could find, cooing in Spanglish the entire time. Natalie stood in a rigid shiver nearby, rubbing her arms through her thick sweater, still wearing her gloves.

"You'll be okay here for a second while I go down the hall to use the phone." A little dazed, Natalie looked around. The kitchen registered a thought. "Maybe some soup? I make great soup."

Caroline nodded and spoke through chattering teeth. "I heard."

A weak chuckle. "Okay. I'll be right back. You're safe here."

A moment later she was bouncing outside Sara Lenty's door, listening to the television through the door without trying, waiting for the ancient woman to get to her door and peer through the peephole. "It's just me, Ms. Lenty. Natalie. I'm sorry it's so late. I need to use your phone again, please."

Chains rattled and the doorknob squeaked a little before it swung open to Ms. Lenty in the thick pink terry robe her niece had given her two years ago on her eighty-first birthday.

"Natalie."

"Hi. I'm sorry to bother you so late. I wouldn't if it wasn't important."

"Oh, for goodness' sake, come in before you wake the nosey parkers." She squinted through thick glasses. "Lord, girl, you're freezing. What's happened?"

As lightly as she could, she said, "Nothing. Really. I walked back from the church. It's much colder than I thought it would be, is all. Mmm. It's nice in here though." Like an oven. Natalie was envious.

The old lady nodded, pointing loosely in the direction of the phone with her arm, saying, "Devin Donahue, that new young weather boy they hired to do the local predictions on Channel Three, he's saying there's another big snow coming. Your homeless folk are not going to want to be out in it. Worst in years, he says. Freezing rain coming hard on its heels, he's sayin'." She half-sat, half-fell back into her lounger. " 'Course he's young so I checked around on the other channels and they're all sayin' the same. Bad night for the bums."

Natalie shook her head and tapped in the number to Miles's cell phone. *Bums* was a word from a different generation that, despite her good heart, Ms. Lenty couldn't seem to shake. She heard only one ring before he picked up.

"Did you lose it or put off paying your phone bill again?" Apparently, she'd used Ms. Lenty's phone often enough that it was on Miles's caller ID.

"Hi. Are you busy?"

"A little. Why?"

"Are you on duty tonight?"

"No. Why?"

"Are you like . . . on a date or something?"

"No." Impatience put a strain on his voice. "Why?"

"I think I might need your help with something."

Chapter Five

Having ascertained on the way home that the girl had barely over a hundred dollars to her name, Natalie made a quick side trip to the hidden tea tin of money she kept in her storage unit.

Yes, yes, a bank would be safer, but banks charged fees and had stiff overdraft penalties . . . There was more than one way to be robbed. Besides, her funds were never around long enough to collect any interest so there was no need for that sort of middleman.

She counted out what she thought would be enough to get a one-way bus ticket to Colorado — another unexpected, unavoidable, and overriding circumstance — and re-revised her budget to squeeze out, not all, but the greater part of her rent with not a penny left over.

"Take it," she said, when the girl made half of a halfhearted protest. "My address is on the paper. You can pay me back. And that's Miles's phone number. Please call him when you get to your cousin's house."

The navy bean soup Aldene heated up for them took the chill from her bones and helped her think clearer — her short gap of free time was slipping away. Aldene had very kindly done her laundry and kept the apartment tidier than Natalie ever had, but the stockpile of soup in the basement was sorely depleted; the rest of the coats and blankets she'd been squirreling away all year should be taken down to the car, and she wanted to go over the volunteer list to see who could take her place making sack lunches for the Backpack Buddies at the elementary school this week.

She found Caroline a larger, thicker coat; a scarf; and sturdier shoes in the donation box, and was pulling her own red-print ear flap stocking cap over her head when Miles knocked on the door.

The broad-shouldered man in her doorway set her defense shields to rattling before they slipped away, and she relaxed her guard against the world. Despite his loose, easy posture, she felt protected and perfectly safe whenever he was near.

"Hi."

"Hello." He was frowning but, as always,

his eyes were affable and kind. "What are you up to now?"

Over her head he spied the women and children inside her apartment and took a deep breath in preparation of explaining to her, yet again, what a generally bad idea it was — not to mention dangerous — to take homeless people into her own home; how once the precedent was set and word got out, it would become less and less a choice for her and more and more something people expected of her. And once that happened . . . well, she'd gotten the memo a few times before.

So before he could get the first word out, she placed her hand flat on his chest and gently pushed him back into the hall, stepped out with him, and closed the door.

"Natalie —"

"I know, I know. But it's temporary, only a few days, and we've been discreet. I promise." They shared a soft spot and she had no problem poking his. "The baby's only a few months old."

He stared into her eyes for a good long minute and then finally looked away with a small indulgent smile and a whispered, "Itchy rash."

"What?"

"Never mind." He took a deep, bracing

breath. "So what's up? How can I help you?"

"I need another favor."

He nodded, reconciled. "Are you in trouble?"

"No. I'm not. But that girl — Caroline is her name — she is. She's pregnant and she says the father, her boyfriend . . . I'm getting pimp from the way she's talking so . . . well, it doesn't matter. She says he's not a nice person and definitely not the type to be a good father to her baby. She wants to go home to Colorado." Her pause was merely to take a breath — there was no one she trusted more than Miles. "Actually, her parents live in Phoenix but she's certain he knows that so she's going to a cousin in Denver just in case he follows her . . . which isn't usually the case, I know, but she's so afraid and frantic that it'll be better for the baby, and hopefully her, too, if she goes somewhere she feels more secure."

"You've given her money." Not a question — more of an inference.

"Some. Not a lot. *But* if you take her to the bus station, to ease her worries about the boyfriend, you can also make sure she uses the money on a *ticket.*" She grinned and pointed, first, to her head and then at him, saying, "Two birds, one stone."

"Very clever." He was humoring her. "She knows I'm a cop?"

"Yes. And I told her not to hold that against you. I said that while you are an exemplary police officer, you are a much better human being and that she didn't need to be afraid of you unless there was a warrant out for her arrest." She smiled. "She assured me there wasn't."

"And you believe her."

"Of course."

"Of course. And I'm on my own with this. You're not coming along."

"Oh. Well, no. I thought . . ." She was surprised. It sounded to her like he wanted her along. "I mean, I can. No problem. I'll go with you if you'd like."

She'd like it. She simply hadn't thought of it — assuming, she supposed, that it would be easier for him to drop Caroline at the bus station and go straight home again rather than doubling back to her place once more.

Logical and practical, just like Janice Poser said . . . No wonder she had no dates.

Half-turning back toward her door, she quickly rearranged her night off in favor of the ride to the bus station and back . . . Janice would be so proud! But then Miles surprised her again.

■ ■ ■ ■

"Damn. What is this?" He asked, taking her jaw in hand to tilt and tip it in the dim hall lighting. He examined her face carefully, his expression both angry and concerned. "What's happened? Are you ill?"

"No." She pulled away, self-conscious. "I'm fine."

"If the circles under your eyes get any darker you'll look like a raccoon. I thought it was the lighting at first, but you've lost weight, too. Your face is thinner. When was the last time you ate?"

"Five minutes ago."

"Are you sleeping? Is there room in there for you to sleep, too? Seriously, you look exhausted."

"I'm fine. I've worked a couple extra shifts at work, is all . . . and I might be catching a cold."

"A couple. Technically that's two. You're this wrecked after two extra shifts at the hospital?"

If he wanted to be technical, not all her shifts had been at the hospital. She shrugged. "So maybe it was two couples." He looked disappointed. "Okay, two and a half couples, but three of those were on my weekend off so it's not as bad as it sounds."

"It sounds like you haven't had a day off in two weeks." He recalled the Posers dishing up soup without her last week and considered her. "I know you haven't paid your phone bill . . . What else are you behind on? How much do you need to get by?"

The appreciation in her eyes and the smile on her lips were, he saw, deceptive as her spine straightened and pride set in her jaw. "You're super sweet but too late, Mr. Got Rocks. I'll catch up with everything once I get paid . . . including my sleep. Plus, and this is a Christmas wish come true, that really great women's shelter in Beaumont . . . ? The one with transitional housing and child care? They have a place for Aldene and the children. They'll help her get a job and . . . I'm so pleased for her. They should call any time now." She laughed at the look he gave her. "I told them the Posers' voice mail was more reliable than mine." She let loose a short sigh. "I'm going to miss them. Do you think they'll forget and leave little Franco behind?"

"It wouldn't surprise me one bit." He shook his head. She was hopeless. "All right then, send your girl out, it's getting late."

"Okay. I'll just get my coat and —"

"Not you." Her suddenly crushed and confused expression had his pulses skidding. Had she always looked at him with that sort of vibrant anticipation? What about that eagerness; that fragile combination of hope and faith that was, at this moment, inspiring a similar mix in him? "Not . . . not tonight. You should sleep. You need to rest because . . . well, I was going to ask if you had plans for Wednesday night . . . for Christmas Eve."

"Oh." She was taken aback but he watched as pleasure flowed into her features, poured color into her cheeks, and restored that particular sparkle he cherished — that he abruptly realized was for him alone. "Oh. Well. You know that I usually spend Christmas Eve at the church . . . with you, when you come. Special dinner . . . Santa . . . Christmas hymns. . . ."

"After all that."

"Well, usually when it's my turn to have the holiday off, my brother comes —"

"Didn't you say he was going to Florida this year?"

"Yes. He is." She looked flustered — like she'd forgotten she'd told him . . . or maybe because she hadn't expected him to remember. His heart smiled. He remembered everything about her. "So instead of going home with him to be with family on Christmas morning, I agreed to work a double — volunteered actually, for both shifts because I had nothing better to do . . . and for the money, obviously."

"But you're still going to the church for Christmas Eve, right?" She nodded. "Good. I'll meet you there. We'll go out after."

"Together. Like . . . a date?"

"Exactly like a date." He probably imagined the small, involuntary squirm — but there was no mistaking her delight. "We'll do something special."

"What?"

He had no idea. "It's a surprise." For them both. "A good one."

"I love surprises."

"Of course, you do," he murmured in a deep, low voice before impulsively bending forward to plant a kiss on her cheek. The look on her face was staggering. How could he have been *so* blind for so long?

Eyes locked in longing and easy accord, he leaned past her to open the apartment door. "Let's go."

"Caroline?"

Using the girl's name was as much about respect as it was kindness and care — and Natalie's opinion that while he had plenty of all three, it was sometimes just as important to speak it as to show it . . . their last few minutes in the hallway being a prime example.

"Caroline." He gave a nod, promising to do better — especially with her.

Pulling his gaze away and offering a friendly smile, he said, "We should get going before it gets too late. Have you got everything?"

Bundled as thick and tight as a piker's money roll, Caroline held up the bag lunch Aldene had packed for her and nothing else, nodding.

Natalie escorted them to the main entrance for several reasons — to collect her mail, to make as much noise as possible so everyone knew that what had come in was now going out, and to see if Miles had any other magic up his sleeves. She was mesmerized.

She reminded the girl to call when she arrived at her cousin's and hugged her goodbye. "This is a good decision, Caroline — the kind good moms make." She stepped back. "Good luck." Then she turned to Miles. "Thank you for doing this."

"You're welcome." His gaze dropped from her eyes to her lips and her heart stopped. He put his fist under her chin and barely skimmed her lower lip with his thumb. Her lips parted, and when she audibly drew in a breath, his eyes closed and he sighed. Lowering his hand, there was a rasp in his voice when he spoke. "Get some sleep. I'll be devastated if you nod off on our first date."

She chuckled, still wanting a kiss.

Holding the door open for Caroline but still watching her, he saw the wish and grinned.

"Christmas Eve."

She couldn't remember the last time a happy dance surged through her like current through a live wire — a snappy rumba to the wall of mailboxes, a short version of Riverdance, removing mostly bills from hers, and then she boogied back to the elevator while flipping through them. Still grinning so hard her cheeks ached, she came across one from the DMV — time to renew again already? She peeled back the flap and peered inside — her entire body sagged.

Her car insurance had lapsed.

For the next two days she nursed the sick knot in the pit of her stomach — a canker of worry and stress, inflamed, growing at a frightening rate.

Eight hours of painstaking work at the hospital and another eight toiling at the Doze Off, she arrived home shortly after midnight each night to fall on the couch and sleep like the dead for five hours before getting up to do it again . . . And still, after working herself weary, her financial forecast looked bleak. There was never enough money.

And no one had to tell her how her situation came about — there was plenty of self-blame in the mix. It was as Mr. Fish said: she should have taken care of her own needs first so she could continue to help others, but . . . Well, there was no *but* to it. She should have . . .

But, the fact was she hadn't. And looking back, she couldn't drum up one ounce of regret for even a single penny she'd used to do what she could for those in need — for simple acts of kindness that anyone with a heartbeat deserved, that anyone with a heartbeat could not ignore.

Her one bright spot was Miles. The tightness in her chest would ease away and a dreamy smile curled her lips every time she thought of him . . . every time someone mentioned Christmas Eve . . . every time a surprise was mentioned or a carol hummed or the familiar scent of cinnamon and sugar cookies tickled her nose.

Just one night, one magical night with Miles, was her single Christmas wish. She wanted one night to ignore her plight, just one before she faced the consequences of her actions and had to push him away when he tried to fix everything. This time there was no way for him to protect her, not without ruining himself — which she would not allow.

"This is so exciting," Natalie said early Wednesday morning, giggling with Aldene and watching Arturo and Crista hopping and dancing in jubilation. The night before, the Posers had left the note saying that their place at the women's shelter was ready and waiting for them. Aldene had taped the note to the bathroom mirror so Natalie would see it when she got home. "Christmas in a place of your own . . . but oh, how I'm going to miss you." She jutted out her lower lip briefly.

"It could not have happened without you, my friend." Aldene rocked her back and forth in an exuberant hug. "I will never forget you. Not ever."

"You'd better not. I'll be expecting a dinner invitation in a few months and a full report on everything. This means a new school for you, Arturo. A little scary, I know, but you're a great guy, you'll fit right in wherever you go. And I asked — there's a Parks and Rec football team. Spring and fall."

"But I don't play football." Clearly, he didn't know where she'd gotten that notion.

"Soccer?" Ah! He grinned broadly. She hugged him. "Look at us. You being so American and me trying to be all international and cultured calling it football.

"Okay. So this is what we'll do. I have to leave for work in a few minutes. But I'll be home by four o'clock, and once I've changed for my *date*" — she simpered at Aldene, who beamed back at her — "I can run you over to Beaumont and still be back in plenty of time to catch some of the fun at the church. And meet Miles, of course — for our *date*. It's going to be a surprise. A good one."

They laughed together, and despite her great joy for the Pena family, she felt a pang of sadness. She'd grown accustomed to having a family around her again.

Chapter Six

Working in the lab over Christmas was more of an inconvenience than anything else. No one liked being in the hospital over the holidays, and great efforts were made by both the patients — to be well enough to leave — and the doctors — to safely discharge them — that lab work was minimal and routine, which made for a very slow day.

So when her relief showed up ten minutes early for her shift, Natalie threw her cares out the window and left forty minutes early from hers.

The bus was on time for a lovely change and she broke land speeds getting home. Aldene and the children were patiently restless while she quickly showered and slipped into the red holiday dress she wore every other Christmas instead of the midnight blue one that she sometimes wore for Easter as well. Her one pair of black pumps did duty all year round — she simply didn't dress up enough to need more.

But now that she was dating . . .

She was presenting herself for inspection by her small band of fans when a loud pounding on the door startled them all. Because no one she knew would sound so angry and menacing, she motioned Aldene and the children into the bedroom. She took baby steps to the door and peered out the hole. Someone had put their hand over it. Fear roiled inside her.

She was stealthily sliding the chain onto the door when the knock came again and made it rattle — no more stalling. She cracked the door and looked out.

"Ugh. What do you want?" Paul Morgan and another officer she didn't recognize stood in the hallway looking very official — as alarming as it was aggravating.

"Open up. It's business."

"What kind of business?"

"You want to open the door?"

"You want to tell me why?"

He produced a long white envelope. "This is a summons to appear in court." Clearly he would have preferred to serve it to more of her face but he smirked anyway. "Time and date are on the notice. The complaint is fraudulent checks."

"What?" She closed the door to free the chain and meet him head-on. She snatched the packet out of his hand and started to open it. "You can't just pull this stuff out of your hat, Morgan. I haven't had a checking account in years."

"Like I care? Fact is, someone else filed the complaint. I'm just delivering the good news."

She didn't recognize the name of the plaintiff but the check had been written to one of her favorite wholesale food dealers two years earlier for over two hundred dollars. Obviously, they'd been shut out when she closed her account . . . and she had less money now than ever before to pay them.

"And you just had to deliver it on Christmas Eve," she said, looking into his pitiless scowl. The other officer looked uncomfortable, like he might have put it off for another thirty-six hours.

"My gift to you."

"Why? Why are you like this? Why do you hate me so much?"

His eyes narrowed. "Because you think you're so good. You think you're so much better than everyone else because you're *so-oo* good." He swung his arm wide. "Out there every night feeding the hungry and clothing the poor like some self-appointed saint. Breaking laws because you think you have a higher purpose, because you think you're doing something better, more important than obeying a law. I've known people like you my whole life. Arrogant do-gooders who sit in the dirt for a couple seconds and then imagine they know all about being dirty."

She opened her mouth to object but he wouldn't give her the space.

"I know you: Always looking down your nose at people while you're handing them a stale sandwich — pretending you're some kind of martyr driving around in a crap car, living in a dump . . ." He nodded to the summons in her hand. "Blowing all your money, going to jail . . . making believe you're one of them. And for what? So everyone'll think you're this outstanding citizen. So someone'll give you a plaque for your service in twenty-five years? So you can delude yourself into thinking you're actually making a difference?" He bent slightly to get in her face. "You're dreamin', honey. Wake up. Nobody's watching. Nobody cares. And nothing ever changes."

He made to leave, but before Natalie could find her tongue, he turned back and tossed a small red box of stick matches at her. "You're going to need those." He turned his back and started walking away. "Don't say I never gave you anything."

Stunned, she watched him walk down the hall to the elevator. His partner looked back once, confused but not apologetic, and chose not to disturb the thick quiet that settled in the hall. The ping of the elevator doors opening brought her mind back like the bell at the end of a brutal round for a prizefighter — and everything he'd said came crashing in, blow after blow.

He was wrong. She knew he was wrong. He had to be wrong. That wasn't who she was, but he'd shaken her underpinnings.

Arrogant, self-appointed saint? If that's how he saw her, who else . . . A martyr in a crap car? Making believe she was one of them? Is that what she was? Was that her motivation, to impress other people? *Was* she deluded?

She startled when a gentle hand touched her arm from behind. She turned her head to look into Aldene's dark eyes, soft and understanding. The woman smiled.

"I heard. I listened. What he said, that is not you. And I feel that it is not you he is angry at — only what you do and only because he does not understand your goodness, or how it came to be in you." She turned Natalie to face her more directly. "I know proud men, my friend. Pride is good when it is earned. But there are times when it is possible to be too proud. Then it becomes a sickness. It is hurtful . . . and dangerous. To others, yes, but most to themselves. It chews on them." She looked back down the hall and then back at Natalie. "That one has seen the love in your heart before, I think, in someone else — and he was too proud to let it in. Too proud to let it touch his heart."

Natalie made a conscious effort to choose to believe her. She was no saint — and *she* knew she wasn't arrogant or deluded or out to impress anyone. The pleasure she derived from aiding those in dire straights was always riddled with the frustration of not being able to do more. So if feeling satisfaction in the help she could give was a sin, then she was guilty. Moreover, she didn't have to make believe that she knew what it was to live on the streets — she'd been there.

Maybe Paul Morgan had, too.

She did drive a crap car though . . .

And she was crap with money — she looked down at the proof in her hand and sighed. Glancing up again, she caught the concern in Aldene's eyes and smiled. And the children — standing at the bedroom door, the excitement and anticipation just below the ever-constant worry — brought a grin to her face.

"Well, what are you all waiting for?" She jammed the matches in her coat pocket and tossed the summons into her basket of bills and lapsed insurance policies. It was Christmas Eve and good things were coming, she could feel it. "Let's go! Aren't you excited to see where you'll be staying? Here, Arturo, I can take some of that. Did you let your uncle Luis know where you're going? Good boy. You're a lot of help to your mom, you know that? I'm happy that you'll be there for her — and that I can count on you to call me if you need anything." Her nod was encouragement for him to nod that he promised he would. "Diena, got your *cobija*? Don't want to leave *that* behind."

Fine, fair is fair. Now that it had been pointed out as a glaring reality, she would admit it: She broke a lot of laws.

She had only to take a quick look at Arturo in the seat beside her and glance in the rearview mirror at the woman, baby, and two small girls behind her, riding along through the night in her uninsured car, with no car seats for the younger children and no real visibility out the back window due to the overstuffing of clothes-filled boxes, to see it as an undeniable fact.

Beaumont was an hour and ten minutes away if they took the time to cross town and take the ramp to the highway — ten minutes less if they took the old country road . . . in spite of the slower speed.

But add the violations, the curvy country road, the manner in which the gas gauge was bobbing between low and empty, *and* the fact that it had begun to snow rather heavily, and Natalie found herself wishing she'd planned the trip differently. Planned *for* it, actually. This was just the sort of impulsive recklessness Miles objected to — and rightly so, she thought, checking once again on her passengers.

So when the sign and gate to Hope House came into view, the rapid drain of nervous anxiety added to the breadth of her smile and the bone-deep gladness she felt.

"I am so grateful." Aldene's voice cracked as she turned to face Natalie and the evening counselor standing just inside the door of the unit that consisted of two small furnished bedrooms, kitchenette, bath, and a small living area with a couch, a chair, and a table to outfit it. While the children ran from room to room repeatedly, Aldene walked half its length, forgoing the bedrooms, as if she was in a church — touching the chair and the top of the small, old Formica table like they had come from a queen's attic. "I know no words big enough." She blinked through the pools of tears in her eyes. "Or strong enough to tell you . . . I am grateful." She reiterated for the counselor, and to Natalie she added, "You are a good and true friend. I will not forget what you have done."

When her first tear slipped, Natalie closed the short distance between them to embrace her. Not for the first time, she felt Aldene's strength and courage, and her determination to make a better, safer life for her children.

This was the difference they all made together.

Still high on kid kisses, with her mind tightly wrapped around the idea that, yes, Santa could find you wherever you went to sleep, Natalie set out to collect her next Christmas miracle — Miles.

Having telephoned the Posers and having left a voice mail for Miles from work, she knew they wouldn't worry that she was a bit late. By her calculations she was still going to be there before Charlie Barton — who looked so Santalike in real life he was a shoo-in every year — finished passing out gifts.

She left Beaumont behind. The heater in the car was cranked up to high and the wipers were working furiously to keep the melting snowflakes off her windshield. The noise was an odd accompaniment to her hummed rendition of "Away in a Manger" — the radio having been broken for years.

It had been a long time since her Christmas Eve had held so much hope and soul-stirring joy.

And her mind was full of it when she crossed an icy patch on the road. The tail end of her car slid to the right and she was suddenly traveling the road sideways, the nose of her car too far into the wrong lane. Reflex had her crying out and whipping the steering wheel frantically to the right, overcompensating and swinging the rear radically to the left. She caught glimpses of snow-laden trees as she banked a hard left and then quickly straight on the road to regain an unsteady control of the car. She slowed to a mere crawl — heart racing.

Blowing out a slow, deep breath, she used her teeth to pull off her gloves for better traction on the wheel. And then, flexing the tremors from her fingers one hand at a time, she ever so gradually increased her speed, her senses hyper-alert and focused on the road.

No more humming — head in the car, not in the clouds.

And so it was that she offered extra prayers of thanks when she spotted blinking red lights through the heavy snow a few minutes later. Another car pulled far onto the shoulder. Another victim of the treacherous road conditions, she suspected.

It took only seconds for the hesitation she felt to shock and astound her. She couldn't see the face of her watch by the dash lights but she knew if she stopped to help she'd be even later than she'd planned; later than a girl ought to be on a first date. . . .

But her date was with Miles — the Miles who knew that if she said she'd be somewhere, she would be. The Miles who knew that if she was too late, she'd have a darn good reason for it and forgive her. The same Miles who wouldn't dream of passing by the stranded car without helping.

She pulled off the road but not into the crusty leftovers of previously plowed snow where she might get stuck. She simply didn't have the time for that.

"Huh," she said when she discovered her own emergency lights still worked.

A two-inch layer of snow covered the

compact sedan and there were no fumes coming from the tail pipe. *No gas* was the first thing she thought, and she could certainly identify with the frustration of that. *There but for the grace of God . . .*

There were two people that she could see inside the car — looking back at her and moving around. For a handful of reasons she was loath to get out of the car in her black pumps if she didn't have to, and decided she'd wait to roll the window down until they approached her.

She didn't have to wait long before both doors opened and a couple who appeared to be in their late teens or early twenties got out. The young man waited and spoke a couple times to the girl, who tumbled from the rider's side and floundered through the old and new snow to the front of the car where he joined her and helped her the rest of the way before the two of them started back toward Natalie's car.

Stepping fully into the beam of her headlights, they covered their eyes with their arms. She cut them to parking strength so they could still see where they were going and rolled down her window.

"Hello," she shouted out through the snow and the wind and the night. "Are you stuck or out of gas?"

"It's out of gas," the young man said when they reached the front bumper. The girl stayed there and he approached Natalie's open window. Gripping the frame of the door with both hands, he added, "It's a good thing you came along. We haven't seen another car out here for almost an hour."

"This wretched weather and Christmas Eve are two very good reasons to stay home and off the roads tonight."

"Actually, I can think of one more," he said, suddenly yanking open her unlocked door and reaching inside for her.

She screamed — in surprise, then fear — and struggled against his attempts to pull her from the car. It was only seconds before he thought of the seat belt and realized she wasn't going to be helpful in releasing it.

He didn't think twice. He drew his arm back as he grabbed the front of her coat and brought his fist down squarely on the left side of her face.

There was a sound . . . but if it was bone cracking, brain bouncing, mind splintering, or her cry of pain, she couldn't tell. Her next vague recollection was of hitting the ground sideways, snow scratching at her face. A leg and a boot pushed the lower half of her body out, away from the car, and she rolled onto her abdomen — pulling arms and legs and head inward, into a protective ball.

The sound of ice-crunching steps mixed with the thundering of her heart and the wind tunnel noise of her rapid breathing. The girl spoke like Charlie Brown's teacher from the other side of the car; the young man's voice was more distinct.

"Can't promise I won't hit you if you don't move out of the way," he said, illustrating this by swinging the car door against her hip as she twisted away. From inside the car, with the heater cranked up to high and the wipers working furiously, he added, "That's it, give us some space. You're a real Good Samaritan, you know that?" He laughed. "Santa Claus is gonna leave you something real special under the tree this year."

The timing of the engine changed when it was put in gear and her instincts went into overdrive. In an awkward sprawling crawl she relocated to the middle of the road, shivering, shaken to her core, and crying. There was a twinge of awareness that he was pulling away slowly — whether to avoid hitting her or spinning the wheels on ice she would never know — but desperation compelled her to make at least one appeal to his humanity before it was too late.

She opened her mouth, took a deep breath, and then suddenly it was . . . too late.

They were gone. The taillights of her car vanished almost instantly. Every red blink from the other car was immediately swallowed up by the night and barely holding the blinding darkness at bay. Snowflakes mingled with hot tears as she slowly pushed herself up on one arm.

"Please. Don't do this," she called after them in a whisper. She held her breath, listening with all her might, trusting beyond reason that they'd have a change of heart, that a rescue was nearby, that all was not lost — but she didn't hold on long.

Somewhere between the terror of being killed for her car and the horror of freezing to death, there was a moment of feeling completely stupid and foolish and . . . and betrayed. This was exactly the sort of thing Miles worried about and warned her of frequently. She knew better than to leave her doors unlocked and to roll her window all the way down — *and* she knew even those safety measures were still over the line of caution and common sense for a woman, alone, at night.

Right. Caution and common sense, she thought, plucking those three words from all those pouring into her pounding head and uselessly seeping away. She started a dizzy struggle to get to her feet. Oh yes, rational intuition — like the hesitation she felt about stopping; the instinct she overrode because . . . well, because . . . well, belaboring stupid and foolish wasn't going to keep her warm, she decided.

Staggering toward the emergency lights, the car gave her something to lean on, and even though it was as hard and cold as the road, she felt better on her feet, throbbing face notwithstanding. Looking around, she strained her eyes to see a light in a window, a streetlight, a headlight coming down the road . . . any light at all.

Red snow flurrying through the glow of the taillights held her foggy attention for a second or two, then she felt her way along the side of the car for the handle.

Had it been hours since the young man flipped the door closed or was it hard to open because everything was freezing rapidly?

The odor inside was familiar — stale cigarette smoke, dry sweat, and decayed food — and she took heart. Out of the whipping wind was better than in it, she decided, striving to hold on to her glass-half-full persuasion.

It lasted precisely five seconds. They'd taken her purse, too.

Chapter Seven

Shivering, creating friction between her coat sleeves and her arms, and stomping her feet to make sure she still had feeling in them, she tried to make out the contents of her new shelter.

Visibility was poor to none . . . and intermittent. She used her hands to search what she could reach around her, stretching her field wider and wider with each sweep. Cans, small loose papers, thin cardboard, a trash bag — her fingers brushed cloth and she grabbed up a sweater from the passenger's side floor. She swung her arm broadly across the backseat, feeling nothing, but that's when she remembered her gift from Paul Morgan.

Frantically, she dug into her coat pocket for the small box of stick matches, saying, "Oh man, are you going to hate yourself in the morning, Morgan."

There weren't many, maybe fifteen if she

was lucky — she had to make each one count.

Using only two, she identified one large and two small plastic bags, which she retrieved and emptied in the dark: a stocking cap, which she pulled on immediately, and a stiff, crusty, grease-stained bath towel that she snatched up gratefully.

Contemplating how best to use her treasures, her thoughts hit on the wealth of cozy clothing in the back of *her* car and got the unexpected thrill of recalling the trunk she had now. It could contain an old blanket or a forgotten gallon of gas — she was ever the optimist. Spirits soared. Visions of traffic flares danced in her head. She took the keys from the ignition and broke out of the cold into the bitter freeze again.

The small rear compartment held little — tools mostly, the spare tire — but she removed the thick rubber mat and draped it as well as she could over the driver's seat before she got back in. Once her body heat warmed it, it would hold off the cold and retain her heat better than the cloth seat.

"All right. Let's see what we can do here," she said aloud, combating the torment of silence. She shoved both legs into the large trash bag and tied the sweater loosely around her feet and ankles. Then, after wrapping the towel around her legs, she opened her coat and smoothed one small plastic bag over her lap, the other over her chest, and zipped herself in again. Hunching low and pulling her collar up high and tight, she drew her hands deep inside the sleeves and folded her arms across herself. Taking a deep breath, she closed her eyes and began the hardest part of survival — waiting for help to arrive. "Okay."

While her muscles ached and convulsed she reminded herself over and over that "Sh-Shivering is my friend. This is m-my body expending energy and g-generating heat. It's okay."

When her teeth stopped chattering and the spasms relaxed and became sporadic, the pain in her face was allowed to resurface — it was a challenge to think of it as a good thing.

She kept her head angled to watch for cars from both directions, using the side mirror to check the rear. Her face pulsed. She got warmer. The red lights blinked . . . blinked . . . blinked . . .

It rocked her awake — the wake of air the large van created when it passed by, shook the car, and startled her eyes wide open.

"No! No!" Her recollection was immediate, her panic acute. "Stop!"

Arms flailing, she untangled herself and went straight for the horn. She pounded on it, and then swore violently. She watched the van's taillights turn to red pinpoints in the dark. Inside her frenzy she noted the increase in visibility — the snow had stopped. She also registered the total lack of light around her. The battery was dead. "Shit and damn."

Tears stung her eyes before spilling over to her cheeks, and for the first time that night she felt real despair. Two solid minutes of good hard crying ensued — she was hopelessly stupid and naive and irresponsible and stupid and reckless and impulsive and stupid . . . *and* she was going to miss her date with Miles *and* she was going to die because anyone looking for her wouldn't know to look for her in someone else's car . . . *with* a dead battery and no emergency lights to draw their attention . . . and they'd drive right by like the van did and Miles would never know that she was in love with him and . . . She was stranded. She was going to die. She was going to miss their date and . . . She sniffed. Stranded.

"What I needed is a rescue fire." She sat up straight. "A big one. The kind stranded people on desert islands make for passing ships to see."

She sniffed again and slipped her hand into the pocket of her coat; smiled through the last of her tears. "The gift that keeps on giving."

She carried small boxes of matches everywhere she went; bought them in bulk and passed them out freely, liberally. To people on the streets, matches meant fire and fire meant warmth and warmth meant not freezing to death. Natalie knew this. She also knew a fire was as good as red flashing lights.

She didn't know how long she'd dozed off but she was awake now.

Removing the layers of her cocoon with care to be used again once the fire was made, she then stuffed one of the small plastic bags with shreds of paper and other miscellaneous pieces of trash from the floor that might burn and braced herself for her next mission.

There were no stars to be seen but the sky was more a dark gray than black — not useful to her ability to see but a comforting point of reference. She could see where up was.

The wind had subsided considerably as well — blowing biting, irregular gusts that seemed almost tropical to those a while earlier.

Using the car to feel her way inland, away from the road, she climbed over the brittle plow pile and then slipped and fell off the shoulder of the road. "Shit." Getting to her feet again, her pumps no help and no protection against the snow, she envisioned the trees she'd seen earlier as she skidded sideways down the highway.

She guesstimated they were twelve to twenty-five feet from the road and started counting her steps; hoping she was traveling in as straight a line as possible. Everyone knew that rule number one was don't leave your car, but she couldn't very well set it on fire, so staying nearby was as good as she could do.

With her survival kit rolled up under one arm, she used the other to feel her way through what had become shades and shadows of darkness. Her only chance at a fire was to find a tree. If it was evergreen there was a good possibility of relatively dry ground — at least snowless ground — at its base. If not, she could push her luck and check for a second tree or clear space alongside the trunk and do her best.

After twenty paces she made contact with a low-hanging limb; her cry of joyful surprise, soft as it was, echoed in the emptiness. Trailing the direction of the branch until her arm reached high over her head, she lost the connection and it was faith alone that powered the last few strides to the tree's torso.

And then, just as she was swallowing her disappointment that it was small and deciduous, her foot caught on something and had her tumbling again . . . into a low bush. Backing out quickly, needing most to stay dry, her hearing fixed on the sound of dry leaves rustling as she moved.

"Dry leaves. Dry ground."

She half-chuckled when she couldn't tell if she was trembling from cold or excitement but knew she needed to handle both simultaneously. So she went to work on a mental plan for the fire while she unrolled the rubber mat from the car adjacent to both the tree and bush. Feeling her way through every step, she used the not-so-crunchy-anymore towel to dry her feet and legs and pulled the large trash bag up over them; tying the sweater loosely around her feet and ankles once again. Not wanting to lose anything, she stuffed all but her bag of trash inside her coat, then got to her knees and sat back on her legs — her head went into the bush as far as she could get it.

Missing the gloves she'd left in her car, she was aware of the pain in her numbing fingers as she walked them over the ground, gathering leaves the size of her thumb, searching for the driest spot. She spoke to them encouragingly. "That's it, take your time. One more, good job. See how easy this is?" And when her search rustled the bush enough to drop snow down her neck, she came up straight again, brushed the top free of snow, and started over with a patience Job would admire.

When at last she had her spot, she held one hand in place to guard it and reached back with the other for the precious box of matches. With only the tip of her finger to tell, she judged ten or twelve matches left in the box.

"Okay." After closing her eyes to concentrate — and pray — she used trembling, unfeeling fingers to open it, painstakingly fumble for a stick, and close it. She held her breath and waited for a break in the wind. Adrenaline put tip to box and forced the stroke to make a small explosion of light . . . that was gone as soon as it appeared.

A frustrated moan popped in her throat and she swallowed it. She needed to stay calm. She lowered her forehead to the tops of her outstretched arms to gather herself and then began once more from the beginning, closing her eyes to concentrate, to pray . . . to arrive at the same result.

Her head shot up suddenly, like an alert rabbit. She heard a new whirring sound, a not-wind drone coming her way, getting closer. A look back at beams of light coming up the road shot electricity to the tips of her toes and out her fingers — made her muscles spastic as she scrambled to get to her feet. Could she make it to the pavement in time to flag it down? Her first step brought her down with a cry and shout. "No, no, no!" Her feet were tied up in the sweater. "No, no, no. I'm here. I'm here." Bag and sweater were off in a flash. "Help! Help me! I'm here." She made it to her feet in time for its approach; to jump waving and screaming and to stagger into snow before it passed her by without slowing down.

Natalie stood, stunned and confounded. What now? The question circled in her mind until her feet were shrieking in pain and instinct alone had her back-stepping to the mat. Hardly aware of it, she searched the dark for the towel and went about the business of surviving.

She discovered that cupping her hands around the box provided marginal protection from the wind — but marginal wasn't enough. She made a mini-dome with a hamburger wrapper — another blowout. But when a second attempt produced more than a spark, an actual flare, she gave it two more chances before moving on to option four — matchstick nine — which was to dig a small hole, a tiny fire pit of sorts.

With fewer matches in the box it became easier to count them — there were four left.

Looking up, she was startled to see . . . to be able to see, actually. The ambient light from the gray skies reflected off the white snow making it almost as bright as day. That which had been hidden from her in darkness had come to light. Trees and bushes had magically materialized while her attention had been elsewhere. Trees heavy with snow, balancing inches of snow on tiny limbs; the car at the road, a snow-topped boulder a few yards away; the road and the fields beyond — empty and stretching for miles — it all glistened as if littered with millions and billions of tiny diamonds.

If she wasn't so cold or so terrified it might have been exquisite — as it was: "It's a good sign."

Putting the box back in her pocket for safekeeping, she took some time to scrape away as much of the frozen ground that a dull stick would allow and used more leaves and papers from the trash to build up the walls around it; tugged the paper canopy into place. Blindly, she skimmed stiff fingers over her handiwork and when she was sure she could do no better, she went for the matchbox once more.

Match four was impressive but three looked, for a whole second, as if it might catch — charring the edge of a leaf. It was worth another try . . . but proved another failure.

She squeezed tears from her eyes and clutched the matchbox, and the last of its contents, tight in the palm of her hand. The near-constant shivering was taking a toll on her strength; she was fatiguing. Even the choice to use or to save the last match was an extraordinary chore . . . until she came to understand that she wasn't going to get any warmer, that conditions weren't going to get any better than they were at that moment. There might not be a later in which to use it.

"I've never been much of a saver anyway."

Sluggishly she came to the decision that, no, no better preparations could be made — what's more, she didn't have the energy. This time the lighting ceremony held more desperation than expectation; much less faith in the outcome. And when it was over, it was something of an odd relief.

She'd done her best. She had fought . . . fought the young man, fought the cold and the night. She hadn't given up . . . not on herself, not on her hope of surviving . . . not on her dream of being with Miles. She still hadn't. As long as her heart beat there was always a chance — she truly believed that, with every molecule in every cell in her body. She believed. The thing was, she simply didn't know what else she could do. She was too tired to walk; she wouldn't make it to the road. The last best thing she could do was to stay as dry and as warm as she could for as long as she could, and wait, and trust that help would come before sleep.

The mat had snow on it now, and while brushing it off still gave her some protection from the moisture of the snow, it had become a conductor of its freezing temperature. Wrapped in plastic and pieces of cotton and wool, she settled the least amount of her body mass on the mat as possible — the poorly covered soles of her feet and the base of her spine, with her back against the small slumbering tree.

All that remained was the time it would take for her body to exhaust itself and stop shivering.

"It'll be all right," she said, though it didn't sound any more convincing out loud than it did in her head.

Gently, slowly, and cherishing each one, she began to sort through memories of love and laughter, recalled friends both old and new. She prized her accomplishments and the gifts she'd received from others — her lids grew heavy and a warm, calm contentment spread through her at simply having known Miles.

One corner of her mouth tipped upward and her heavy-lidded gaze lifted to the sky. The radiance, the soft lighting of the sky that she'd noticed earlier was . . . *more,* she thought, fancying that the once solid mass of heavy cloud cover that had unburdened itself of its snow was now pulling apart, separating and plumping up. Small patches of star-studded sky spread slowly as she watched through air so clear and crisp it all but crackled.

As a matter of fact, everything around her was shimmering, shining . . . the word *heavenly* came to mind. Her lazy gaze fixed on two particular stars, low in the sky, moving, coming closer, and . . . no, not stars. Headlights registered. A car traveling in the far lane, on the other side of the median toward Beaumont . . . too far away to see her . . . too far away . . .

"I'm still here." The words floated from her in a cloud of warm air and were just as audible.

In a trance, she tracked the vehicle with her eyes between slow, long blinks — until it drove into what looked like a spotlight on a stage — a curio that penetrated her groggy awareness.

Once again, her vision turned aloft. Her lips, stiff and cracked, bowed at the sight of brilliant crepuscular rays streaming from the heavens. God rays. But not from the sun . . . not even from a full moon.

More and more of the comet's tail appeared before the last of the clouds broke away to reveal its true magnificence — a staggering light in a moonless night sky with a gloriously long, luminous tail.

"The Christmas Comet."

She'd never seen anything like it. No one alive had seen it before — racing along on its epic orbit around the sun; pulling and rolling and shifting the molecules in the air, trailing ancient and magical dust in its wake.

She'd read about it, seen pictures of other comets . . . There were those who believed ISON was the return of what was named the Star of Bethlehem — that it was this brilliant comet the magi followed so very,

very long ago. And who knew, maybe it was.

All Natalie knew, for sure and for certain, was that anything so extraordinary and beautiful was a singularity — a miraculous event. A miracle.

"It just has to be . . ."

Chapter Eight

"I couldn't believe it." Miles wasn't sure how many times he'd said it in the last three days but he *still* couldn't believe it. "There she was, sitting under a tree, sound asleep. I couldn't believe it."

See?

Having made it through the worst of her ordeal, Natalie was now stable — all she had to do was wake up.

"What made you turn around and go back?" asked Special Agent Palmer, sitting casually in the chair at the end of her hospital bed. He'd arrived several hours earlier on an assignment to first check on her condition and then give her some good news.

"When I found her car at the side of the road, out of gas, with her not in it, I wanted to wring her neck. She knew better than to get out . . . and to stay in one place so we could find her. God, I was so mad." Instantly, his remembered anger bubbled in his veins, but it didn't belong to Natalie anymore. "The best I could hope was that she'd set out for town, not too far, a few miles — I thought I'd catch her on the way in. Maybe she thought she could hitch a ride . . .

"The first thing I found was an open convenience store with a couple police cruisers parked outside. Turns out two kids — a girl and a boy — did hitch a ride into town and when the driver stopped there for gas they took off in his van . . . with the gas he hadn't paid for yet, which is what caught the attendant's notice and why he called the cops so quick. By some miracle there was a patrol in the vicinity. They were collared inside twenty minutes. The kids and the van were then brought back for identification and that's when I rolled up. When the driver said he'd picked 'em up a couple miles outside town, that they'd run out of gas, I asked him to describe the car. It was Natalie's."

Agent Palmer chuckled and nodded. "So the kid didn't really slip on the ice, land on his face, and break his own nose." It wasn't a question.

Miles shook his head once and clenched his still sore fist. "Technically, I suppose, he slipped *after* his nose was broken." He looked back into Palmer's face, saw no judgment, and knew the infinitesimal dollop of guilt he felt was all his. "I haven't hit anyone since I got out of the army thirteen years ago."

"So then you went back to her car," said the DEA agent, leaping over the subject with ease, needing no further explanation.

"I went back to *their* car where they'd left her."

"That's when you saw her."

He nodded, perplexed. "I don't know why I didn't see it the first time I passed by. The storm was over." Again he shook his head in wonder. "There she was, plain as day. I couldn't believe it."

"Well, you weren't the only one out looking . . . or the only one who missed seeing her. We were watching for her, too. We took that same road — we even saw the car, slowed down. It looked abandoned. Kills me to think she was only a few yards away." His gaze shifted toward the bed. "She's good people."

Miles sighed and went back to watching her breathe. She was more than just a good person to him.

After a short time the Posers returned from the cafeteria with coffee for both Miles and the agent, and once they'd extracted a promise to be notified when Natalie woke up, they left for the night. A little while after that, Palmer got up to stretch his legs and went down the hall to the visitors' lounge to check in with his office and call his wife.

Miles leaned forward to take up Natalie's hand. He'd always liked the way she talked with her hands; they were almost as expressive as her face. Gloveless, they'd been nearly purple when he found her — in fact, everyone had marveled at how well she'd pinked up and had sustained no frostbite at all. The words *amazing* and *miraculous* and *most uncommon* were repeated often, in wonder and speculation.

Miles smiled. He'd often used the same words, in the same way, just watching her ladle soup or pester a man to go to the free clinic or slip a burner phone to a kid to call home with when she thought no one else was looking . . . or simply walking down the street, done-in and ready for sleep.

Come to think of it, he was dead on his feet, too. Bouncing high and low like a hard rubber ball for the last few days was taking its toll. After that night at her apartment he soared so far above the ground he could have painted the sky blue by hand, which made his fall into hell when she didn't arrive at the church all the more violent and chaotic. Elated when he found her, knocked down by her condition, and back to overjoyed when she was out of the woods was a monster roller-coaster ride unlike any he'd taken before — but there was no one in the world he'd rather take it with than her.

"Ruined." At least that was the word her murmur sounded like.

"What?" He leaned closer, waiting for her to speak again. "Natalie?"

Eyes closed, she drew her chapped lower lip into her mouth to wet it, then tried again. "It's ruined."

"What's ruined?"

"My dress."

His chuckle was silent. "That's okay," he said, sympathetically. "You're going to need a completely different one for our reception, anyway."

She frowned, confused enough to blink her eyes open several times before they came to focus on him. Her immediate smile was warm and affectionate — and then it drooped as she took in the space over his shoulder, the strange bed, the TV on the wall, the tray table, the out-of-place hotel picture on the wall . . . Her gaze came back to and clung to the one thing in the room she recognized: Miles.

He smiled, caressed her face without touching it — then realized he could, and did. "I can't believe you stood me up on our very first date."

The furrow between her brows deepened. Gradually, as she glanced away and recalled *why,* her expression relaxed and her gaze met his. "Car trouble."

His eyes opened wide; he grinned and nodded at the understatement.

They might have been smiling at one another but the current between them was spiked with fear and relief: It conveyed the terror and panic they'd each endured, the hope they had stretched to its limits, and the love that had driven them to this moment.

She turned her hand over so they were palm to palm and she could clasp his tighter. Softly and sincerely, she said, "I'm so sorry."

He knew it wasn't for missing their date or for ignoring his repeated advice to be cautious or for being herself and doing what came natural to her: helping those in need. Her only regret was having caused him distress and the pain that accompanied it.

"Well, you're here and you're safe," he said, then attempted a grudge. "I'll forgive you this time."

"Even if I can't promise there won't be a next time?"

He sobered and answered seriously. "Yes, even if . . . though I hope you won't test me." In her expression he saw that she knew she was no longer alone, that her life and his life were one life now, and what one did the other would feel. But he also saw *her,* and he smiled. "And I can't promise I'll be this nice about it next time, so keep that in mind when you do."

She laughed, then hissed at the stiff pain on the left side of her face and reached for it.

"A couple of minor scratches there . . . and one hell of a shiner," Miles said, his voice easy and light despite his tense expression. "A few other bruises, too. You got off easy."

"Better than you, I think." She reached up to palm his cheek. "I don't think I've ever seen you unshaven." She grinned at him. "You're a mess."

There was a noise at the door and they both looked that way.

"Good. You're back," Miles said to the dark-haired man in blue jeans and winter jacket standing mostly in the hall. "Come in. She's awake."

■ ■ ■ ■

Natalie was curious about the man, of course, but even more intrigued by the sudden rush of excitement rolling off Miles.

"Natalie, this is Special Agent Palmer from the DEA. He has a story to tell you."

"Please don't." Not too curious and not at all apologetic, she said, "I'm sorry, Agent Palmer. No offense. I do sometimes wish I could help you guys out. I do. But I can't risk getting between you and the dealers and the addicts who might come to me for help. They need to be able to trust me." She chuckled, hoping to take some of the sting and insult out of her rejection. "Plus, I just promised Miles I'd try to stay out of trouble for a while."

The agent had a nice smile. "Good. And I'm glad you're feeling better. You had us worried." He skipped a beat. "And I'm not here to ask for your help. You've already helped us more than you know, without even knowing it."

"Oh no."

"Without anyone knowing it," he said quickly. "Except for those you helped. And they are extremely grateful." Okay. Now she was curious. "So grateful they've asked us to help set up a rather large trust in your name so that you can start up your soup kitchen and . . . well, whatever else you want to do with it to continue to help people, like you helped them."

"Who?"

Again, he smiled. "Aldene and the children?"

"Aldene? She has money for a trust?"

"A big trust. And her name isn't Aldene."

"What is it?"

He shook his head. "For your safety I can't tell you who she was and I can't tell you who she is today because she and the rest of the family are in protective custody with the DOJ and I don't know. But I can tell you that the man that you met, Luis Pena — also not his real name — is her father and his sons are her brothers."

"Okay." Still family, though why they'd lie about the order of it was still confusing. "I never asked about a husband. I guess I just assumed he'd passed away or . . . or was off somewhere looking for work or . . . I try not to pry too much."

He nodded, aware that her friendship and help had been unconditional. "He's why they fled Mexico." He sat, took a breath, and began the story. "Wealthy people in Mexico, affluent families that have lived there for generations, are prime targets for kidnapping and ransom by the drug cartels. They pay street taxes to leave their homes and spend fortunes on bribes and protection for their families. And for the most part, if they don't get in the way or cause any trouble, they manage to keep what is theirs and stay in the country they love.

"I can't get specific about the Pena family, but Aldene's husband, her oldest son —"

"Arturo . . . not his real name, right?"

He nodded. "Also one of her brothers . . . they were out together and witnessed a cartel execution. He sent the boys running in one direction and took off the other way. He was captured and killed. The man, Luis, gathered his entire family and smuggled them over the border that night and didn't stop running until he got here and could safely contact the authorities. We were called in first and they were given temporary S-5 permits — for witnesses and informants in criminal or terrorists cases. We, and certain people in the Mexican government, have been after these guys for years.

"Turns out the kid, Arturo, didn't see the actual murder but his young uncle did and he was willing to testify in exchange for witness protection for himself and his family."

He looked away briefly. "*But* sometimes risking your life isn't enough, and somewhere between the DEA, the DOJ, and Homeland Security, it was decided that a legal and permanent residence — and *then* witness protection — was going to require an EB-5 visa." There was an angry tick in his cheek when he paused to gather an explanation. "EB-5s are what you might call a rich man's visa that gets their wheels greased to the front of the line by investing five hundred thousand dollars or more in American business projects — what they call economic growth projects for rural and high unemployment areas. *Or* a million for projects outside those areas." He hesitated, rethinking what he was about to say, and then tipped his head regrettably to say, "Money."

She could see he didn't approve of the deal Aldene and her family had to make to stay safe for doing the right thing . . . to stay alive. She liked him for it.

"Anyway, Luis apparently didn't feel secure without a solid deal in place so he used some connections he had to slip away and drop out of sight until the financial arrangements could be made. *Way* out of sight, because by the time we found his connection he'd stashed the kids and he was the only one making periodic contact with them." He shook his head. "Considering the long fingers of the cartels in this country, it's hard to believe he felt safer on the streets than in a temporary safe house . . . but he said that was exactly why he thought it was best to be able to separate and move around than to sit all together in one place." He shrugged. "Who knows? Scared is scared and you do what you do to keep your family safe. And with the money thing . . . ? Hard to tell who you can trust when money's involved."

"I like money . . . and I never have any. How'd they know I wouldn't sell them out? I mean, if I somehow found them out."

Agent Palmer's gaze shifted to Miles, who then grinned at her. "You're as well known for being a soft touch as you are for your soup, sweetheart. And, apparently, you *can* do discreet better than I gave you credit for, because the father was keeping his ear to the ground. He knew his daughter and grandchildren were safe with you as long as he didn't hear anything about them, or get wind of anyone staying with you."

"See?" She played proud, but only to cover the deep gratification she felt in having been a part — albeit unknowingly — of the family's escape from danger.

"Don't get cocky," he said with a loving frown. "It was still risky and dangerous."

"It was," the agent agreed, and shifted his weight in the chair he was sitting in. "Which is why, when we finally connected with the family again, we thought it would be safer if you never knew who they were and they simply disappeared. Aldene told her father you were trying to get them into a shelter so we accelerated that process a little . . . and it would have worked out perfectly except she knew you were behind in your rent and working extra jobs to make ends meet. She and her father, as I said, are extremely grateful to you for helping them — and with no ulterior motive." Yet another disparaging reference to the special visa — she *really* liked him for it.

"Long story a little shorter, they insisted that they wanted to give you money . . . outside of that entailed by their EB-5. For your dreams, they said. They planned to send you a fortune anonymously through the mail." He chuckled. "We explained how conspicuous and possibly hazardous that might be for you, and a little about taxes and all that, and they finally agreed to let us arrange for a trust to be set up in your name. It has its own background and cover story and can't be traced to them."

He stood and pulled a long white envelope from a pocket inside his jacket. Stepping around to the side of the bed opposite Miles, he handed it to her. His expression was serious but his eyes were twinkling with goodwill.

He cleared his throat and began to recite: "*On behalf of the Pena family* — not their real names — *please accept this token of their gratitude and friendship. They will never forget you or your kindness to them.*" He smiled and reached back into his jacket. "And neither will I. Please, take my card. If you ever need me for anything, I want you to call. I get the position you're in but you never know — having a friend in the DEA might come in handy someday."

She took his card; they all shook hands and then he was gone.

For one entire minute, Miles and Natalie stared at the white envelope on her lap.

"Aren't you going to open it?" he asked finally. She turned her head and scrutinized him until he became a little uncomfortable. "What?"

"What sort of reception?"

He was surprised into laughter, but didn't hesitate to answer. "Our wedding reception."

Her brows rose over sparkling eyes.

"Aren't you getting a little ahead of yourself?"

"No. I'm way behind where I should be with you. I should have asked you to marry me three years ago, about a week after I met you, when I first realized I was hopelessly in love with you."

"It took you a whole week?" For her it was that first night when he'd helped her, all battered and bruised, out of the back of his police car and then, needlessly, he'd picked her up in his arms and carried her into the ER. Literally, he'd swept her off her feet.

"Only to realize it . . . and then that night, the night I finally asked you out . . . that's when I realized you felt the same. That look on your face? I'd seen it so often, waited for it, worked for it, hoped it would be there every time I saw you. It just didn't occur to me, until then, what it meant." Suddenly, he was so overcome with emotion she thought he might cry. She reached to smooth her hand over the side of his face, through his hair, and to rest on the back of his neck. He smiled and leaned into it. "The other night, shortly before I found you . . . I was a little bit out of my mind, but life was never so clear to me. It's short. Way too short. I vowed then and there that if I found you alive I wouldn't live another second without you. I'd marry you and we'd live happily ever after." He leaned in, mere inches from her face. "Please marry me."

"Tonight?" she asked, being facetious.

"Yes. Tomorrow at the latest."

"Okay."

The kiss they shared was everything she knew it would be — soft and demanding; conquering and offering; rousing and freeing — it fused her soul to his.

At last, Miles smiled between sweet, sipping kisses and pulled away to say, "I can't wait to start bragging about my wife's survival skills."

She nodded, dubious. "My luck is fantastic, but I don't think luck is a skill."

"Trust me, building a fire like that in the middle of a snowstorm isn't just luck."

"Fire?"

"I couldn't have built it on my best day in the army. It had clearly been burning for a while. I couldn't believe it — the broken branches and twigs still burning in the pit, the embers red hot. I was amazed by the heat it was putting off."

"What fire?"

"The one you built to stay warm . . . also a good signal fire, by the way. It was so bright I couldn't believe I missed —"

"I used up all my matches . . ."

"I'm not surprised. It couldn't have been easy."

"No. I mean, I didn't . . . It didn't . . . I . . ."

She saw it again. That staggering light in a moonless night sky with a gloriously long, luminous tail crossed her mind in all its true magnificence. So unique, so powerful and moving. So unearthly and magical.

"What is it?" Miles asked, watching as clarity lit her expression.

Accepting the fire as real, she looked down at the unopened envelope on the bed and back at Miles.

Life, purpose, and love — all she'd ever wished for.

"The Christmas Comet."

Author's Note

Originally I chose Hans Christian Andersen's *The Little Match Girl* as my fairy tale for this novella. However, while most fairy tales are not exactly funny and upbeat, most, in their most common versions, don't end quite so grimly or without a happy ending. I soon discovered that the Brothers Grimm had also been inspired to write a story about an impoverished little girl in *The Star Money* that ends on a much lighter note. Inspired by both, my story is a mix of the two.

P.S. Comet ISON is real and should be visible from Earth from approximately November 2013 through about February 2014. Watch for it. And if it passes through your part of the sky, make a wish.

■ ■ ■ ■

Stroke of Midnight

R. C. RYAN

■ ■ ■ ■

To my daughter-in-law Maureen,
whose generous heart makes all who
meet her fall in love.

And in memory of my Tom,
who forever owns my heart.

Prologue

Ten Years Previous

"Sydney." Margot stared in surprise at her sixteen-year-old stepdaughter, dressed in her school uniform, carrying an armload of textbooks. "What are you doing home from school so early?"

"I told you we were having a half-day for teacher conferences." Sydney watched, wide-eyed, as workers swarmed over the barn her father had converted into his artist studio, efficiently wrapping dozens of his paintings. "What are they doing?"

"Preparing them for shipment."

"Shipment? Where? Why?"

"We've been over this, Sydney. With your father dead, we have no use for this big farmhouse and this barn" — Margot waved her hands to indicate the cavernous surroundings — "where your father used to hide away for hours on end. Not only was I fortunate to find a buyer for this place, but someone who obviously has more money than brains offered a fabulous sum for the entire collection of your father's art. I was hoping to have it out of here before you got home."

Sydney turned away to hide the tears that sprang to her eyes. She hated the way the grief could sneak up on her and make her weep at the worst possible time. "But Dad promised me they would all belong to me one day."

"He said no such thing to me." Margot's hand shot out, grabbing the girl by her shoulder, her fingers gripping painfully. The woman's eyes flashed the way they always did when she was challenged. "As your father's widow, I don't need your permission. I'm free to dispose of his estate as I choose. I have to think about the future. It was hard enough when I had only my own two daughters to worry about. Now, thanks to your father's untimely death, I have one more to feed and clothe and educate." She gave a dismissive look at the girl's prim navy jumper and white blouse. "There will be no more private schools for you. Not with Hester and Hilda ready for college and all the expense that will entail. I told your father he was spoiling you, but he was determined to make it up to you because you'd lost your mother at such a tender age. Now that I'm in charge, there'll be no more of such pampering. You're old enough to be exposed to the realities of life. The money from your father's paintings will allow me a comfortable lifestyle, but money can't be stretched forever. We'll move to the city where you can walk to school, and Hester and Hilda can pursue their dreams of careers in fashion in New York City."

"Dad said . . ."

"Enough." Margot lifted her hand in a dismissive gesture. "I know your father fancied himself a true man of the earth while painting all those pastoral scenes. He made it plain that he wanted you to grow up in the country as he had. That life is gone now, Sydney." Margot narrowed her eyes on the girl. "It's time to stop mourning our loss and move on. Thank heavens some foolish collector thought those paintings were worth more than the paint and canvas, though I must say, your father was such a dreamer, I was afraid we'd all be left destitute." Her tone sharpened. "The buyer of this farm wants to take possession by the end of the month. I've already contacted your school to let them know you won't be back for the next term."

She turned away with a swish of skirts.

"Pack only what you absolutely must have. Since your sisters will be living on campus in the fall, you and I will make do with something much smaller and more manageable."

When she was gone, Sydney walked among the remaining unwrapped paintings, allowing her fingers to trace her father's familiar signature at the lower right-hand corner of each canvas.

How she'd loved being here, working alongside her father, learning the craft from a master. He'd patiently taught her how to mix the paints to make the sky that perfect shade of blue, the meadows so green and lush, she could imagine herself lying in the grass, watching the clouds overhead turning into castles and carriages and kings. While they'd worked, he'd spoken lovingly about his happy childhood in the tiny town of Innismere, in the west of Ireland, where he'd honed his craft along the lovely river Glass, which meandered across his beloved valley.

She could hear his voice, as clearly as though he were still here beside her. "I'll take you there one day, Sydney, and we'll walk the hills and forest glades, and you'll see that marvelous light that shines down on Ireland in a way that it shines nowhere else on Earth. I want you to feel the peace and the love that I knew in that sweet, magical place."

"Oh, Da, I can't wait." She ran a hand along the scarred old table that held his tools and cans and rags, and breathed in the familiar scents of paint and turpentine that were forever imprinted on her mind and heart.

Feeling the press of that familiar hand on her shoulder, she paused. As though moved by invisible strings, she picked up a small framed photo of her father that she'd taken one day here in his studio. He was wearing a paint-smeared shirt, his hair mussed, his smile bright as he worked on one of his many canvases. He'd loved the photo so much he'd had it framed.

"Take it, Sydney. Keep it close and think of me often. And remember this, darlin': Believe."

Had the words been spoken aloud, or had she merely heard them in her mind?

No matter. Whether or not she could see or hear her father, she knew he was here beside her, watching out for her, keeping her safe. She could hear his voice inside her head and feel the gentle touch of his hand on her shoulder.

Wrapping the picture in one of his paint-stained rags, she tucked it in her pocket.

Margot had said to pack only the important things. This was all Sydney needed. For the rest of her days, this little memento would keep her father close, and hopefully, one day help mend her broken heart.

CHAPTER ONE

"I've finished, Sydney. Take a look." Kamal, one of the students in Sydney's evening community center art class, paused to dip his brush in turpentine before wiping it on a rag.

Sydney stepped up beside the solemn, dark-haired man to study his completed canvas.

As usual, Kamal had ignored the still life she'd set on a table, consisting of an empty wine bottle, a bunch of grapes, and a wedge of cheese on a pretty plate, and had instead chosen to paint a waterfall. Kamal was obsessed with waterfalls. Throughout the entire year he had painted half a dozen of them, explaining that it made him happy to look at them.

"Well, as waterfalls go, I think this is one of your better ones."

His smile was radiant. "Thank you, Sydney. I think so, too. I'm going to give it to my wife."

"Sydney, what do you think of this?" Mrs. Martinez motioned for Sydney to come closer.

"Very nice, Mrs. Martinez." Sydney paused beside the white-haired woman who was wider than she was tall. "But why did you paint the grapes red?"

"I didn't want grapes in my picture, so I made them hot chili peppers. See?" The old woman pointed to the blobs of red paint bleeding into the orange cheese. "My grandchildren love red hot chili peppers."

"Very nice. But maybe they love the music group more than the vegetables."

"I don't understand," the older woman said.

"A little joke, Mrs. Martinez." Sydney was grateful when the bell sounded, signaling the end of the evening's class. "I'll see all of you next week."

She picked up her bulging backpack and headed toward the little flat above Colosanti's Deli. During her college days, she'd worked two jobs because Margot had said more money was needed for Hester and Hilda as they established themselves in their new careers. Now she continued working two jobs, teaching second grade while also teaching art at the community center five evenings a week, just so that she could afford to live alone. Though it was small and cramped, it was her very own private space. Heaven, she thought. Sheer heaven to be finally free of Margot's controlling nature and angry, hurtful words.

"Ah, Sydney." Mr. Colosanti greeted her outside his deli. He stood less than five feet tall, with sharp, blackbird eyes and a head covered with gray curly hair that reminded Sydney of steel wool. His white apron fell to his ankles. "Look what I have for you." He picked up a perfect ripe peach and rubbed it on his sleeve before handing it to her. "I've been saving this one just for you."

"You sweetie." She accepted the peach and brushed a kiss over his weathered cheek, causing him to blush clear to the tips of his ears.

As she turned he added, "You have a visitor." He lowered his voice. "Your stepmama. She insisted that I let her in."

Sydney had to fight to keep her smile in place. Everyone in the neighborhood was aware of Margot's sarcasm, and most had sampled it a time or two. "It's all right. I know you had no choice. Thanks for the warning, Mr. Colosanti."

She climbed the steps to her flat and pushed open the door.

Margot stopped her pacing to turn and glare. "How can you bear this dreary place?" She wrinkled her nose and pointed to the fat brown guinea pig in a cage by the window. "It smells like a barnyard in here because of that . . ."

"Gus. The class guinea pig. Nguyn was supposed to have him this week, but his mother is out of town, so I offered to keep him until she got back."

"Of course you did. Just like you used to offer to keep all the stray puppies and kittens that you claimed 'followed you home from school' all those years ago. You still can't resist taking in every stray you meet. I'm surprised you didn't offer to take Nguyn home with you while his mother was away."

"I did. But his aunt is with him."

Margot rolled her eyes. "I swear, Sydney, this place is so depressing."

"I'm sorry you feel that way, Margot. I like it. It's close enough to walk to work in the mornings, and look at my bonus." Sydney held up the peach. "Mr. Colosanti always saves me a piece of fruit. And sometimes, when a customer doesn't pick up a deli order, he lets me have it for my supper."

"And well he ought to, considering the

rent he charges for this dump. He should be ashamed of himself. And you. Look at how you spend your days. Teaching second graders who can barely speak English, and then wasting your evenings teaching art to senior citizens."

"They're not all seniors. It's the community center, Margot. Some of my students are young. And you'd be amazed at their talent."

"I don't care if they're all Picassos. You're never going to be anything more than a second-rate, old-maid teacher if you persist in this foolishness."

"I'm single by choice. And I happen to love my job, Margot."

"Do you hear yourself? It's a job, Sydney, not a career. How can you hope to ever meet anyone of substance here? Take Hester, for instance. Since going to work for that new fashion designer, she's been introduced to several famous actors and musicians. She told me that a drummer who plays with the Hot Hunks asked her to meet him for drinks after his band's concert next week. The Hot Hunks. Their music is topping the charts. And my beautiful Hilda is dating Anthony Bellair, the star of that new police drama on TV."

"I believe he's married, Margot."

"He's divorcing. And he's hinted that Hilda could become wife number two."

"That would be number three. He was married briefly to that pretty blond model that he dumped for . . ."

"Whatever." Margot waved off her remark with a quick lift of her hand. "At least Hester and Hilda are putting themselves out there to find men worthy of consideration. How are you ever going to improve your life if you stay in this garbage pit?"

"I didn't realize my life needed improving. I like my life. In fact, I love it."

"Of course you do. Doesn't everyone yearn for a cheap upper flat in a run-down, dreary neighborhood? Doesn't every young woman hope to grow old alone, surrounded by immigrants and losers?"

Margot shot Sydney that icy stare that always managed to freeze Sydney's heart. At least it always had when she was young. These days she was working very hard to move beyond her childish fears of her stepmother, though in truth, she found herself reacting much the same way as she had when she was that frightened child who'd first met the woman and her two angry daughters who would share her life with her father. Deep inside, a lump of fear lodged like a stone in the pit of Sydney's stomach. And though she knew the things Margot said were untrue, she was helpless to fight them. Each insult hurled, each cruel word spoken, grew like an insidious seed in Sydney's soul.

Sydney's best friend, Melanie, called it Margot's venom. Once unleashed, that snakebite poison rendered the unlucky recipient unable to think or act rationally as they recoiled from the attack.

Sydney had to blink back tears. "Do you enjoy saying cruel things, Margot?"

"I say them because someone has to remind you to grow up and be sensible. Just look at you. You may as well wear a sign that says, *Take advantage of me. I'm gullible.*"

"I'm not . . ."

"Oh, please. Don't deny the obvious. Mark my words. The first down-on-his-luck guy who gives you the time of day will have you wrapped around his finger before you can blink. You'll be bringing him home and feeding him like . . ." She turned toward the cage. "Like your guinea pig there. And if he turns out to be a gigolo, you won't even know what hit you until he's taken your time, your money, and your virtue. When that happens, don't come running to me for help."

"I wouldn't think of asking you to help

me." Stung by Margo's cruel words, Sydney crossed her arms over her chest. "I'm sure you had some reason for this visit."

"Two reasons, actually. I'm moving again."

"To a better neighborhood?"

"As a matter of fact, I am. Unlike you, I won't be satisfied until I'm at the very top. I've been packing, and I found a couple of dusty boxes in storage." She pointed to the boxes she'd dumped unceremoniously just inside the door. "I don't know how they survived my first move, since they belonged to your father and I'd thought I had already tossed everything of his. I don't have time to deal with them, so I was hoping you'd set them out with your trash."

"Do Da's things mean so little to you, Margot?"

"They're tattered and torn and filthy." Margot gave one of her famous phony, teeth-baring smiles. "But if you'd like to keep them, for sentimental reasons, be my guest."

She walked to the door, eager to escape what she considered little more than a dungeon. "Maybe after I'm settled we can meet at Hester and Hilda's town house. It has a magnificent view of the river. I'm sure they could introduce you to some of the important people they know. There must be someone who can add a little luster to your drab little life."

When the door closed behind Margot, Sydney dropped down onto a chair, feeling drained and useless, her typical reaction to Margot's litany of petty complaints.

Deciding to forgo supper, Sydney set the kettle on the stove while she nibbled on the peach. Making a cup of tea, she carried it to the coffee table and opened the dusty boxes. Inside was a pile of her father's paint-stained shirts and pants, dull and faded from years of storage. They were too damaged to consider giving to a charity. Though it caused a pain around her heart, she knew she would have to dispose of them with the trash, as Margot had so coldly suggested.

Feeling tears welling in her eyes, she gathered a handful of her father's shirts to her face, wishing she could still smell him. Hearing the faint rustle of paper, she fumbled in the folds and found an envelope in one of the shirt pockets. Inside the envelope she found a fat roll of hundred-dollar bills and a note, written in her father's distinct script.

With eyes brimming, she read the note.

My darling Sydney,

My greatest wish is that you will one day

visit my birthplace and discover the love I feel for it. The little village of Innismere is a magical place, as is all of Ireland. Each time I sell one of my paintings, I intend to put a percentage into this special hiding place, the pocket of my favorite shirt, which you gave me. My hope is that, by the time you've grown into a woman, there will be enough for you to travel to that grand country in style and to stay as long as you choose. While you're there, darlin', feel the magic. And believe.

Sydney studied the shirt. It was the one he'd worn in the photograph she still prized above all else. With a smile she unfolded the bills and counted them out. Five thousand dollars. Compared with her meager salary, it was a fortune.

She thought of her stepmother's hurtful words. This was enough to change her life if she chose to. Enough to move to a more modern apartment. To take time away from her job to apply for something more challenging, more glamorous.

If she chose to.

The thought came to her with absolute certainty. She knew without a doubt what she would do with this windfall.

Instead of being sensible, as Margot had suggested, she would throw caution to the wind. She would follow her father's dream and go to Ireland. To Innismere. To find the love that had shone through her father's eyes every time he had spoken of that grand old place. She would sit beside the river Glass and sketch, just as her father had in his youth. And she would feel her father's presence there beside her.

A brief visit to Ireland may not change her life, but it would enable her to store up some glorious memories to warm her heart during the long years to come.

It may be a foolish waste of money in Margot's eyes, but Sydney would have the satisfaction of knowing that she was using the money as her father had wished.

And really, wasn't that worth any price?

Chapter Two

"Welcome aboard Allied America's Flight Two Twenty-seven bound for Ireland."

As Sydney settled into her seat, the flight attendant's voice began the preflight welcome. Sydney fidgeted with her seat belt and then took out the laminated sheet of instructions to follow along in case of an emergency.

When the voice faded, Sydney sat back and took a deep breath. Minutes later, as the plane began to taxi along the runway, she white-knuckled the armrests.

The passenger beside her chuckled. "I've tried that. It never works, you know."

She turned to him with a puzzled frown.

"Trying to lift the plane with the sheer force of your determination." He shot her a rogue's grin. "Half the passengers aboard are doing the same. But it's all up to the pilot now, you see."

She gave a quick laugh, as much at his

brogue as that devilish smile, and very deliberately released her death grip on the armrests, folding her hands in her lap. "I didn't realize I was so transparent."

"Oh, it's natural enough. I've done it myself a time or two. But the more I travel, the more I've begun to realize that once I strap myself into one of these big birds, I've given up the control to someone else."

He was wearing torn jeans and a faded tee beneath a rumpled plaid shirt. He was badly in need of a shave and a haircut. Thick, dark hair spilled over the collar of his shirt. The rough stubble of beard added to his shabby appearance. His eyes were a smoky gray, and at the moment they sparkled with unspoken humor.

Sydney found herself drawn to those deep, soulful eyes, while ignoring his unkempt appearance. It was a result of her years of tutoring. At the community center, some of her most talented pupils turned out to be those who least looked the part.

He patted her hand and indicated the sea of puffy clouds outside their window. "You see? We're already airborne."

It was a jolt to Sydney's system to realize the truth of what he'd said. Now that they were high in the air, her fears began to subside. She let out the breath she'd been holding and opened the folder containing the various tours she was considering at the end of her flight.

Seeing them, her seatmate smiled. "Your first trip to Ireland?"

She nodded. "How about you?"

"I'm headed home after two weeks of holiday spent biking, hiking, and touring your lovely land."

She heard the pleasure in his voice. "Your first time here?"

He shook his head, sending shaggy hair dancing. "I've been a time or two. But this time I pushed myself to the limits, climbing higher, biking until I thought my legs would fall off. I can honestly say that the best thing about a holiday is looking forward to soaking my aching muscles once I get home."

"I've heard grand things about your home."

"Have you now? And who's been bragging about Ireland?"

"My father was born there. When I was little, he used to tell me stories about his wonderful, carefree childhood to cheer me up. He used to say he couldn't wait to show me his birthplace."

"Ah. And are you meeting him there?"

Sydney's smile faltered, the grief a sudden, sharp pain around her heart. "He died when I was a teen. But I've never forgotten the joy he felt whenever he talked about Ireland."

"And you're going alone?"

Sydney nodded. "Well, not exactly alone." She indicated her travel bag. "I carry my da's photo tucked away in a little pocket of my purse. I suppose it sounds silly, but I feel like a little part of him is with me."

Her seatmate nodded. "Not silly at all." He lifted a silver chain he wore around his neck. On it dangled a small silver locket. "This was worn by my grandfather, and then my father. Wearing it makes me feel close to both of them."

"That's nice. Are they still living?"

He shook his head. "My grandparents died when I was twelve. My parents when I was in my teens. I miss them still."

"I know what you mean. Even after a lifetime, I'll be able to see my da's face and hear his voice."

"Though you're American, there's a hint of the Irish in your voice, especially when you speak of your da."

Sydney smiled. "I know I should say Daddy or Dad, but it just seems right to call him Da."

The brogue beside her softened. "Mine were Da and Mum. And Granda and

DeeDee."

"That's sweet." She leaned her head back and felt her nerves begin to subside until she was pleasantly drifting. Not only had the liftoff gone smoothly, but her seatmate was turning out to be a charming distraction. A distraction that was badly needed at the moment. She was still reeling from her out-of-the-blue decision to leave home, so uncharacteristic for the usually conservative young woman, and from the blistering anger when her stepmother had learned of her plans.

It had been, as always, an ugly scene. But now, she would put aside all the unpleasantness and just think about what was to come.

It was her last coherent thought before she slept.

"Enjoy your nap?"

At the deep voice beside her, Sydney's head came up sharply.

She glanced down at the blanket covering her lap. "Did you do this?"

Her seatmate's smile had her heart doing a slow somersault. "I asked the flight attendant to fetch a blanket. They have the air blasting in here."

"Thank you." She sat up straighter. "I can't believe I slept so soundly. I guess I was more tense than I realized."

"Traveling can be stressful."

Especially if your family members call you a fool for even thinking about taking a trip. Though Sydney thought the words, she didn't speak them. It was too personal, too painful, to say aloud. Perhaps because she wasn't at all certain whether Margot had been right or wrong.

"My name is Cullen." Her seatmate offered a handshake.

"Sydney." She felt her hand enfolded in his big palm.

"No ring, I see." He glanced down at her hand, still firmly held in his. "Does that mean no husband?"

"No husband. Are you married, Cullen?"

"I'm afraid I haven't found that special one, yet."

"I'm sure there will be a lovely Irish colleen who will suit you perfectly."

"Someday." He shrugged. "Do you live in New York, Sydney?"

"Yes."

"And what do you do there?"

It was all the push Sydney needed to begin telling him about the children she taught, and the fascinating countries they'd lived in before coming to America, and the harrowing tales they told about their struggles to begin a new life so far away from the troubles and turmoil they left behind.

While she talked, he caught the glow that came into her eyes. "You love your work."

"I do. Is it that obvious?"

"It is, yes. And how do you fill your nights after teaching second graders all day?"

"I teach art at our local community center."

"You're an artist?"

"Not much of one. My da was a gifted artist. I wish I could be like him. But I'm afraid I'm better at teaching than doing."

"But you love teaching others?"

She blushed. "Guilty as charged."

"Don't make light of it. I think teaching is a wonderful gift."

Feeling a wave of self-consciousness, she tried to divert attention away from herself. "Do you live in Dublin, Cullen?"

"I do when I'm working. But my home is in Innismere."

She knew her jaw had dropped. But she was so startled, all she could do was gasp.

Cullen arched a brow. "Have I said something wrong?"

"No. It's just that . . ." She gave a toss of her head. "That's where I'm headed. Innismere. That's where my da was born."

His smile deepened. "Now what are the

odds of such a coincidence?"

As the flight attendant began preparing the passengers for their descent into Dublin's Shannon Airport, Cullen laid a hand over Sydney's. "As long as we're both heading in the same direction, why don't you let me drive you to Innismere?"

"I thought you worked in Dublin."

"I do. But for now, I'm still on holiday. Since this is your first time in Ireland, I'd love to show you around. I have a car at the airport," he added. "It would save you the cost of hiring a car and driver. And I promise to deliver you right to the door of your inn. I assume you're staying at the Inn of Innismere, since it's the only decent place in town."

"I am."

"Well then. What do you say?"

She bit her lip. This man was a stranger, after all. Did she risk riding with a stranger for an hour or more?

She knew all the reasons why she ought to refuse. But there was something about this charming stranger that had her warming to him, despite all the little warning bells that were going off in her head.

Sydney shrugged. "Thank you for the offer, Cullen. I'd love to ride with you to Innismere. But only if you let me pay for the gas."

She saw the look of surprise that came into his eyes.

"Now why would you do that?"

"You said yourself you'd be saving me the cost of a car and driver. The least I can do is pay for the gas, since you're providing the car."

He took a moment to consider before the smile returned. "All right. If you insist."

"I do."

And then she was fetching her carry-on and following Cullen from the plane. She pushed aside the nagging little worry that her rumpled seatmate had charmed her into breaking her first rule — to take on no more strays. But after all, she did need a ride, and he was going to the very same town where she was headed. It made perfect sense to pool their resources. And he certainly looked as though he could use the gas money.

Still, she'd broken her first rule.

And to think she'd done it before even setting foot on Ireland's soil.

Tomorrow was another day. A clean slate. Tomorrow was soon enough to swear off strays. Both the two-legged and four-legged variety.

Chapter Three

They drove along narrow ribbons of highway, past ancient ruins, and sailed through pretty little towns and villages with their church steeples gleaming in the sunlight. Everywhere Sydney looked, there were people walking and shopkeepers chatting. They drove by fields of sleek cattle or leggy horses, and Sydney exclaimed over the acres of glorious flowers that grew alongside the roads.

"There's so much to see. And all of it so grand."

Cullen smiled and nodded. "I love traveling the world. But best of all, I love coming home."

"How could you not?" She pointed to the tumble of giant stones in a pasture. "Think about the hundreds of years that have passed, and still those stones remain to let us know that someone once lived there, and made it their home."

"And fell in love there, and married and raised their children. It's easy to forget the very real people who lived and loved, just as people have from the beginning of time."

Sydney sighed. "When you say it like that, it all sounds so romantic."

"Not to spoil your illusions, but people fought and died here, too. Our people were forced to go to war on this very land. We Irish have a bloody history."

"But you endured. You remain. And you thrive."

"We do indeed."

Cullen drove up a long, curving driveway and came to a halt in front of the steps of a charming old two-story inn. The walls were covered with ivy. Flowers of deep purple and palest pink spilled from urns that lined the long front porch and wide steps — a porch dotted with several cushioned rocking chairs.

"Here we are." Cullen popped the trunk and a white-haired man with a ruddy complexion, wearing a fisherman's knit sweater and charcoal cords, opened Sydney's passenger-side door and offered his hand.

When she stepped out, the older man called, "Welcome to the Inn of Innismere, miss. I'm Sean McCarthy. My wife, Bridget, and I manage the inn."

"Thank you, Sean. It's nice to meet you. I can't wait to see the inside of your lovely inn."

Before the man could remove her suitcase, Cullen was there first, hauling it out and carrying it up the steps where he set it down.

"Thank you, Cullen." Sean clapped a hand on the young man's shoulder. "Home from your latest jaunt, are ye, lad?"

"I am."

"Bridget and I have missed you."

Cullen winked at the old man. "Then I'll have to make it up to you by spending more time here." He turned to Sydney. "I'll leave you here to settle in. You're in good hands with Sean and Bridget. If you'd like, I could come by in the morning and show you around the town."

"You're just being polite. I'm sure you have better things to do than act as tour guide for me."

"Nothing would make me happier than to show you my town."

Sydney hesitated for only a moment. "If you're sure you can spare the time, I'd like that. Where shall we meet?"

His smile was quick and easy. "I'll pick you up right here at nine."

Whatever doubt she was entertaining was forgotten under the spell of that smile.

"Nine it is." She removed some bills from her wallet. When he tried to refuse them she closed his fingers around them. "A deal is a deal." She offered her hand. "Thank you for driving me here, Cullen."

Seeing the arched brow of the old man, Cullen shot her a wicked grin and a wink before accepting her money and her handshake.

"It was my pleasure."

Sydney felt the quick tingle along her arm, like magic fingers brushing her skin, and she was forced to absorb a rush of heat before he released her hand.

"I'll see you in the morning." With a jaunty salute to them both, Cullen turned and settled himself behind the wheel and was gone before Sean managed to climb the steps and hold the door for her.

If she had any concern about her unexpected agreement to spend more time with a man who was still a perfect stranger, it was swept away by the business of signing in, examining her room, unpacking, and going down to a light supper before finally falling into bed and drifting into a sound, dreamless sleep.

"Ah, good morning, Sydney." the innkeeper, Bridget McCarthy, wore a fashionably tailored navy dress and pearls at her throat and ears. Her white hair, short and neat, bobbed at her shoulders. She had the sunniest smile Sydney had ever seen, and a comforting warmth that seemed to radiate from her in waves.

Sydney felt drawn in by that warmth.

"I hope you found your rooms comfortable."

"More than comfortable, thank you, Bridget. They're lovely. I especially love the view from my window."

"Ah, yes. The courtyard. You're here at the best time of year to appreciate it. The gardens are always lovely, but I was just saying to Sean that this year they seem to be at their very best. 'Tis as though pixie dust was scattered over all of Innismere, turning it from pretty to picture perfect." The innkeeper pointed to the front steps, where Cullen stood talking to Bridget's husband. "I believe you have company, Sydney."

"Cullen." Sydney turned hopeful eyes to Bridget. "Do you know him?"

"Know him?" The woman gave a delighted laugh. "Sean and I are his godparents. We've known him from the day he was born. But that's true of most everyone here. Innismere is a small enough town that everyone knows everyone."

"What can you tell me about him, Bridget?"

"Tell you?"

"About Cullen. About his family."

"Why . . ." The woman blinked and seemed to search for something to say to fill the sudden silence. "Why, I can tell you what I'd say about all our young people. Cullen's a fine man who makes us all proud. But then, I'm sure the same could be said about you and yours." She began fussing with the papers on her desk. "Isn't that so?"

"Yes. Of course." Sydney couldn't decide if the innkeeper was flustered or merely being polite. She seemed clearly at a loss for words.

"Will you be joining him now, Sydney?"

"Yes. Thank you." Sydney walked out the door and the two men, who'd been conversing in low tones, abruptly looked up before turning to greet her.

Cullen stepped up beside her. "Ready for your grand tour of Innismere?"

"More than ready." Her heart gave a sudden hitch, and she blamed it on the fact that she was actually here in Ireland, and about to see her father's birthplace. It wasn't, she told herself, because of her handsome tour guide, or the fact that his lips curved in a fascinating smile that reminded her of a rogue. And though he'd shaved, and had exchanged his torn denims for a fresh pair of faded khaki pants and a soft knit shirt, those smoky eyes and killer smile still gave him the look of a dashing hero of one of her favorite romantic novels.

He put a hand beneath her elbow. Instead of guiding her toward his car, he turned toward the ribbon of sidewalk. "I thought we'd walk through the village first, and I can show you a few of my favorite places. Would you like that?"

She'd seen the price of gas, and understood completely. She was glad now that she'd chosen comfortable shoes over stylish ones. "I'd love it, as long as we can stop and eat along the way. I slept in and didn't bother with breakfast."

"I know the perfect place." He kept his hand at her elbow and moved along beside her as they headed toward the heart of town.

It was pleasant, Sydney thought, having this man as her own personal tour guide. His charming brogue, his warm laughter, and those strong fingers brushing her skin were a lovely bonus.

"This is Kelly's Bakery." They paused to return the smile of a young girl placing a pretty platter of cupcakes in the display window. "Mary Francis Kelly bakes the finest barmbrack."

At her questioning look he chuckled. "You aren't familiar with barmbrack?"

"I never heard of it."

"It's a sort of tea cake, with bits of fruit that are soaked in a pot of tea overnight."

"It sounds . . . interesting," Sydney said with a very doubtful look.

"Oh, you of little faith. I can see that you'll have to give barmbrack a try another day. Mrs. Kelly's is the finest in the county. And she's passing her skill along to her three lovely granddaughters." Cullen lifted a hand to the older woman behind the counter, who waved back. "We'll stop by later and indulge ourselves."

They walked on, strolling leisurely, as though they hadn't a care in the world. And, thought Sydney, she didn't. Right this moment, there was nothing more pressing than a walk through her father's hometown. And wasn't that grand indeed? For a person who'd known nothing but hard, demanding work since she'd been a teen, it was a particularly pleasant feeling.

"This is Brennan's beauty shop."

Three women in smocks seated in chairs while their hair was being cut or colored or permed waved their hands, and both Cullen and Sydney waved back.

"Is everyone always so friendly?" Sydney avoided a dip in the sidewalk and Cullen's hand was instantly there beneath her elbow to keep her steady.

"And why not? They know everyone who passes them on the street, unless" — he turned to her with a grin — " 'tis a visitor like yourself, in which case they'll make it a point to get to know you soon enough." His eyes danced with laughter. "Could you say the same about New York?"

She chuckled. "Don't be fooled by the throngs of people. New York's not as big and impersonal as you may think. Though there are a lot more strangers walking the streets of my city, those of us who live there have formed our own sort of bond. Take Mr. Colosanti, who rents me the flat above his deli. It's a comfort to know that he looks out for me. And though he doesn't say much, he takes care of me in his own fashion."

"And why wouldn't he?" Cullen looked her up and down. "I'm sure there are any number of men in New York who'd be wanting to look out for the likes of you."

She nudged his shoulder. "I don't think you mean that in the same way I do."

"Trust me." He caught her hand. "If I were your neighbor, I'd be looking out for you, Sydney."

It seemed the most natural thing in the world for him to continue holding her hand as they walked along, talking and laughing. She found herself telling him about the special fruit Mr. Colosanti always saved for her, and the way he offered her any leftover deli orders, especially when she'd arrived home too late to think about fixing dinner.

"Does he charge you extra for the food?"

"He wouldn't think of doing such a thing."

"Well, I've heard that big-city businessmen often take their customers for all they can."

"Mr. Colosanti isn't like that. He's more like my uncle or grandfather than my landlord."

"I see." He smoothly changed the subject. "It's glad I am to be sharing this visit with you."

As they rounded a corner they breathed in the wonderful fragrance of freshly ground coffee that drifted on the breeze.

"I promised you breakfast," Cullen said. "And it doesn't get any better than Riley's. Will Riley's brother, Frank, has a farm just outside of town, which guarantees that the eggs are fresh, as is the bread his wife bakes every morning."

Instead of going inside the small restaurant, Cullen indicated a pretty arrangement of tables and chairs in a small courtyard. The minute they were seated, a young girl hurried over carrying a tray containing cups and carafes, one of coffee and one of tea. After taking their orders, she disappeared inside, leaving them alone.

"Good timing." Cullen sipped his tea. "With the workers already at their offices, and lunch still hours away, we have the place to ourselves."

"It's such a clean, pretty town." Sydney looked around with interest. "And everyone so friendly and cheerful."

They enjoyed a leisurely breakfast in the sunlight, and laughed at the antics of a bird determined to snatch a few crumbs from beside Sydney's chair. Hunger overcame fear and the bird stayed until every last crumb had been devoured.

When the waitress brought their bill, Sydney snatched it off the table and set some money on it.

Cullen shook his head. "Have you forgotten? I invited you to breakfast."

"But it's my vacation. I came here fully prepared to pay my own way."

"And now you're paying mine, too."

She laughed. "You had an egg and some toast. I don't think it will break the bank.

I'll let you buy next time."

"Promise?" He laid a hand over hers.

"Promise." She looked up into his laughing eyes and felt the curl of heat all the way to her toes.

If there were a photograph of charm in the dictionary, it would be a picture of Cullen at this moment, Sydney thought. He could melt her heart with nothing more than the touch of his hand and that wonderful, heart-tugging grin.

If she weren't careful she'd start to believe in silly fairy tales, and happily-ever-after endings. But in truth, everyone knew that vacation romances were like wisps of fog, evaporating into the air without a trace. Vacation romances lasted for a few days or weeks, and then ended in strained goodbyes.

"Well." She got to her feet and reluctantly took leave of the little restaurant. "It's been a lovely tour, Cullen."

He caught her hand. Squeezed. "The tour has only just begun. The best part is yet to come."

Chapter Four

"Now you'll see the rest of Innismere," Cullen said with a smile. "All three square miles of it."

"It may be small, but the streets are so clean." Sydney studied the scene before her. It was a busy, bustling little town. Windows of shops sparkled. People smiled as they greeted one another.

Cullen paused to pick up a torn brown paper bag that had blown across the sidewalk in the breeze.

As he tucked it into his pocket, Sydney laughed. "Do you always pick up litter?"

At her question he arched a brow. "Doesn't everyone?"

Sydney thought about his remark as they continued along. No wonder the little town looked so clean. If everyone did as he did, there would be no litter. Not just in a small town like this, but everywhere.

Such a simple thing, but she found herself

admiring him for it.

She looked up at the church on the hill, its ancient silver cross gleaming in the sunlight. To one side was a low building.

Before she could ask a question, Cullen explained. "Classrooms."

"Ah. A school for the parishioners."

"Not at all. This school is available to all the children." At Sydney's look of surprise Cullen added, "Some years ago the church and the city fathers agreed that it would be a better use of money if the church would donate the school to the town. Before that, students who wanted a public-school education had to take a tram to nearby Kerryville. Now they can remain in their own town and simply walk to school."

"Their parents must be thrilled."

"Indeed. As are the teachers."

Sydney pointed. "What's on the opposite side of the church, in that little fenced enclosure?"

"Come on. I'll show you." Keeping her hand tucked in his, Cullen led the way up the hill. As he swung open a gate, Sydney could see that they were in a little cemetery. Rows and rows of old and new grave markers were neatly spaced in a lovely area beside the church, on a sliver of land that looked out to the water.

Letting go of Cullen's hand, Sydney moved eagerly among the gravestones, searching for her father's family plot. When she found it, she dropped to her knees and stared hungrily at the names and dates of her father's ancestors.

Cullen stood a little away, allowing her some privacy.

She glanced over her shoulder. "I'll never be able to remember all these names and dates."

He pulled some papers from his pocket and produced a pencil. "Hold this over the engravings, scribble with the pencil, and you'll have a perfect replica."

She did as he suggested, and held the papers up, reading the names and dates of birth and death as clearly as if they'd been photographed.

"Oh, Cullen. What a fine idea. I'd have never thought of this."

He made a grand bow. "Happy to be of service. Now you have the names of your ancestors, and their dates of birth and death."

Her eyes brightened as she got to her feet and tucked the papers in her pocket. "Tell me about the river below."

" 'Tis the river Glass."

She nodded. "My father used to tell me

stories about it. How he loved sitting along the banks of that very river and sketching all the lovely sights that caught his eye."

"And now you're here and you can do the same, if you've a mind to."

She hung her head as a wave of sadness washed over her. "I'd always hoped to do it with my da beside me."

He put a hand beneath her chin, lifting her face to his. "You said yourself his picture holds him close. Who's to say he won't be right there with you as you sketch?"

He could see her mood beginning to lighten once more.

"Come on." He caught her hand, swinging it as they turned back toward the town. "I believe I promised you some of Mary Francis Kelly's barmbrack."

"Yes, you did."

"And I'm known to one and all as a man of my word."

Long before they reached the heart of town Cullen had her laughing at the silly stories he told her about his antics as a child.

"It sounds as though you were a handful for your parents."

"They were up to the challenge. I'm told my own father was a wee bit wild, until my mother tamed him." He looked at their joined hands. "How about you? Did you ever drive your parents to despair? Or were you always the perfect child?"

"Perfect?" That had Sydney laughing and shaking her head. "According to Margot, I'm a perfect failure."

"Who is Margot?"

"My stepmother. My mother died when I was five, and my father told me he was overwhelmed with grief and guilt, thinking he'd never be able to do all the things a mother should do. When he met Margot, she had twin daughters who were older than I, and he was convinced that by marrying Margot, I would be surrounded by, not one, but three substitute mothers."

"That sounds like the perfect solution to a motherless child."

Sydney shrugged. "You know what they say. Man makes plans while the universe laughs."

He arched a brow. "Trouble in paradise?"

She struggled to shake off the sad mood that always seemed to grip her when she thought about her relationship with her stepmother. "Something like that." She took in a deep breath. "Bridget McCarthy told me that she's your godmother."

"That she is. She claims she put a hand on my wee head in church and vowed to see me safely through this world. I'll tell you this. She's worked tirelessly to keep that vow."

"It must be wonderful to have someone so devoted to you."

"It's grand. She was a dear friend of my parents, and I've always considered her a second mother." Cullen looked up. "Ah, here we are."

Seeing the sign outside the bakery, they paused before stepping inside.

The room smelled of bread baking, and the wonderful fragrance of cookies and cakes.

"I've been expecting you." Before they could say a word, Mrs. Kelly reached across the counter. On a small crystal plate were two slices of what appeared to be some sort of fruitcake.

Cullen shot her a wicked grin. "I haven't said what I wanted yet."

"No need," she said with a laugh. "It's always the barmbrack for you, Cullen."

"So it is. Mrs. Kelly, I'd like you to meet a visitor to our town. Sydney, this is Mary Francis Kelly."

"It's so nice to meet you, Mrs. Kelly. Cullen's been teasing me all day with promises of your excellent baking."

"That's so like our Cullen. 'Tis lovely to meet you, Sydney. Welcome to Innismere."

Sydney accepted a small slice of cake from the plate and, as she bit into it, couldn't stop her sigh of pure pleasure. "Oh, this is delicious. It absolutely melts in my mouth."

"Thank you. I needn't ask Cullen what he thinks. He samples one every time he stops in."

"I don't think one slice will be enough today, Mrs. Kelly. You'd better give us three or four, at least. And two cups of your special herbal tea in those carryout cups."

When she'd filled a pretty little handled bag with two lidded cups of tea and several slices of barmbrack, Cullen accepted the bag. Before he could reach into his pocket, Mrs. Kelly stopped him. "Not a penny, Cullen. Now be on your way, the two of you."

She turned to Sydney. "I hope you'll come back often while you're a guest in our town."

As Cullen held the door, Sydney called over her shoulder, "You can count on it, Mrs. Kelly."

Cullen caught Sydney's hand and led her toward a small park overlooking the river. Seated on an old stone bench, they sipped steaming tea and nibbled their cake, tossing the crumbs to the birds that darted about their feet.

"Do you come here often, Cullen?"

"Every chance I have. Whenever I'm in town, I find myself drawn to the park and the river."

"My father had such fond memories of this town."

"Did he tell you why he left?"

Sydney shrugged. "He used to tell me that as much as he loved it here, he was driven to seek fame and fortune in America."

"It drove so many of our fine citizens to leave their beloved homeland. And did he find what he was seeking?"

Sydney looked away. "I think, after my mother died, he lost that drive to succeed. He took solace in his work, and I know that he loved being with me as much as I loved being with him. But nothing was the same after her death. It was as though he was simply marking time until he could be with her again."

Cullen took her hand, his thumb running lightly over her wrist. "Theirs must have been a great love."

"It was. Though I've forgotten so much about my mother, I can still see the way she glowed when my father walked in the door. And I can hear the catch in his voice when he called her his special angel."

Cullen picked up the last slice of cake and held it to her mouth. "Take the first bite.

We'll share."

She did as he asked, and watched as he popped the rest in his mouth.

"I guess this means it's time to head back to the inn. I'm sure Bridget and Sean will be wondering if you're ever coming back."

"I hope they're not worried."

"They know you're safe with me."

Something in the way he said it had Sydney glancing up at his face. He merely smiled down at her before taking her hand and leading her back along the curving sidewalk, regaling her with tales of his teen years in town.

At the door to the inn, Cullen paused. "I wish I could join you for dinner here tonight. Bridget's pot roast is the finest in town. But I have an appointment."

"You don't need to apologize. You've given me an entire day. And for that I thank you. But I'm sure you have better things to do. It's time you got back to your busy life."

His grin was quick. "My busy life can wait. I can't think of a better way to spend my time than with you, Sydney."

Before she had time to realize what he was planning on doing, he lowered his head and brushed her mouth with his. It was the merest touch of lips to lips, and yet she felt the heat of it all the way to her toes.

Caught off guard, her eyes went wide as she clutched his waist.

His eyes remained steady on hers as his arms came around her and he drew her closer, covering her mouth in a kiss so hot, so hungry, she felt all her breath backing up in her throat. A sizzle of pure energy rippled through her, heating her blood, speeding up her heartbeat until it was throbbing at her temples.

As she returned his kiss, she had the strangest sensation. As though she'd found home in this man's arms. A haven in his kiss.

Very slowly he lifted his head and stared down at her with a probing, almost fierce look in his eyes.

With her head still swimming, she heard the deep timbre of his voice. "Spend tomorrow with me."

"You have a life . . ."

He touched a finger to her lips to still her protest. At once she felt another quick rush of heat and stepped back, lifting her face to his.

"How about a picnic on the banks of the river Glass? You can bring along your paints and canvas, and you can sit and sketch, just as your father did."

"Oh, Cullen. I can't think of anything I'd

rather do."

"Good." He lifted a hand to brush a strand of her hair from her eyes. At that simple touch, his eyes narrowed on her, and she felt certain he was going to kiss her again.

She wanted him to. Wanted that tingle of warmth, that feeling of belonging in his arms.

Instead he took a step back. "Tomorrow then. I'll be here around ten."

"I'll be ready."

She watched him walk away, wondering at the way her heart was thundering.

How would she ever be able to wait until ten o'clock to see him again?

How had she lived so long without a warm, vital, exciting companion such as this?

Fanciful, she thought, with a hand to her heart. Hadn't she always been too much of a dreamer?

Now she was seeing way too much in a man who was simply being generous to a visitor to his town.

Still, a girl could dream, couldn't she?

CHAPTER FIVE

"Ah, there you are. Good morning, Sydney." Bridget McCarthy, wearing a fresh red and white polka-dotted dress and her ever-present pearls at her throat, greeted Sydney as she descended the stairs. "There's breakfast in the dining room."

"Thank you, Bridget." Sydney followed the wonderful fragrance of coffee to a sunny room, where the table was set with fine crystal and lace, and a sideboard displayed bacon, omelets, toast, and an assortment of jams.

As Sydney filled her plate, Bridget called, "With the weather so fresh, feel free to take your meal out to the courtyard if you'd like. We've a lovely old table and chairs set up amidst the gardens."

Sydney couldn't resist the offer, and found herself sitting on a cushioned chair, breathing in the wonderful perfume of flowers as she enjoyed steaming coffee and a breakfast fit for a queen. A cheese and spinach omelet, with strips of thick, crisp bacon, and cinnamon toast slathered with strawberry preserves. It all seemed so rich and decadent, considering her usual breakfast consisted of an apple or occasionally a slice of toast with peanut butter, eaten on the run.

As a fountain splashed nearby, she sat back. What if she had resisted the urge to follow her heart and come to her father's home? What if she'd done as Margot suggested and used the money for something practical? She would have never known such a beautiful, magical place as this existed. She would have missed this amazing adventure.

Amazing? It was priceless. And there was no denying that Cullen added to the magic. Without him she would have never stepped into Mary Francis Kelly's bakery and sampled her marvelous barmbrack. Without Cullen she may have missed the tiny church cemetery where her ancestors were buried.

And today . . . Her heart skipped a beat at the promise of a picnic along the banks of the river Glass. That tantalizing thought had kept her awake for hours last night. Or had it been something . . . or someone . . . else that had robbed her of sleep?

She glanced at her watch and hurriedly

finished her breakfast. It was because of her nerves that she'd overslept again this morning. Of course, she could blame her sleep pattern on the distance she'd traveled, and the time change. But in her heart, she knew the truth. Her interrupted sleep was the fault of her very handsome, attentive guide who'd begun to haunt even her dreams.

She carried her dishes indoors, then hurried up to her room to fetch her paints and canvas. With everything packed neatly in a handled carryall, she descended the stairs to find Cullen conversing easily with Bridget and Sean.

He looked over with a quick smile. "Right on time. Ready?"

"I am." She turned to Bridget. "Did Cullen explain that I won't be back in time for lunch?"

"That he did."

Sydney arched a brow, but Cullen merely smiled and offered his arm. On the porch he paused to pick up a large wicker basket. And then, hand in hand, they left the inn and walked along the curving walkway until they came to a stone path leading down to the river.

Cullen guided her down the steep slope. "Did your father tell you how the river came by its name?"

Sydney nodded. "He said the river is so named because it's always clear as glass. Even in the deepest part of the river, you can see clear to the bottom."

"That's so." When they reached the river's banks, Cullen pointed, and Sydney paused to study a jumble of silvery pebbles at the very bottom of the river. As she watched, a school of fish, swimming by in perfect symmetry, caught sight of her shadow and broke ranks to dart in different directions. The sight of them, nervously flitting about, had her laughing.

She set her carryall in the grass and knelt alongside the water.

Cullen was watching her. "Did your father tell you about the river Glass's famous Slipper Rock?"

"Only that it's so named because it's shaped like a lady's slipper. Is there more?"

"Much more." Cullen stared into the distance. "The light shining through the waterfall gives the rock the look of crystal. But up close, it's made of natural granite, with bits of quartz and mica that add the shimmer of jewels. Slipper Rock stands guard in the middle of the river, and has for as long as the town has been here. Many here believe it possesses magical powers."

"Magic?" Sydney was instantly intrigued.

"What sort of powers?"

"For one, it's said that when lovers are touched by the light shining through Slipper Rock, they remain true to that love for all time."

"Do you know of any such lovers?" Intrigued, her eyes widened.

"I do indeed. Both my parents and grandparents claimed to have been blessed by the light. Of course, that's true of many of our good citizens. But the story took on greater importance several generations ago." Cullen's voice lowered. "People still talk about the beautiful young maiden in our town who wed the great love of her life. Within days of their marriage, her young husband went off to war, leaving her with his babe growing within her. On that sad day he promised that one day he would return and look for her on the banks of the river Glass. She gave him her word that she would wait for him here. And so she waited, day after day, month after endless month, until at last her wee babe was born."

"Did her husband ever come back?"

"He did. Gravely wounded, he saw his love swimming in the river and, heedless of his wounds, called out to her, tore off his bloody tunic, and leapt into the water, eager to join her. She, in turn, began swimming toward him. By the time they came together in the deep, he'd lost so much blood 'tis said the river ran red with it, and Slipper Rock reflected that same bloodred hue from the setting sun. The young husband was too weak to continue. And though his wife made a valiant effort to get him to shore, the weight of his dead body dragged her down to the depths. They were found the following morning, still locked in one another's arms."

Sydney looked stricken. "How sad to think, after waiting so long, they had no time to be together."

Cullen arched a brow. "When you think of all the lovers torn apart by war, these were the lucky ones, for they died together, and together they remain for all eternity."

"At least there's that." Sydney thought about it for a moment. "What about their baby?"

"My grandfather? He was raised by some good villagers and lived a long and productive life."

"Your grandfather!" Sydney's hand flew to her mouth to stifle her little cry. "What an amazing story. And what good friends and neighbors." She glanced at the sparkling water. "Do you believe the lovers are still here?"

"I believe their spirits remain."

"What makes you believe? Have you ever seen them?"

"I haven't. No. But there are many who claim to have seen them on a moonlit night. And they say that whoever is lucky enough to see them feels a sense of peace and quiet joy that soothes even the most broken heart and soul."

"What a sad and lovely story." Sydney held a hand to her eyes to shade the sunlight glinting off Slipper Rock. "Is that a waterfall?"

"It is." Cullen offered his hand. "If you'd like, we can cross the bridge and get a better view from the other side."

Sydney took his hand and walked with him across a lovely old wooden bridge that spanned the river at its narrowest point.

"Oh, my." She drew in a breath at the spectacular view from this side of the river, with the town and its church spire up on a hill reflected in the still, quiet waters. Slipper Rock, gleaming in the sunlight, appeared to be made of spun glass.

"I really have to paint Slipper Rock from here. With the light just so, and the water shimmering around it."

"All right." Cullen watched as she began setting up her easel and opening her paints.

"If you've no need of me, I'll leave you to it."

A short time later Sydney glanced around to see Cullen lying in the shade of a tree, hands beneath his head, eyes closed, peacefully sleeping. He looked, for all the world, like a man who hadn't a care.

Was that why she was so drawn to him? Was it the fact that he wasn't driven to spend all his time charging full-speed ahead, eager for more and more success, like most of the men she knew?

She couldn't think of another man who would be willing to spend his days in the company of someone he'd just met on a plane, content to show her around his town instead of getting back to his own life.

She'd expected to feel self-conscious having him around while she painted. But as she began to sketch Slipper Rock, and then apply paint to canvas, she was soon so absorbed in her work, she completely forgot about the man dozing in the shade of a tree. But his grandfather's story would remain in her heart forever.

From beneath half-closed lids, Cullen watched Sydney as she lost herself in her work. The sun bathed her in a halo of light, turning the ends of her hair to burnished flame. She was slender as a willow, her head tilted at an angle as she studied the scene before her. There was an ease, an unhurried rhythm to her movements that fascinated him as she sought to capture the flow of the river, the shimmering rock, and the trees that lined the shore.

She was born to paint. It was obvious in the dreamy smile that played on her lips, the joy that danced in her eyes. This was no weekend artist, hoping to take home a memento of her trip to a new land. This was a woman whose entire being was focused on capturing the scene before her.

Though he could hardly wait to see the finished product, he forced himself to remain where he was, pretending to sleep. A gifted artist like Sydney needed her own space, her own time, to fulfill her creation.

He thought about the strange twists and turns his life had taken. His trip to America had been a spontaneous decision, spurred by the urging of his friends. But he hadn't realized how much he needed to get away until he'd been gone for over a week, and found himself hiking trails that challenged him as nothing had before.

He'd needed that. Not only the challenge, but the time spent in the wilderness, clearing his mind of all but the essentials. He felt he was returning home with a clear sense of purpose.

And then he'd met Sydney. Sweet, innocent, generous Sydney.

He was a firm believer that there were no accidents in life.

His lips split into a warm smile as he drifted on a cloud of contentment.

Sydney set aside her brushes and stretched her arms over her head.

The motion had Cullen sitting up abruptly.

She turned to him. "Sorry. I woke you."

"I had a lovely nap. Have you finished?"

"Yes. Would you like to see?"

He stood and walked close, studying the painting with a critical eye.

"You've captured it perfectly."

For someone like Sydney, who had spent a lifetime being criticized for her attempts to emulate her father's craft, Cullen's words wrapped around her heart like a warm hug. "Thank you."

"You're welcome. Hungry?"

She nodded.

"Good. While you clean your brushes, I'll prepare our picnic."

From the hamper Cullen removed a blanket, which he spread beneath the tree.

While he worked, Sydney kicked off her shoes and sat on the bank of the river while she cleaned her brushes, and then her hands.

As soon as her fingers touched the water, it began to ripple and shift, as though a boat had passed by. She looked up, but there was nothing and no one around. Still, the water rolled and tumbled on shore, directed by some unseen source.

Sydney watched as the images that had been reflected in the river changed. Instead of the trees, the bridge, and Slipper Rock, the reflection became a blue sky and clouds that shifted and changed until they resembled old-fashioned robe-clad figures that reminded Sydney of characters from her childhood stories about kings and queens, knights and maidens.

She looked across the river, expecting to see the town and the church, with its steeple. What she saw was a lovely castle shimmering in the sunlight.

"Cullen."

Hearing the urgency in her voice he hurried over. "Something wrong?"

"No. I just want to know the name of that castle."

She pointed to the hill.

Cullen gave her a gentle smile. "I see it's

true what they say about an artist's imagination."

"Are you telling me you don't see the . . . ?" She blinked and looked again, only to see nothing but the church and the town.

"Come on." Laughing, Cullen caught her hand. "Your picnic awaits you, m'lady."

She joined in the laughter and allowed him to lead her to the shade.

When she dropped down on the blanket, he handed her a stem glass.

"Champagne?" Her laughter faded. "Is this a special occasion?"

"It is. Didn't I tell you?" He touched his glass to hers. "Just being with you has made this day special, Sydney."

As she sipped the bubbly champagne, she felt her heart do a little hitch. Though his words were spoken lightly enough, she'd seen something in his eyes. Something smoldering that had her blood heating, and her pulse racing.

Even though he'd given her no reason to think otherwise, she had the most overwhelming sensation that this was about to become, indeed, a very special day for both of them.

Chapter Six

Sydney sipped the champagne, loving the feel of it, like bubbly liquid silver on her tongue.

Seeing the dreamy smile on her lips, Cullen paused. "You've had champagne before, haven't you?"

She shrugged. "Once, on my twenty-first birthday. But I don't remember it being this smooth." She stifled a laugh. "Or this fizzy."

Cullen uncovered a plate of tender chicken, and another of freshly baked croissants.

Sydney's eyes widened. "I think I see the handiwork of Mrs. Kelly's bake shop."

"Busted. I guess I won't try to take credit for any of this." He shot her a wicked grin. "I told her I wanted to impress a very special person, and she promised to take care of everything."

A very special person.

At his words, Sydney felt her heart do a

little dance. Had that been a slip of the tongue? Was he aware of what he'd revealed?

She held the words close to her heart. Cullen thought she was a very special person.

Cullen lifted yet another lid. "Let's just see what else she made for us."

Sydney gave a laugh of delight. "Surprise. Barmbrack."

"I'd have been very disappointed if she hadn't tucked a few slices of it in the basket." He opened a covered container and held up two perfect peaches. "I suppose these are here to make us feel healthy."

"This is an absolute feast." Sydney dug into her chicken and sighed with pleasure as she buttered a croissant.

Beside her, Cullen enjoyed the meal before sitting back, sipping champagne, and nibbling his favorite treat. "I'm so glad I had this chance to show you some of my town."

Their eyes met over the rims of their glasses, and Sydney's heart took a quick, hard bounce at the look in Cullen's eyes.

"I'm glad, too. I can't think of a better tour guide."

"The tour's not over yet. Have you had enough food?"

At her nod, he gathered up the remains of

their picnic and returned it to the hamper. Setting it at the base of the tree, he caught her hand. As she got to her feet, a man stepped from the woods, leading two horses.

"Just in time, Patrick." Cullen hurried forward and exchanged a few words with the man before accepting the reins of the two horses and leading them toward Sydney.

He indicated a white mare with streaming mane and tale, bearing a fancy saddle trimmed in silver and gold braid. "This is Princess."

Sydney reached up to rub the mare's forelock. "She looks like a princess."

"And has the regal bearing of one, as well. I hope you can ride."

"I grew up in the country. Margot used to refer to my father as a gentleman farmer."

"My kind of man." Cullen offered his hand and Sydney easily pulled herself into the saddle.

Beside her, Cullen mounted a roan stallion. "And this is Prince."

"I should have known. He looks every bit a prince."

Cullen leaned over and caught Sydney's hand. "I thought you'd enjoy seeing parts of my village that most tourists never get to see. The terrain is rough, but the horses are surefooted, and I promise you, the view is worth the effort. Are you game?"

She squeezed his hand. "I wouldn't miss it for the world."

Cullen wheeled his mount and Sydney did the same. With Prince leading the way, Princess easily followed as they disappeared into the cool darkness of the woods.

As she followed along, Sydney had a sudden memory of her favorite childhood dream. She was a princess, riding a white steed beside her prince in their magical kingdom. Though she knew it was just a fantasy, she couldn't shake the feeling that this day had become more than special. It was, in fact, a magical day.

The trail climbed up and up until at last the hills leveled off and the dense wall of trees thinned, giving way to a spectacular view of the land far below.

They dismounted, and Cullen tethered the horses to a small sapling before leading her to a flat, rocky promontory overlooking the valley.

Sydney's voice was hushed, as though in a sacred place. "Look at the waterfall below. And see the way the sunlight sparkles on Slipper Rock. It looks as though it's made of glass. Oh, and there." She pointed. "Your village looks like a beautiful miniature under a Christmas tree." She touched a hand to his sleeve. "Oh, Cullen, what a wonderful place. It's all so lovely, it takes my breath away."

Cullen closed a hand over hers and turned to look directly into her eyes. "It isn't the only thing that takes my breath away."

When she started to draw back he lifted his hand to her cheek. Just a touch, but she couldn't move. Could hardly dare to breathe, as he lowered his face to hers and covered her mouth with his.

This kiss wasn't at all like the first time. The heat, the fire, was instantaneous and so all-consuming it had them both trembling with need.

The hands at her shoulders were strong as she was drawn against a solid chest. The mouth moving on hers was warm and seductive, making it impossible for her to resist. Not that she thought about resisting. From the moment Cullen touched her, she found herself wanting more.

With a sigh, she wrapped her arms around his waist and gave herself up to the pure pleasure of his touch.

He framed her face with his big hands and pressed soft, moist kisses over her forehead, her cheek, the corner of her mouth. When he moved lower to her throat, she nearly purred with pleasure.

"Sydney." His fingers tangled in her hair and he drew her face up while he stared down into her eyes. "What am I going to do about you?"

She smiled. "You make me sound like a problem to be solved."

He lowered his hands to her shoulders, holding her a little away. With a puzzled frown he muttered, "Or an unexpected treasure to be cherished."

She reached a finger to the frown line on his forehead. "I don't think a treasure would bring a look like this."

"That's just it. You are a treasure. One that deserves only the best." He surprised her by tugging on her hand. "Come on."

"What about the horses?"

"Patrick will return them to their stable. I want you to see my secret place."

A secret place. Sydney was so excited by his words she found herself speechless.

Without a word, she allowed herself to be led deep into the woods.

He led her along a steeply curving trail through low-hanging branches of flowering trees and across a field of waist-high wildflowers until they stepped out into a meadow lush with grass. Far below was the river Glass, and shining like a clear-crystal sculpture was Slipper Rock. All were bathed in the most amazing light.

Sydney caught her breath. "Oh, Cullen. This is an artist's paradise. I have to come back here one day with my supplies and paint that scene."

"I'll bring you whenever you'd like. For now, come and see this." Cullen pointed to a spot a short distance away. It was a small, circular ancient stone ruin.

She turned to him with shining eyes. "I wonder how old this is."

"Ancient. I've always considered it holy ground."

"Do you know anything about its history?"

He shook his head. "Only that whenever I'm here, I feel as though I'm in another world."

"Is that what makes this your secret place?"

He shrugged. "Ever since I was a boy I've been drawn to this spot. I used to climb here whenever I could." He led her toward a low, flat rock and settled himself beside her. "I'd sit here and wonder what my life would be like when I was all grown up."

"And now, here you are." She wrapped her arms around her drawn-up knees and smiled at him. "Is your life everything you'd hoped it would be?"

"It is, yes. And now that you're here, it's even better than I'd hoped." He lifted a hand to her face, tucking a stray strand of hair behind her ear.

She plucked a shamrock that had grown up the side of the rock, and then a second and a third. "I used to make daisy chains when I was a little girl. I believe I'll make a shamrock chain for you."

She braided the vines and twisted them about Cullen's wrist.

"I love it. Thank you." He touched his palm to her cheek and smiled down into her eyes.

When she returned his smile, he leaned close and brushed her mouth with his. Suddenly he drew back as though burned and got abruptly to his feet.

Sydney was startled by his sudden mood shift. "What's wrong?"

"This isn't wise." He took a step back. "Every time we're together, I tell myself to take care. But whenever I get too close to you, all my good intentions go out the window."

"And you think being here with me is wrong? Are you afraid of a little thing like a kiss?"

"If you think a kiss is a little thing, you're

wrong." His frown grew. "What I'm thinking, what I want, would shock you. And a fine woman like you deserves better. We'll go now."

She stood her ground and touched a finger to the frown line that marred his brow. "What if I want the same thing you want, Cullen?"

He shook his head in denial. "That's the champagne talking."

She caught his arm when he started to turn away. "The champagne hasn't affected me. My head is every bit as clear as the air up here."

"Sydney . . ."

She placed her hand over his mouth. "How can I convince you of what I want?"

Her eyes sparkled with humor as she lifted herself on tiptoe to brush her lips over his. At once her smile dissolved as his arms came around her, crushing her to his chest.

His mouth moved over hers with such hunger, all she could do was return his kisses with the same urgency.

When at last they came up for air, his eyes narrowed on her. "Now do you understand? This isn't a game, Sydney. If you insist on staying here, you know where this will lead. Is that what you want?"

Because she couldn't seem to find her

voice, she merely nodded.

"I'm giving you a chance to refuse." His words were little more than a whisper. "I want you to be sure, Sydney. For once we cross this line, we can never go back."

"I'm sure."

He framed her face with his big hands, staring into her eyes. When at last he lowered his face to hers, Sydney anticipated the heat that always accompanied his kiss. What she hadn't counted on was the sudden shocking sexual jolt that had her body trembling with need.

As he drew out the kiss, her fingers tightened around the front of his shirt, drawing him ever closer, needing desperately to feel his body against hers.

"You taste like ripe peach," he whispered inside her mouth.

"And you taste . . ." Like sin, she thought, as he took the kiss deeper, causing her mind to go blank.

His hands moved over her, bringing the most amazing heat. She could feel her flesh growing hot, her blood flowing like fire through her veins. Even her breath felt too hot, burning her lungs, causing her to gasp for air.

"I want you, Sydney." His words were a growl against her throat, causing her heartbeat to roar in her temples. "Only you."

She thought of all the things she wanted to say to him, but her thoughts disappeared like wisps of fog when he began nibbling kisses in the little hollow between her neck and shoulder. And when his mouth moved lower, to her breast, she was incapable of any thought at all. All that was left to her was need. This grinding, primitive need that had her arms wrapping around his neck while she offered him everything.

Greedy, desperate, they dropped to the soft cushion of the meadow and lost themselves in the wonder of their unleashed feelings. Like two starving wanderers, they feasted. And like two lost souls they came together, filling up all the lonely places inside themselves.

His kisses were by turn soft and seductive, and then, without warning, fierce and demanding. His hands — those big, clever hands — moved over her, bringing her the most amazing pleasure. And still, she wanted more. She wanted everything he had to give.

"I've known," he whispered against her throat, "since I first met you, that I would have to have you. But I want you to know that I fought it. I wanted this to be your choice."

"It's what I want, Cullen. You're what I want. Only you." Her voice, choked with emotion, nearly broke on a sob as he took her up and over the first peak.

There was no time to catch her breath before he took her again, up and up until she clutched at him, desperate for release.

As he entered her she went very still, and for a moment the only sound was their breathing, as he stared down into her eyes with a look of such passion, such desperate longing, it pierced her heart.

"Come with me, Sydney. Stay with me. Love me."

She did. Moving with him, climbing with him, as they scaled a high, steep mountain peak until their lungs burned from the effort. And when at last they reached the very pinnacle, they seemed to step back for the space of a heartbeat, savoring the intense pleasure that was building until it was almost pain. Then, unable to hold back a moment longer, they stepped over the very edge. And soared.

They lay together in a tangled heap of arms and legs, breathing labored, heartbeats ragged.

"That was . . ." Cullen leaned up on his elbow and reached a hand to the damp hair at her neck. "Incredible."

She managed a dry laugh. "Did the earth move?"

"It did. Yes. I felt it."

"Good. At least I'm not the only one."

"Ah, but you are the only one, my love. The only one who has ever touched my heart like this."

In the silence that followed, he looked down at her. "Am I heavy?"

Instead of waiting for her reply, he rolled to one side, drawing her into the circle of his arms.

She lay perfectly still, absorbing the feel of being held in his embrace. She could hear the strong, steady beat of his heart inside her own chest, keeping perfect time to hers. His warm breath feathered the hair at her temple.

She could lie just so forever. The thought was so comforting, she let out a long, low sigh.

He laid a big palm on her cheek. "Are you weary after such a day? Do you want to go?"

"No. Do you?"

"What I want . . ." He smiled before brushing his mouth over hers. "Is you, love. Just you."

And then, without a word, his kisses became more urgent, as did his touch, as he led her down and down to a deep, dark cavern of sensual delight, to the most exquisite secret place of all. A place where only lovers can go.

Chapter Seven

"When I was a lad, I hiked all these fields." Cullen held Sydney's hand in his as they followed the trail back to the spot beside the river where they'd left the picnic hamper.

She liked having her hand held. Liked the easy way he'd caught it, and then continued holding it, even swinging their hands as they walked. In fact, she liked everything about being with him. "It's fun to think about you out here, doing all the things kids do, Cullen. It's such a peaceful place. But so rugged. Did you ever get lost?"

"Never. How could I, with the river Glass to show me the way back?" At the bank of the river he paused to pick up the hamper before leading her across the bridge.

As they headed toward town, Sydney turned for a last look at the majestic river, meandering about the countryside like a shiny ribbon. Slipper Rock gleamed in the setting sun, a beacon of light as dusk began settling over the land. "I know what you mean. My father said he could follow the river for miles and never feel as though he'd left home." She sighed. "I felt that way about the farm when I was young. When Margot sold everything and we moved to the city, I wandered around feeling like a lost soul for such a long time."

"What happened to finally make the city feel like home?"

She thought about it. "The friends I made. Gradually they took the place of my family. And the big city that I'd found so overwhelming eventually narrowed down to a few blocks of shops and apartments. My neighbors, my students, became the family I craved."

Cullen nodded. "It was the same for me. When I lost my parents, I knew I could always count on the good people of Innismere to fill the hole in my heart, the same way they'd once cared for my grandfather."

"How did your parents die?"

"In a plane crash over Scotland."

"How awful."

He nodded. "But it comforted me to know they'd gone together. It had always been their wish to be together for all time. And now, they are."

"That's such a lovely thought. And the townspeople watched over you after you lost your parents?"

He nodded. "They were my aunts and uncles, cousins and godparents. My family and my friends." He squeezed her hand. "But friends can only do so much. They can't ever replace that special someone every heart craves."

Sydney felt a tingle of warmth all the way to her toes. Could she be that someone for him? Could he be that someone for her?

As they passed beneath a wooden pub sign, Cullen paused. "How about a pint at O'Malley's?"

Sydney laughed. "If you'd like."

He led her through a rowdy crowd, pausing at every table to call out a greeting, and to introduce Sydney to one and all. After a few minutes it became impossible for her to remember so many smiling faces, so many happy people, and all of them like old friends, so warm and easy with both her and Cullen.

They managed to squeeze into a small, cramped booth near the kitchen. As a pretty blonde in a bright green apron passed by, Cullen held up two fingers, and within minutes she set down two frosty bottles. In the space of half an hour, nearly every patron of the pub had stopped by to joke with Cullen, and to give his pretty date a few lingering looks.

"They approve," he whispered.

"Of what?"

"Not what. Who. You, of course."

"Oh." She managed to blush. "And here I thought maybe I had grass in my hair, or a piece of chicken stuck in my teeth."

"Well, you do." He rubbed his thumb over her lips and saw her eyes widen before her laughter returned. "But I still say they were looking over my lady."

My lady. The phrase did something strange to her heart.

"Here you are." A giant of a man, with red hair and a smile that turned his craggy boxer's face from stern to that of a jovial pixie, caught Cullen's hand in a death grip and squeezed. "Annie said she'd seen you come in with" — he turned to Sydney — "a rare beauty. And my Annie doesn't lie."

"Sydney, this is . . ."

"O'Malley," the giant said. "Welcome to my pub."

"Thank you. It's wonderful."

Seeing their bottles empty, the man signaled for a waitress. "Will you have another?"

"Sorry. One's my limit." Cullen got to his

feet and reached for Sydney's hand.

As he dug his hand in his pocket, O'Malley closed a hand over his arm. "Not on your life. Your money's no good here." He reached around Cullen to offer a handshake. "It was lovely meeting you, Sydney. I hope you'll come back again often."

"Thank you. I'd like that."

As they maneuvered their way through the crowd, there were shouts and calls of good-bye.

After the wall of sound inside the pub, the silence of the evening was a welcome relief.

They walked through the town, smiling and answering those who called out a greeting. It was, Sydney realized, so pleasant to feel like a part of the ebb and flow of this pretty little country village.

I could easily make this town my home.

The thought caught her by surprise, though she couldn't say why. But then, after all, this had been her father's home. Why couldn't it be hers, as well?

She was so deep in thought she was caught by surprise when she found herself outside the inn.

Cullen released her hand and set down the picnic basket before retrieving her art supplies.

He studied the painting of Slipper Rock

before asking, "Would you mind if I kept this?"

She arched a brow in question.

He merely gave her a devilish smile that wrapped itself around her heart and squeezed until she could hardly breathe. "A memento of this very special day. Do you mind?"

That had her blushing furiously. "Not at all. If you'd really like it, it's yours."

He brushed a quick kiss over her mouth just as Sean stepped through the door.

The old man looked from Cullen to Sydney. "Well, here you are. Bridget and I were just wondering when you'd be home."

Home. Sydney couldn't help smiling. After only a few days, wasn't that exactly how this lovely inn was beginning to feel?

Cullen gave the old man a wink. "I knew I'd better get her back before you and Bridget sent out a search party."

Sean chuckled. "We knew she was in good hands with you, lad." He turned to Sydney. "Bridget has tea and scones, if you've a mind to join her."

"Thank you. I'd like that." Sydney glanced at Cullen, feeling suddenly shy. "How about you?"

He shook his head. "I'll be leaving now." With Sean watching, he leaned close to drop a quick kiss on her cheek.

Swinging the hamper in one hand, he lifted the other in a jaunty wave before walking away.

Sydney stayed where she was, staring after him until she realized that Sean was watching her a little too closely. Her cheeks felt suddenly hot. Lifting her hand to her face, she turned away and strode into the inn.

"So, you spent the day at the river?" Bridget filled a lovely china cup with tea and passed it across the table to Sydney, before indicating the plate of scones. "Did it cast its spell?"

"Spell?" Sydney looked up from her tea in surprise.

"Most first-time visitors to our town find the river Glass one of our most intriguing points of interest. Not only because of the lovely bridge, which offers a very different view from the other side, but the river itself, which has the most calming influence on people. It's especially appealing to people from big cities who hear only automobile horns and sirens and voices raised in anger."

Sydney smiled. "I can relate. And to tell you the truth, I thought the river did cast a spell over me." Her smile grew. "I thought I saw a castle instead of the church on the hill, and robed women and men coming down out of the clouds."

Bridget took her time selecting a scone. "Did you tell Cullen what you thought you saw?"

Sydney nodded. "We shared quite a laugh at my artist's imagination."

"Ah, yes. You're an artist." Intrigued, Bridget set aside her tea. "Tell me what you painted."

Sydney shrugged, feeling suddenly self-conscious. "I'd intended to paint everything. The river, the trees reflected in its water, even the town up on the hill. But in the end, all I found myself drawn to was Slipper Rock."

"You painted our rock? May I see it?"

Again that self-conscious shrug. "Cullen asked if he could keep it. He said he wanted it as a memento of our day together."

Bridget was fairly beaming. "Why, I think that's quite romantic."

Sydney relaxed. "I'm glad you think so." She blushed furiously. "I mean . . . I thought so, too, but I was afraid I was just being silly."

"Romance is never silly." Bridget gave her a gentle smile. "Why don't we take our tea out on the patio, where we can sit and watch the setting sun?"

Sydney followed the older woman outside, grateful for the shifting shadows that would cover the range of emotions she knew were visible in her eyes.

This entire day had been like a lovely dream. She only wished she and Cullen could have spent the night together, as well.

Later, as she made her way up to her room, she shivered with anticipation. There was always tomorrow.

It was early morning when Cullen paced the back room of the gallery while an old man sat at a table peering at a canvas through a lighted magnifier. Cullen had wanted to come by the previous night, but he'd known it was too late for his old friend to be up. And so he'd waited, and counted the hours until he'd felt it safe to assume that Paddy would be up and dressed and would have finished his morning tea.

Now he counted the tiles on the floor, and then the overly loud tick-tock of the clock on the far wall. It was the only sound he could hear. The room, like the old man, had gone eerily silent.

When at last the old man looked up, his lips curved into a wide smile. His eyes behind the thick lenses of his spectacles glinted with unrestrained excitement.

"It's as you thought, lad."

Cullen released the breath he'd been holding. "You've no doubt, Paddy?"

"None at all, lad."

The two shook hands before Cullen plucked the now-framed canvas from the worktable and tucked it under his arm. "Thank you, Paddy."

"You're welcome, lad. Shall we begin the celebrations?"

"It's a bit premature for that, Paddy. I haven't said a word to her."

"Then ye'd better get crackin', lad. Yer father and grandfather would've never taken this long."

At the mention of his father and grandfather, Cullen touched a hand to the gold locket tucked beneath his shirt and felt the warm shimmer of heat in his palm. Just the mere thought of those two old scoundrels had him sweating.

"You're right, Paddy. But Sydney's not like any other woman I've known. Despite the fact that she's been on her own for some time now, there's something very shy and sweet about her."

Just thinking about her had him smiling broadly. She was such a contradiction. Independent, yet somehow sheltered. So smart and sure of herself, and yet it was obvious that her stepmother still managed to exert a great deal of control over her life. Cullen sensed that this journey to her father's place of birth was her first halting step toward a declaration of independence. But a woman like Sydney needed time.

"If I move too quickly, she may run like a rabbit."

"I say go for it, lad. Ye could always sugarcoat it with a bit of romance. Women just can't deny that need for a romantic interlude, especially while on vacation in a foreign land. Hearing a man declare his love shouldn't cause a lass to bolt now, should it?"

The two shared a laugh.

"You're right, Paddy. I've been so focused on taking this one step at a time, I almost overlooked the obvious. After yesterday, I'm pretty certain that she could be persuaded. Especially if I remember the romance."

"Then stop wasting time with an old man like me and get yerself back to the lass before ye lose her altogether."

With a light heart Cullen let himself out of the gallery and drove away from town and out into the wild Irish countryside.

When he arrived at his home he carefully set the painting on the mantel and stepped back to study Sydney's work. Hadn't she perfectly captured Slipper Rock, right down to the way the iridescent light shimmered through the bits of stone, making it appear as though made of glass?

He stood, hands in his pockets, gaze centered on the painting. It fit. It all fit. If he'd had any doubts before, there were none left.

Suddenly he turned away and headed out the door.

He'd spent most of the night tossing, turning, and finally pacing his room. Before dawn he'd been up and about, seeing to mundane things until he was sure Paddy would be available. All these hours he'd been too anxious to think about eating. He'd barely paused to shower and dress before heading to the gallery. Now he couldn't think of a thing except this need to see Sydney.

He'd wanted to tell her what he suspected yesterday, but something had held him back.

No more hesitation, he thought resolutely. He would tell her now.

And then he would ask her the question.

Her answer would definitely change both their lives forever.

Chapter Eight

"What are we to make of this weather?" Bridget cleared the glass-topped patio table, setting their empty breakfast dishes on a silver tray before refilling Sydney's cup with steaming tea. "It's as though you brought endless sunshine with you." She settled herself across the table and glanced at the lush flowers in her gardens. "I've never seen my planters looking so fine."

"Just admit that you have a green thumb." Sydney nibbled a scone, wondering if Cullen would call.

"I'd like to take all the credit, for I dearly love to garden. But I've never seen them looking like this before." The older woman peered at Sydney over the rim of her cup. "Are you sure you haven't brought some sort of enchantment?"

"I feel like I'm the one who's been enchanted." At Sydney's confession, the two shared a laugh.

"So." Bridget picked up the thread of their conversation from the previous night. "You're an artist like your father."

"Oh, how I wish that were true. I'm afraid I'm much better suited to teaching than to actually painting a masterpiece."

"And what makes you think that?" Bridget looked up sharply.

"My stepmother, Margot, never lets me forget it. She constantly reminds me that artists and teachers don't earn as much as tradesmen, and that my father's pursuit of his dream denied her the life she deserved. She said if my father had been a truly gifted artist, they would have lived like the rich and famous, instead of spending a lifetime on a farm in upstate New York."

"Is your stepmother poor then?"

That had Sydney chuckling. "Not by most standards, but then, nothing is ever enough for Margot. To hear her tell it . . ."

Sydney's words trailed off as Cullen came charging out the back door of the inn looking like a man on fire.

He descended the steps and halted in front of Sydney, struggling to catch his breath.

"Well, look at you . . ." Bridget fell silent when she realized that Cullen wasn't even aware of her presence. His fierce gaze was fixed on Sydney as though she were the only person left on Earth.

"I'll just take these dishes out of your way." Bridget picked up a tray laden with the remains of Sydney's breakfast and let herself into the kitchen.

Once there she summoned Sean, and the two of them remained by the open window, unconcerned about the fact that they were blatantly eavesdropping.

Sydney's first reaction was a sense of alarm. The fierce look in Cullen's eyes, and the fact that he was breathing heavily, had her hand going to her throat. "What's happened, Cullen? Tell me what's wrong."

"Wrong?" He blinked, and in that instant, his frown gradually turned into a smile. "Oh, there's nothing wrong, Sydney. Everything is so right."

"You're not making any sense."

He walked closer and caught her hands in his. "What would you say if I told you that you're a very gifted artist, Sydney?"

"I'd say you were crazy."

"I am. Crazy for you. A friend of mine who is an art critic looked at your work. He called it brilliant. I know now that you're the one."

"The . . . one?"

He nodded. "The one I've been waiting for."

"Cullen . . ."

He touched a finger to her lips to silence her protest. "Just listen, Sydney. I need to say this. All of it. Before I lose my nerve." He took in a deep breath. "When I met you on the plane, I sensed there was something special about you. I tried to dismiss it, but each time I was with you after that, the feeling became stronger. Your kindness. Your generosity. Especially your generosity. And then yesterday . . ." He shook his head, remembering. "Yesterday convinced me. Please believe me when I tell you that I really wanted to wait until I could make this as special as you deserve. But I've been up all night thinking about you, about us, and I couldn't wait another hour. So . . ." Still holding her hands he dropped to his knees on the stone patio. "Sydney, will you do me the honor of being my wife?"

"Wife?" The word came out in a whoosh of air, as though at any moment she would stop breathing altogether. "We've only just met. We barely know one another."

"I know everything I need to know about you, Sydney. Please say yes."

"You . . . want to marry me?"

"I do. More than anything in this world."

"Cullen." Sweet heaven. She felt her eyes fill with tears, and found that she couldn't speak a word over the sudden lump in her throat.

He got to his feet and gathered her close. "I've made you cry."

"It's all right." Her words were muffled against his chest. "They're . . . happy tears."

"Truly?" He lifted her face to his and stared into her eyes. "Then you won't reject me out-of-hand like some crazy man? Even though I've caught you by surprise, you'll consider my proposal?"

"Consider it?" She sniffed and felt more tears springing up. "Oh, Cullen." She wrapped her arms around his neck and held on fiercely. "Yes. Oh, yes." Against his cheek she whispered, "If you're crazy, then so am I. Of course I'll marry you. I'll marry you any time, any place you say."

"Oh, my darling girl." His hands encircled her waist and he swung her around and around before setting her once more on her feet and kissing her soundly. "You've made me the happiest man . . ."

The ringing of his cell phone had him looking startled, until he suddenly reached into his pocket and stared at the number. "No. Oh no. Not Dublin. Oh my sweet Sydney, in all the excitement, I forgot about one of the most important meetings of the year. I can't afford to miss this."

He turned away slightly to say into his phone, "Sorry. Running late. I'll be there in an hour."

He pocketed the phone. "I had it on my calendar. I should have waited. But I was so blinded by . . ." He dug into his shirt pocket, looking puzzled. "Not this, too. I've left it on the dresser."

"It?"

He framed her face with his hands. "The ring. Actually my grandmother's ring, and then my mother's. And soon to be yours." He leaned close and brushed his mouth over hers.

They came together in a blaze of passion, kissing, clinging, until at last they moved slightly apart, both laughing like children. Both struggling for breath.

Cullen pressed his forehead to Sydney's. "I have to leave, but only for a few hours. When I get back, I swear I'll do this the right way. I'll make it up to you. It will be as romantic as you deserve. We'll marry at the city offices today."

"Today? You want to marry today? So soon? Is that even possible?"

"Of course." He nodded. "Now that I've found you, I'm not about to let you get away. And if we don't wed today, we'll have to wait the entire weekend, until they open again on Monday." He had a sudden thought. "But if you'd like to have your family witness our wedding, we could have a second wedding, a church wedding, later. Would you like that?"

She gave a breathless little laugh. "This is all happening so fast, I can't think." She brought his hand to her heart. "Feel what you've done to me."

At the wild beating he lifted her hand to his heart. "Listen to mine. It's thundering even harder."

"That's from running."

"All right. It's from running. But it's also because of you, my love. You've made me the happiest man in the world, Sydney."

He started to turn away, then turned back with a look of horror. "The ring wasn't the only thing I forgot. In my excitement, I left my wallet at home, too, along with all my money. I'll never make it to Dublin and back with half a tank of gas. I'll have to go back . . ."

"Here." Sydney reached into the pocket of her skirt and peeled off a number of bills. "This should do it."

He was already shaking his head. "I can't accept . . ."

"You have no choice. You said yourself you're already late. Go ahead, Cullen. If we're about to get married, my money is yours anyway."

He laughed and accepted the money before lifting her hand to his lips. "Not only are you the sweetest woman in the world, but you're the most generous, too." He started away, calling over his shoulder, "No matter how late I get back, we'll make it official. And then, if you'd like, we'll celebrate with the entire town."

He turned back and rushed to her side. "I just had a thought. Here." He slipped the wilted shamrock chain from his wrist and placed it on Sydney's. "Wear this to remind you of me until I can replace it with diamonds and rubies."

And then he was gone, racing around the side entrance of the inn as though the very devil himself were after him.

Minutes later Sydney heard the roar of his engine. And then there was only silence.

Bridget and Sean turned to one another with matching looks of astonishment.

Before her husband could say a word, Bridget touched a finger to his lips. Her words were a hushed whisper. "Not a word of this to anyone. 'Tis none of our business.

Not until Cullen chooses to make it public."

The old man nodded, before turning away and going off to find something that would keep him so busy he wouldn't have time to enjoy a bit of gossip with his neighbors.

Sydney danced up the steps and let herself into the inn. Seeing no one around, she felt a tiny twinge of disappointment. She would burst if she didn't soon share her news with someone.

Her family. However distant Margot and her daughters were, they were all the family Sydney had. And at the moment, she needed to tell someone about Cullen.

In her room she dialed her cell phone, seeing Cullen's dear face before her. He'd been so happy, so eager when she'd accepted his proposal.

And why wouldn't she accept? Hadn't she known, almost from the beginning, that he was a very special man? Every moment spent with him had become magical. He made her laugh. Made her feel as though she were the only woman in his world. And yesterday her heart had been overflowing with love for him.

To think that he returned that love. It was almost more than she could take in.

"Yes. Hello."

At the sound of Margot's voice, Sydney was forced to swallow before she could say, "Margot, it's Sydney."

"I can read my caller ID. You sound out of breath. Are you in some kind of trouble?"

"Trouble? Oh, no. In fact, I called to tell you my good news. I'm in love. His name is Cullen. And he's asked me to marry him."

For the space of several seconds there was an ominous silence.

"Did you hear . . . ?"

Margot's tone was sharper than usual. "I suppose this Cullen is a native?"

"Native? You make him sound like some sort of savage."

"He lives there? In Ireland?"

"He does. In Innismere."

"I see. Your father's sleepy little hometown. I suppose that would make him seem all the more attractive to you."

"What's that supposed to mean?"

"You can't deny that you've spent a lifetime fantasizing about visiting your father's birthplace. I would think any man living there would seem . . . a larger-than-life romantic figure."

"That isn't what attracted me to him."

"Really? Is it his success then? What does this Cullen do for a living?"

Sydney stared up at the ceiling, wondering just how to respond. "I'm not sure. He works in Dublin."

"As a banker? A lawyer?"

"He didn't say."

"He didn't say?" Margot's tone hardened. "You're about to marry a man and you don't even know what he does for a living. What about his family? Do they approve?"

"I . . . don't know. His parents are dead."

"Any siblings? Aunts? Uncles? Cousins?"

"I'm not . . ."

"I certainly hope you've met at least some of his family and friends."

"I haven't, but . . ."

"Wait. You've met nobody important in his life?"

"Well, Bridget, the innkeeper here, is his godmother."

"Would that be a fairy godmother?" Margot's tone grew more sarcastic by the word. "You've done it again, haven't you? You've taken in a stray, and now you can't part with it."

"Stop that, Margot. Don't be so cruel. Cullen is no stray. He's a lovely man who . . ."

"Just tell me this, and I'll be convinced, Sydney. Tell me that he's spent a fortune taking you to the finest restaurants and clubs."

"I'm not interested in such things."

"All right. Has he presented you with an engagement ring fit for a queen?"

Sydney lifted her wrist, to examine the wilted shamrock chain around her wrist. "Margot . . ."

The voice on the other end of the line sucked in a deep breath. The voice was pained. "And above all, please don't tell me that you gave him money."

"Well, I . . ." Sydney's words came out in a rush, eager to explain. "Maybe a little. But I was the one who insisted. He didn't want . . ."

"Stop right there. You've said enough. Let me finish the story for you. He made romantic overtures, but never happened to have any money when the bill came, so you insisted on paying. Maybe you've even loaned him more money for one reason or another, whenever he had another sad story. And all you got from this man was an empty promise. Can you deny any of this?"

"I can't, but . . ."

"No buts, Sydney. I'm betting that he even suggested that you rush into a quick marriage, so that he can claim half of everything you own."

At the silence that followed that statement, Margot's voice grew ominous. "Don't you see? He has you pegged for a rich tourist, who won't miss a few hundred dollars here or there. All he has to do is give you a few hours of his time, and take you to some local places that don't cost him anything, and you're hooked. And now he's even coaxed you into considering marrying him. It's the oldest scam in the world and you've fallen for it. Didn't I warn you before you left? You're so easy to read. You may as well have 'sucker' tattooed on your forehead. My advice to you is to get out of there as quickly as possible, before this gigolo relieves you of the rest of your money."

"He's not like that at all. He's not what you think, Margot."

"Isn't he? What's Cullen's last name, Sydney?"

At the silence that followed, Margot's tone seemed to lower a full octave. "I see. Another detail you can't supply. You're such a silly, romantic, love-starved fool. Go ahead, Sydney. Stay there in that fabled hometown of your father's. Marry your Prince Charming, who will turn out to be a fortune hunter. But don't come running home to me when you wake up alone and humiliated, without a penny to your name."

"You don't understand . . ." Sydney's only thought was to defend Cullen, and to defend herself. But even as the words formed in her mind, she couldn't speak them aloud. All of them sounded pale and empty beside the rich, ripe, colorful accusations Margot had just hurled. "It isn't like that at all, Margot. It's just . . . Oh, how can I make you see . . ."

With tears streaming down her cheeks, she struggled to find the words to convince her stepmother. It was several minutes before Sydney realized the line had already gone dead.

But not as dead as her poor heart.

She dropped the phone and sank to the edge of the bed, sobbing into her hands as Margot's hateful words played over and over in her mind.

Chapter Nine

Once the seed of mistrust had been sown in Sydney's mind, it began to grow and fester like a poisonous weed until it took over everything good and beautiful. It became impossible for Sydney to think about anything else. All the sweet and wonderful things she'd found so lovable about Cullen were swept aside by the venom of Margot's words.

Margot's questions demanded answers. Answers that had Sydney inwardly wincing.

Had she ever seen Cullen actually pay for anything?

At Mrs. Kelly's bake shop, that sweet woman had refused his offer to pay for his barmbrack. Why? She appeared to be a successful businesswoman. It was her job to accept pay for her work. How could she make any money if she gave away her pastries? Unless, of course, she already knew that Cullen couldn't afford to pay.

What about the lovely picnic basket? Had that good woman provided that free of charge as well? Or had he suggested that he would pay her later, when he came into some money?

And then again at O'Malley's Pub. Cullen had appeared to make an effort to pay, but the owner had stopped him. Why? What was going on here?

Now that she thought about it, other than the picnic, and O'Malley's and Riley's, Cullen hadn't taken her anywhere. At least no place where she could actually meet his friends and have a conversation.

She'd begun their relationship by insisting on paying for his gas, and he'd appeared to grudgingly accept. Had it all been an act to set a trap for an unsuspecting tourist?

Since arriving in Innismere, they had walked everywhere. Not that she'd minded. She couldn't fault Cullen for that. It had been her wish to see her father's town. And what better way than on foot?

She'd thought it all sweet and charming.

Now, Margot's words gave her no peace.

She knew absolutely nothing about the man who had asked her to be his wife. Not his last name, nor what he did for a living, or even where or how he lived. And hadn't she felt as though his godmother, Bridget

McCarthy, had been keeping secrets about him? She never gave Sydney a direct answer to even the simplest question about Cullen.

Did everyone in this town know him to be a con man? Had they been watching his latest conquest while secretly laughing behind the silly tourist's back?

And on top of everything else, there was his insistence that they marry quickly. Was that designed to keep her from asking any questions?

Shattered beyond belief, Sydney suddenly scrolled through her cell phone until she found the number for the airline. Minutes later she had booked a flight home, even though it would cost a fortune to change her ticket from the original scheduled return.

She glanced at her watch. She had just enough time to pack and get to the airport in Dublin.

Dublin. For a moment her poor heart stopped beating. Dublin was where Cullen had told her he was going. Had that been a lie, as well? And all that business about forgetting his wallet. Forgetting his grandmother's ring.

Lie, upon lie, upon lie. And she had willingly believed every word of it. In fact, she'd lapped it up like a starving housecat.

Or a love-starved fool.

She absorbed the pain around her heart and pressed a hand to the spot.

Then, taking a deep breath, she reached for her suitcase and began hastily tossing her belongings inside.

When the suitcase was closed, she again scrolled through her phone menu and called for a car to drive her to Dublin.

Giving a last look around the lovely room, she opened the door and descended the stairs.

Seeing no one around, she left a note on the closed guest book, saying she was departing at once and was leaving for Shannon Airport in order to catch the evening flight home.

Bridget had her credit card information. Sydney hoped the woman was honest enough to refuse to charge her for the time she hadn't spent there. Of course, she had every right to charge Sydney the full amount. Whatever Bridget's decision, Sydney decided that it would be worth any price just to have this humiliating scene behind her.

A car pulled up to the curb and Sydney climbed into the backseat.

"Dublin, please. Shannon Airport."

"Yes, miss."

As they drove through the town, Sydney found her gaze drawn to the old church on the hill, seeing in her mind's eye the simple cemetery and the neat rows of headstones, many of them bearing the names of her ancestors.

She had nearly shamed all of them. Thank heaven Margot had brought her to her senses in time to spare her any further humiliation.

She blinked, seeing again the lovely old castle of her dreams, and the robed men and women looking like kings and queens riding across the sky on winged clouds.

She would have to do something to curb her wild imagination.

She leaned her head back and closed her eyes, trying to blot out all the images that began playing through her mind. Images of a tall, handsome rogue with the most wonderful smile and that charming sense of humor that never failed to touch her heart.

No wonder he'd been so charming. It had all been a well-rehearsed act. And all of it designed to steal the heart of some pathetic, love-starved tourist, just ripe for a summer romance.

Shannon airport was bustling with people, and all of them in a hurry.

Sydney made her way to the assigned terminal and was surprised to find the passengers already boarding. Grateful that she'd made it in the nick of time, she stepped into line and presented her ticket to the agent before following the others aboard the plane.

Once seated, she leaned her head back and closed her eyes against the sting of tears that threatened. She'd had such hopes for this journey to her father's birthplace. She'd spent all of his hard-earned money for her own selfish gratification. And what did she have to show for it? A few days in Ireland. A visit to her ancestors' gravesites. And . . . she felt the hot sting of embarrassment . . . a romantic whirlwind, designed to dupe anyone foolish enough to believe in love at first sight and happily ever after.

At least she'd managed to escape before the final humiliation. How would she have ever explained marriage to a complete stranger after she woke up to find herself alone and penniless in a foreign land?

"Oh, Da." With a sigh she opened her purse and took out the familiar photograph. Just the sight of her father, shirt rumpled and stained, that wonderful smile on his handsome face, had her pain of embarrassment growing deeper. "I'm so sorry. I should have listened to Margot's warning. I almost fell for the oldest trick in the world."

"Love is no trick."

She looked around, wondering at the sound of her father's voice, spoken aloud.

The seat beside her was empty.

She studied the photograph, seeing her father's face, his wise, loving eyes. "Cullen doesn't love me. Like Margot said, it was all a con. Why, we only knew each other for a couple of days."

She closed her eyes, recalling her father's words, spoken so often after they'd lost her mother. "I knew, the moment I saw her, that she was the one for me. Love, true love, doesn't need time. Nor rhyme or reason. With true love, the heart knows."

Sydney sighed aloud. "I thought I knew. But, as Margot said, I was an easy mark."

"How could Margot know, Sydney? Only those caught in the grip of love can know what's truly in the heart."

"I can't trust my heart, Da."

"If not your heart, what can you trust?"

Sydney stared at the photograph, and would have sworn that her father winked.

"Da . . ."

His words were like a soft, gentle breeze, whispering across her face. "Believe, Sydney. Listen to your heart and believe what it tells you."

As his words washed over her, she unbuckled her seat belt and started up the aisle.

The flight attendant stopped her with a hand to her arm. "You'll need to be seated, miss. We're about to depart."

"I've changed my plans. I need to get off the plane now."

"Sorry. Once the cabin door is sealed, we can't allow anyone to leave. You'll have to take your seat. Hurry now."

"But . . ."

"Now," the attendant said sternly. "Or I'll be forced to call security."

Hearing the roar of engines, Sydney made her way back to her designated seat and fastened her belt. As the plane started along the runway, she could no longer hold back the tears. They streamed down her face as she pressed her father's photo to her heart and whispered, "Oh, Da, I've made a horrible mistake. And now, Cullen will never know why I left him without a word. Oh, what have I done? Da, I do believe in love. I do believe what my heart is telling me, but it's too late. Unless there's a miracle, Cullen will never know."

Choking back sobs, she buried her face in her hands.

She felt a gentle touch to her shoulder,

and her father's voice whispering, "Believe."

A voice came over the intercom. "This is your captain speaking. Due to a mechanical failure, I'm afraid we must return to the terminal. I'm sorry for this inconvenience, but the safety of our passengers is always our primary concern."

Stunned, Sydney lifted her head and watched as the plane made a slow turn and retraced the route to the terminal, where the passengers were ordered to deplane and await transfer to another, later plane.

As she followed the others past a throng of interested bystanders, one man separated himself from the crowd and started toward her.

His eyes showed the strain of tension as he caught hold of her upper arms and drew her close, burying his face in her hair.

"Sydney. I thought I'd lost you."

"Cullen." She took in a breath, wondering where to begin.

Before she could say a word, he gathered her close. "When Bridget told me you'd checked out, I drove like a maniac, desperate to get here in time. When I realized I was too late, I fell to my knees in despair. And then, just as I'd lost hope, I felt someone touch my shoulder and I heard a man's voice say, 'Believe.' I looked around, but there was no one near. And then I experienced this strange sense of peace, and I knew without a doubt that you would return to me. In almost that same instant I heard the announcement that your plane was returning to the terminal, and I knew in my heart that everything would be all right."

She lifted her head to meet his eyes. Her own swam with tears. "It was the same for me. One minute I was filled with despair, and the next I heard the captain speaking and knew that I'd been given a second chance to make things right." She touched a hand to his face. "I need to explain why . . ."

He closed a hand over hers. "Not now, love. There are no words needed. Just come with me. Please," he added when she arched a brow. "And I promise you'll soon have the answers to all your heart's questions."

Chapter Ten

The drive from Dublin to Innismere seemed to take no more than a moment in time. No sooner had Sydney leaned her head back and closed her eyes than Cullen was taking her hand and helping her from his car.

She looked around in surprise. "Where are we?"

"This building houses our town hall and courthouse." He led her up the steps.

Once inside they crossed to a pair of ornate double doors. Cullen held the door for Sydney, and she looked up to see a man in judicial robes just stepping into the chambers.

"Ah. So this is the one?" the stranger said to Cullen.

"Indeed. Thank you for taking care of this on such short notice."

The white-haired judge winked. "Always happy to be on Cupid's side. Especially when Cupid is assisting the history of our fine town." He turned to Sydney. "Do you have any questions?"

"Dozens of them." She nodded. "But first, shouldn't I fill out some forms?"

He held up a handful of documents. "So you have."

When she looked at them, she could see her own handwriting.

The judge smiled. "I must ask if you are here of your own choice."

Believe. The word played through her mind.

She glanced at Cullen before saying softly, "I am."

"And you, Cullen? This is what you desire above all else?"

"With all my heart."

"Let us begin." The judge picked up a book and began reading in a strange language.

"Gaelic," Cullen whispered.

Sydney's eyes widened as she heard her name spoken, and then Cullen's, before the judge returned to the ancient tongue.

When he had finished, he closed the book and held it out to them. "Will you swear upon all that is holy that you will abide by the laws of the land as you begin your journey together as husband and wife?"

Sydney and Cullen placed their hands on

the book while raising their right hands and agreeing.

The judge produced a magnificent ruby and diamond ring. "Bridget McCarthy brought this to me. I remember your mother and grandmother wearing this very ring on their wedding days. It is more than a ring. It is a symbol of hope for all in this town."

"I'm in Bridget's debt," Cullen whispered as he placed it on Sydney's finger before lifting her hand to his lips.

Seeing the braided shamrock bracelet still on her wrist brought a smile to his eyes. "But this lovely vine means more to me than precious jewels."

Before Sydney could respond, the judge said, "Blessings on the two of you." He glanced at his watch. "Just in time. 'Tis the stroke of midnight. A minute more and I'd have turned into a wise old owl."

Adjusting his glasses, he turned away and disappeared into his chambers, while Sydney turned to Cullen with a look of alarm. "Was he joking?"

"You'll have to ask him the next time you see him." With a wink, Cullen caught Sydney's hand and the two of them dashed out of the courthouse.

Despite the late hour, the street was alive with people holding candles who began clapping and cheering as the couple made their way to Cullen's car.

Once inside he turned to her with a smile. "Wave to all the good people."

She did as he'd said, and was surprised by the roar of approval that assaulted her ears. "They make me feel like royalty. Do they do this for every couple who marry in your town?"

His eyes, his smile, were full of mischief. "Not every couple, though I know they're particularly happy for me. I had planned on celebrating here, with the good people of Innismere. But after all this excitement, I think we could both use some quiet time. I'll let them know through Bridget that they can plan a proper celebration for tomorrow." He put the car in gear. "For now, why don't we go to my home?"

Sydney nodded. "Maybe that's best. This has all happened so quickly, my head is spinning."

As he started the car's engine, he caught her hand. "I'm sorry for all the confusion, Sydney. I hope I can make it up to you."

When she said nothing, he lifted her hand to his lips. At once she felt the warmth spreading through her veins. His simple touch was like a potent drug, putting her at ease and erasing all her doubts and fears.

"Sydney, you should know that I've been distracted ever since we met on the plane. I knew there was something special about you. And the more time I spent with you, the more convinced I was that our meeting was no accident. We were meant to meet and fall in love. It was fated from the beginning of time."

She looked away. "How many times have you said those very words to someone, Cullen?"

"Never before." When she turned to him, his smile was dazzling. "You're the first, Sydney. You'll be the last. You are the only one."

Her smile came slowly. "I ran away because of Margot's warning that I'd been taken in by your charm. She called you Prince Charming."

"Your stepmother makes that sound like a bad thing." He squeezed her hand. "I hope it's true. Are you charmed?"

"Completely."

He threw back his head and laughed. "That makes two of us. You're the most amazing, delightful woman I've ever known."

"I've always thought of myself as ordinary."

"Sydney, you're the most extraordinary

woman in the world. I'm completely dazzled by you."

They drove through the darkened countryside, past pretty farmhouses with lights aglow, and Sydney began watching, wondering if she'd be able to spy Cullen's house.

The road began climbing past tall hedgerows that blotted out the twinkling stars, past lovely meandering rock walls with brightly painted doors, until they came up over a rise and drew near a magnificent manor house that resembled the castle of Sydney's vision. Every window was ablaze with light.

Cullen drove to the front door and stepped out. Rounding the car, he opened Sydney's door and caught her hand.

Before she could ask a single question, ornate double doors were thrown open and a silver-haired man in a black suit made a grand bow before saying, "Welcome home, sir."

"Thank you, Egan. This is my lovely bride, Sydney."

"Welcome to Eventide." The old man stood aside as they stepped into the elegant foyer. "Mrs. Maguire is conferring with Cook about the wedding supper you requested, sir."

"Thank you, Egan." Cullen caught Sydney's hand and led her up the wide, curving stairs to the second story.

Once inside, she stared around the elegant sitting room where a fire burned on the hearth. A white marble surround with a wide matching mantel gleamed in the firelight. Above the mantel hung two paintings.

Sydney stared in openmouthed surprise. "Is one of those mine?"

Cullen nodded. "It is, yes. I had it framed so it could hang beside its mate."

Sydney stared at a painting from her childhood hanging beside her own. She stepped closer, before turning to Cullen in stunned disbelief. "Is this my father's? How can this be?"

"My family bought it."

"Your family! When?"

"Years ago. As soon as your father's paintings were offered for sale, our solicitor was told to bid on the entire collection."

"You bought them from my stepmother?"

He nodded. "From her representative, actually. We never dealt with her directly."

Sydney's eyes filled with tears as she stared hungrily at her father's painting of Slipper Rock. "Why did you want this?"

"It belongs here. Your father's talent brought a sense of pride to our town. His early paintings were all about the familiar landmarks of Innismere. And even when he left his home, and painted the lovely scenes around the countryside of his new land, they seemed to speak of his home here."

Sydney glanced around. "Where are the rest of his paintings?"

Cullen caught her hand. "Come. I'll show you."

The majestic hallway was lined with paintings, and every one of them had been painted by her father's hand. Just seeing them, she was transported back to her childhood, and all the joyful hours she'd spent in her father's company.

She touched a hand to each painting, feeling again the dips and curves of her father's scrawled signature.

Beneath a huge skylight rested her father's finest creation. This one was a scene of the river Glass from the far shore. On the hill, instead of the church, her father had painted this castle. In the clouds above were robed figures of a king and queen.

Sydney's hand flew to her mouth. "Look, Cullen. It's the vision I described to you."

He was smiling. "So it is."

She shook her head. "I know this canvas bears my father's signature, but I never saw him paint this castle, or those royal figures."

Cullen's smile grew. "That's because this

was commissioned by my grandfather when your father was just a lad. Even at a young age, he shared the magic of this place, for he'd seen it with his own eyes."

He caught her hand and led her back to his suite of rooms, where he urged her to sit beside him on a white sofa. "I owe you an explanation. You've been so patient with me, Sydney. But now, it's time I told you everything."

She clasped her hands together, wondering what he was about to reveal. Though she'd gone this far with him on faith, there was still that tiny seed of doubt that Margot had planted.

"There's much about this town, and its people, that is never revealed to outsiders."

"Am I an outsider?"

"You never were, Sydney, thanks to your father. But until we were certain, we did our best to keep our secrets to ourselves."

"And now?"

"I owe you the truth. My ancestors are direct descendants of ancient Irish lords. At one time they were considered royalty. Through the generations they've protected the land either as warriors, or, in more peaceful times, as elected officials. I've been asked to run for Parliament, or at least to be mayor of Innismere, but I choose instead to simply run my software company, which employs hundreds of people both here and in Dublin, and a few thousand more employees abroad."

Sydney's jaw dropped. "You're a successful businessman?"

"You seem surprised."

She nodded. "You never seemed to work. And you never had any money. Mrs. Kelly wouldn't take your money. Neither would O'Malley. So I thought . . ." Seeing the laughter in his eyes, her words trailed off.

"You thought I was unemployed?"

She shrugged. "Worse."

"Worse?" As the realization dawned, he burst into laughter. "You thought I was using you?"

She looked away. "Not at first, but when I told Margot that I was in love with you, she persuaded me that you were a con artist who was playing me for a fool."

"Sydney, the reason Mary Francis Kelly and O'Malley wouldn't take money from me is because, when they were about to be foreclosed, I loaned them enough to pay off their mortgages to the bank."

"Oh, I'm so relieved. You'll never know . . ."

They both looked up as a plump woman in a black dress, her cheeks bright pink, eyes alight with curiosity, charged into the room and nearly skidded to a halt.

"Ye're home then." She seemed delighted. "I was in the kitchen, and telling Cook that ye wanted yer wedding supper up in yer rooms. Little did I know ye were already here until Egan found us gossiping and told me ye needed me."

"Mrs. Maguire, I'd like you to meet my bride, Sydney."

"Sydney. Of course." The older woman seemed absolutely delighted as she stepped closer and offered her a handshake. "It's very welcome indeed ye are to Eventide, Mrs. Rella."

"Rella?" Sydney shot a sideways glance at Cullen. "When the judge officiated at our wedding, he called you something else."

Cullen chuckled. "In Gaelic, it's an ancient and noble name, and folks in Innismere prefer the Gaelic to the English translation."

"I'll be fetching that wedding supper now," the old woman said as she fairly danced from the room.

Sydney glanced at her beloved father's painting, and then at her own. The two were identical.

Seeing the direction of her gaze, Cullen said, "It all fit, you see."

"Fit?"

"The things you'd seen. Only a chosen few have ever had the vision of our ancestors. The castle. The royal figures. And, of course, there's your painting of Slipper Rock. That fit perfectly."

"I don't understand."

He took her hand and lifted it to his lips. "Your painting exactly matched one your father painted when he was a lad, when it had been commissioned by my grandfather. A seer, who was an advisor to my ancestors, said that Slipper Rock had magical powers. He assured my family that one day, a slipper would fit an amazing woman who would become the great love of my life. I took his prediction literally, and thought I ought to try fitting a slipper on your foot. But then you chose to paint Slipper Rock, and I knew at once what he really meant. Your painting has been measured against the one painted by your father. An expert has examined and measured, centimeter by centimeter, to be certain that it fit. For, you see, once the slipper fit, I knew I'd found my one and only true love."

Sydney's eyes widened with sudden knowledge. "Are you suggesting that this is like some sort of fairy tale? The handsome, charming son of royalty? His godmother, who runs the inn? The slipper that fits? It's all . . . magic?"

"I'll leave that for you to decide, my beautiful bride. I know only that I've waited a lifetime for you. Your love has rescued me from a life that was empty and meaningless. Even though I have a good life here, with many friends, I yearned for that one special person who would mean more to me than life itself."

That lovely rogue smile lit all his features as he leaned close to brush her mouth with his, sending a tingle of warmth along her spine. "And because you're American, I'll say this in your tongue. Welcome home, my lovely Sydney Rella."

"Of course. Sydney Rella. Sydney Rella." She was up and dancing around like a girl, clapping her hands as the final piece of the puzzle fell into place.

And then she was in Cullen's arms, laughing and crying as the truth dawned.

"You love me. Truly love me. And I love you. And we really are going to live happily ever after, aren't we?"

Cullen didn't bother to answer. He was too busy kissing her, and showing her, in the way of lovers from the beginning of time, the true magic of love.

The employees of Thorndike Press hope you have enjoyed this Large Print book. All our Thorndike, Wheeler, and Kennebec Large Print titles are designed for easy reading, and all our books are made to last. Other Thorndike Press Large Print books are available at your library, through selected bookstores, or directly from us.

For information about titles, please call:
(800) 223-1244

or visit our Web site at:
http://gale.cengage.com/thorndike

To share your comments, please write:
Publisher
Thorndike Press
10 Water St., Suite 310
Waterville, ME 04901